MELLYBEAN
AND THE
GIANT MONSTER

W9-AOV-383

MIKE WHITE

RAZORBILL

RAZORBILL

An imprint of Penguin Random House LLC, New York

First published in the United States of America by Razorbill,
an imprint of Penguin Random House LLC, 2020

Copyright © 2020 by Mike White

Penguin supports copyright. Copyright fuels creativity, encourages diverse voices, promotes free speech, and creates a vibrant culture. Thank you for buying an authorized edition of this book and for complying with copyright laws by not reproducing, scanning, or distributing any part of it in any form without permission. You are supporting writers and allowing Penguin to continue to publish books for every reader.

RAZORBILL & colophon is a registered trademark of Penguin Random House LLC.

Visit us online at penguinrandomhouse.com

LIBRARY OF CONGRESS CATALOGING-IN-PUBLICATION DATA
Names: White, Mike (Children's author), author, illustrator.
Title: Mellybean and the giant monster / Mike White.
Description: New York : Razorbill, 2020. | Series: Mellybean; book 1 | Audience: Ages 8–12. |
Summary: While trying to bury a shoe in the backyard, a young dog who lives with two humans and three cats is transported to a world filled with magic, adventure, and one giant, grumpy monster.
Identifiers: LCCN 2020020473 | ISBN 9780593202807 (trade paperback) | ISBN 9780593202548 (hardcover) | ISBN 9780593205730 (kindle edition) | ISBN 9780593205747 (nook edition) | ISBN 9780593202791 (epub) Subjects: LCSH: Graphic novels. | CYAC: Graphic novels. | Dogs—Fiction. | Monsters—Fiction. | Adventure and adventurers—Fiction. Classification: LCC PZ7.7.W5415 Me 2020 | DDC 741.5/973—dc23 LC record available at https://lccn.loc.gov/2020020473

Manufactured in China.

ISBN 9780593202548 (hardcover); ISBN 9780593202807 (paperback)

3 5 7 9 10 8 6 4 2

Design by Mike White.
Colors by Valery Kutz.
Text set in Evil Genius.

Dedicated to:
Carol, Melody, Butternut,
Charlie, & Tugs

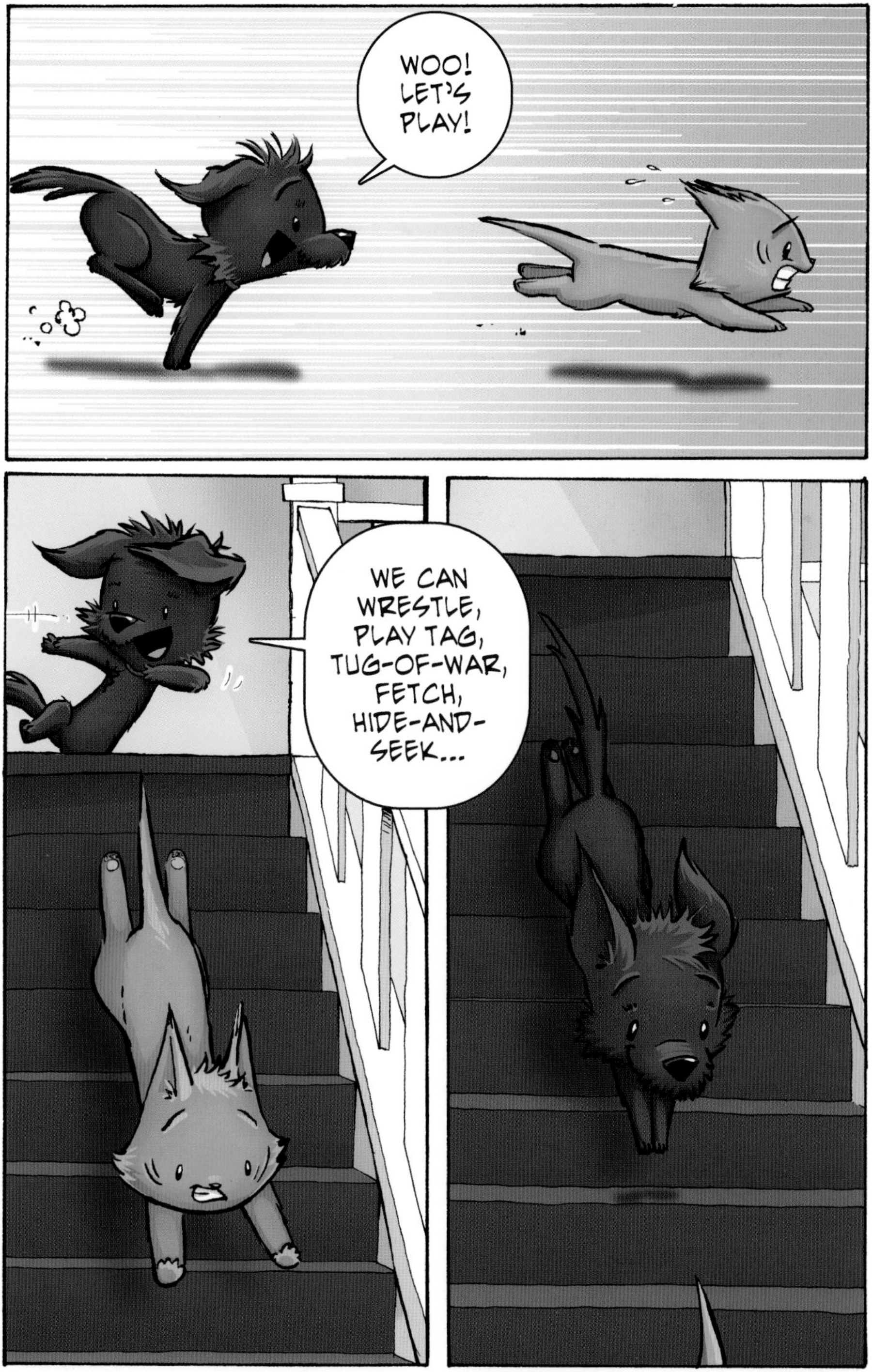
WOO! LET'S PLAY!
WE CAN WRESTLE, PLAY TAG, TUG-OF-WAR, FETCH, HIDE-AND-SEEK...

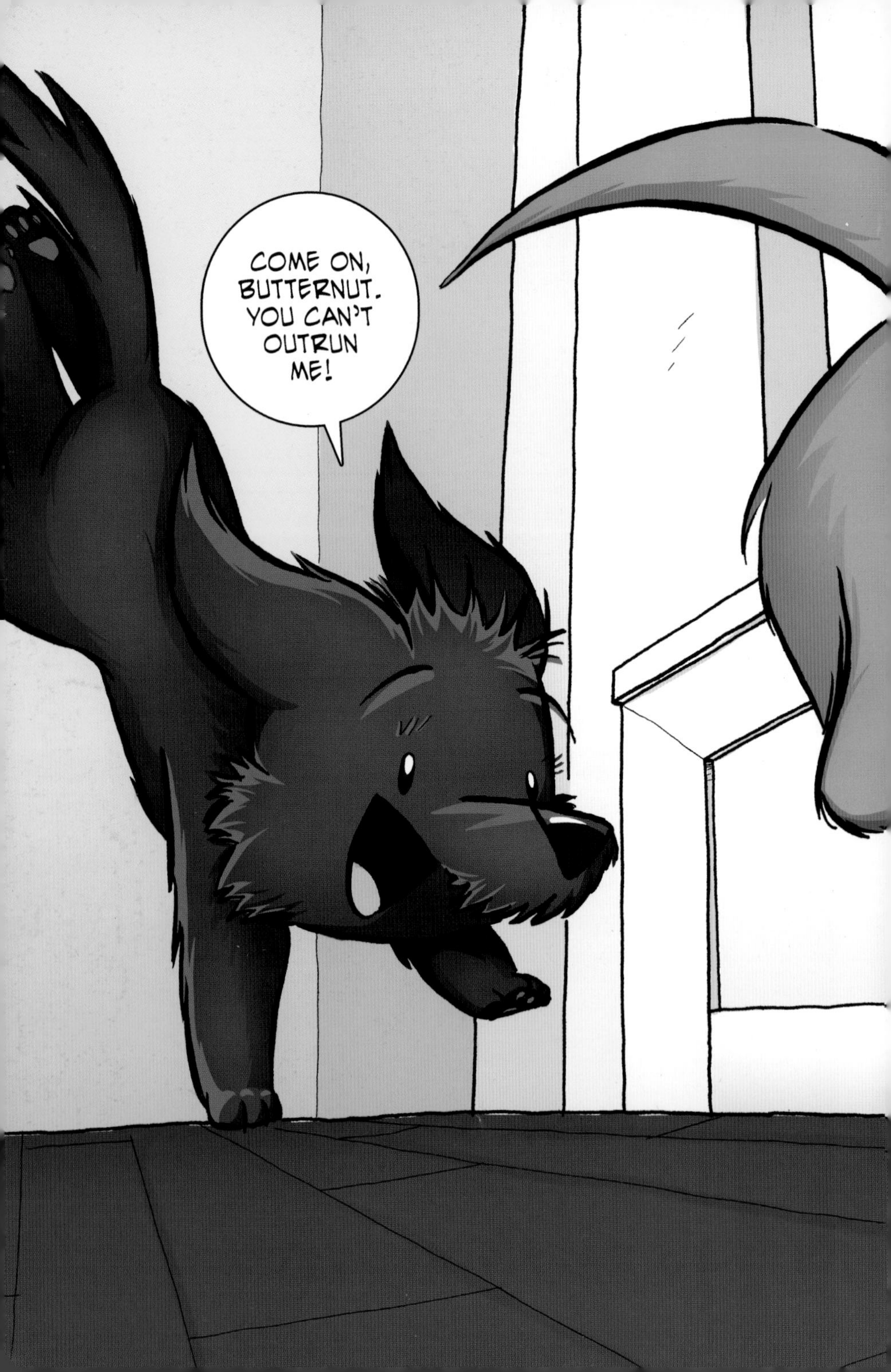
COME ON, BUTTERNUT. YOU CAN'T OUTRUN ME!

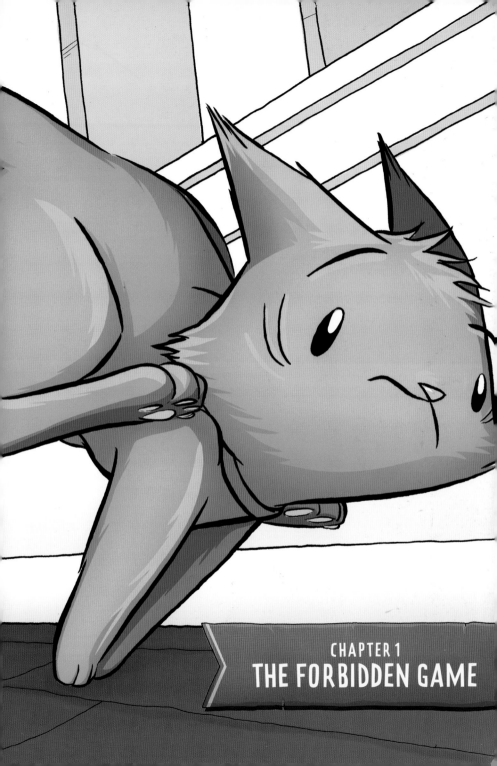

CHAPTER 1
THE FORBIDDEN GAME

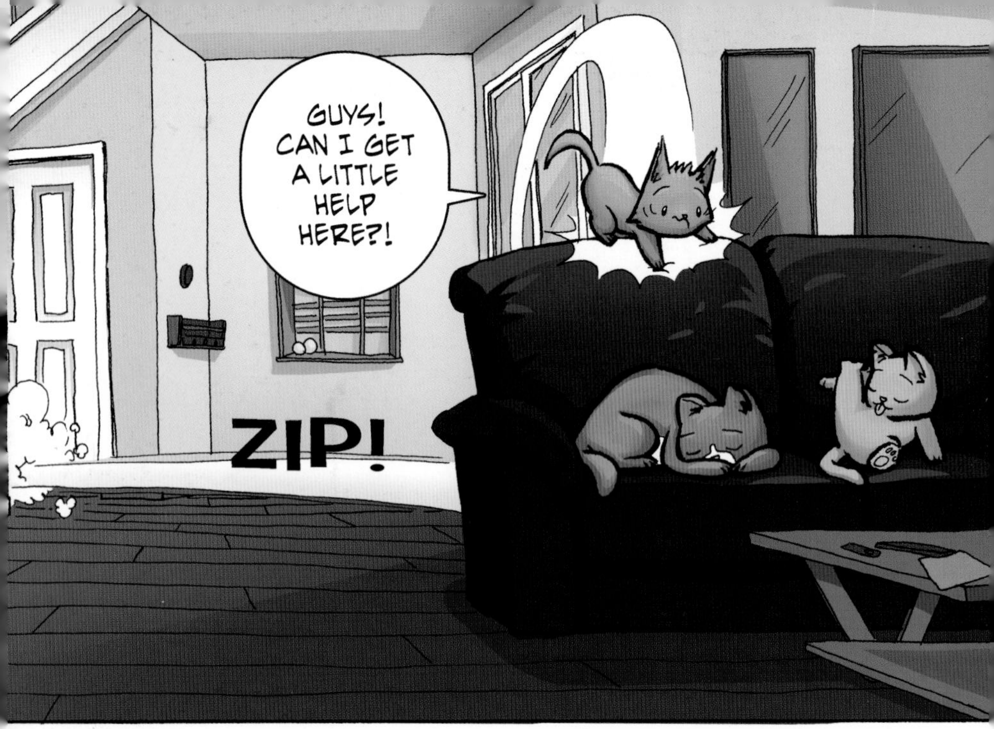
GUYS! CAN I GET A LITTLE HELP HERE?!
ZIP!

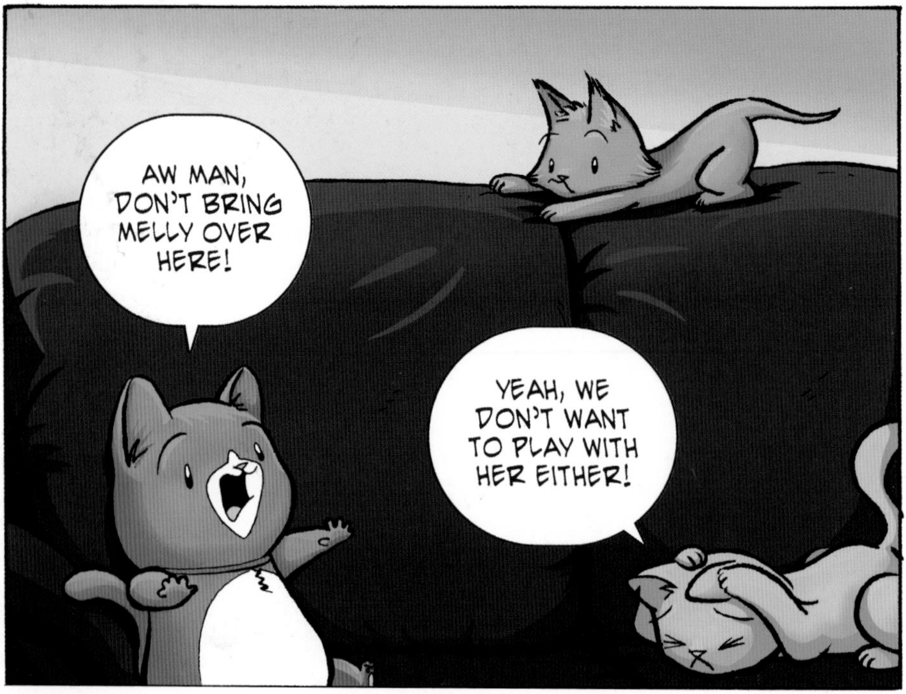
AW MAN, DON'T BRING MELLY OVER HERE!
YEAH, WE DON'T WANT TO PLAY WITH HER EITHER!

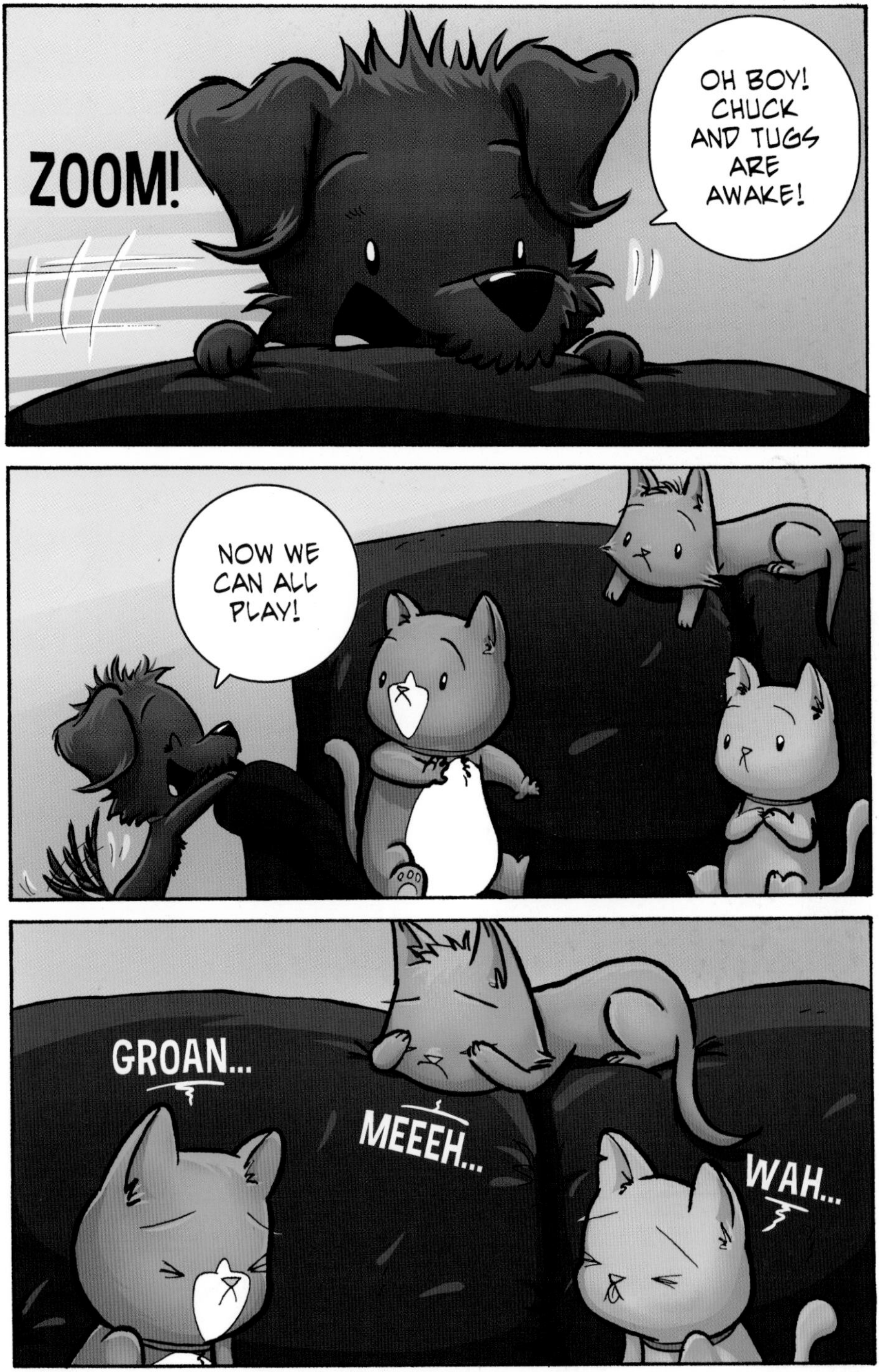
ZOOM!
OH BOY! CHUCK AND TUGS ARE AWAKE!
NOW WE CAN ALL PLAY!
GROAN...
MEEEH...
WAH...

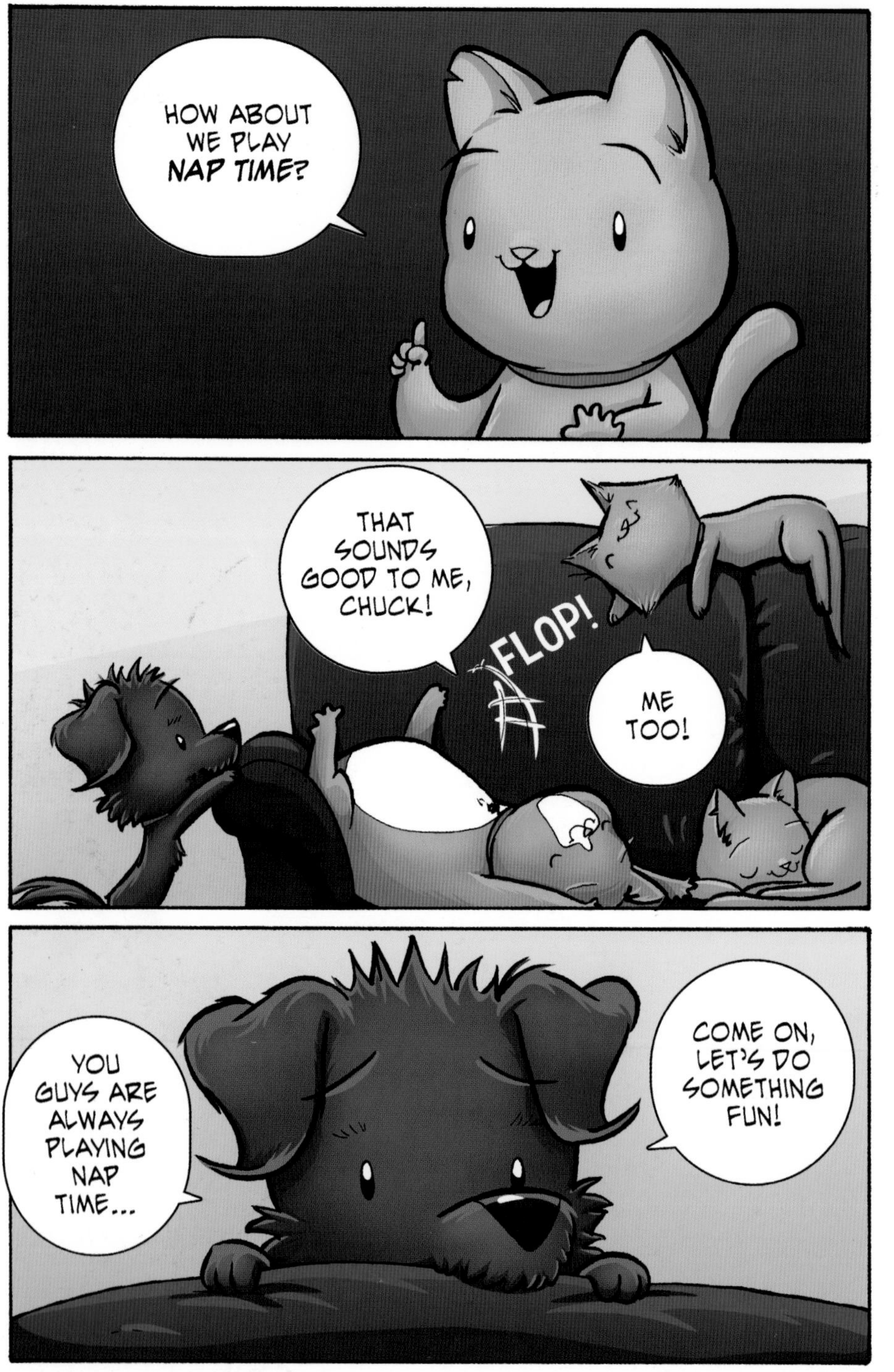
HOW ABOUT WE PLAY NAP TIME?
THAT SOUNDS GOOD TO ME, CHUCK!
FLOP!
ME TOO!
COME ON, LET'S DO SOMETHING FUN!
YOU GUYS ARE ALWAYS PLAYING NAP TIME...

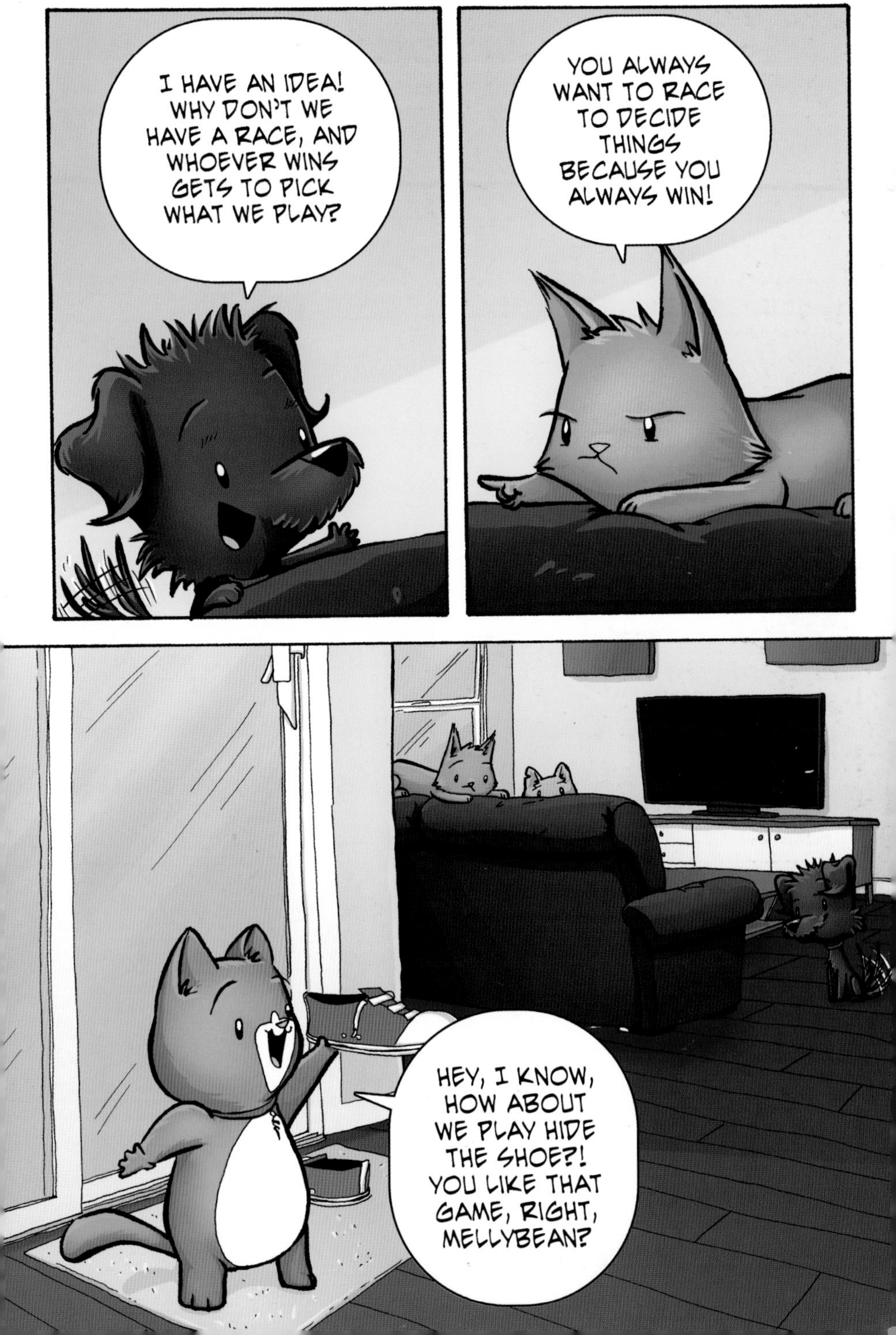
I HAVE AN IDEA! WHY DON'T WE HAVE A RACE, AND WHOEVER WINS GETS TO PICK WHAT WE PLAY?
YOU ALWAYS WANT TO RACE TO DECIDE THINGS BECAUSE YOU ALWAYS WIN!
HEY, I KNOW, HOW ABOUT WE PLAY HIDE THE SHOE?! YOU LIKE THAT GAME, RIGHT, MELLYBEAN?

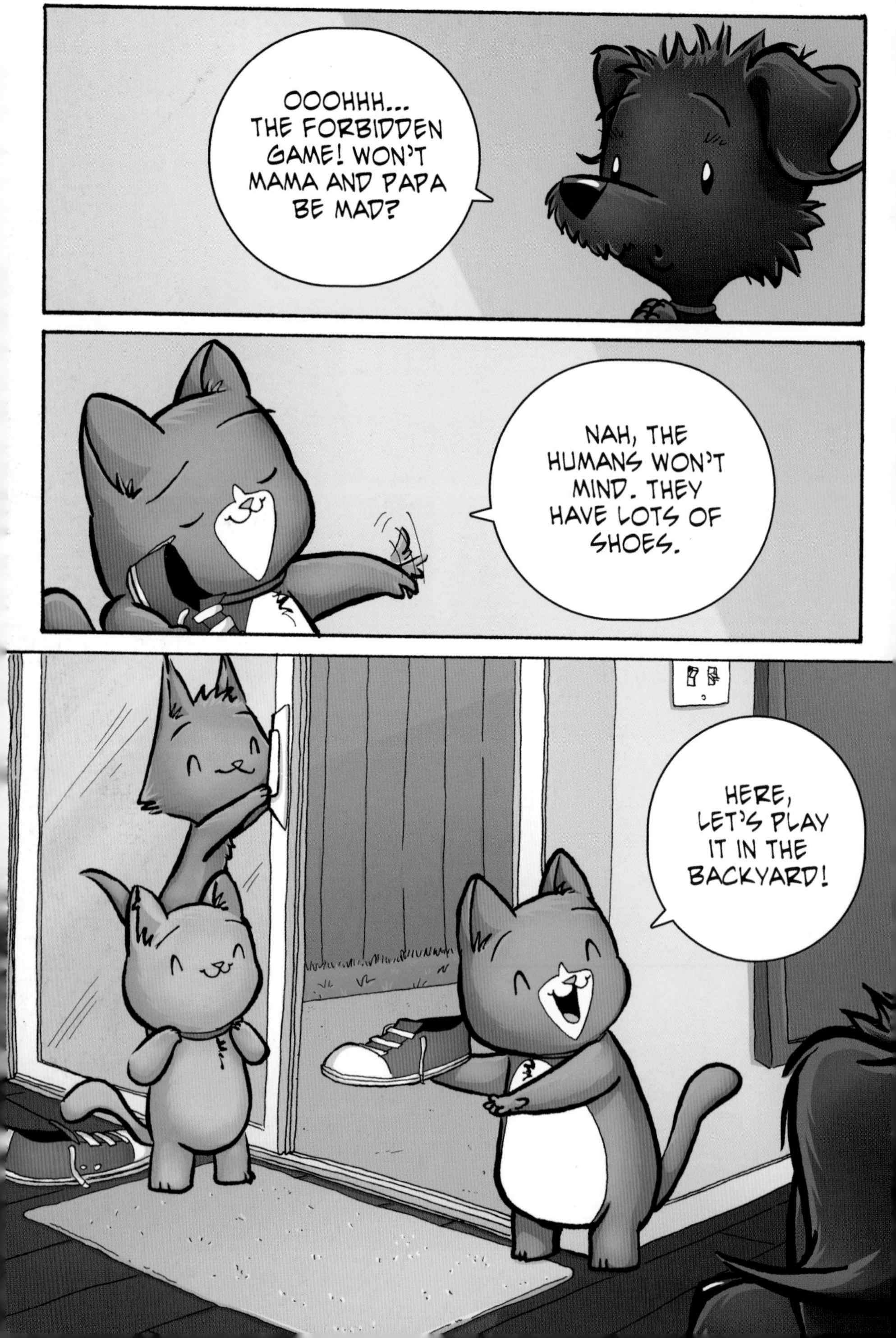
OOOHHH... THE FORBIDDEN GAME! WON'T MAMA AND PAPA BE MAD?
NAH, THE HUMANS WON'T MIND. THEY HAVE LOTS OF SHOES.
HERE, LET'S PLAY IT IN THE BACKYARD!

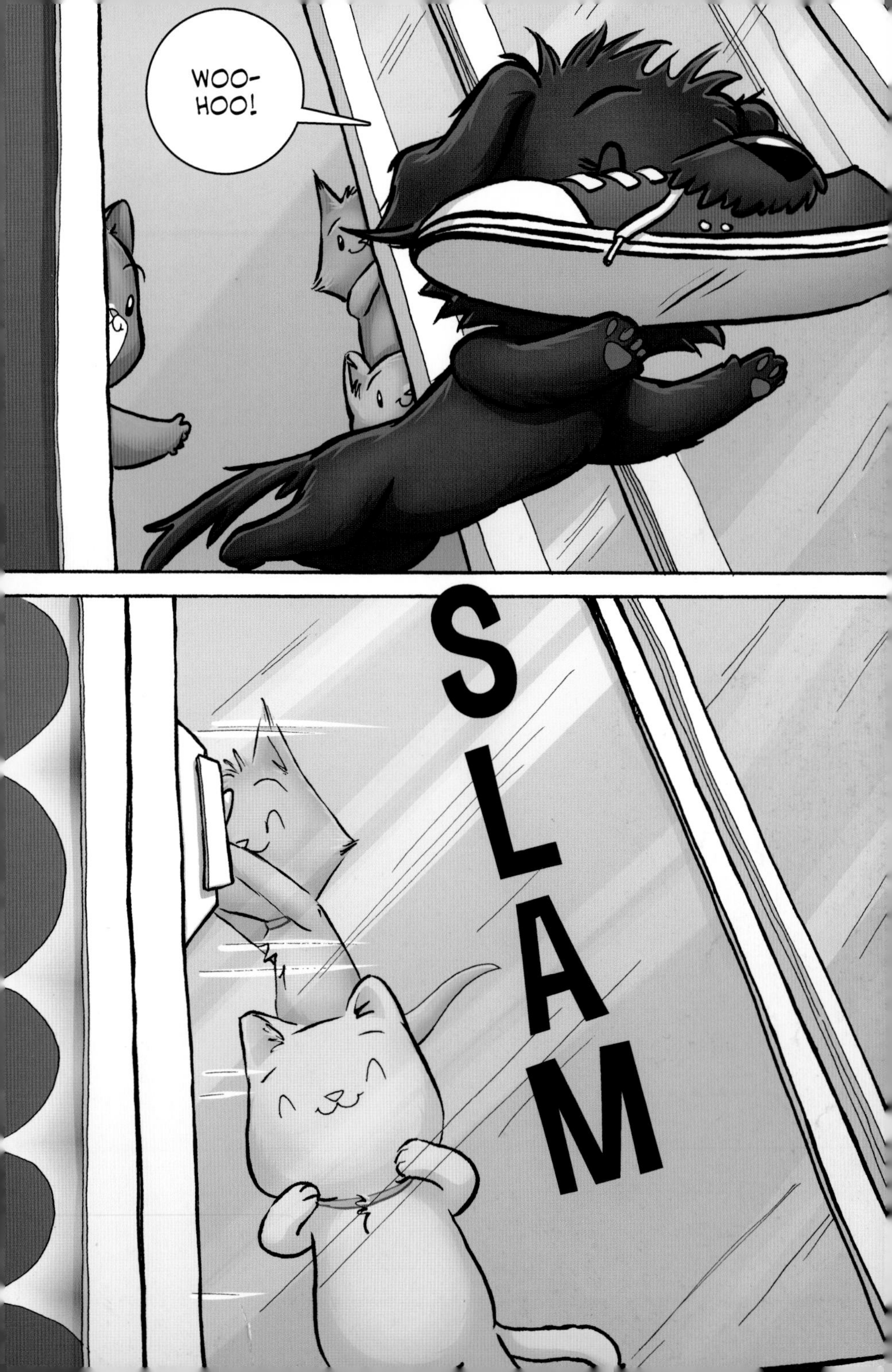
WOO-
HOO!
SLAM

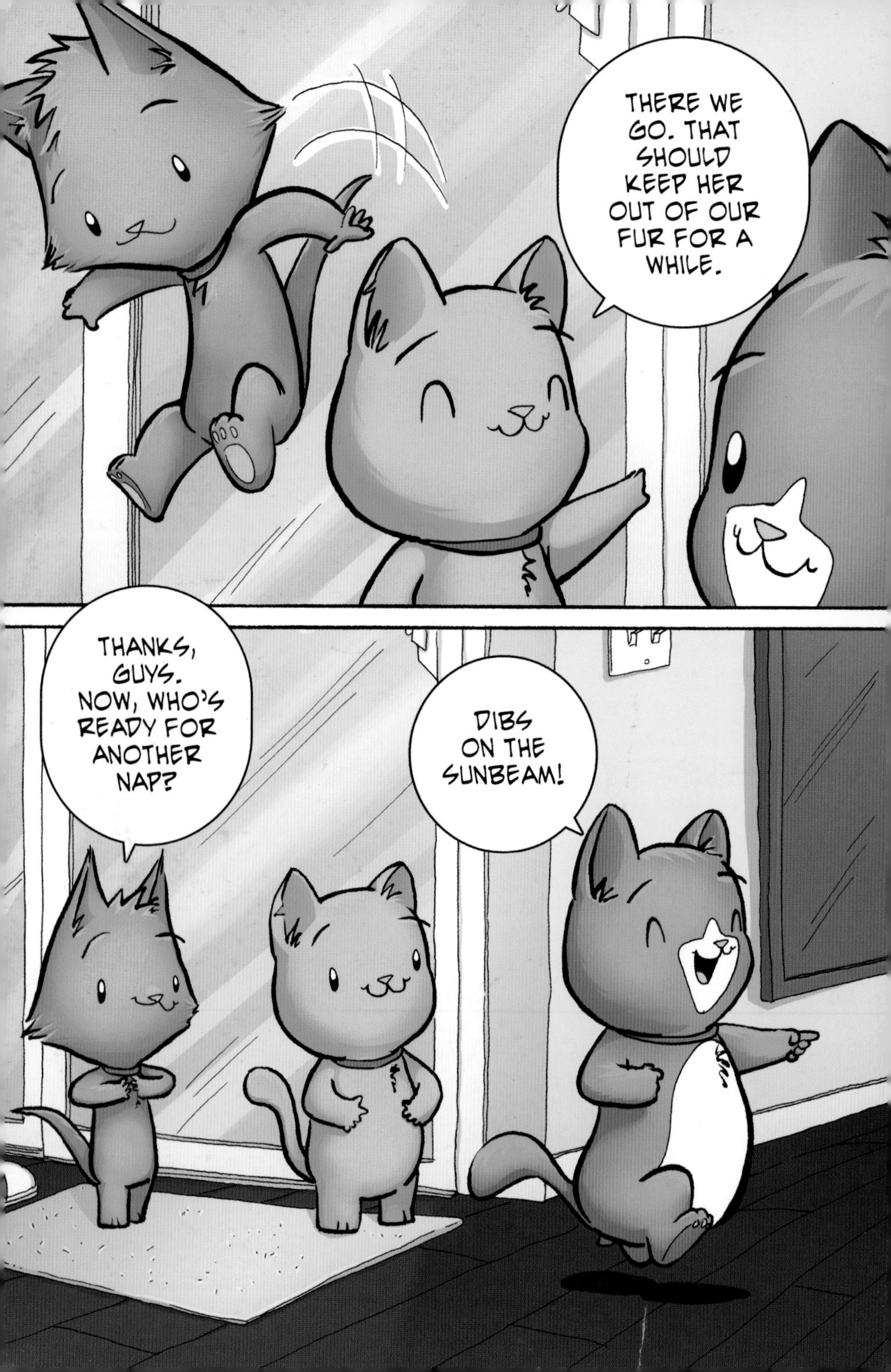
THERE WE GO. THAT SHOULD KEEP HER OUT OF OUR FUR FOR A WHILE.
THANKS, GUYS. NOW, WHO'S READY FOR ANOTHER NAP?
DIBS ON THE SUNBEAM!

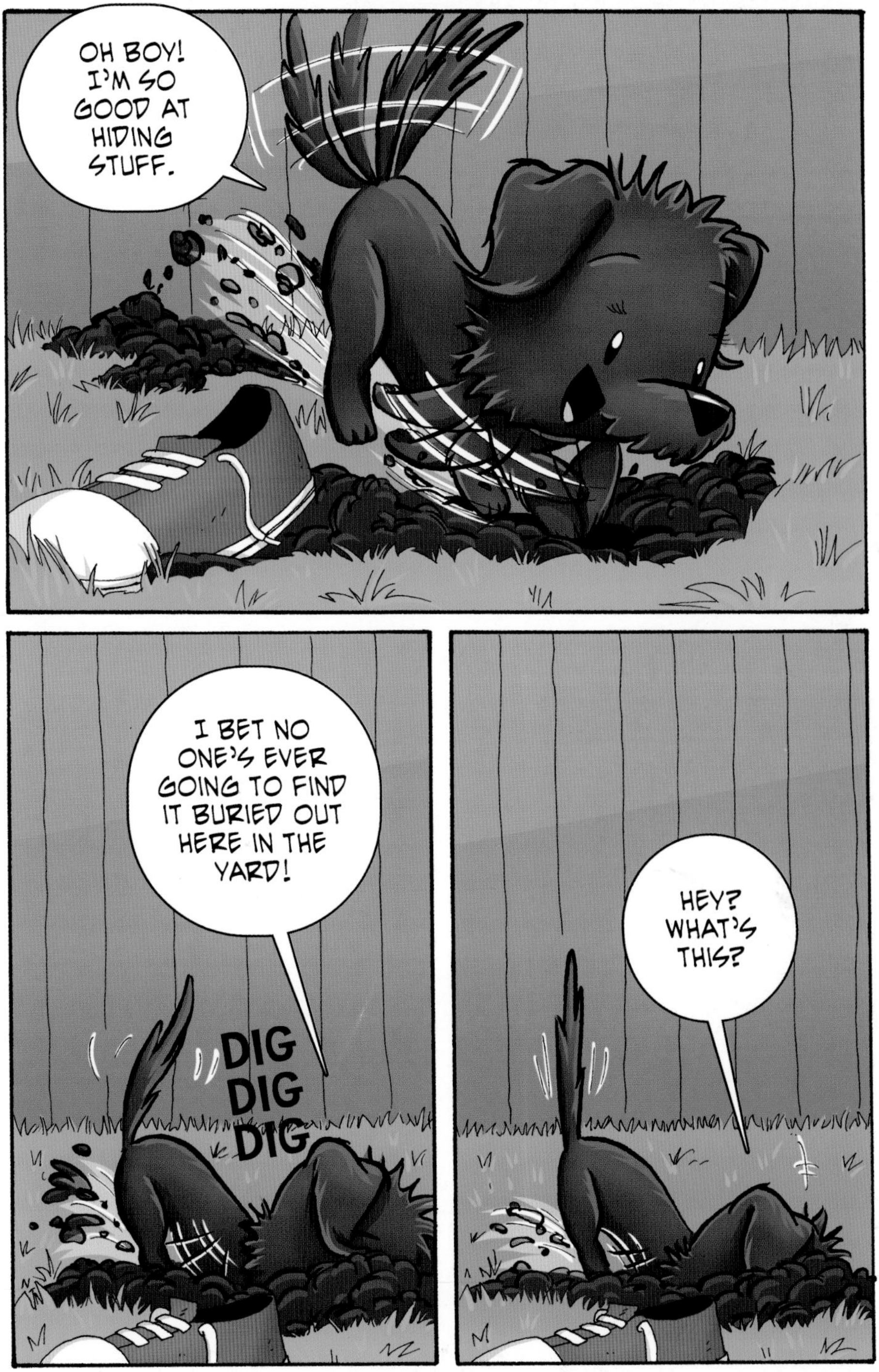
OH BOY! I'M SO GOOD AT HIDING STUFF.
I BET NO ONE'S EVER GOING TO FIND IT BURIED OUT HERE IN THE YARD!
DIG DIG DIG
HEY? WHAT'S THIS?

THERE'S ALREADY A GIANT HOLE DOWN HERE...

MUST BE THOSE PESKY SKUNKS AGAIN. THEY'RE ALWAYS DIGGING UNDER OUR HOUSE.

SNIFF SNIFF SNIFF

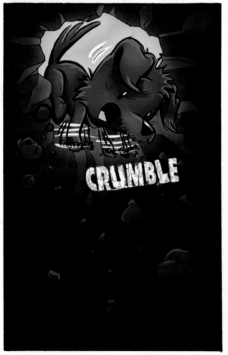

CRUMBLE

WHOA!

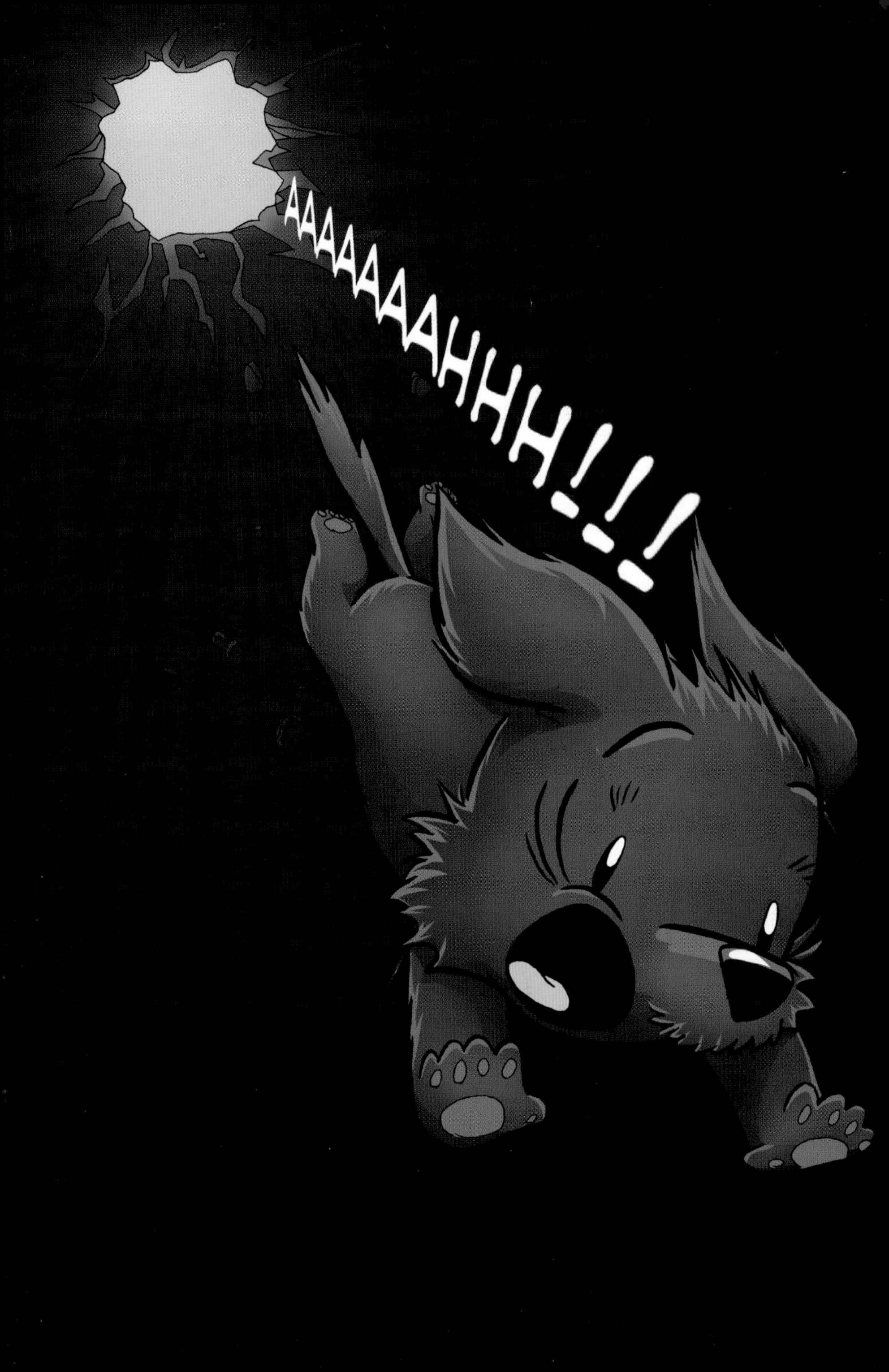
AAAAAAAAHHHH!!!!

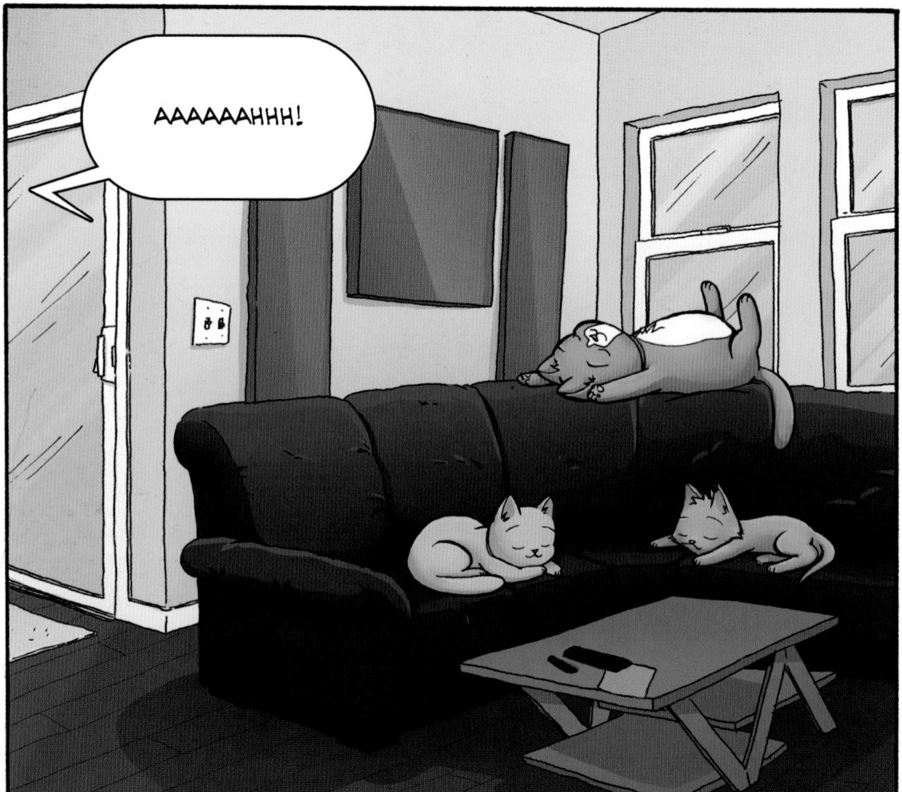
AAAAAAHHH!

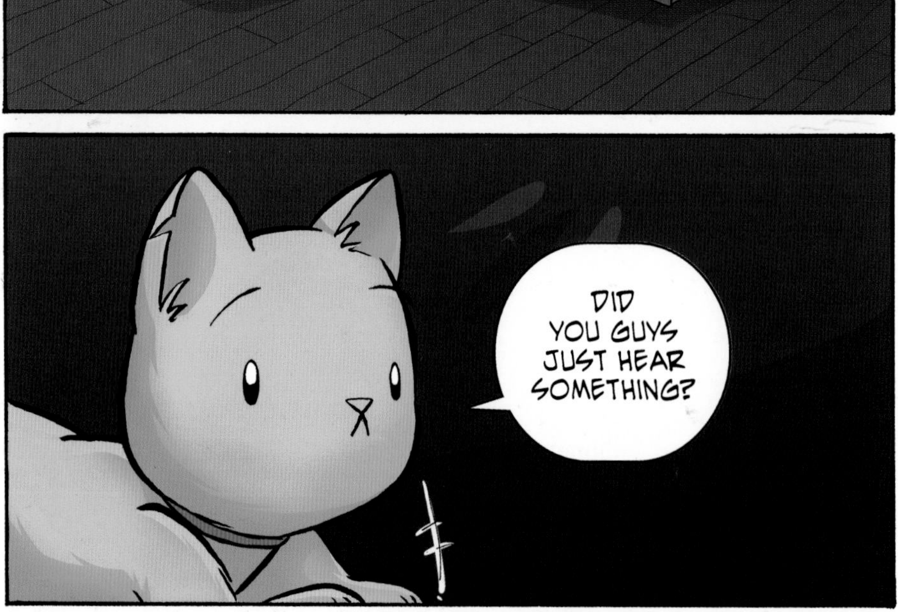
DID YOU GUYS JUST HEAR SOMETHING?

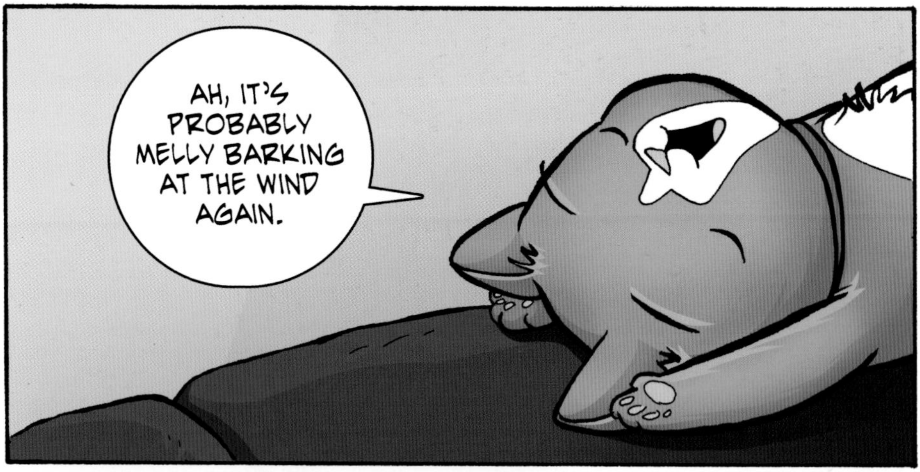
AH, IT'S PROBABLY MELLY BARKING AT THE WIND AGAIN.

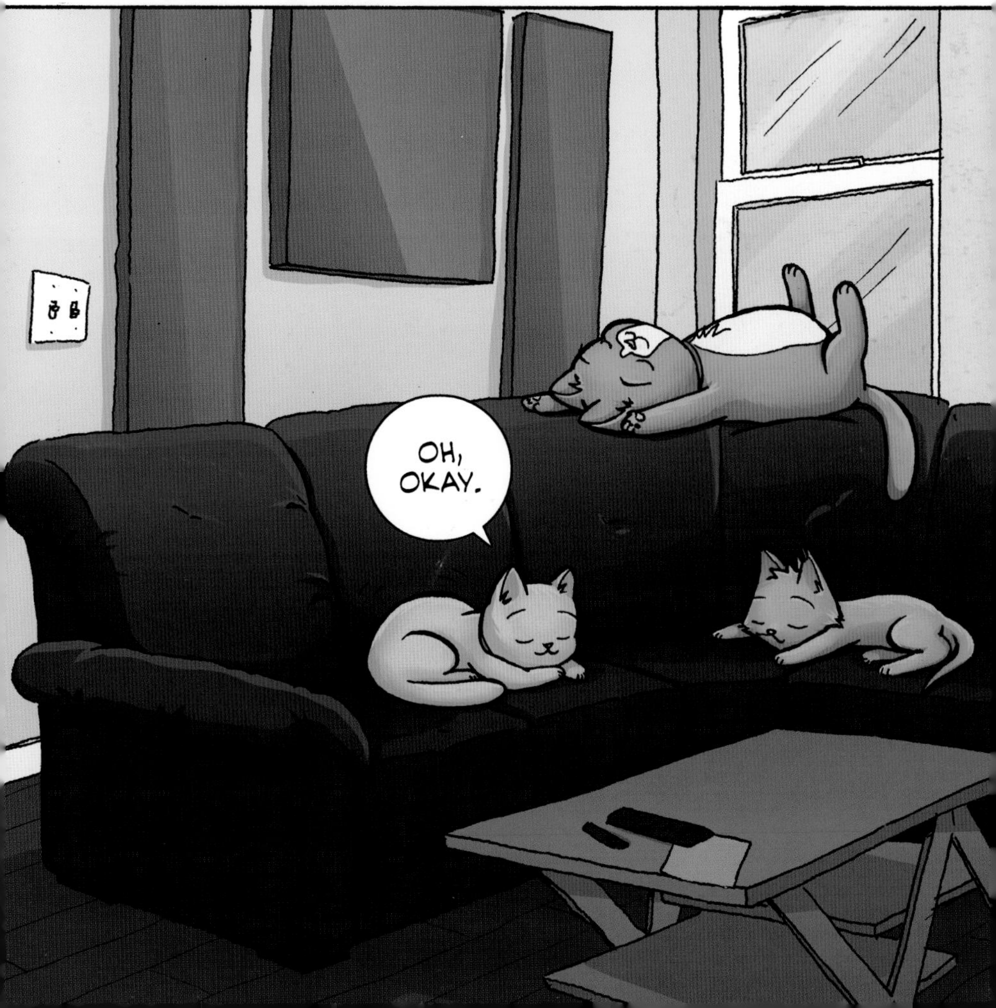
OH, OKAY.

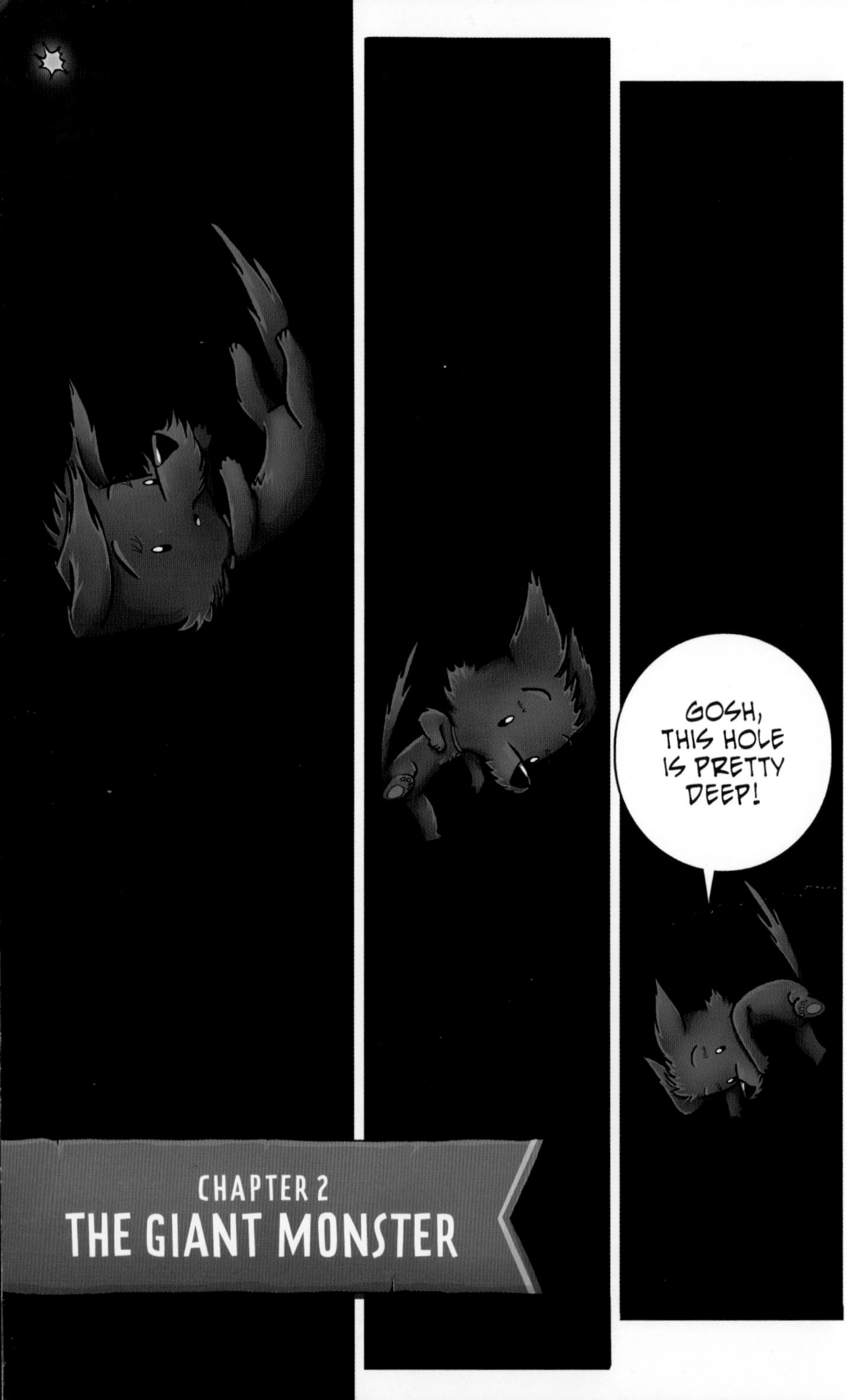
GOSH, THIS HOLE IS PRETTY DEEP!

CHAPTER 2
THE GIANT MONSTER

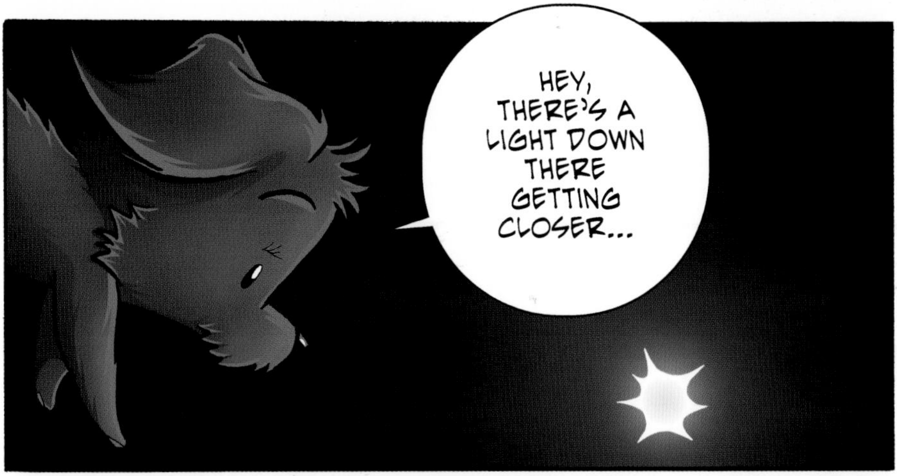
HEY, THERE'S A LIGHT DOWN THERE GETTING CLOSER...

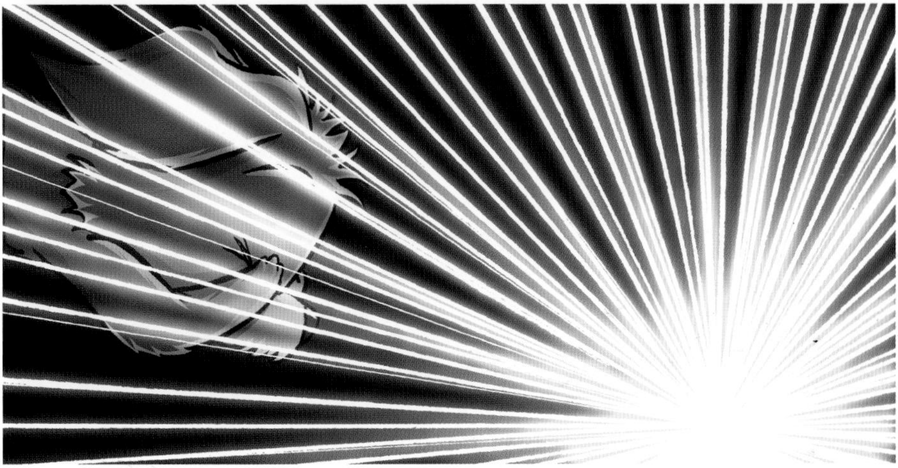

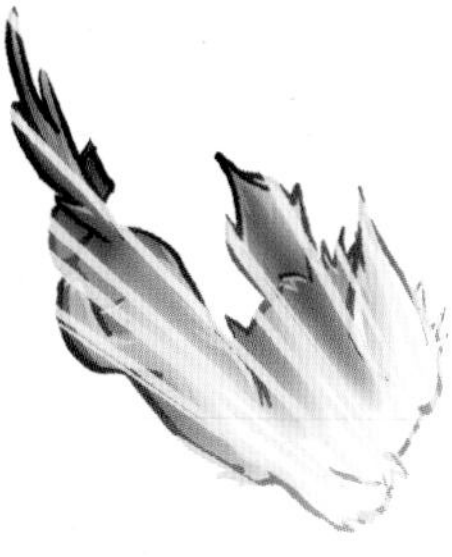

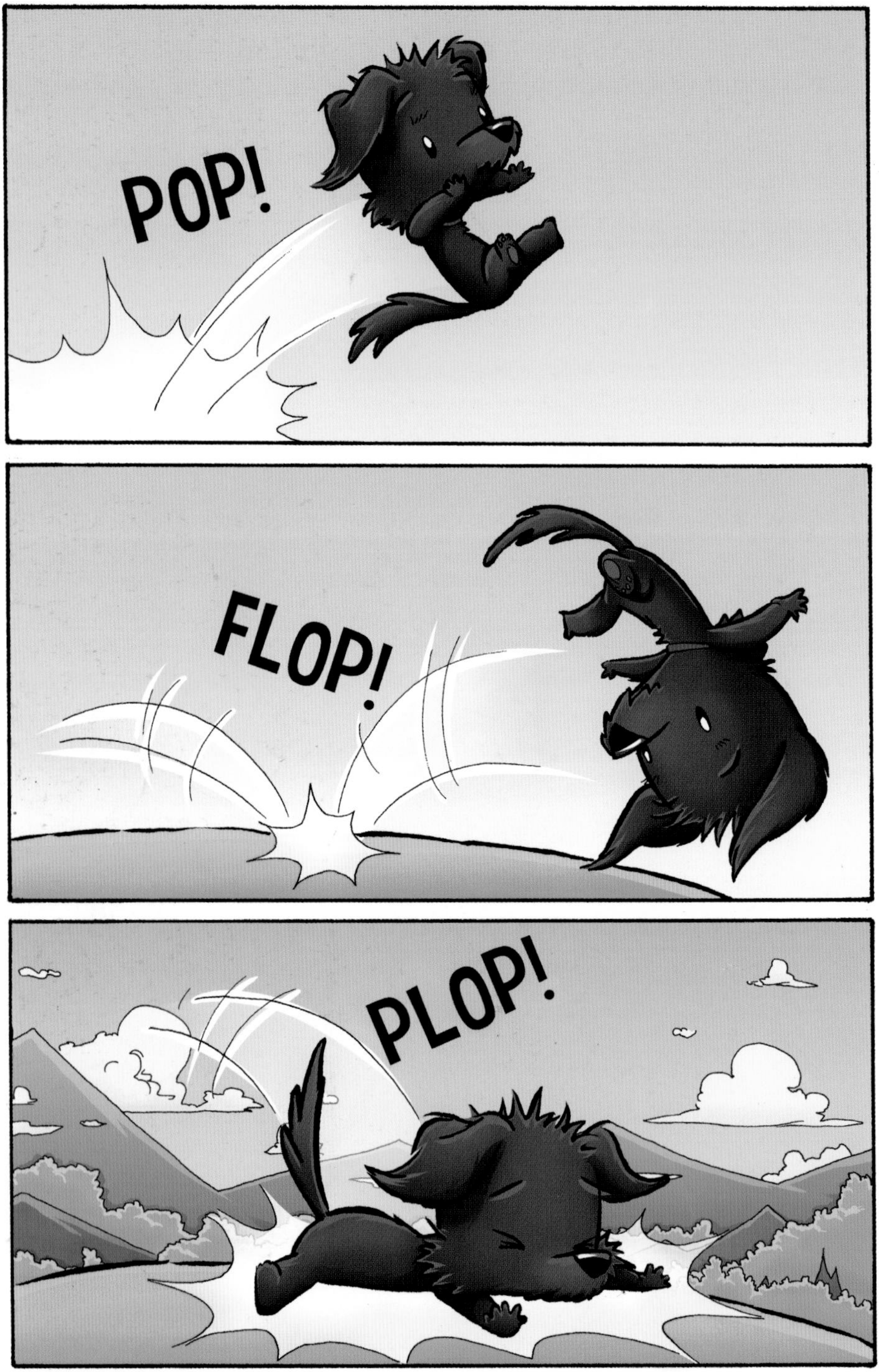
POP!
FLOP!
PLOP!

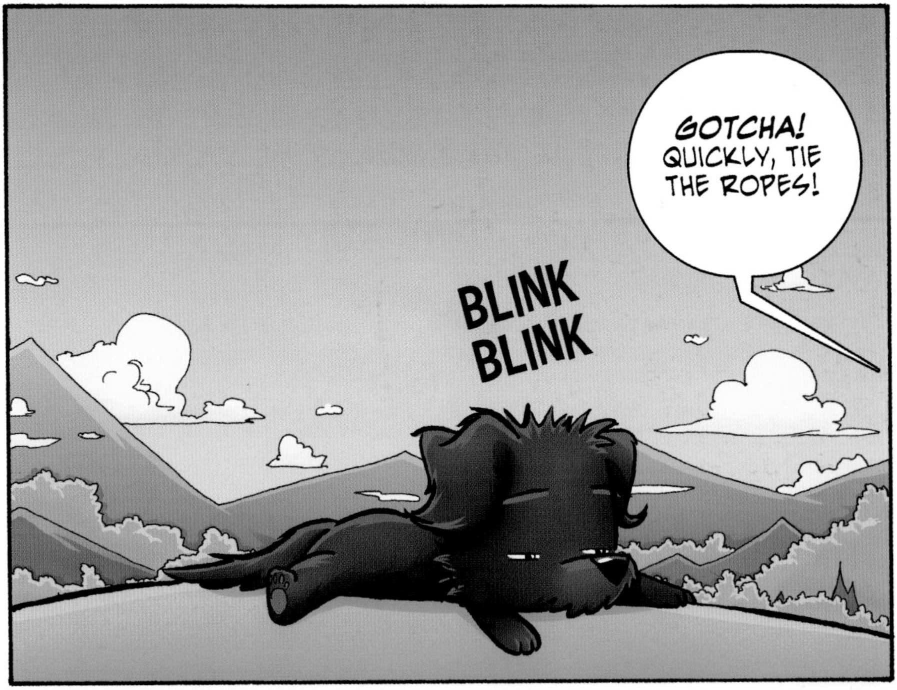
GOTCHA! QUICKLY, TIE THE ROPES!
BLINK BLINK

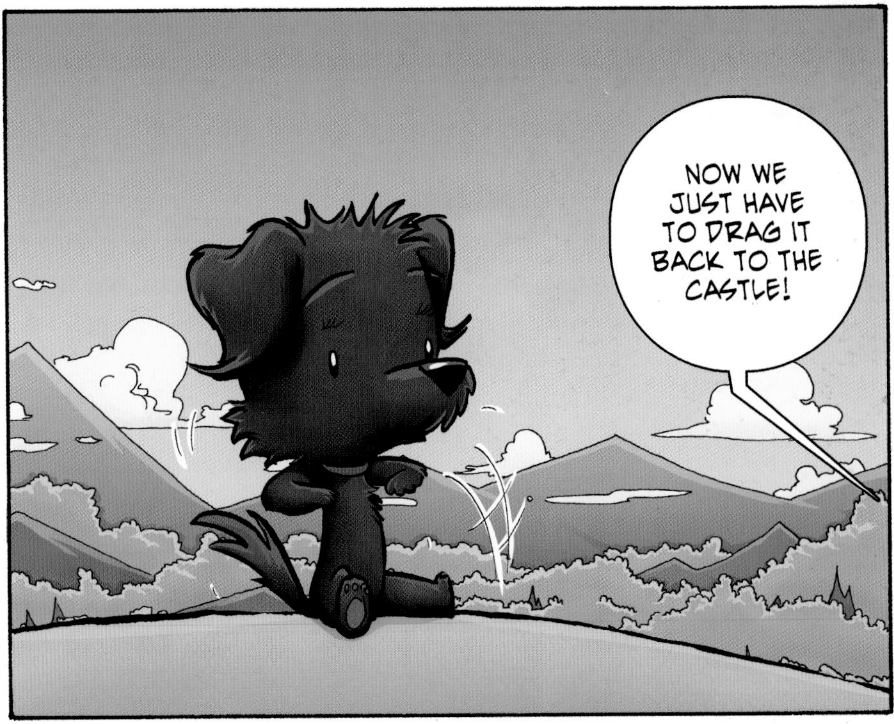
NOW WE JUST HAVE TO DRAG IT BACK TO THE CASTLE!

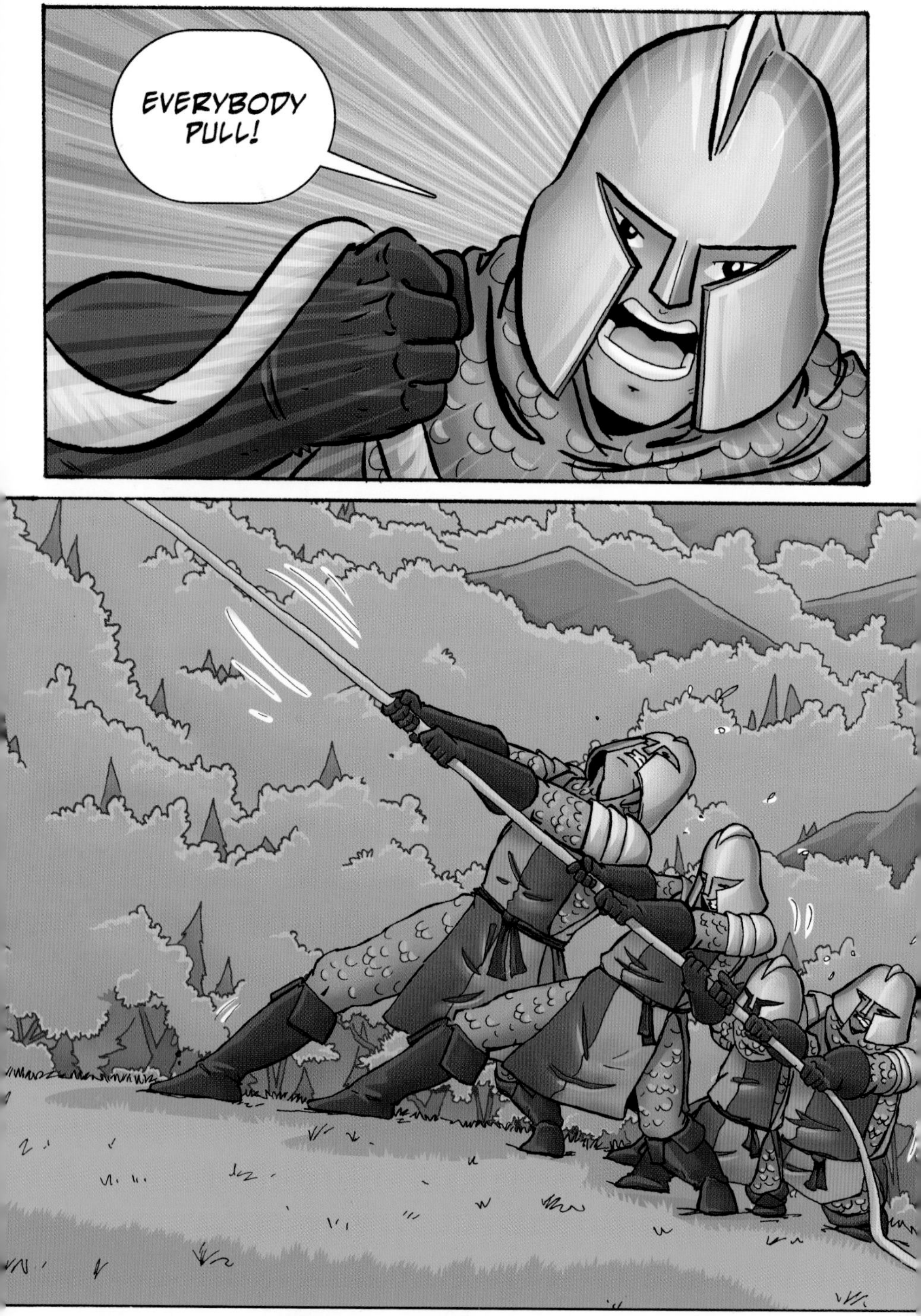
EVERYBODY PULL!

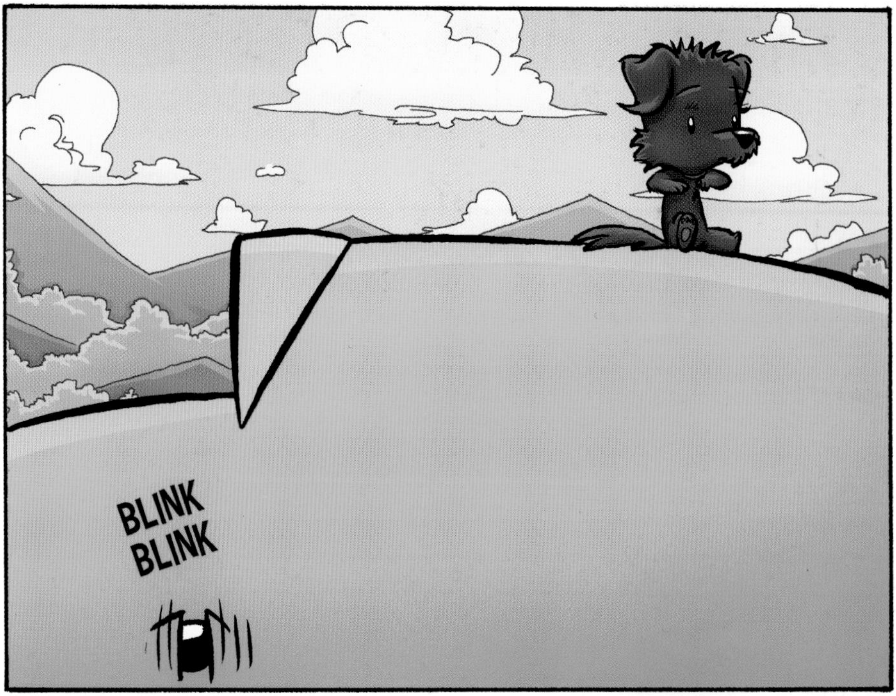
BLINK
BLINK

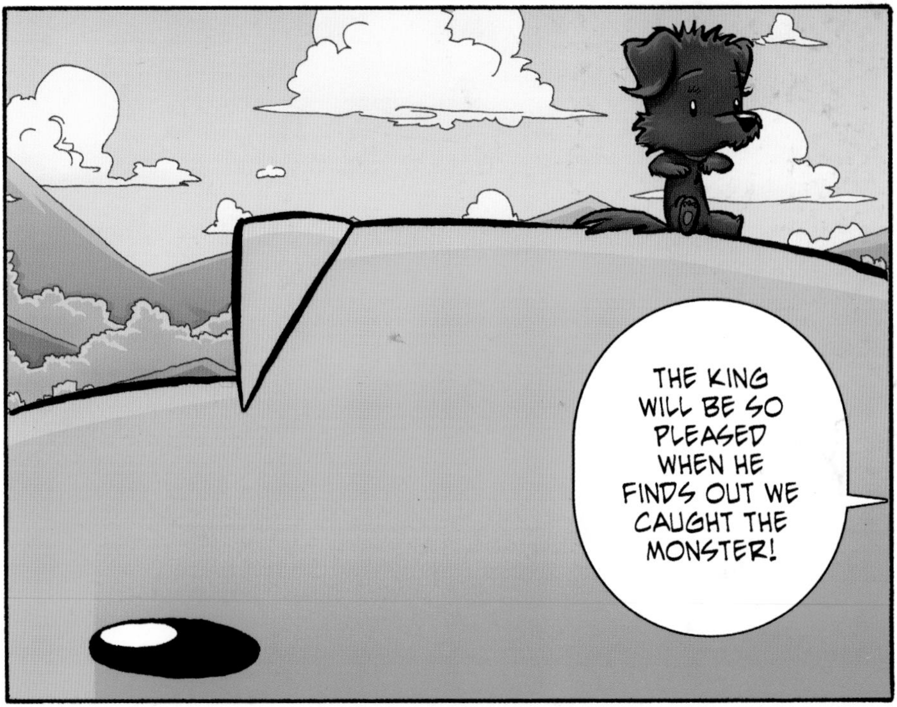
THE KING WILL BE SO PLEASED WHEN HE FINDS OUT WE CAUGHT THE MONSTER!

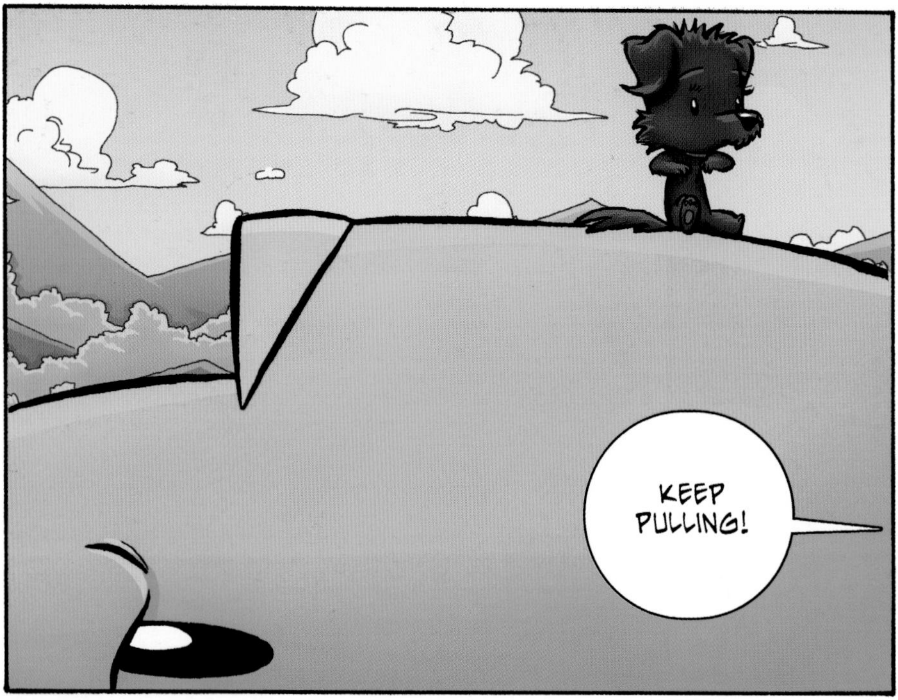
KEEP
PULLING!

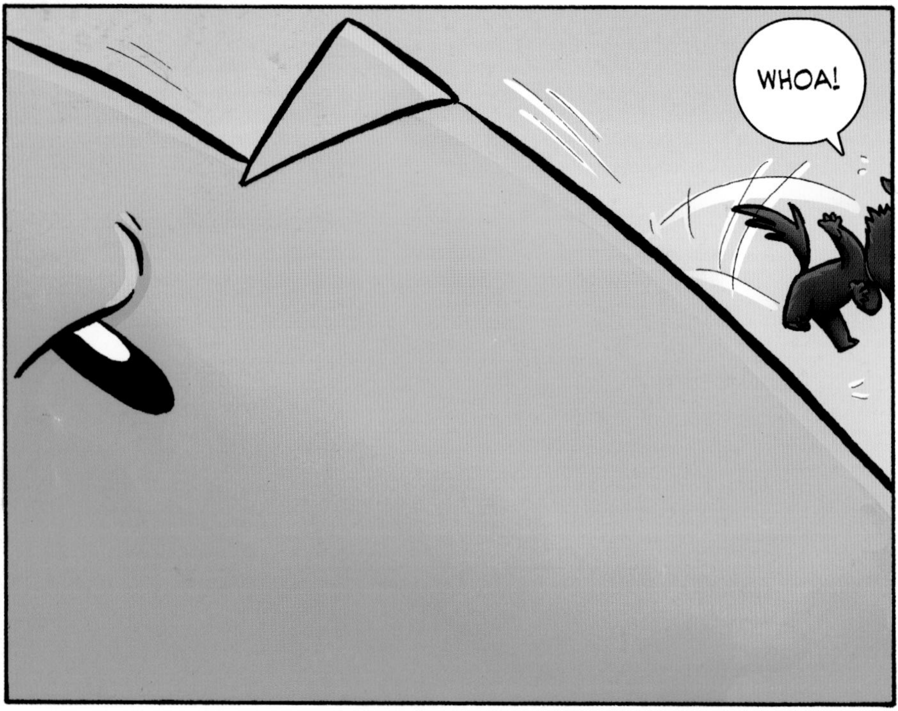
WHOA!

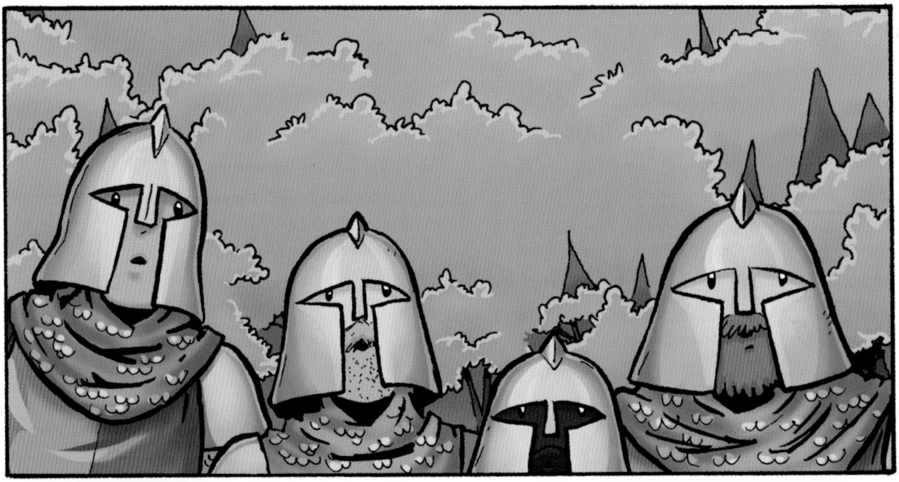

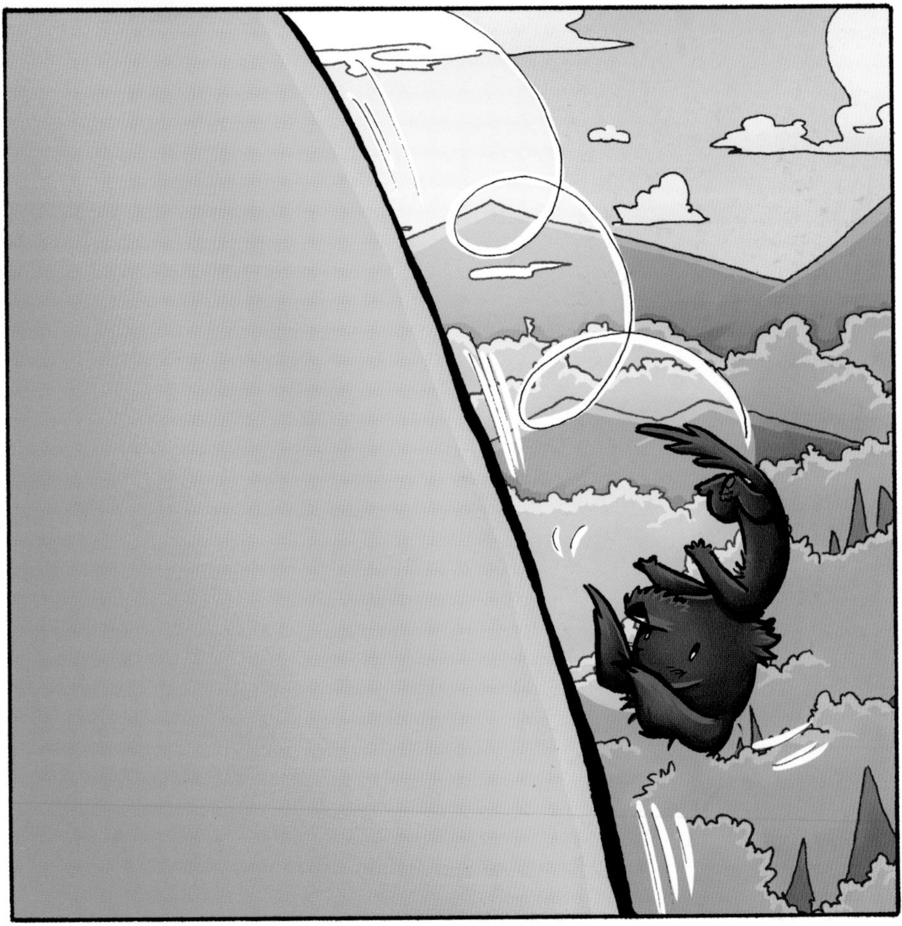

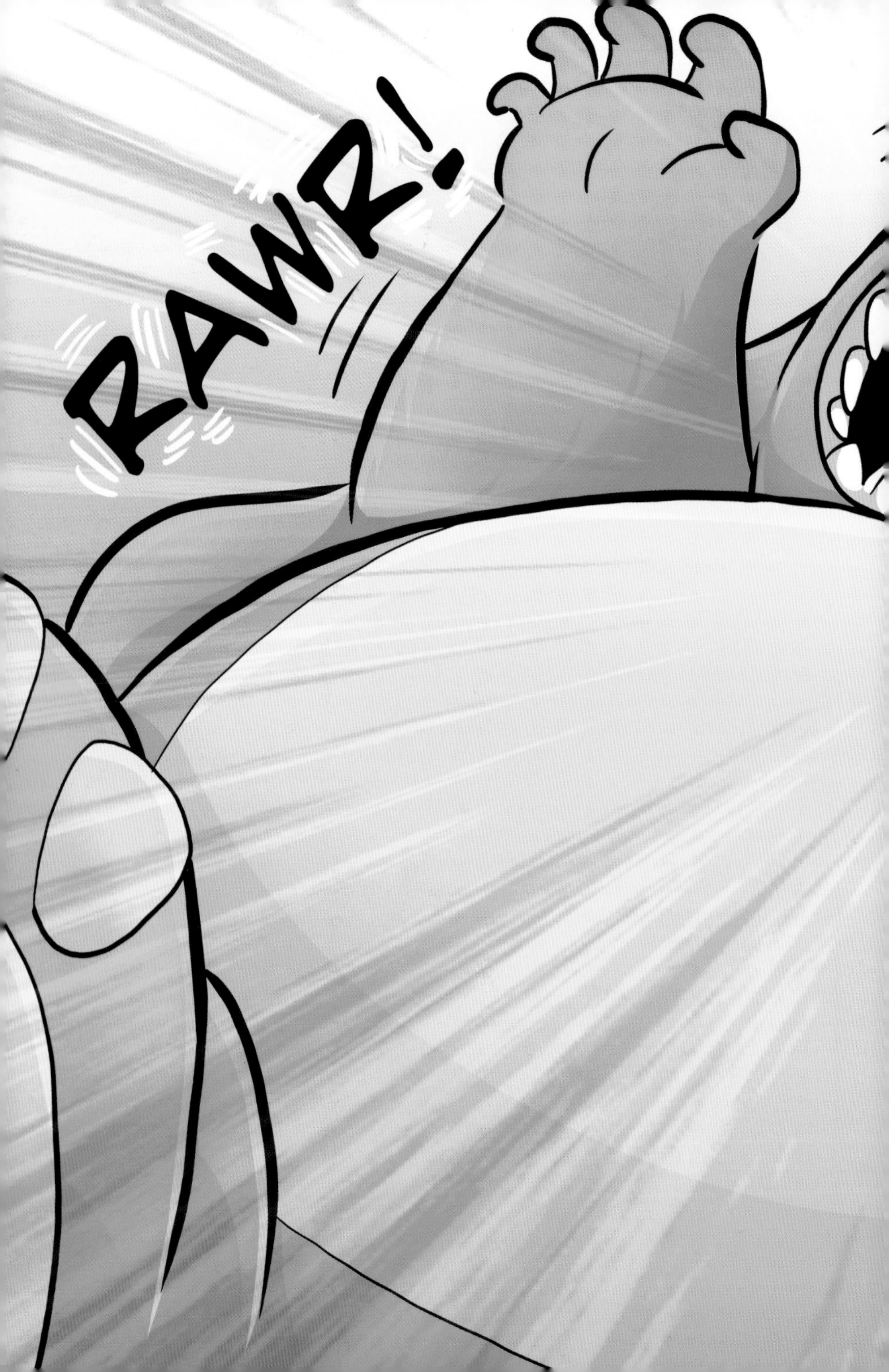
RAWR!

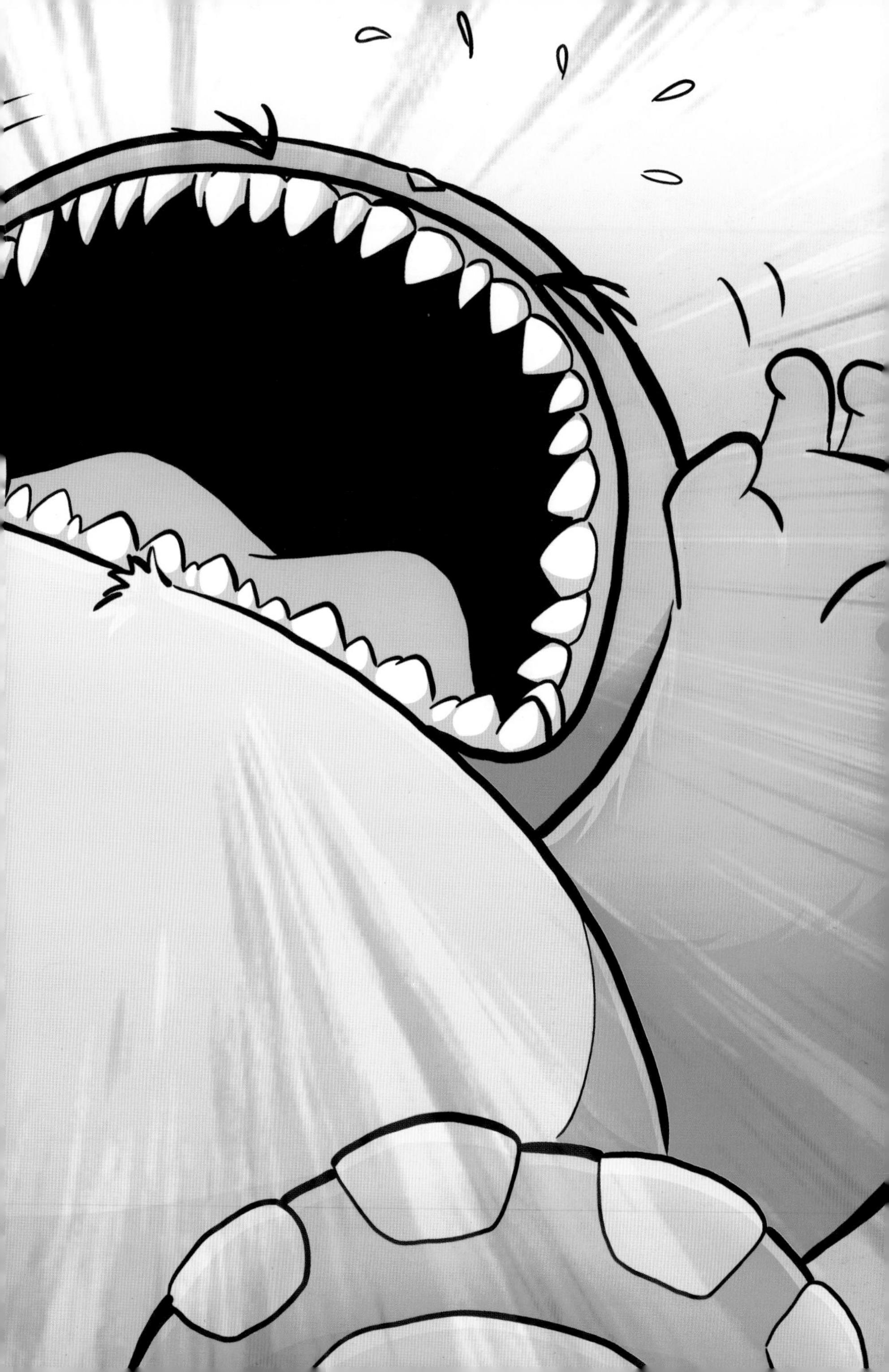

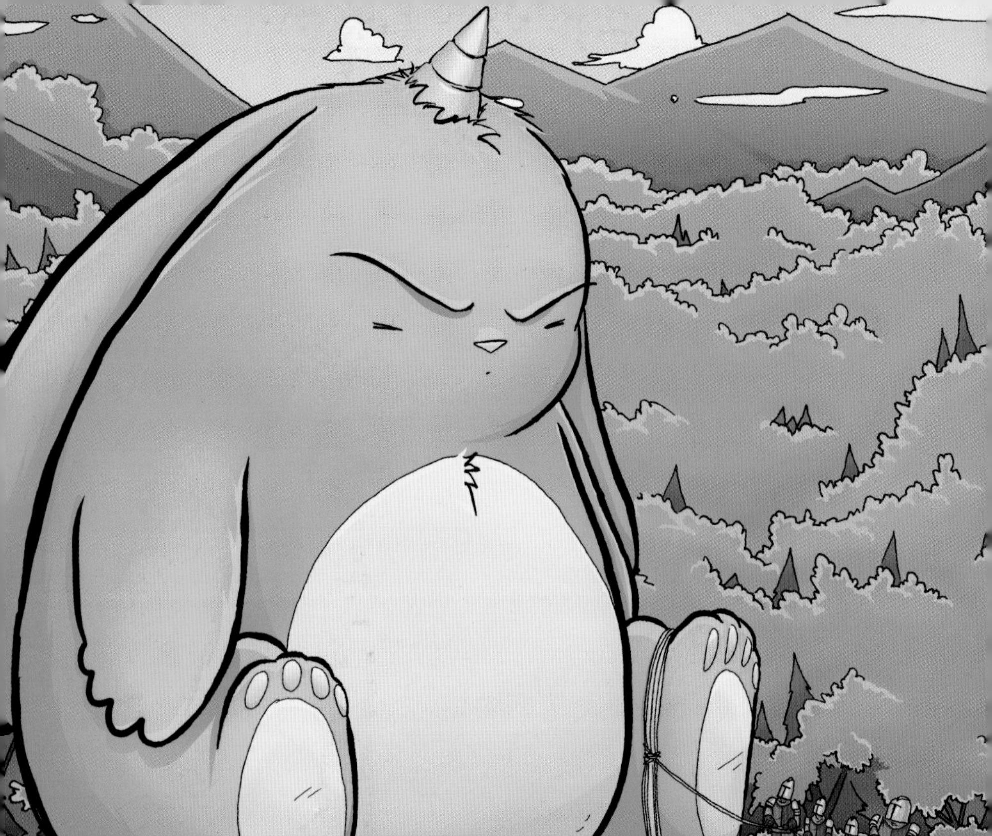

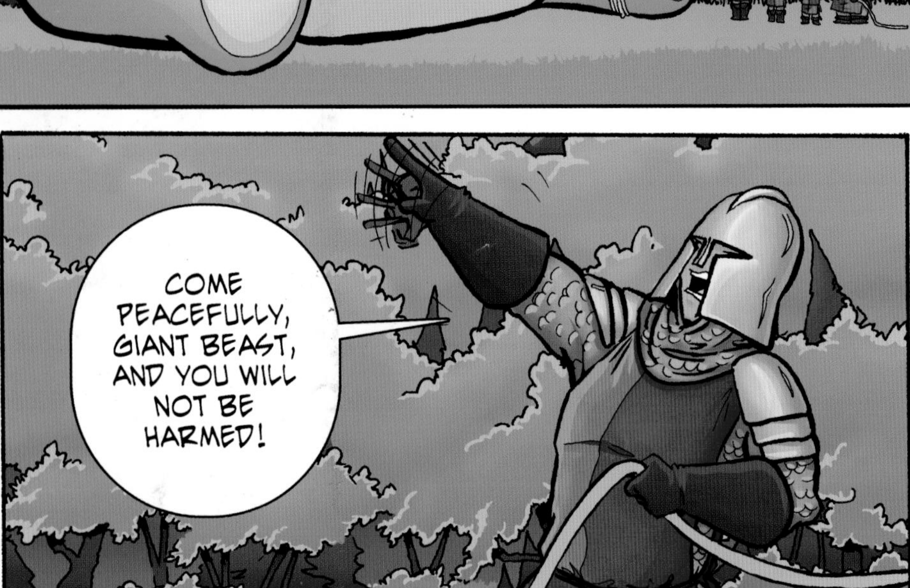
COME PEACEFULLY, GIANT BEAST, AND YOU WILL NOT BE HARMED!

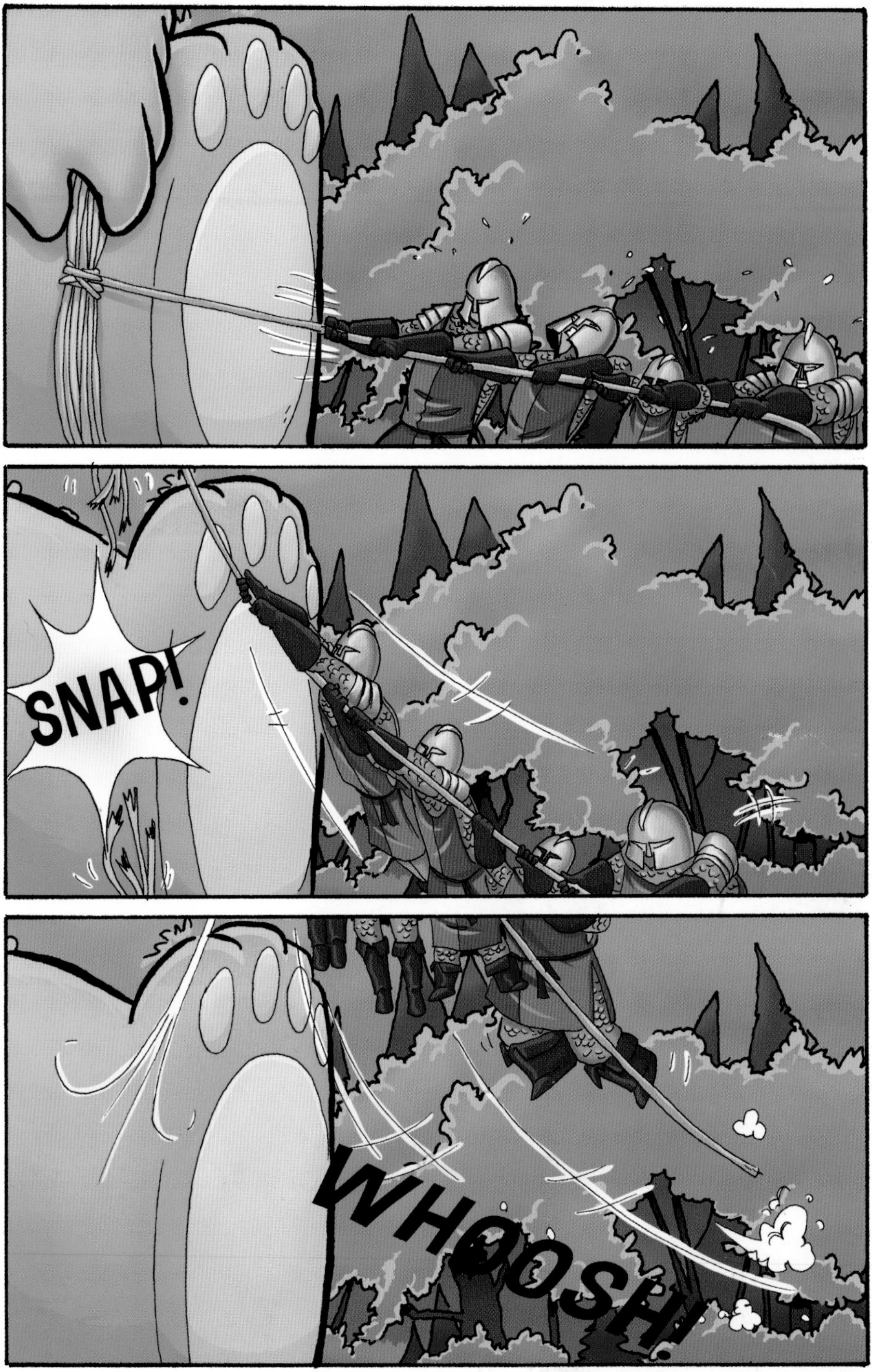
SNAP!
WHOOSH!

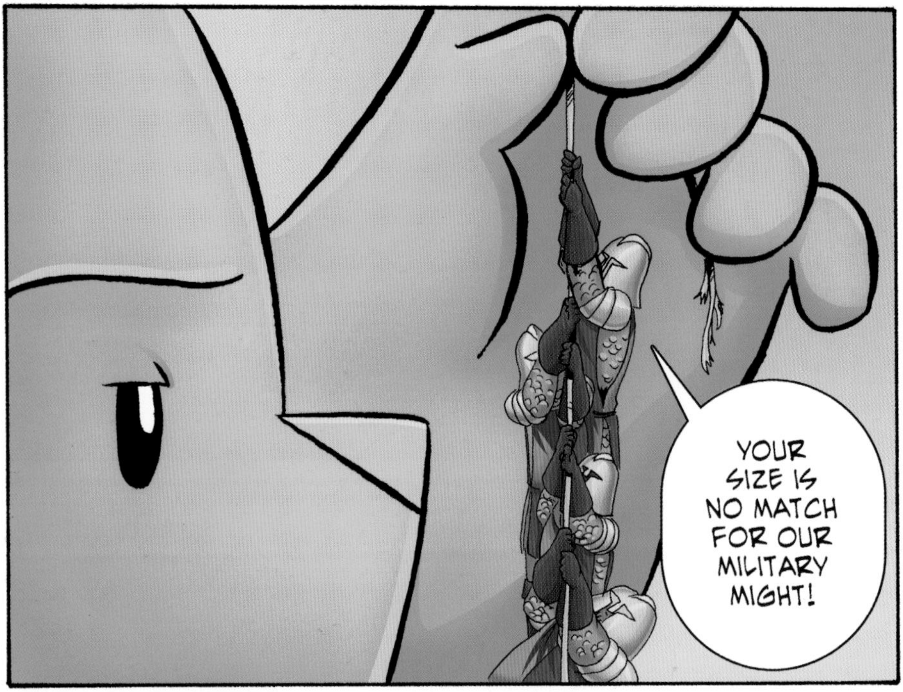
YOUR SIZE IS NO MATCH FOR OUR MILITARY MIGHT!

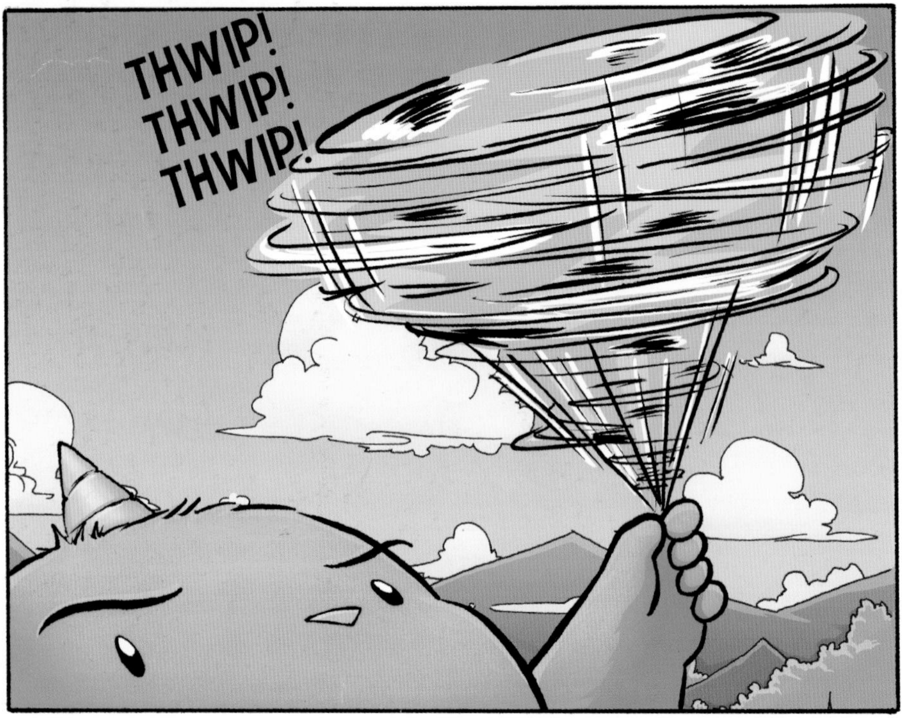
THWIP! THWIP! THWIP!

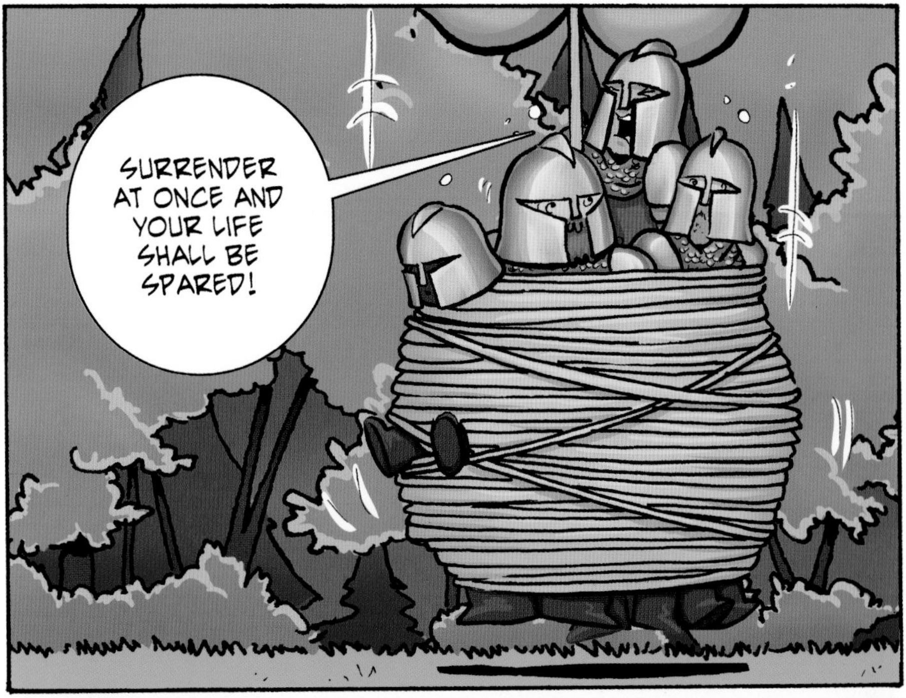
SURRENDER AT ONCE AND YOUR LIFE SHALL BE SPARED!

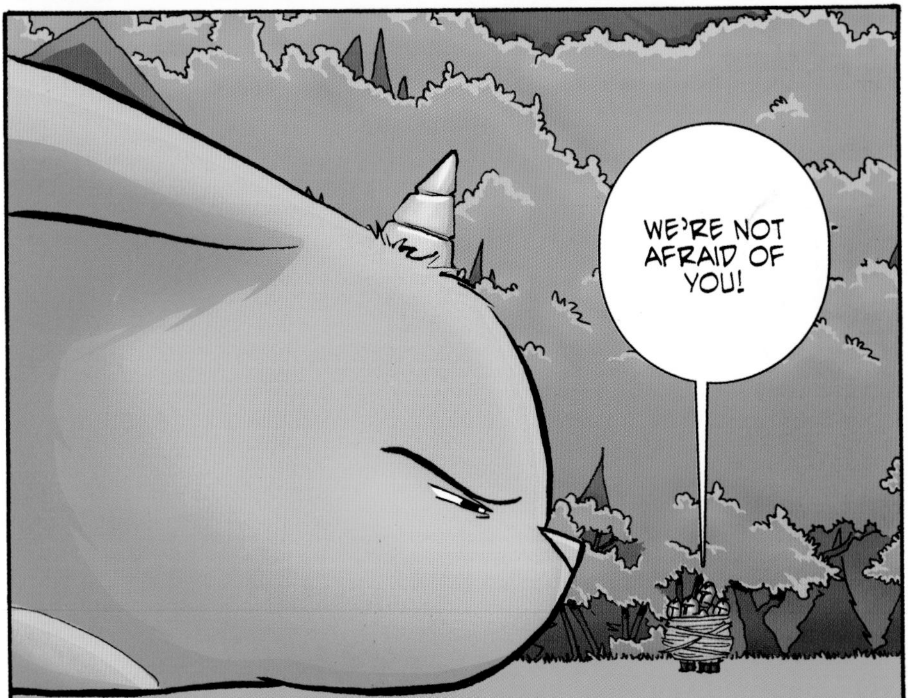
WE'RE NOT AFRAID OF YOU!

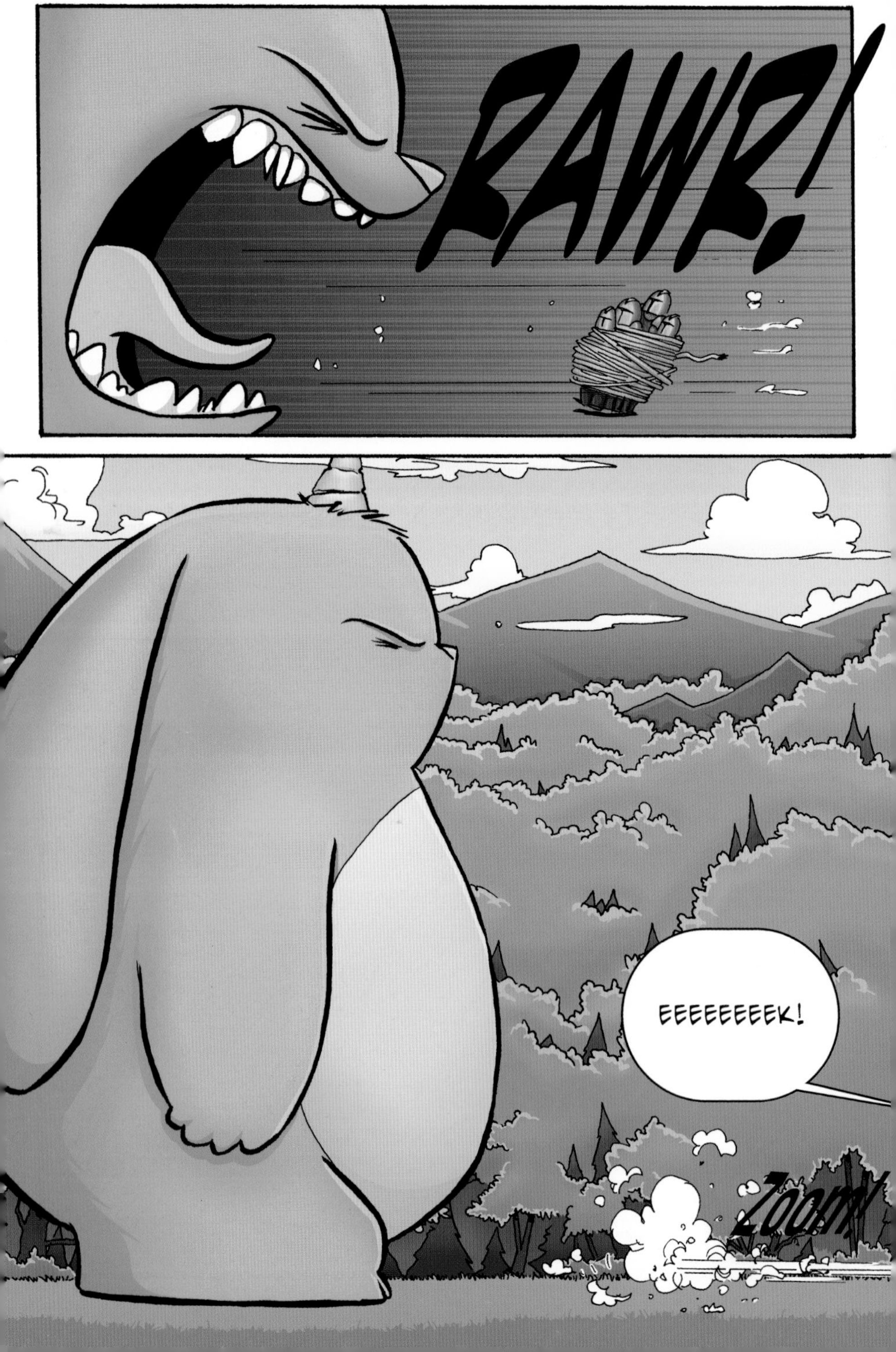
RAWR!
EEEEEEEEK!
ZOOM!

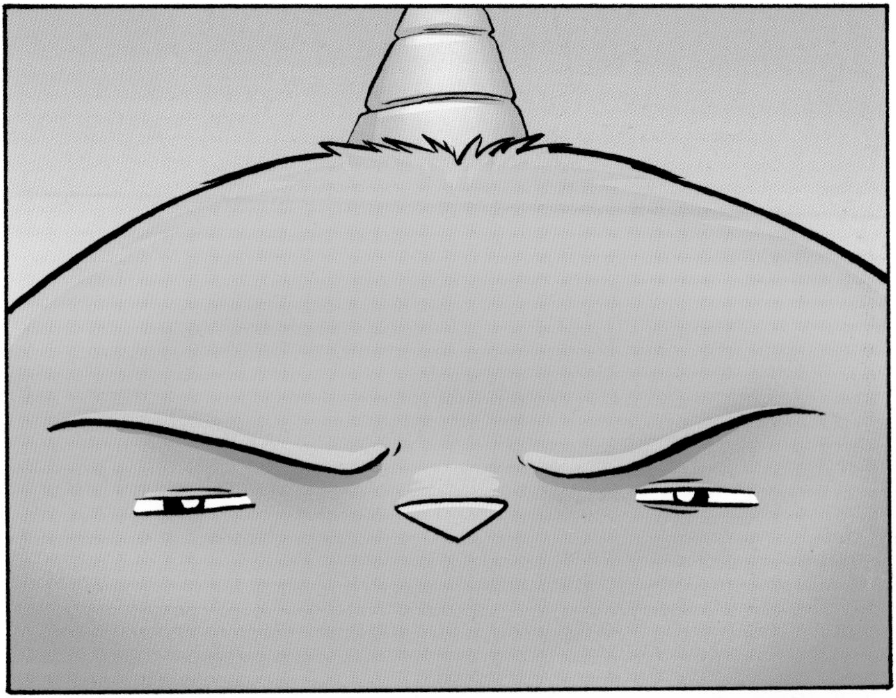
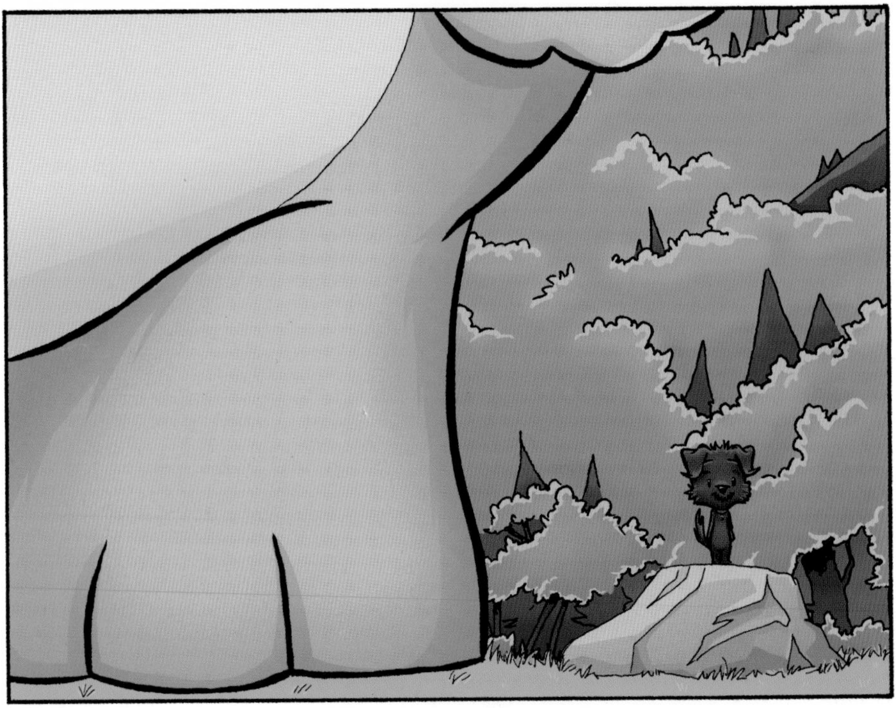

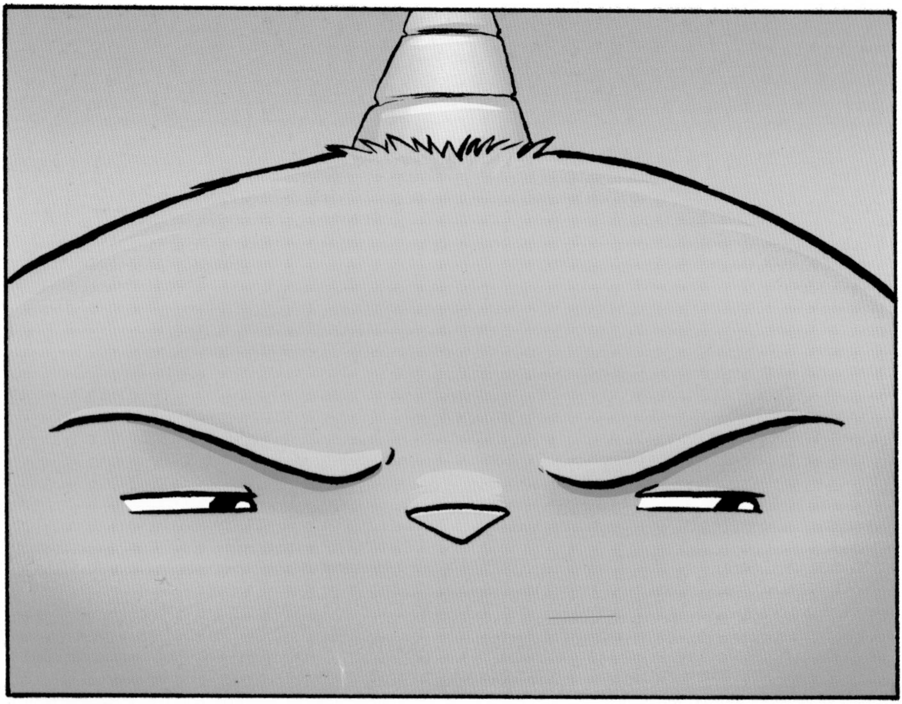

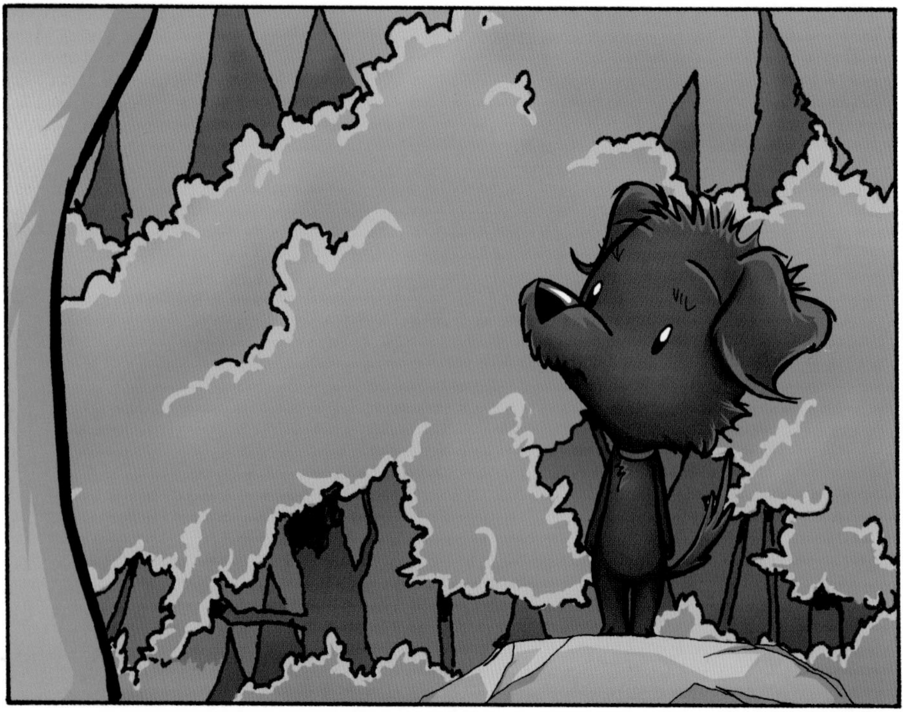

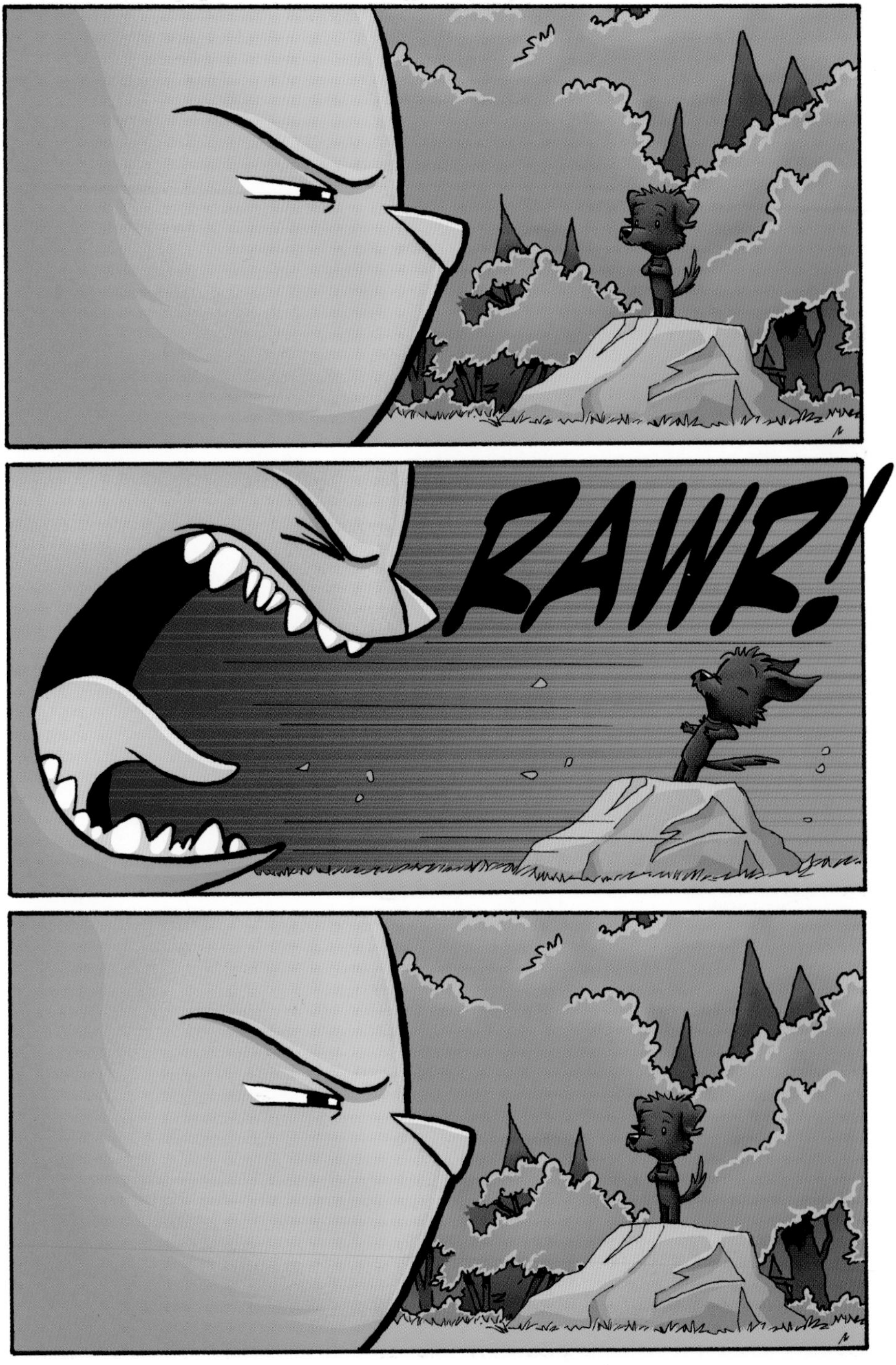
RAWR!

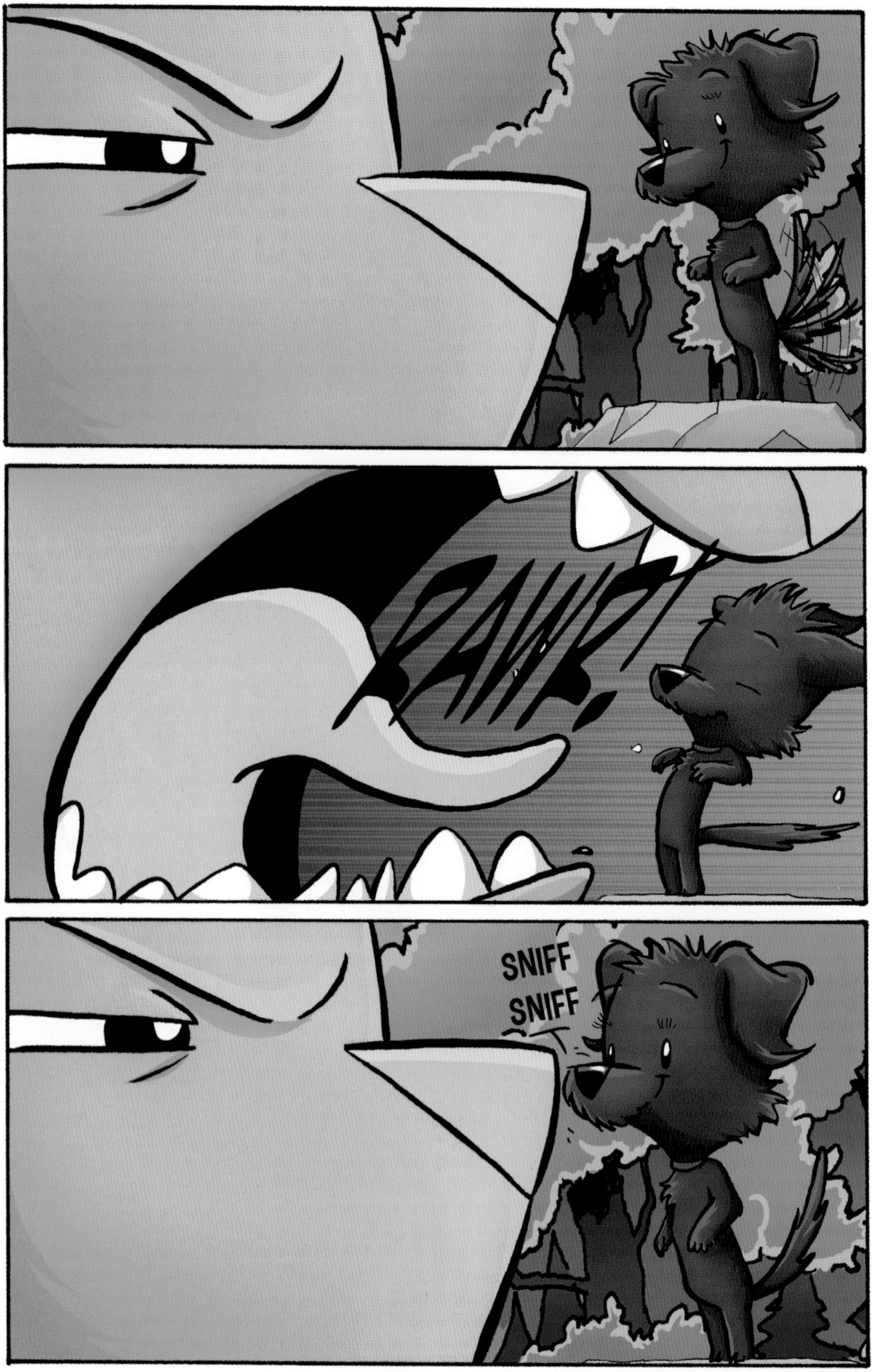
RAWR!
SNIFF
SNIFF

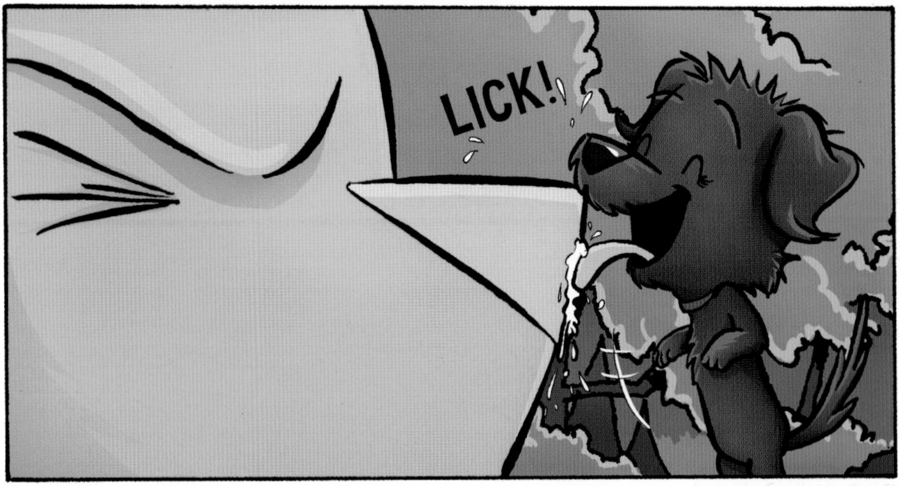
LICK!

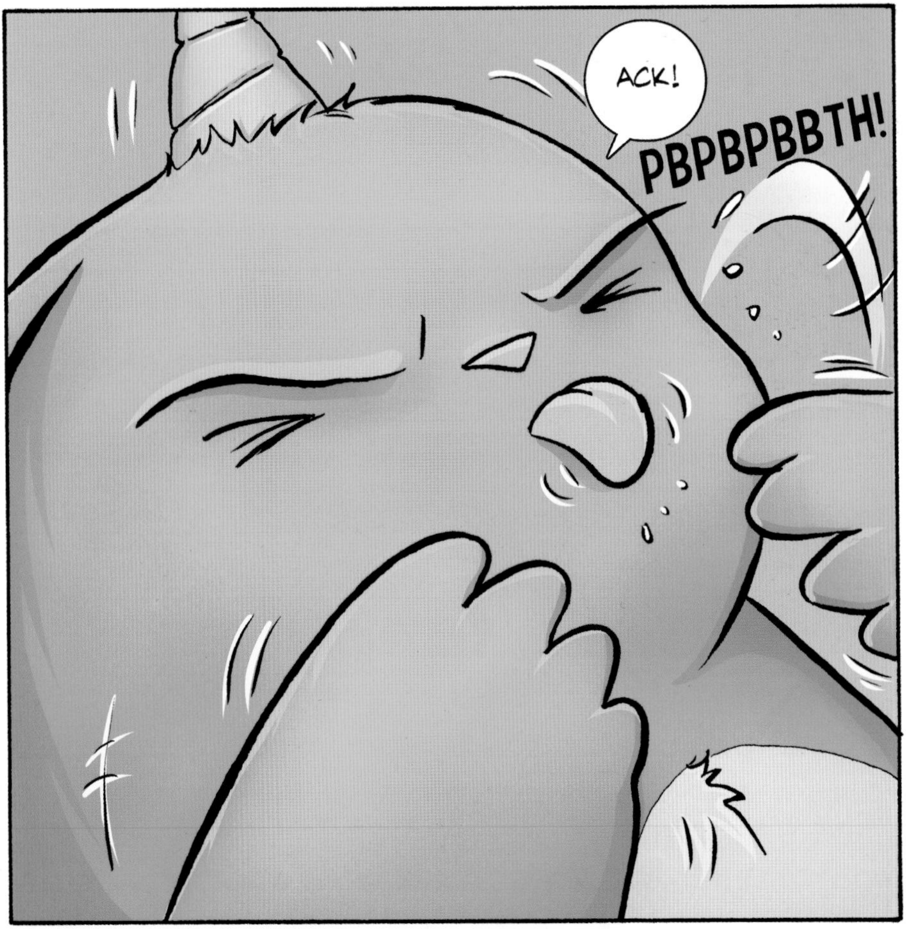
ACK!
PBPBPBBTH!

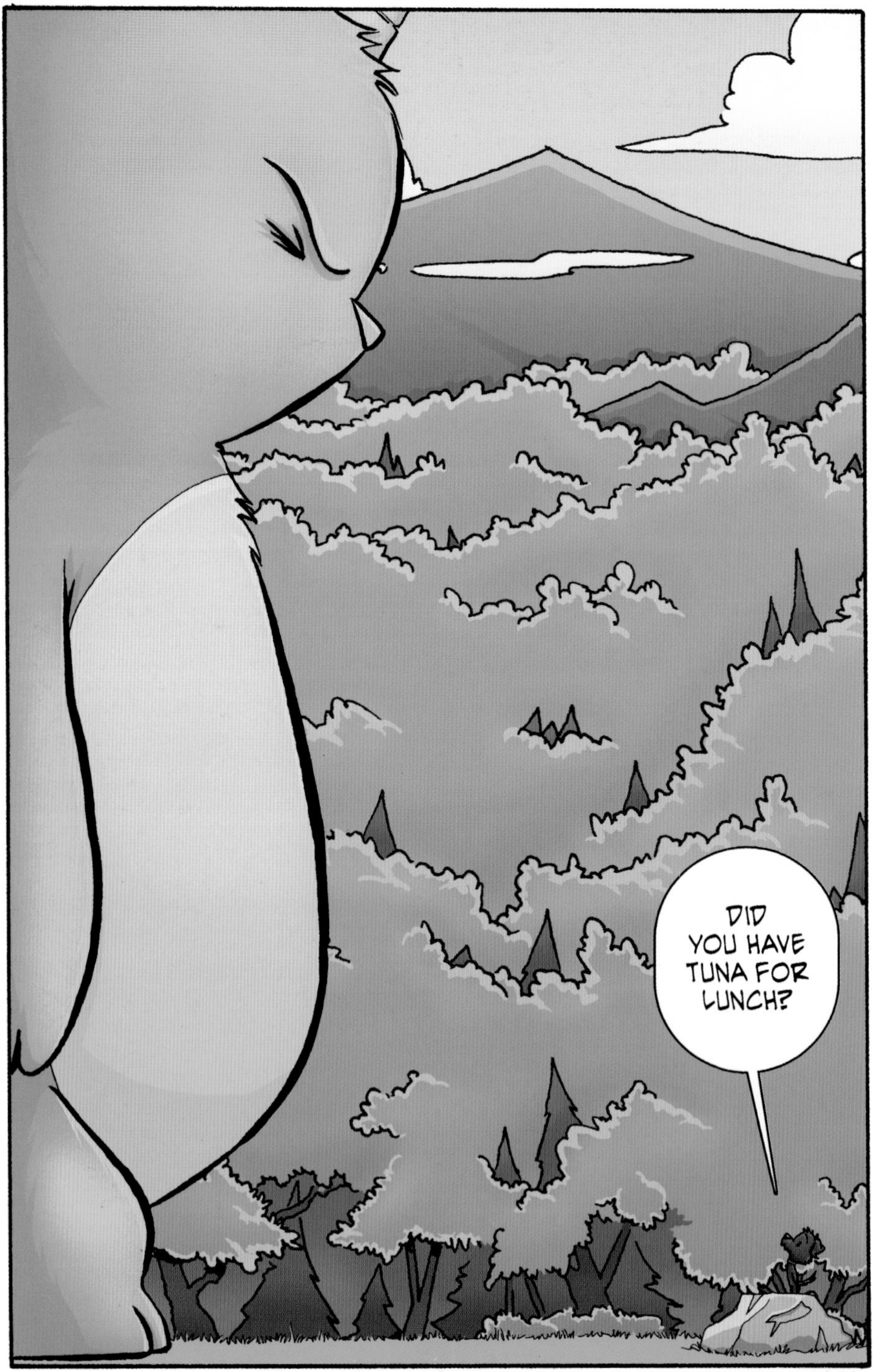
DID YOU HAVE TUNA FOR LUNCH?

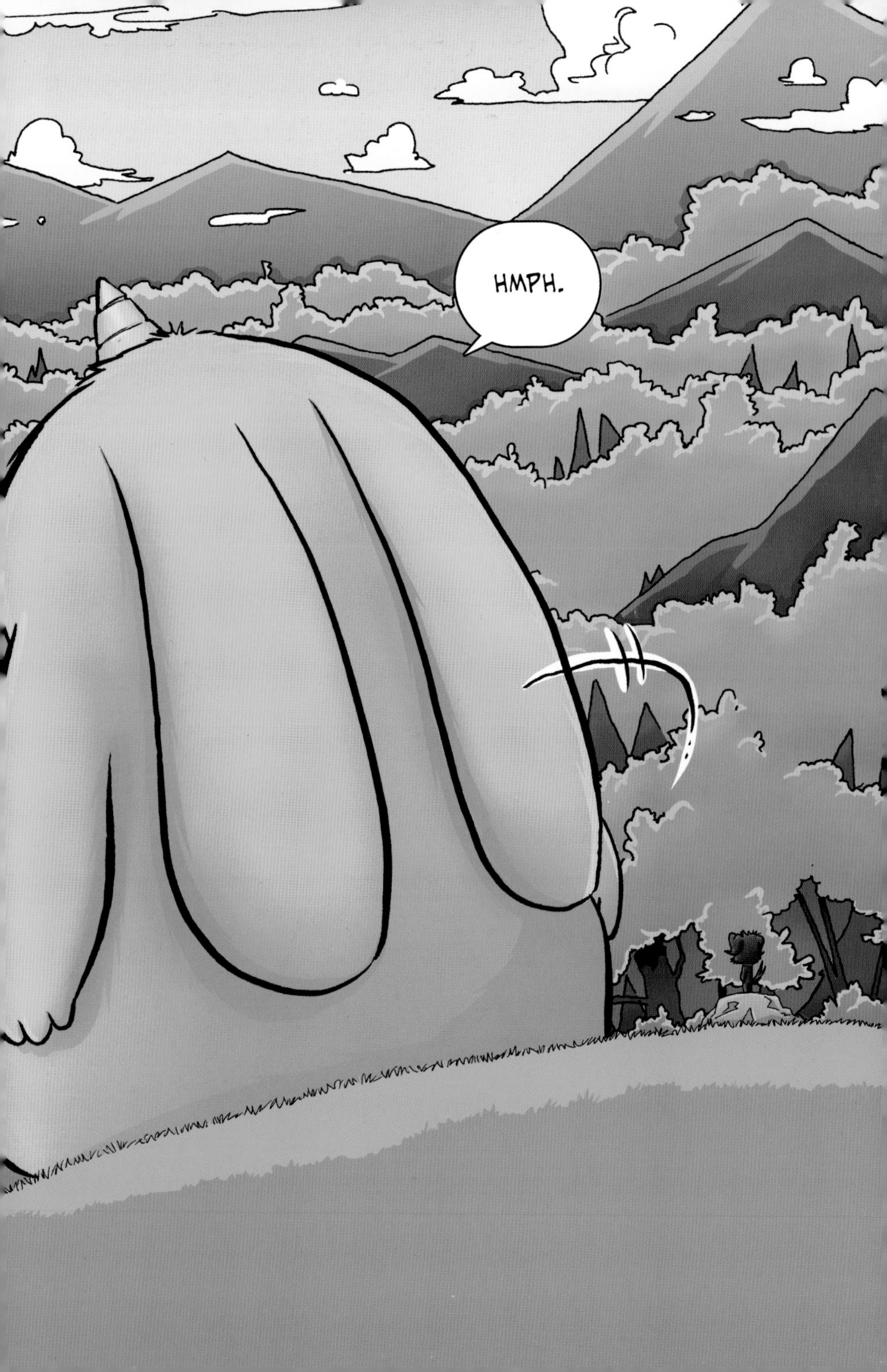
HMPH.

CHAPTER 3
A PERSISTENT PUP

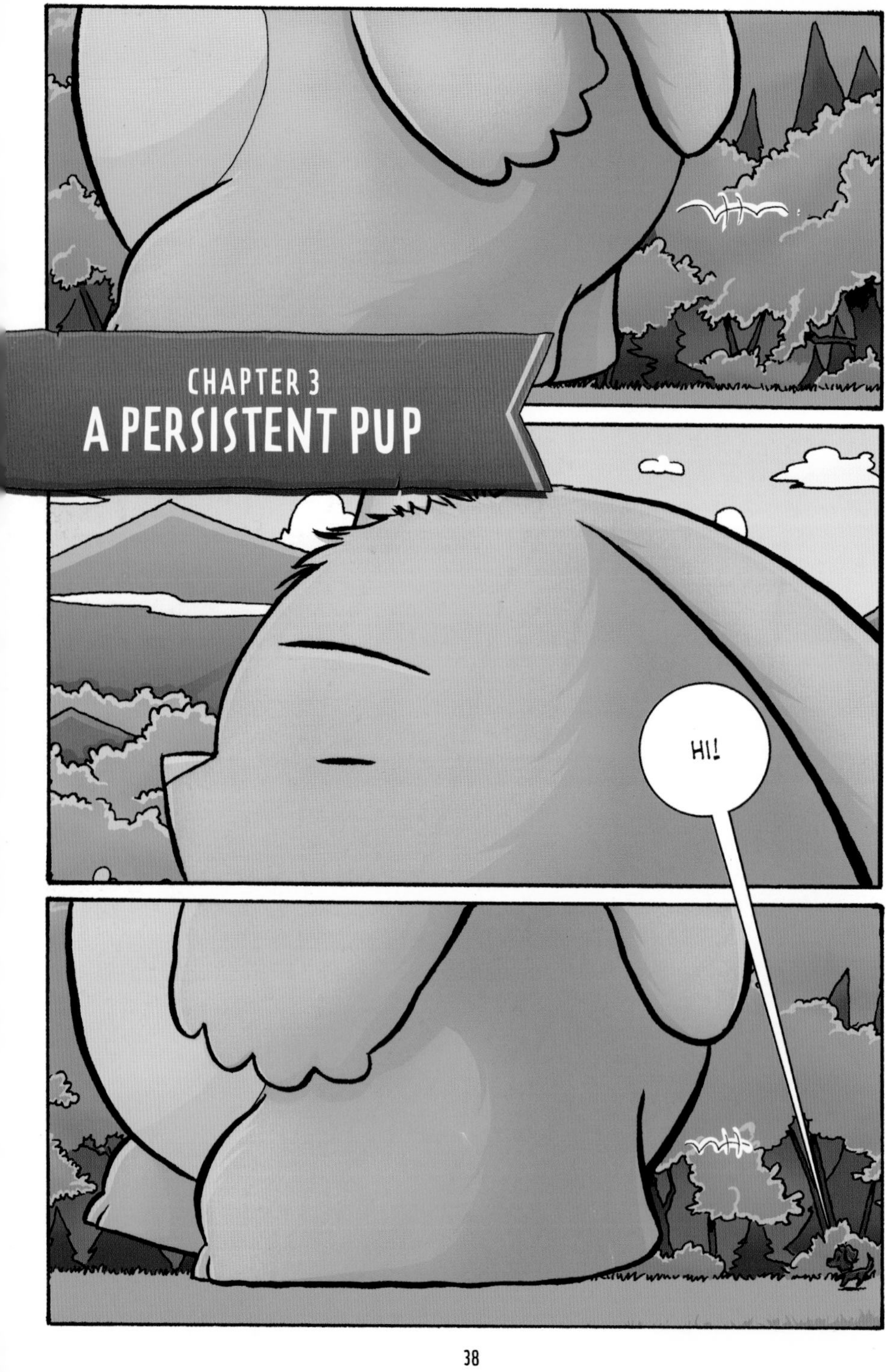
HI!

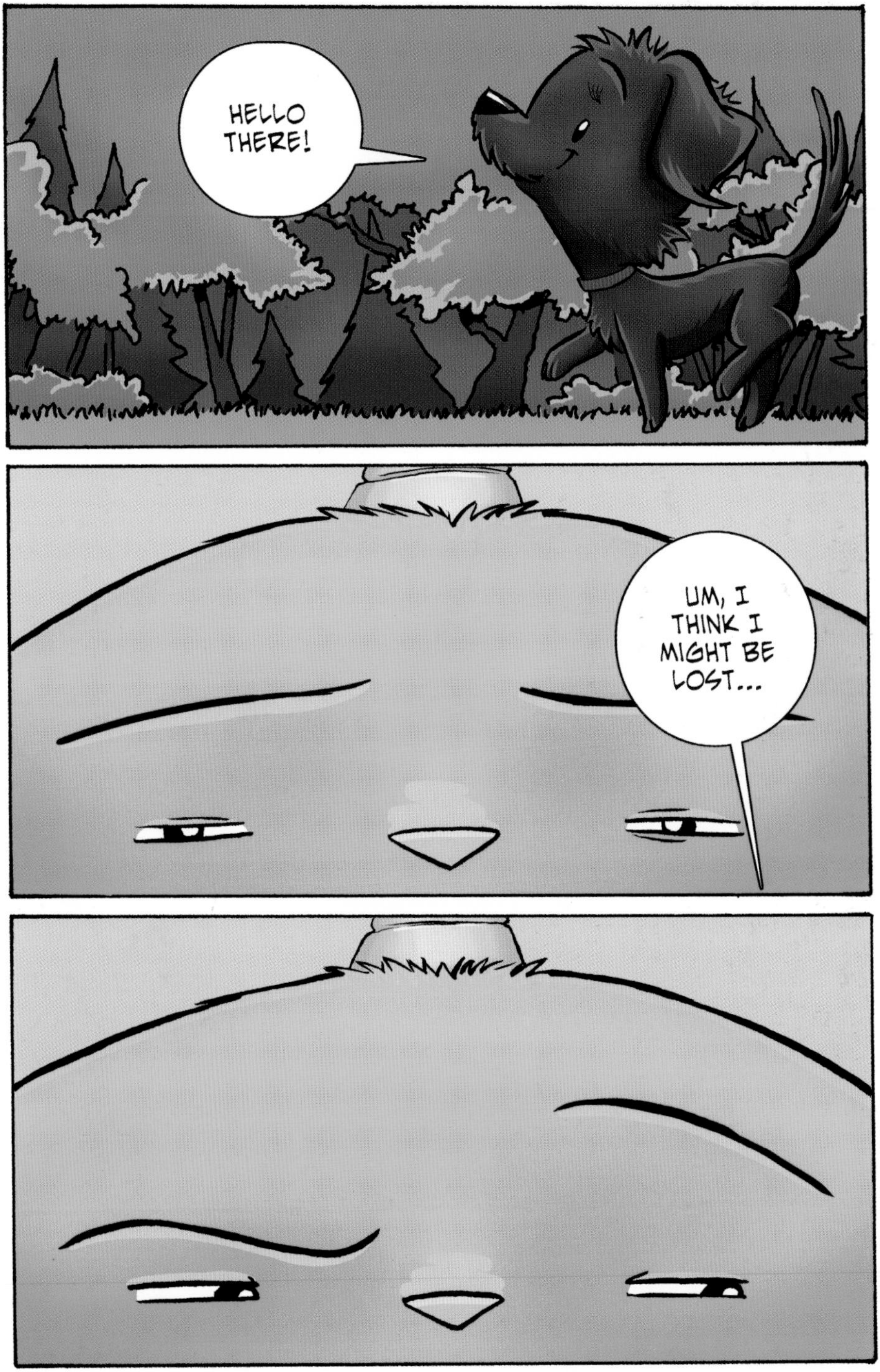
HELLO THERE!
UM, I THINK I MIGHT BE LOST...

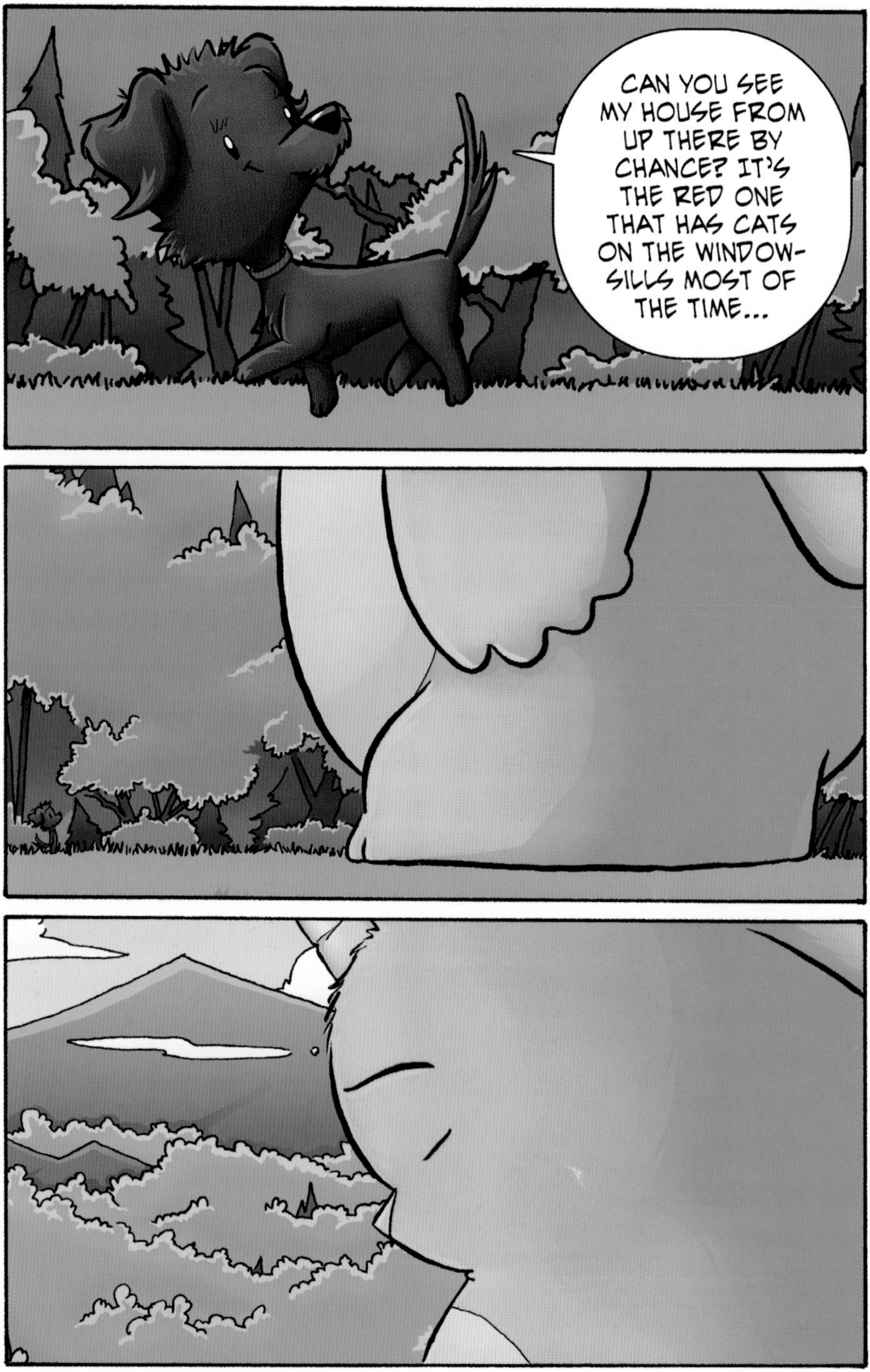
CAN YOU SEE MY HOUSE FROM UP THERE BY CHANCE? IT'S THE RED ONE THAT HAS CATS ON THE WINDOW-SILLS MOST OF THE TIME...

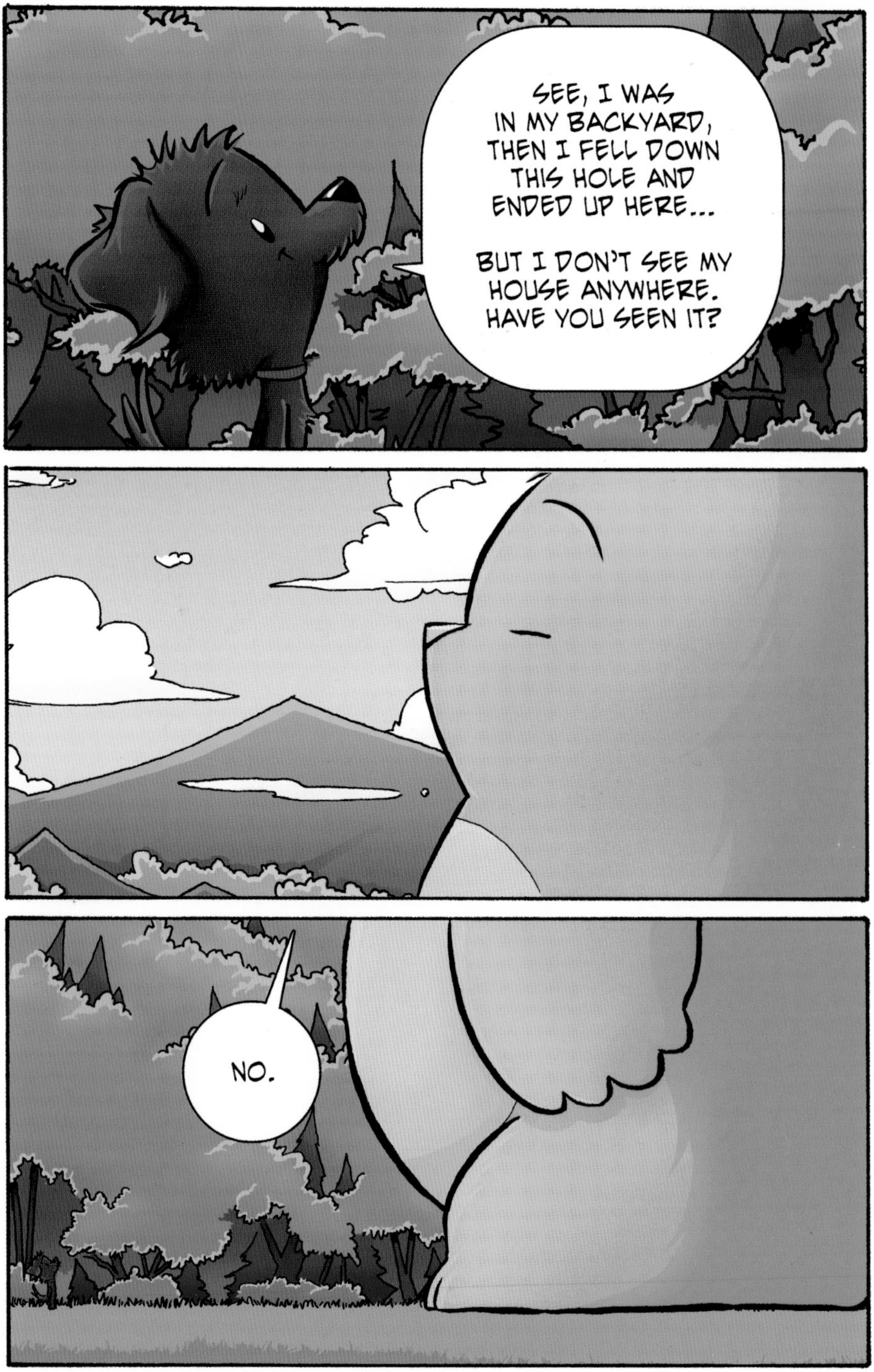
SEE, I WAS IN MY BACKYARD, THEN I FELL DOWN THIS HOLE AND ENDED UP HERE...
BUT I DON'T SEE MY HOUSE ANYWHERE. HAVE YOU SEEN IT?
NO.

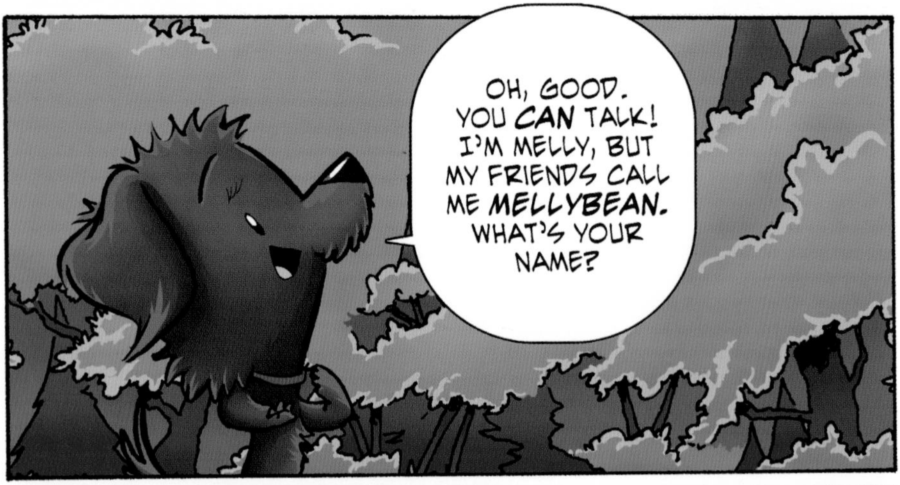
OH, GOOD. YOU **CAN** TALK! I'M MELLY, BUT MY FRIENDS CALL ME ***MELLYBEAN.*** WHAT'S YOUR NAME?

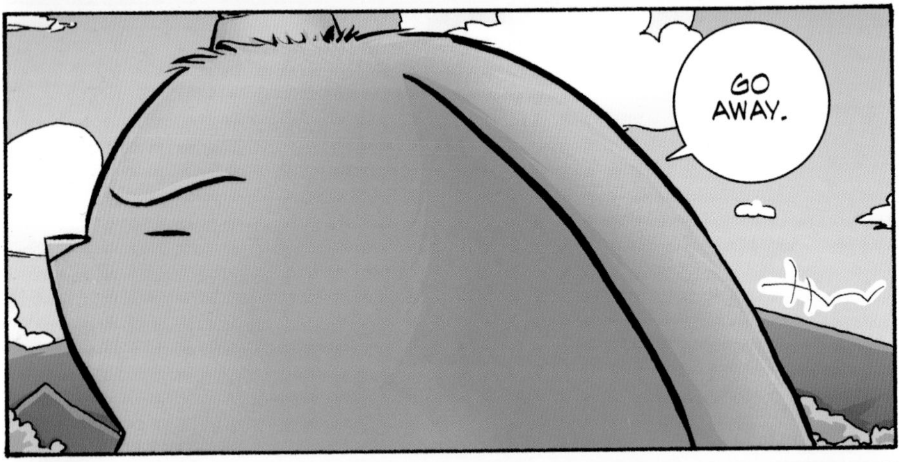
GO AWAY.

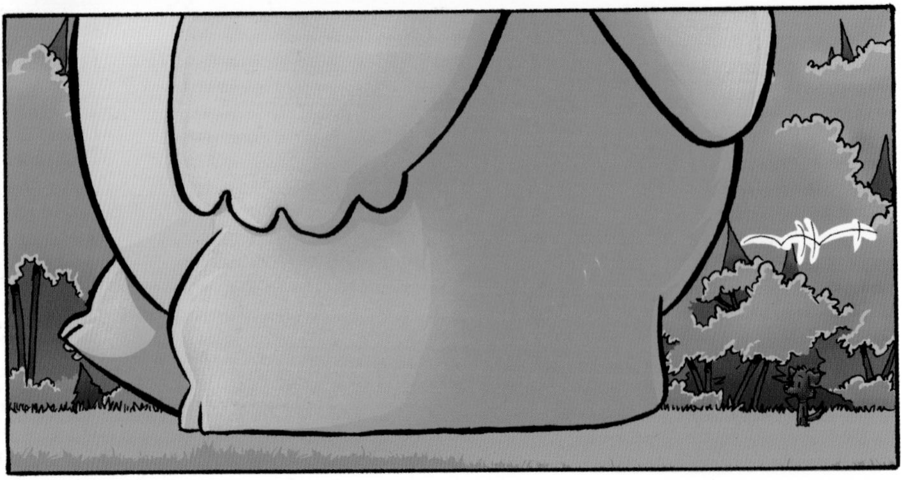

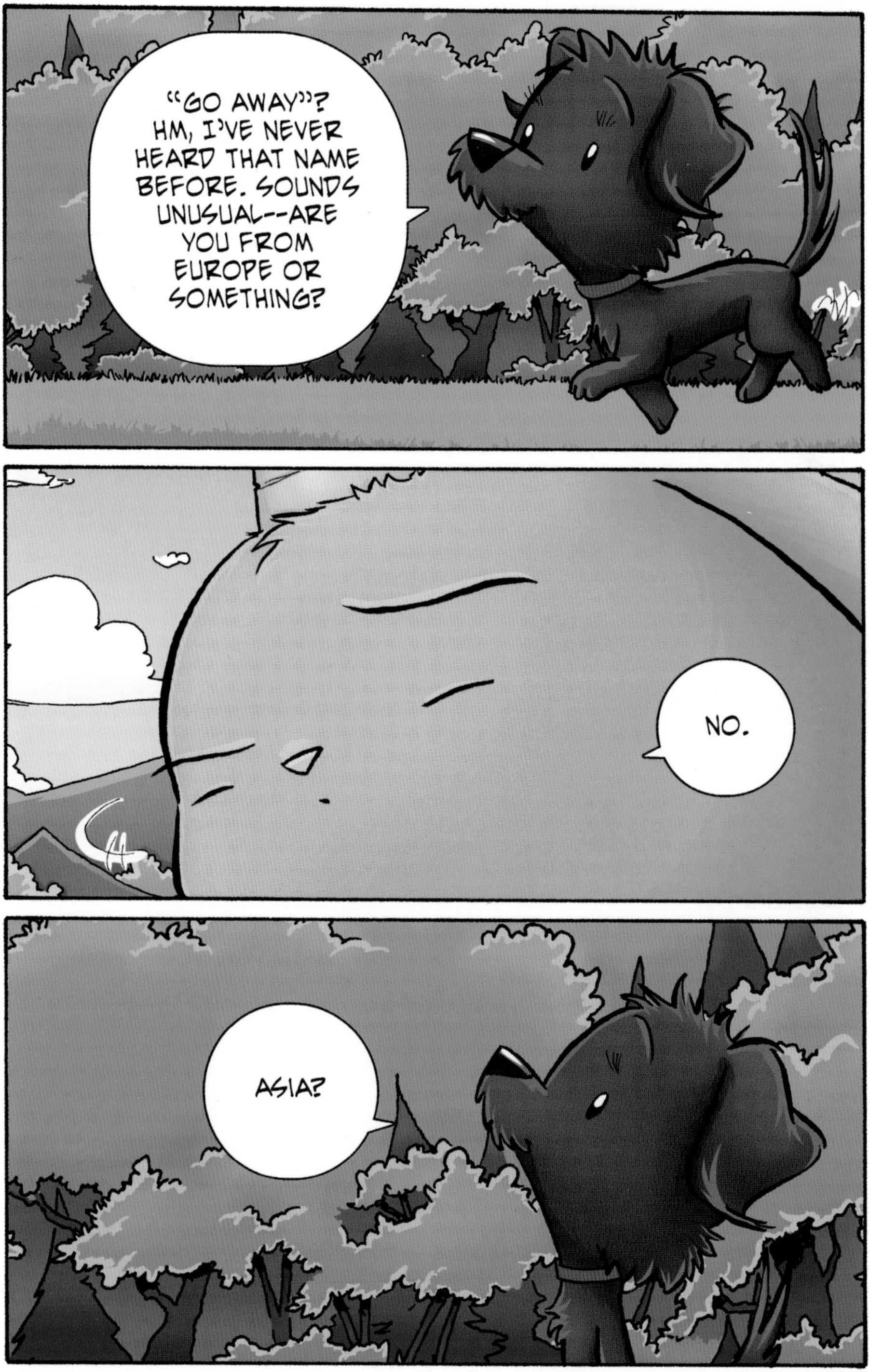
"GO AWAY"? HM, I'VE NEVER HEARD THAT NAME BEFORE. SOUNDS UNUSUAL--ARE YOU FROM EUROPE OR SOMETHING?
NO.
ASIA?

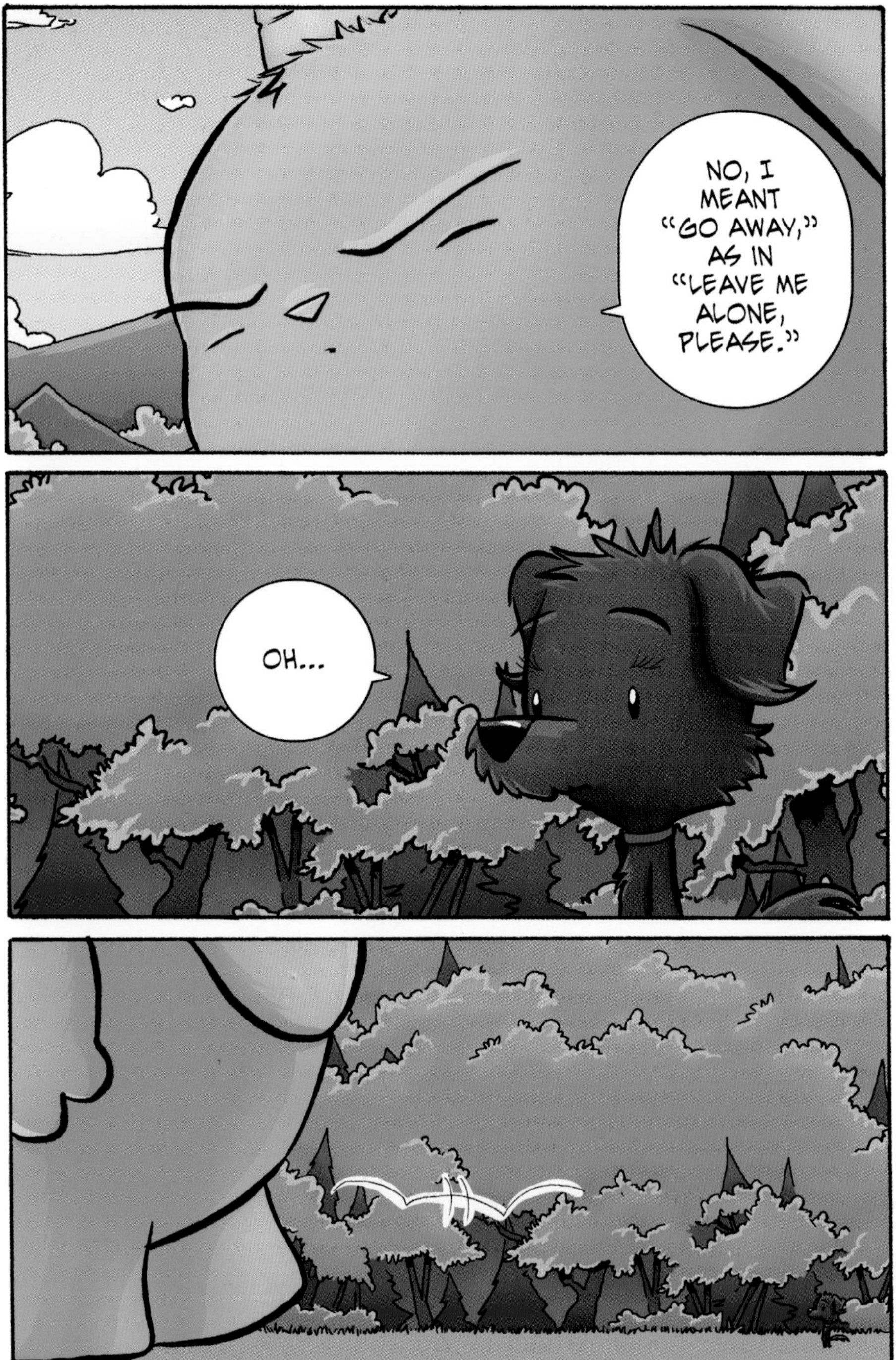
NO, I MEANT "GO AWAY," AS IN "LEAVE ME ALONE, PLEASE."
OH...

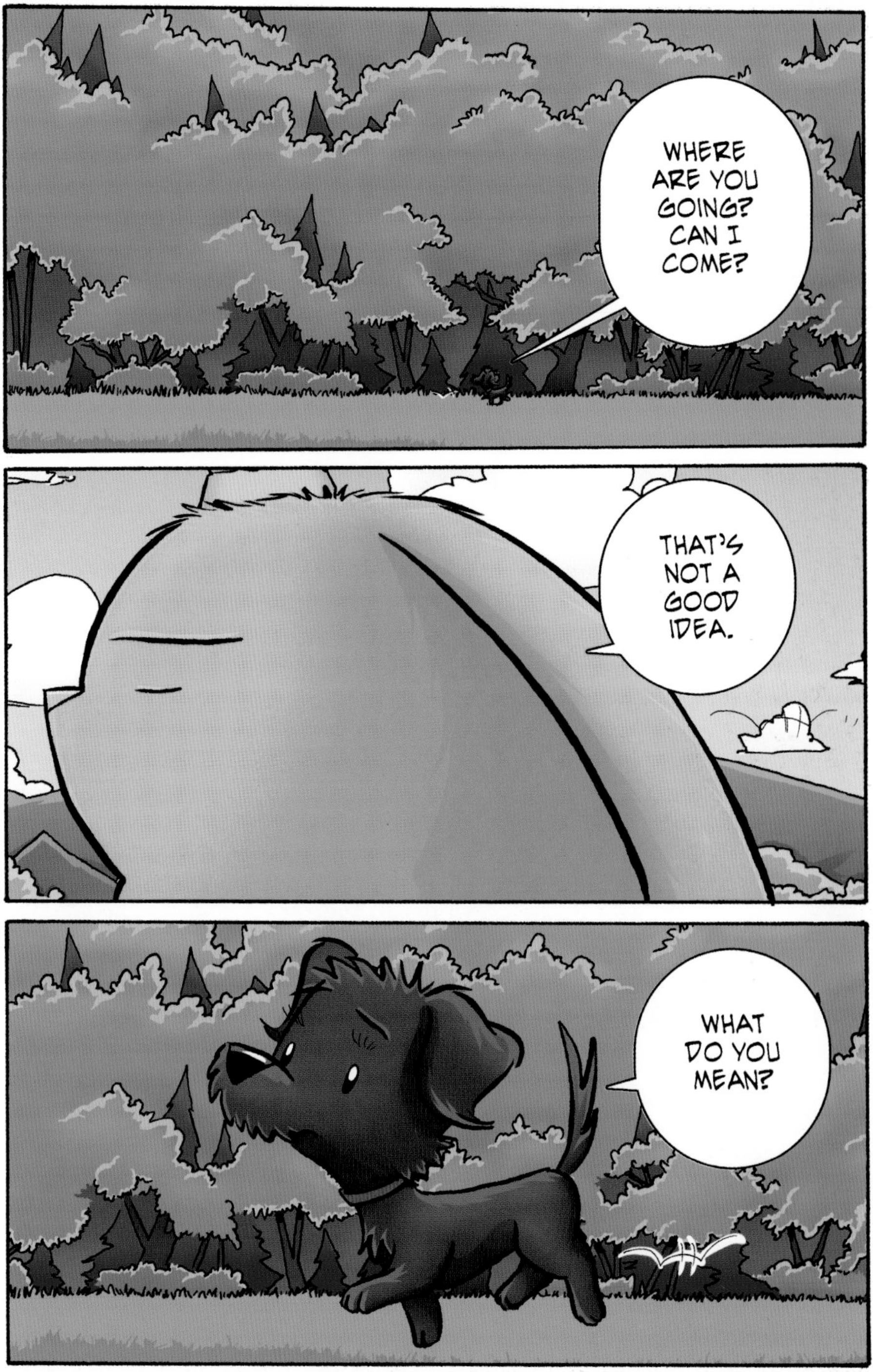
WHERE ARE YOU GOING? CAN I COME?
THAT'S NOT A GOOD IDEA.
WHAT DO YOU MEAN?

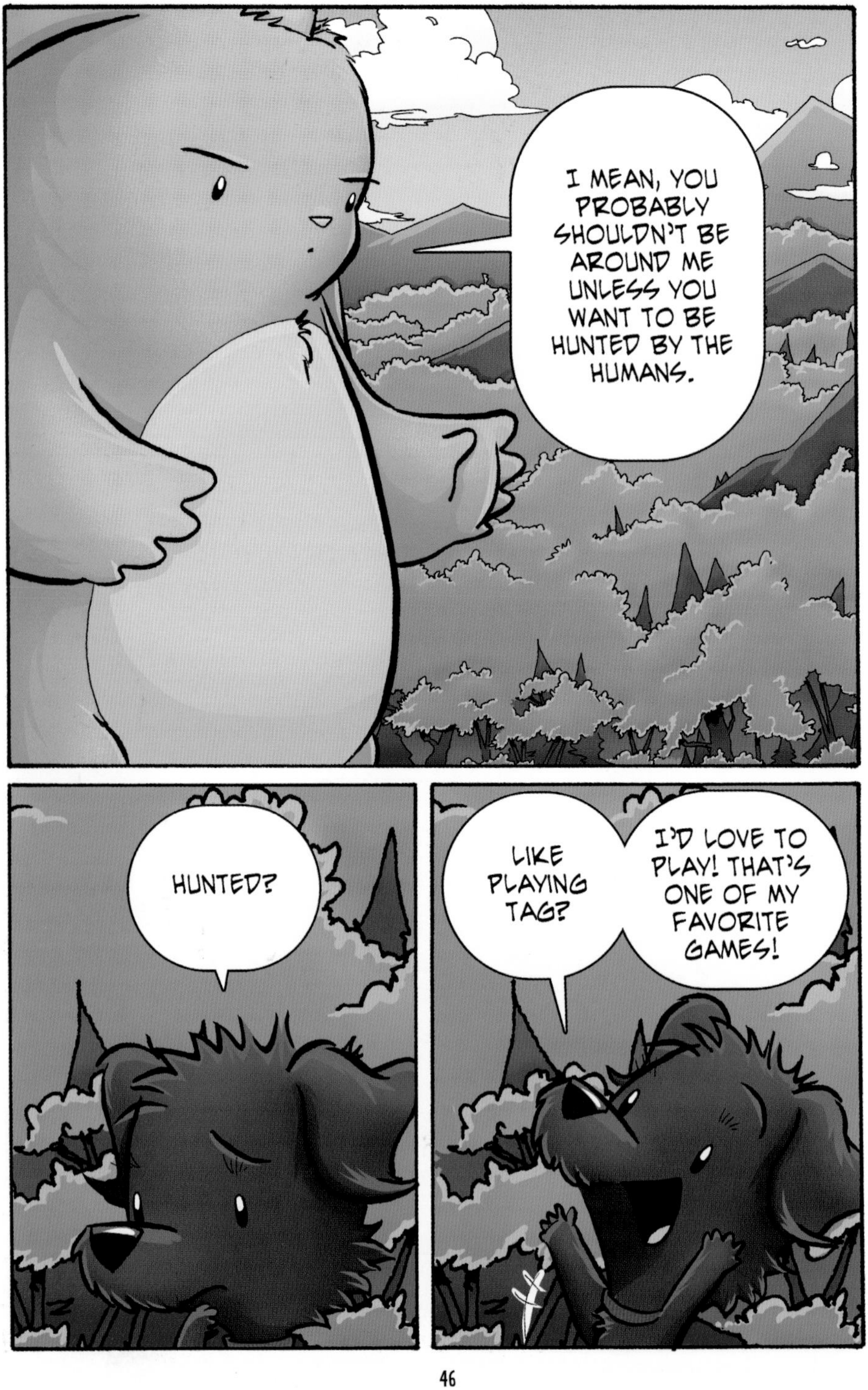
I MEAN, YOU PROBABLY SHOULDN'T BE AROUND ME UNLESS YOU WANT TO BE HUNTED BY THE HUMANS.
HUNTED?
LIKE PLAYING TAG?
I'D LOVE TO PLAY! THAT'S ONE OF MY FAVORITE GAMES!

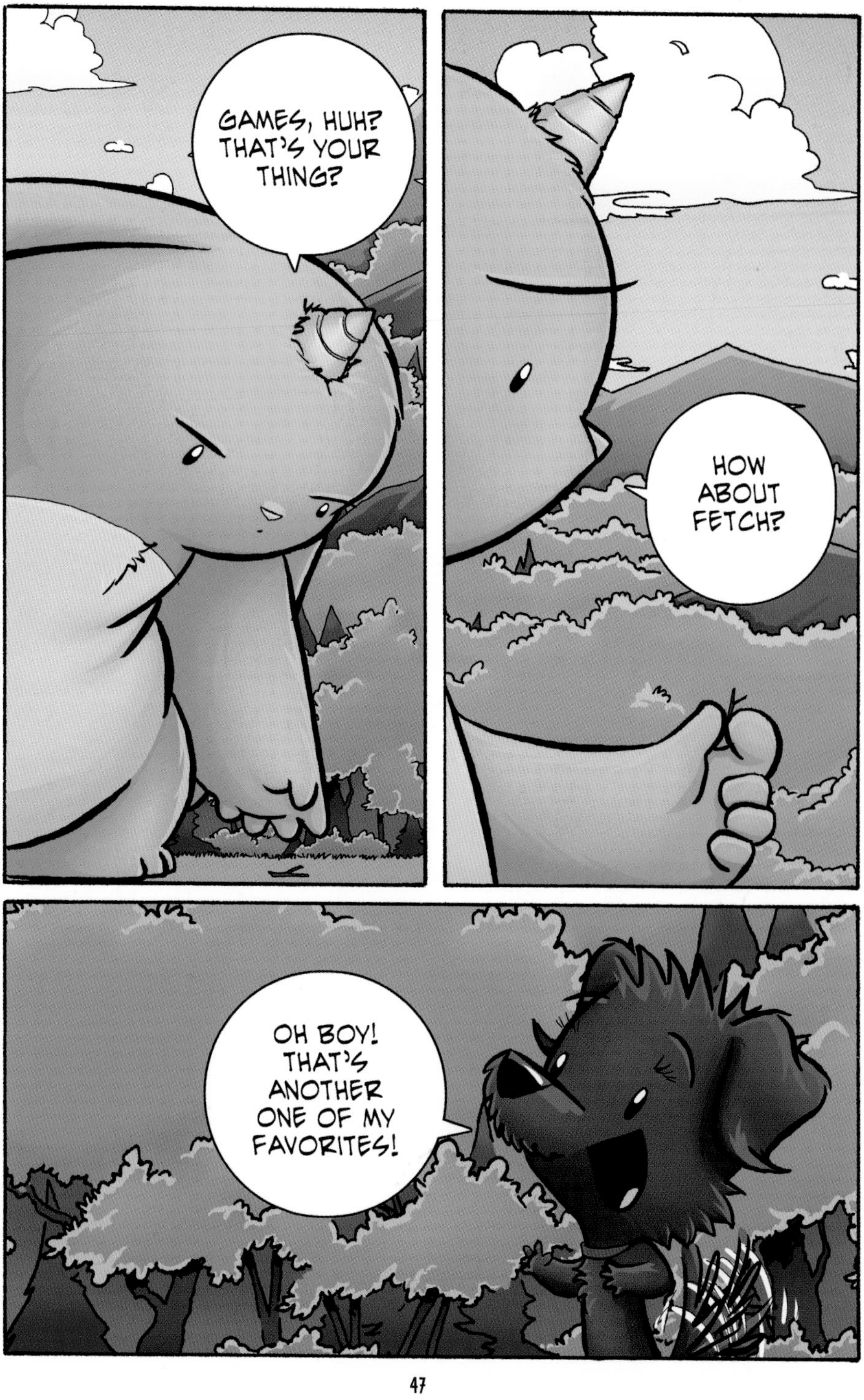
GAMES, HUH? THAT'S YOUR THING?
HOW ABOUT FETCH?
OH BOY! THAT'S ANOTHER ONE OF MY FAVORITES!

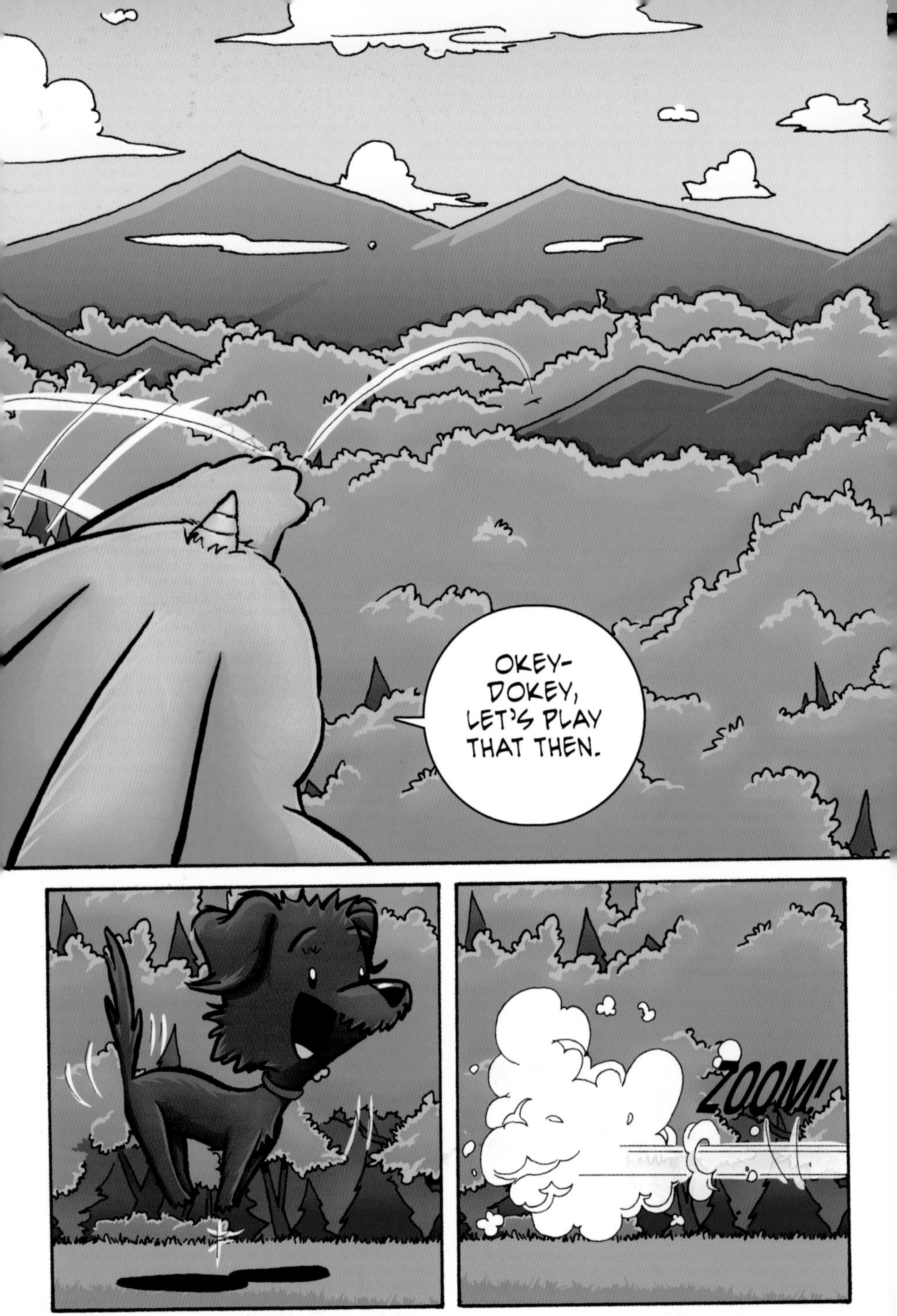
OKEY-DOKEY, LET'S PLAY THAT THEN.
ZOOM!

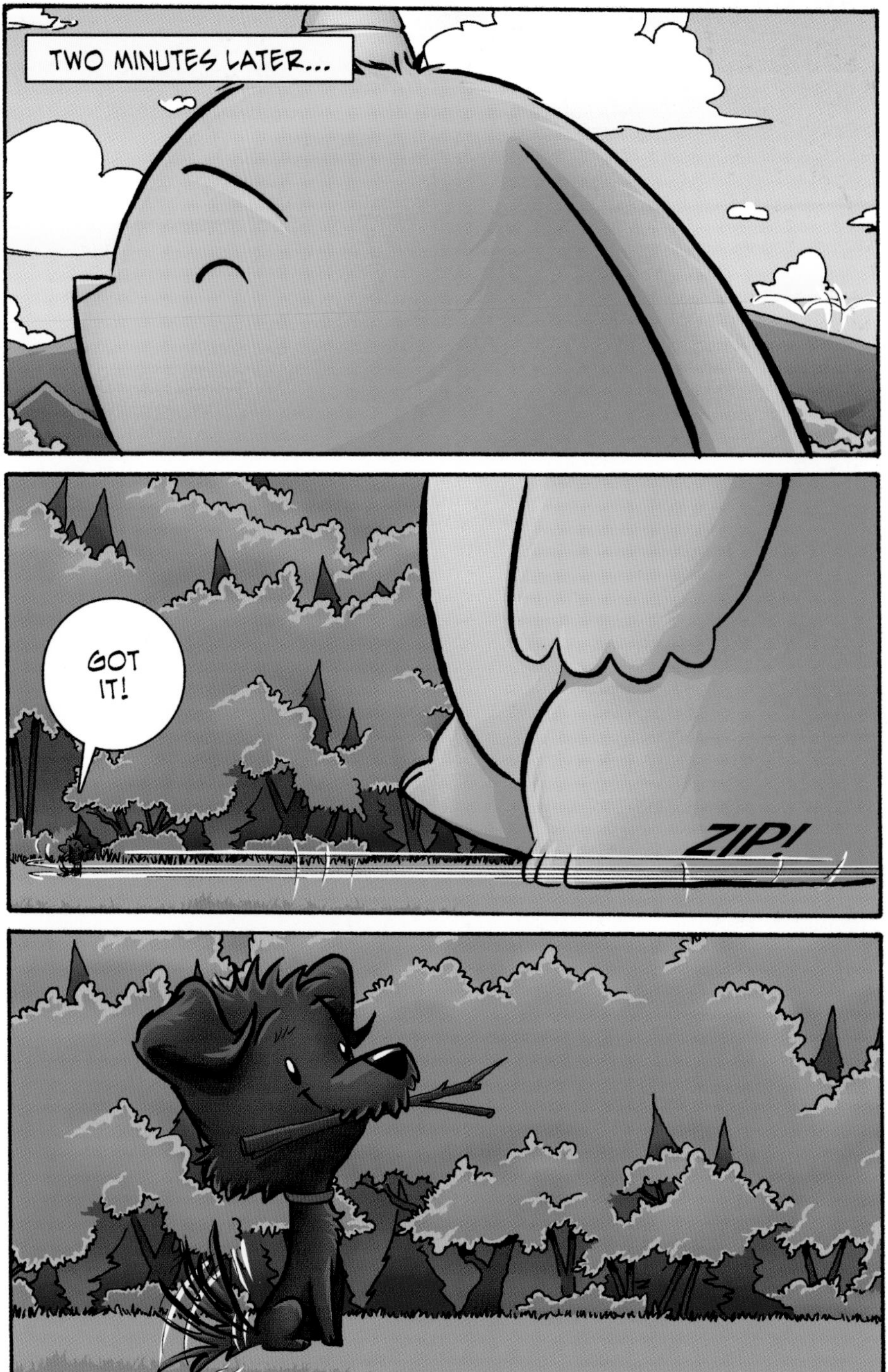

TWO MINUTES LATER...
GOT IT!
ZIP!

THAT, UH... THAT WAS PRETTY FAST...
THROW IT AGAIN!

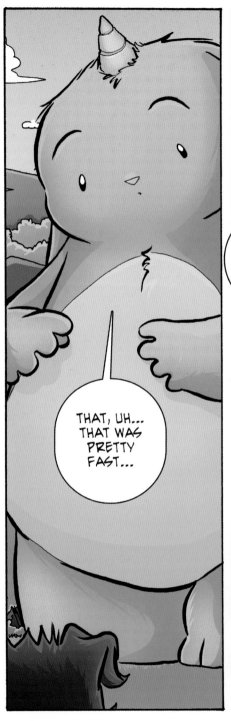

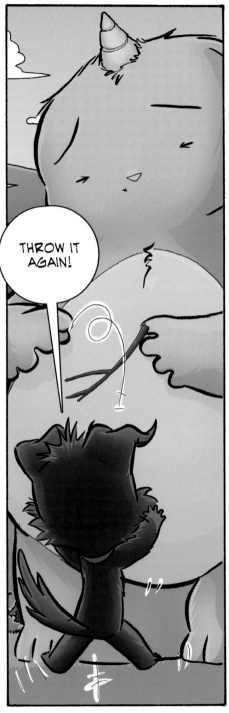

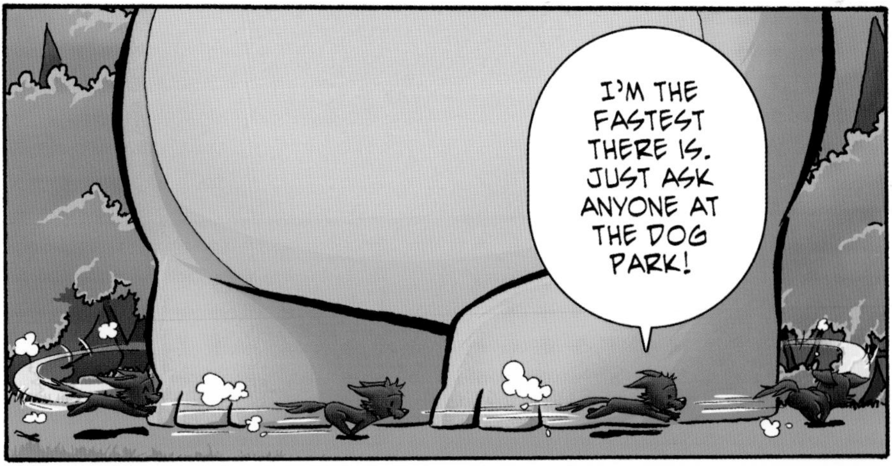
I'M THE FASTEST THERE IS. JUST ASK ANYONE AT THE DOG PARK!

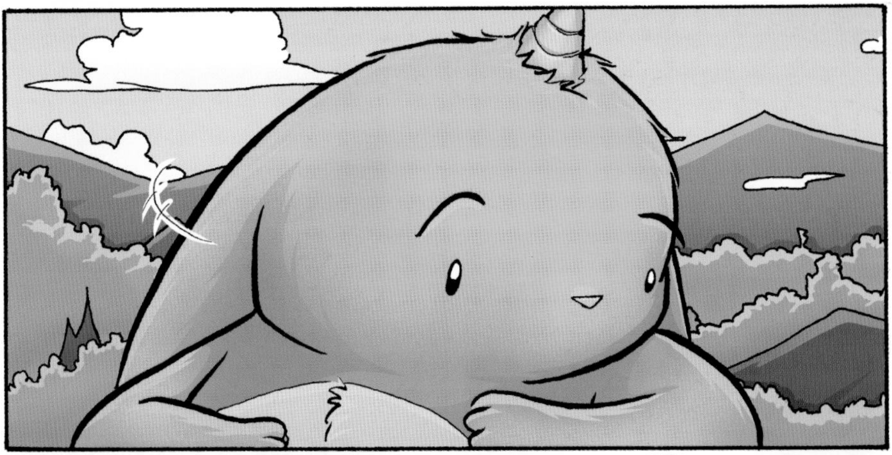

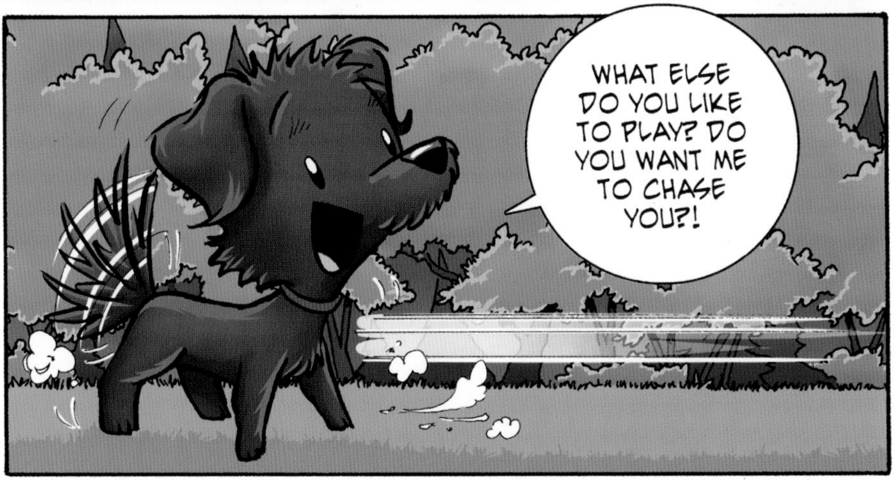
WHAT ELSE DO YOU LIKE TO PLAY? DO YOU WANT ME TO CHASE YOU?!

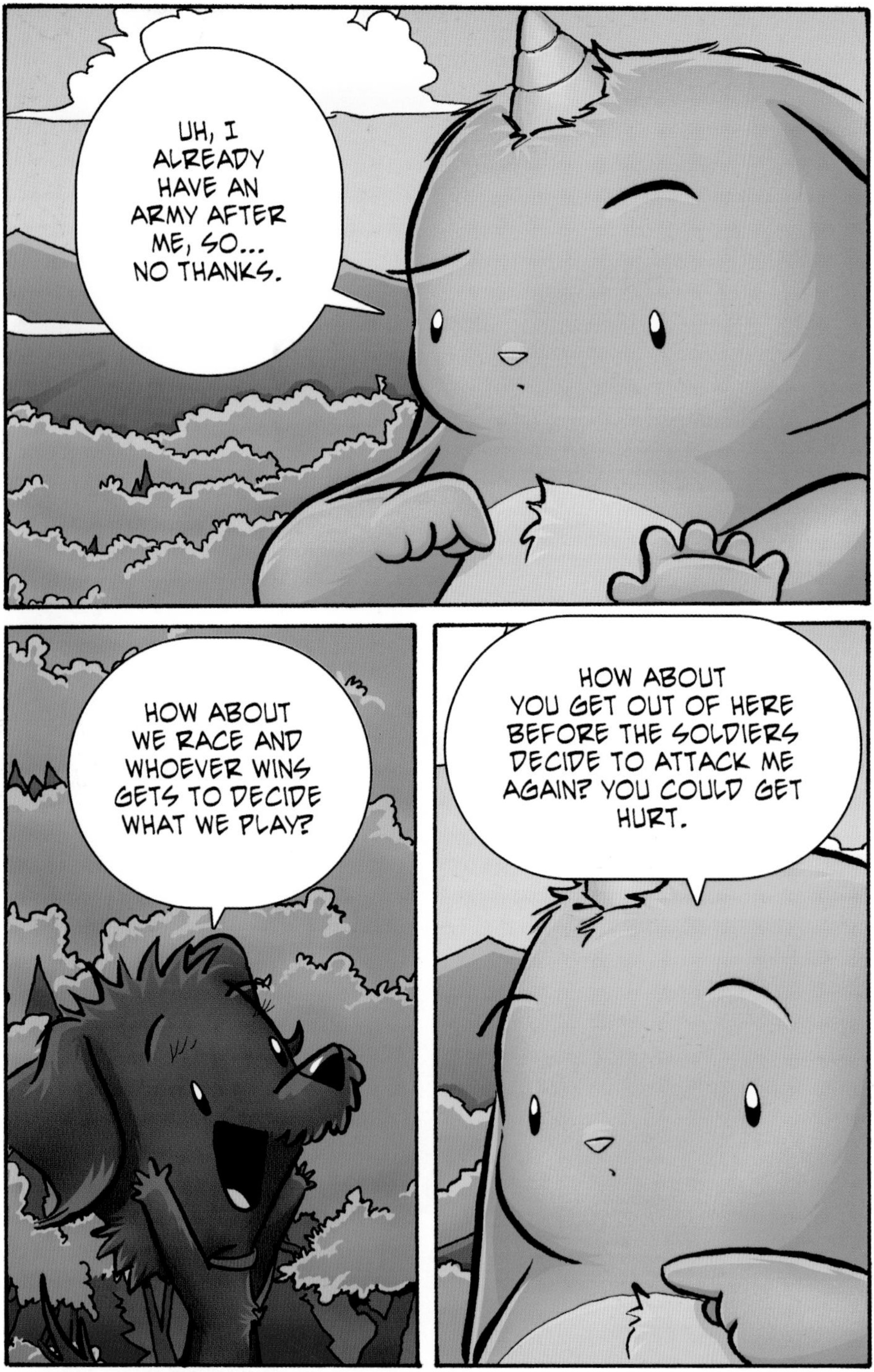
UH, I ALREADY HAVE AN ARMY AFTER ME, SO... NO THANKS.
HOW ABOUT WE RACE AND WHOEVER WINS GETS TO DECIDE WHAT WE PLAY?
HOW ABOUT YOU GET OUT OF HERE BEFORE THE SOLDIERS DECIDE TO ATTACK ME AGAIN? YOU COULD GET HURT.

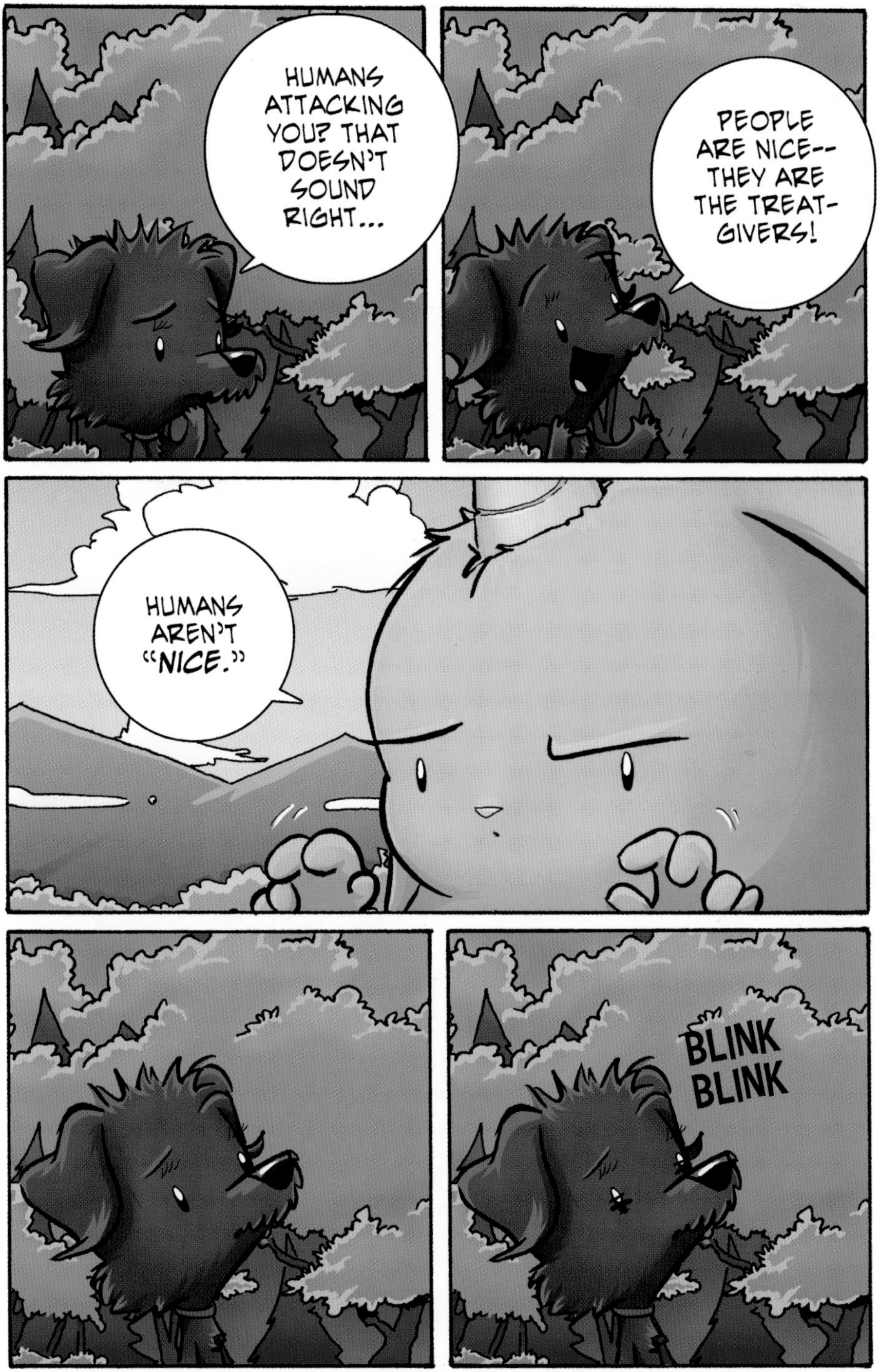
HUMANS ATTACKING YOU? THAT DOESN'T SOUND RIGHT...
PEOPLE ARE NICE-- THEY ARE THE TREAT-GIVERS!
HUMANS AREN'T "NICE."
BLINK BLINK

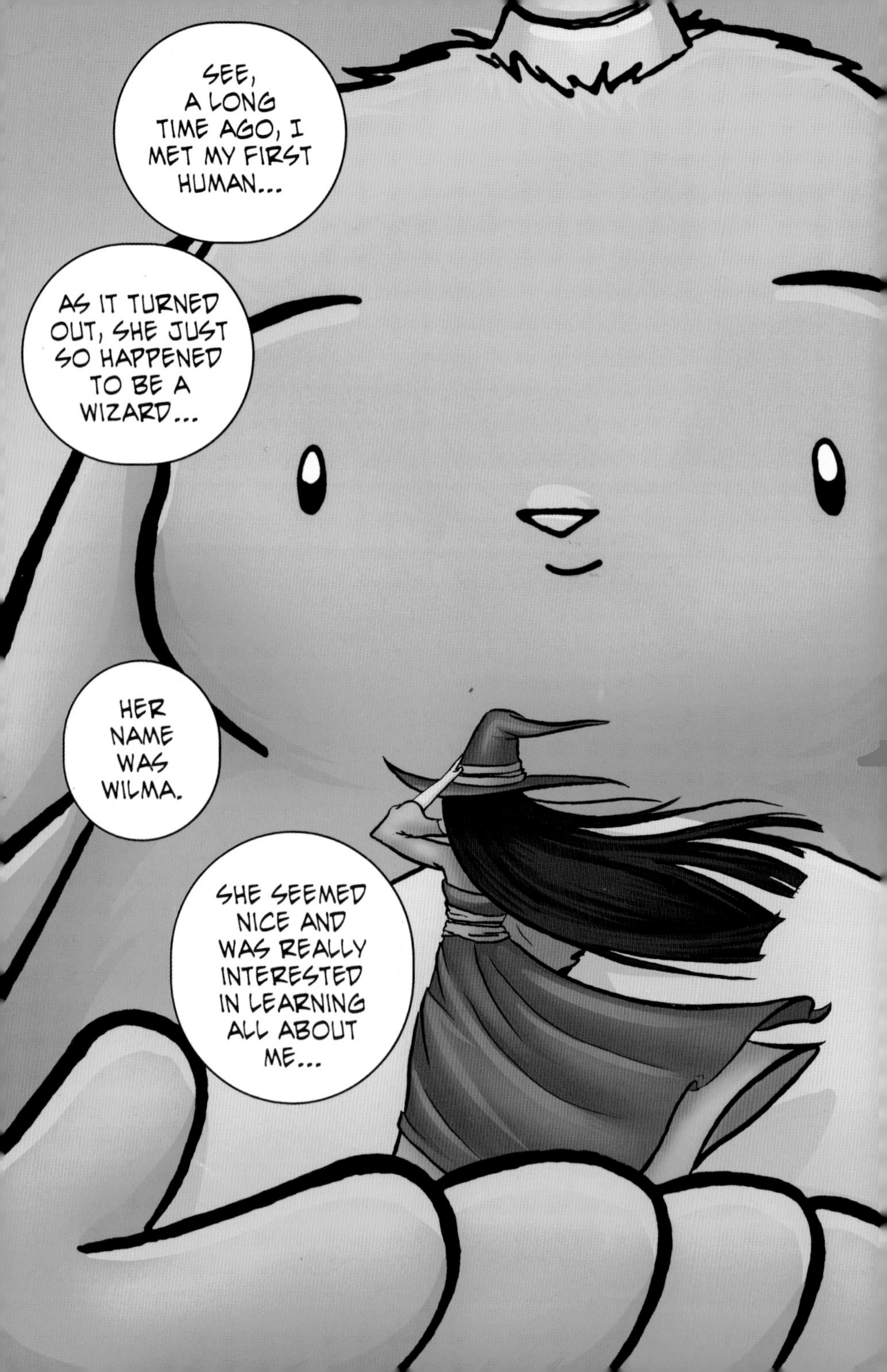
SEE, A LONG TIME AGO, I MET MY FIRST HUMAN...
AS IT TURNED OUT, SHE JUST SO HAPPENED TO BE A WIZARD...
HER NAME WAS WILMA.
SHE SEEMED NICE AND WAS REALLY INTERESTED IN LEARNING ALL ABOUT ME...

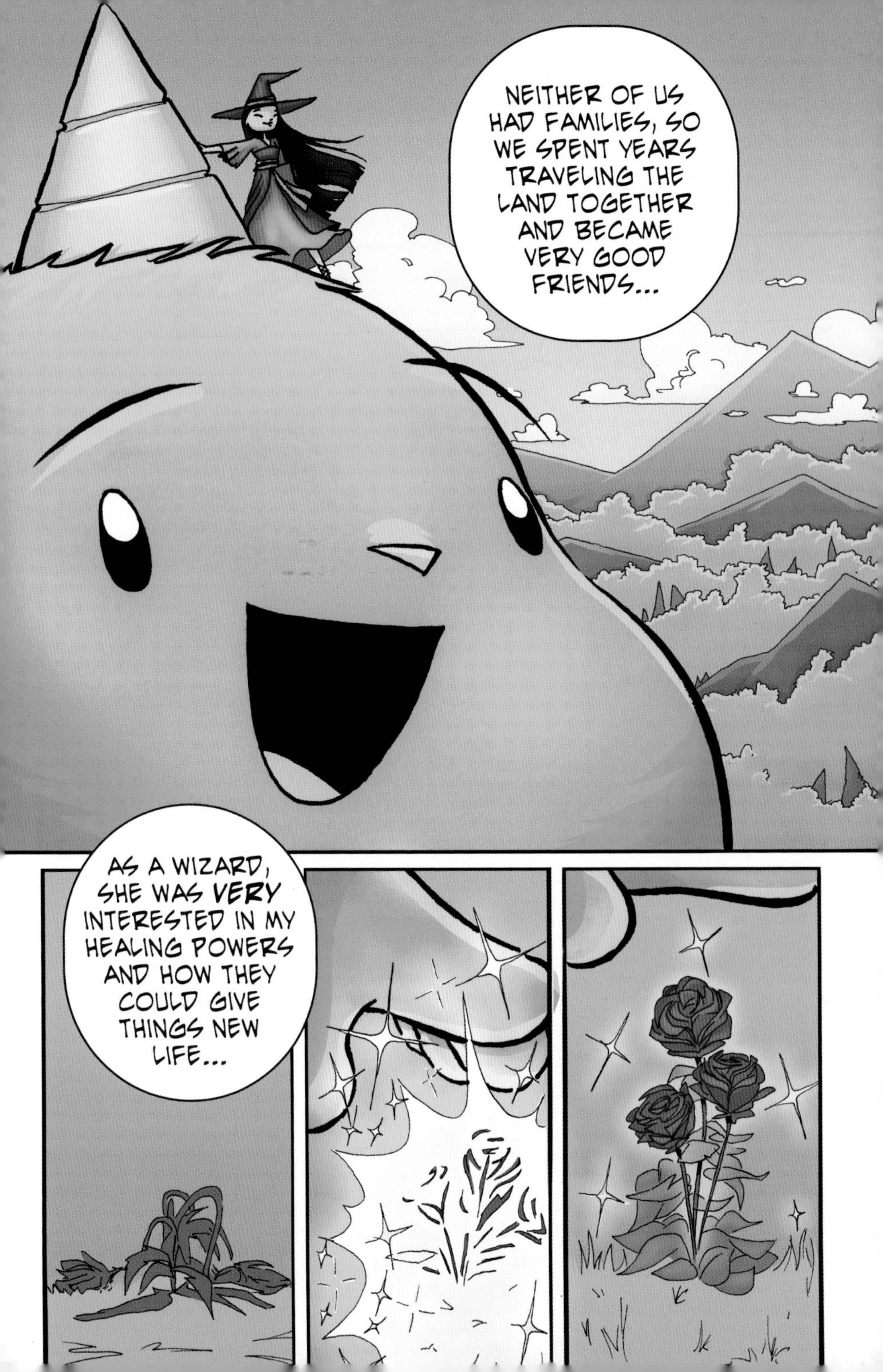
NEITHER OF US HAD FAMILIES, SO WE SPENT YEARS TRAVELING THE LAND TOGETHER AND BECAME VERY GOOD FRIENDS...
AS A WIZARD, SHE WAS **VERY** INTERESTED IN MY HEALING POWERS AND HOW THEY COULD GIVE THINGS NEW LIFE...

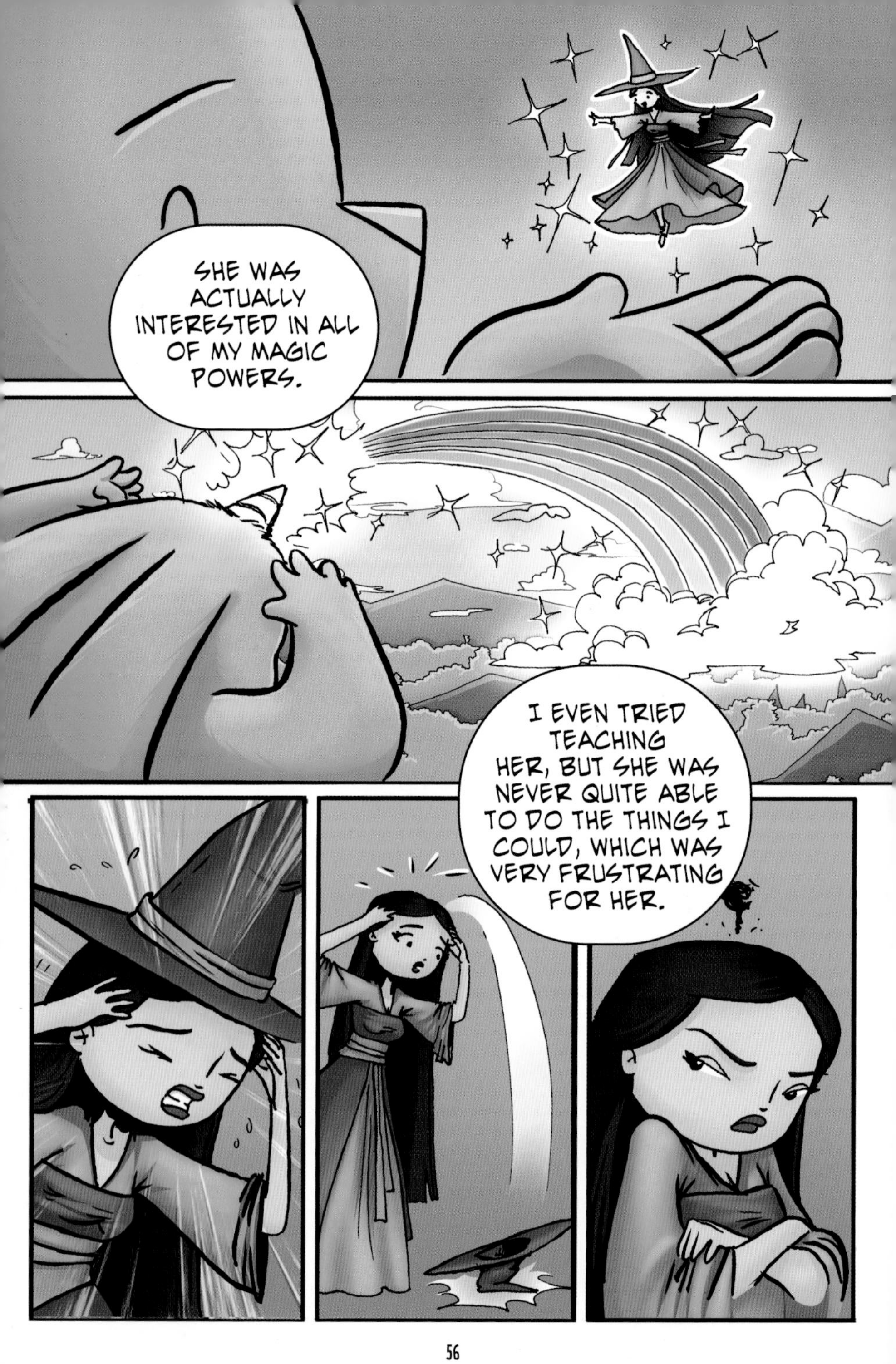
SHE WAS ACTUALLY INTERESTED IN ALL OF MY MAGIC POWERS.
I EVEN TRIED TEACHING HER, BUT SHE WAS NEVER QUITE ABLE TO DO THE THINGS I COULD, WHICH WAS VERY FRUSTRATING FOR HER.

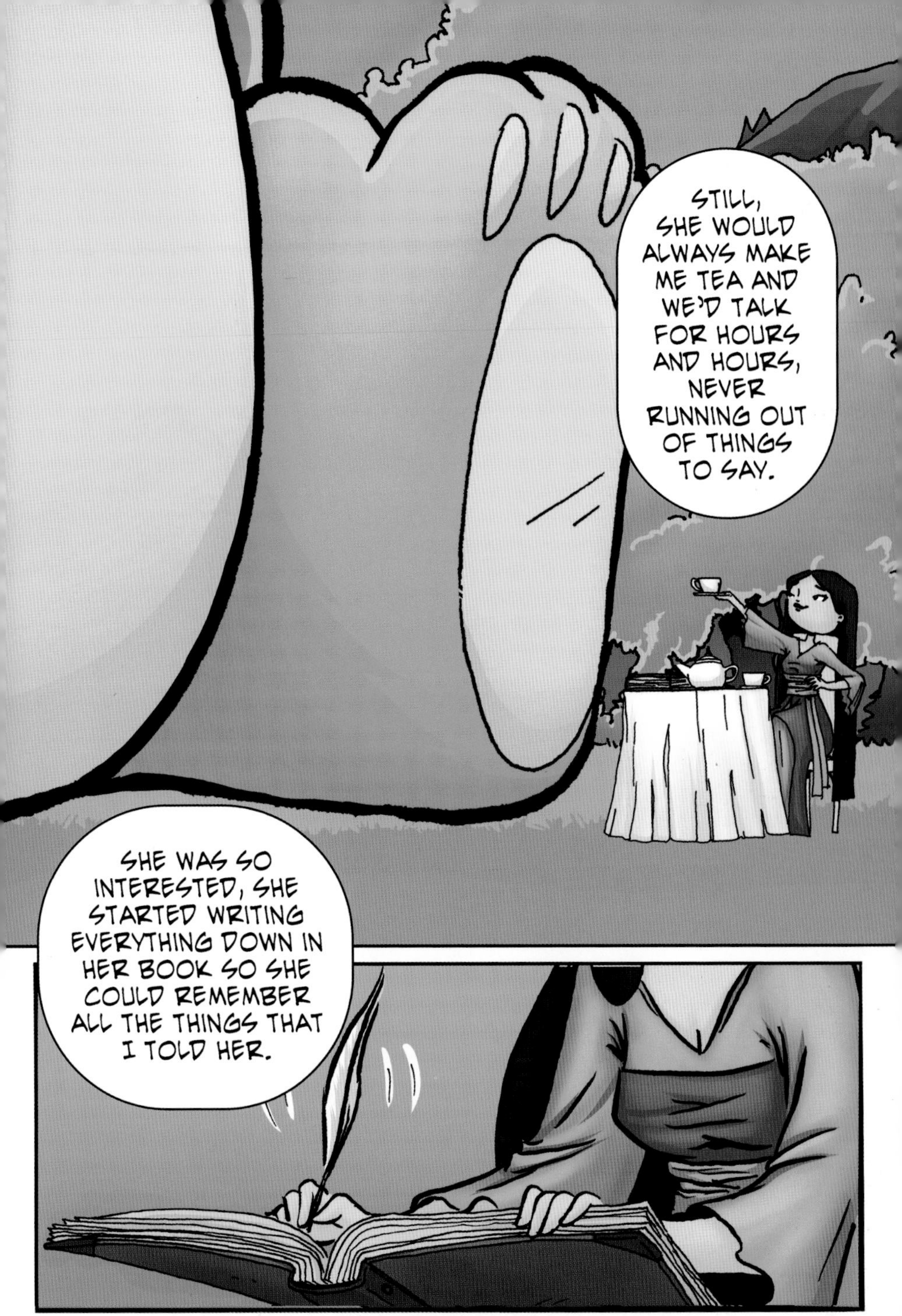
STILL, SHE WOULD ALWAYS MAKE ME TEA AND WE'D TALK FOR HOURS AND HOURS, NEVER RUNNING OUT OF THINGS TO SAY.
SHE WAS SO INTERESTED, SHE STARTED WRITING EVERYTHING DOWN IN HER BOOK SO SHE COULD REMEMBER ALL THE THINGS THAT I TOLD HER.

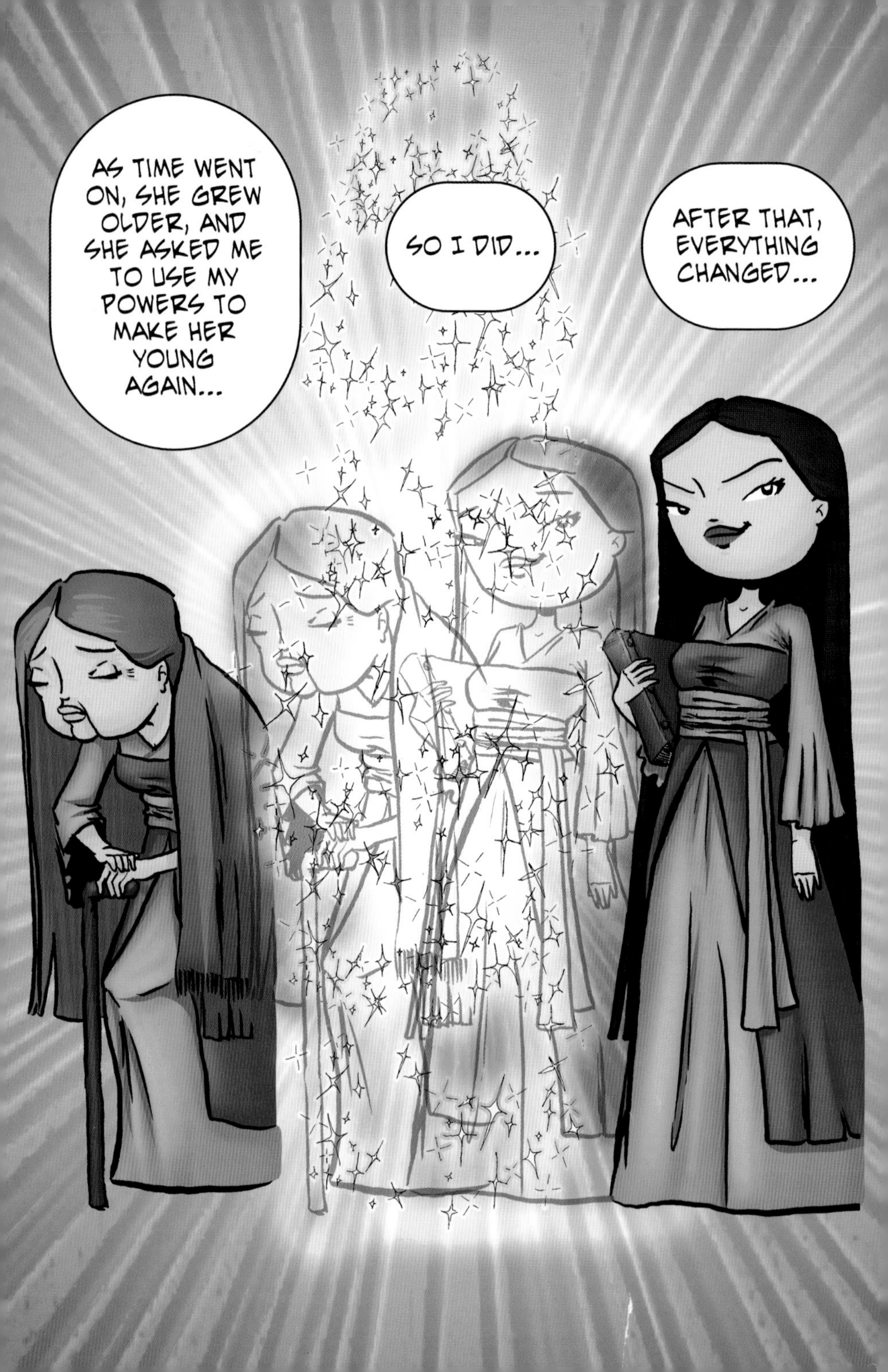
AS TIME WENT ON, SHE GREW OLDER, AND SHE ASKED ME TO USE MY POWERS TO MAKE HER YOUNG AGAIN...
SO I DID...
AFTER THAT, EVERYTHING CHANGED...

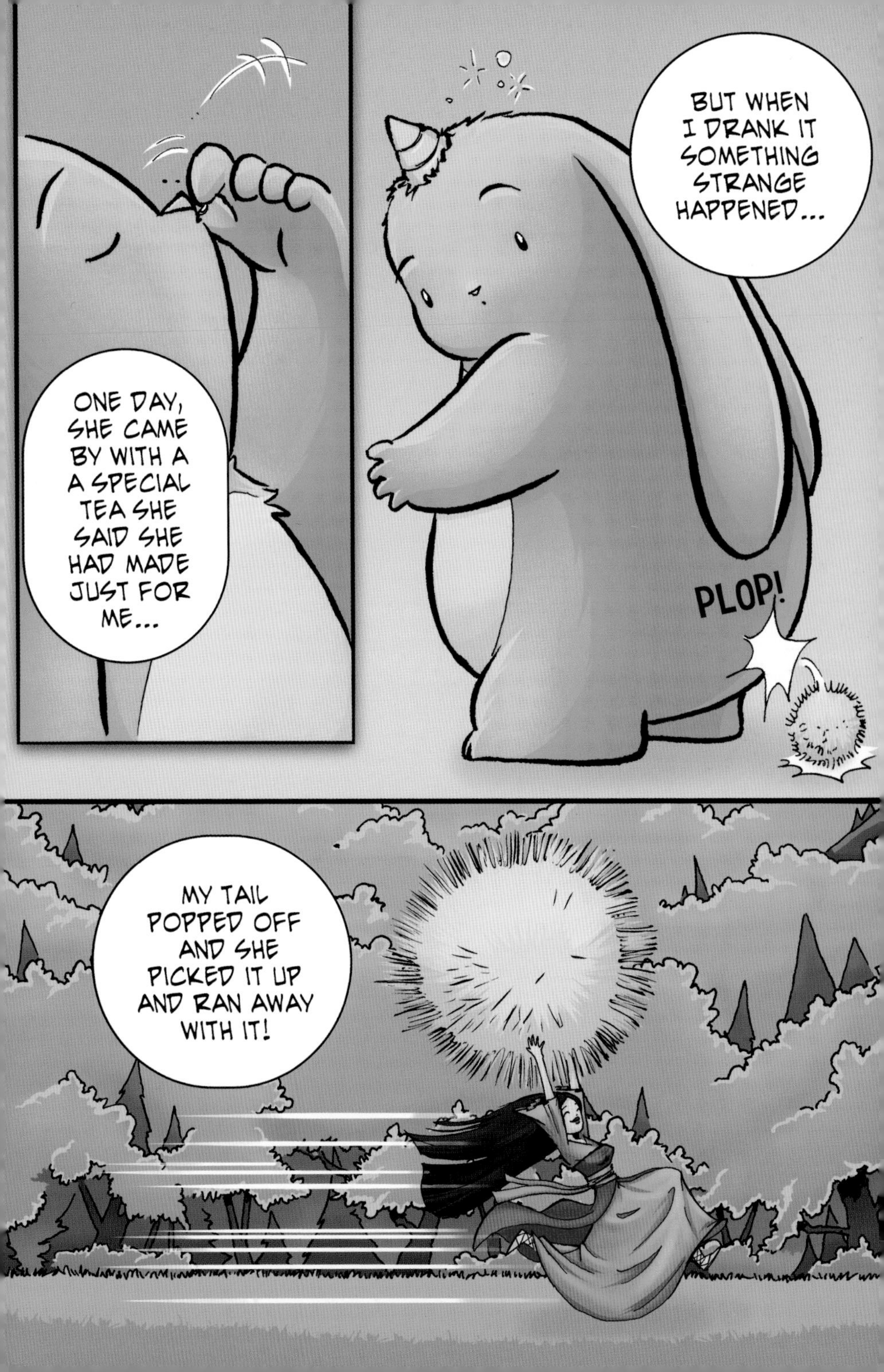
ONE DAY, SHE CAME BY WITH A A SPECIAL TEA SHE SAID SHE HAD MADE JUST FOR ME...
BUT WHEN I DRANK IT SOMETHING STRANGE HAPPENED...
PLOP!
MY TAIL POPPED OFF AND SHE PICKED IT UP AND RAN AWAY WITH IT!

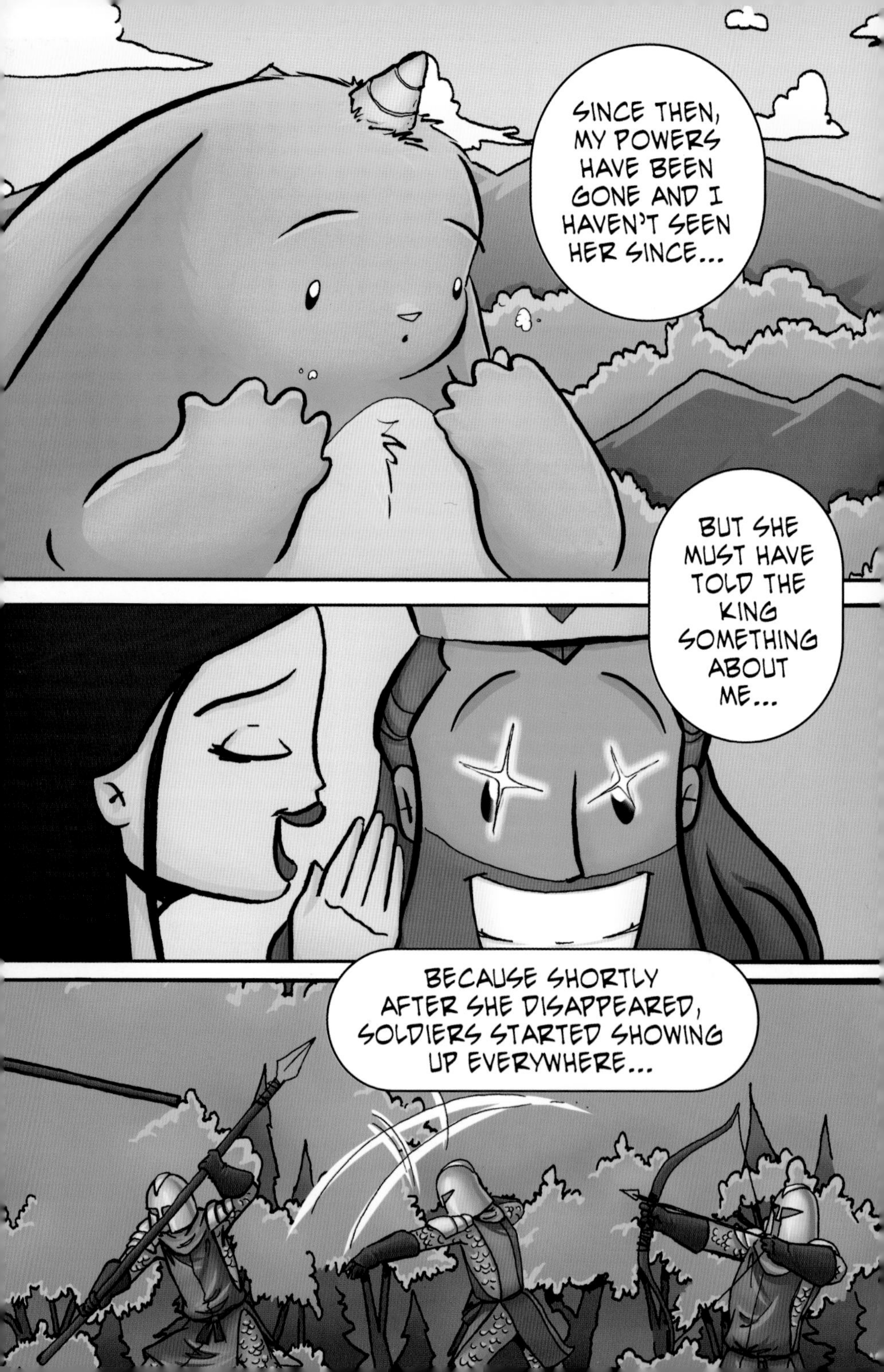
SINCE THEN, MY POWERS HAVE BEEN GONE AND I HAVEN'T SEEN HER SINCE...
BUT SHE MUST HAVE TOLD THE KING SOMETHING ABOUT ME...
BECAUSE SHORTLY AFTER SHE DISAPPEARED, SOLDIERS STARTED SHOWING UP EVERYWHERE...

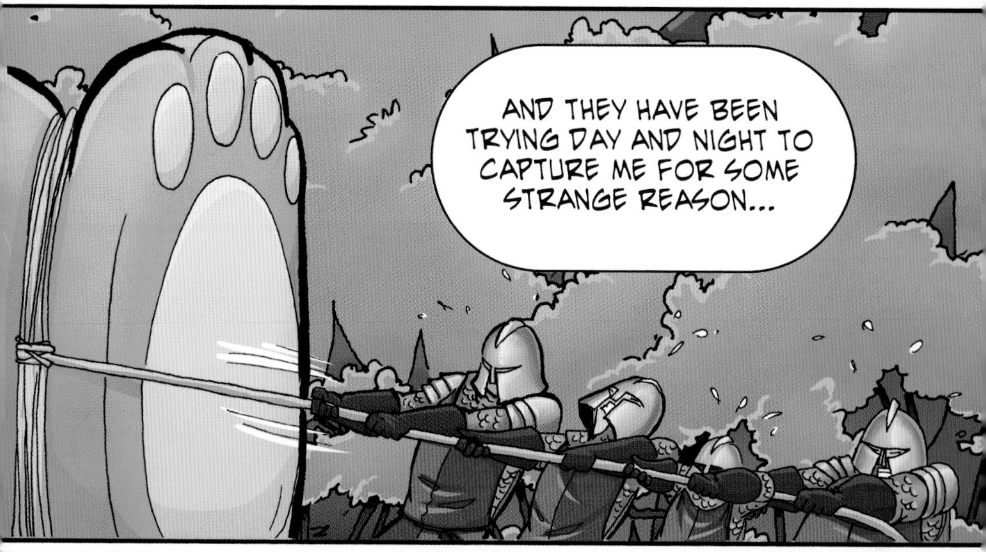
AND THEY HAVE BEEN TRYING DAY AND NIGHT TO CAPTURE ME FOR SOME STRANGE REASON...

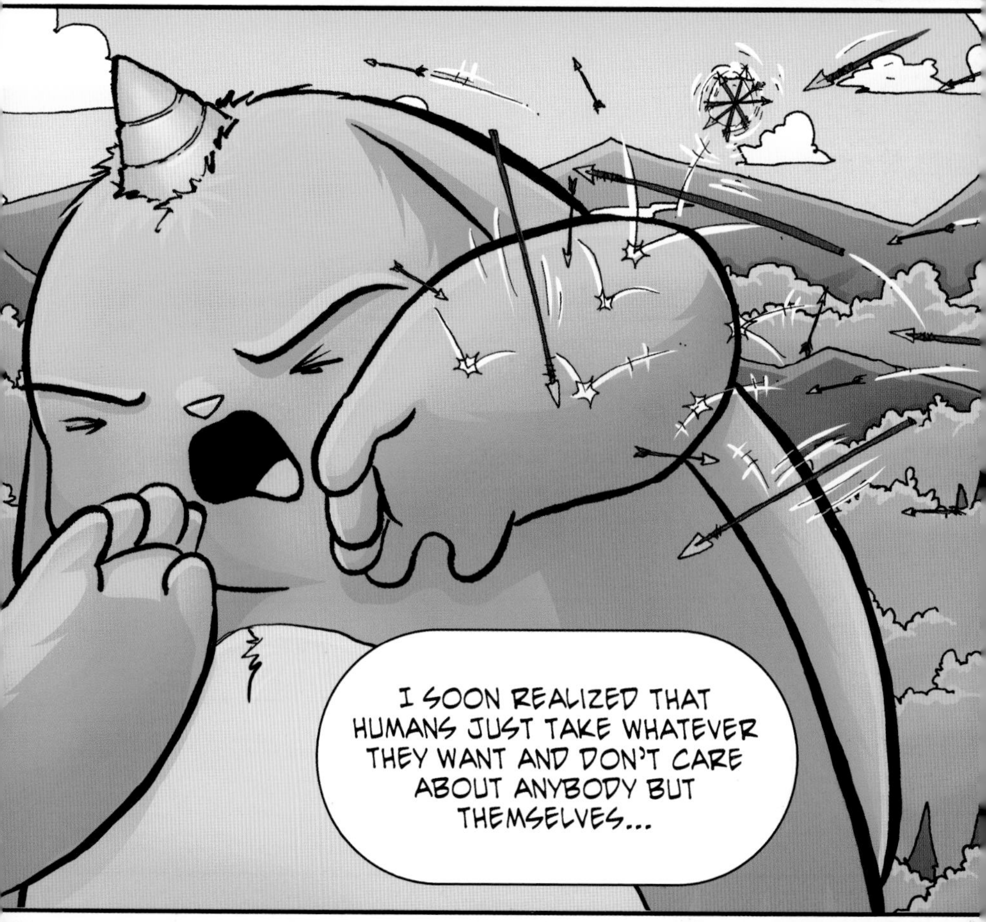
I SOON REALIZED THAT HUMANS JUST TAKE WHATEVER THEY WANT AND DON'T CARE ABOUT ANYBODY BUT THEMSELVES...

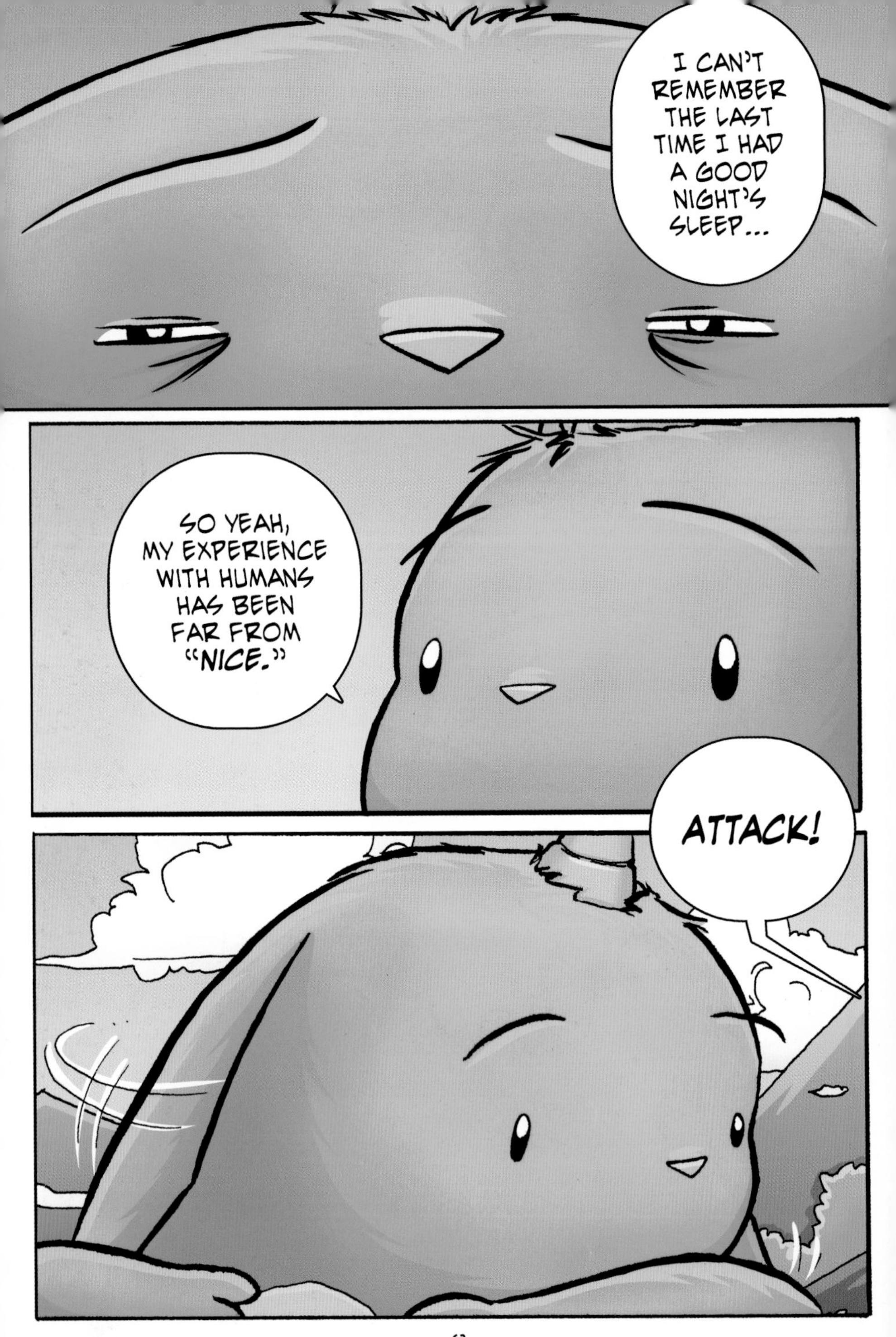
I CAN'T REMEMBER THE LAST TIME I HAD A GOOD NIGHT'S SLEEP...
SO YEAH, MY EXPERIENCE WITH HUMANS HAS BEEN FAR FROM "NICE."
ATTACK!

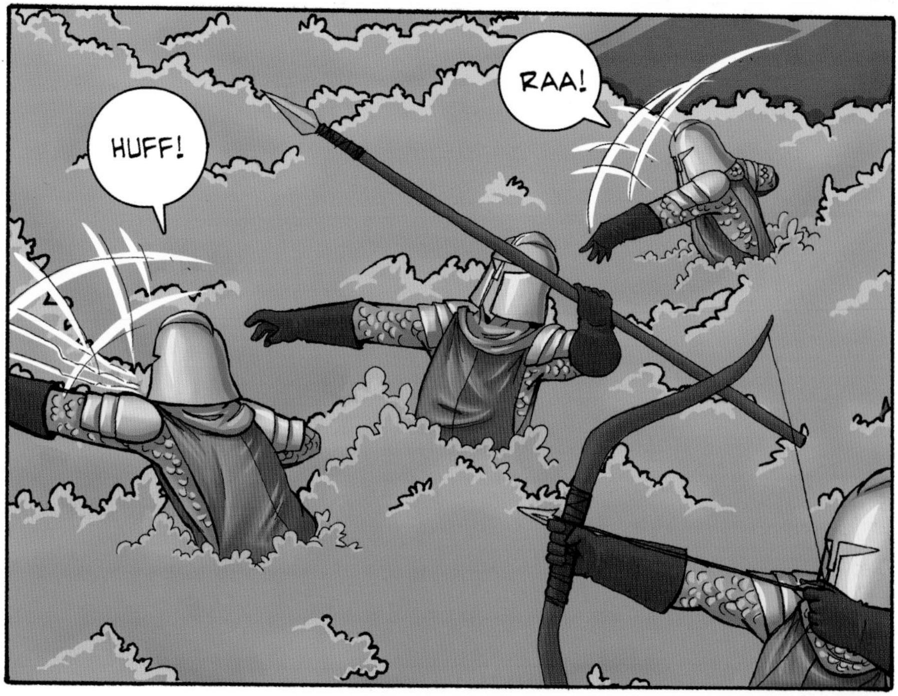
HUFF!
RAA!

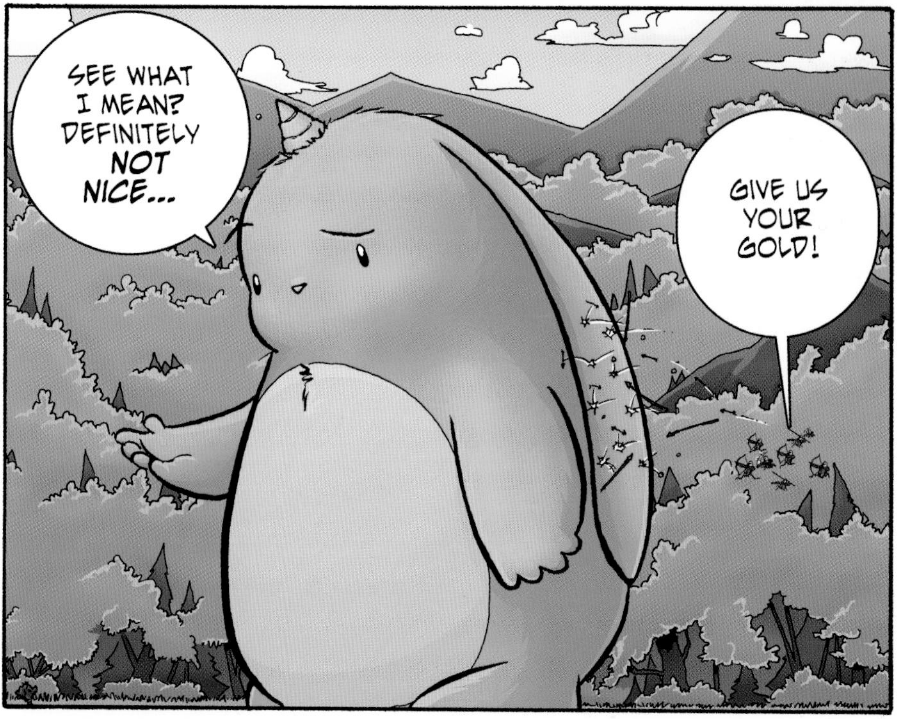
SEE WHAT I MEAN? DEFINITELY **NOT** NICE...
GIVE US YOUR GOLD!

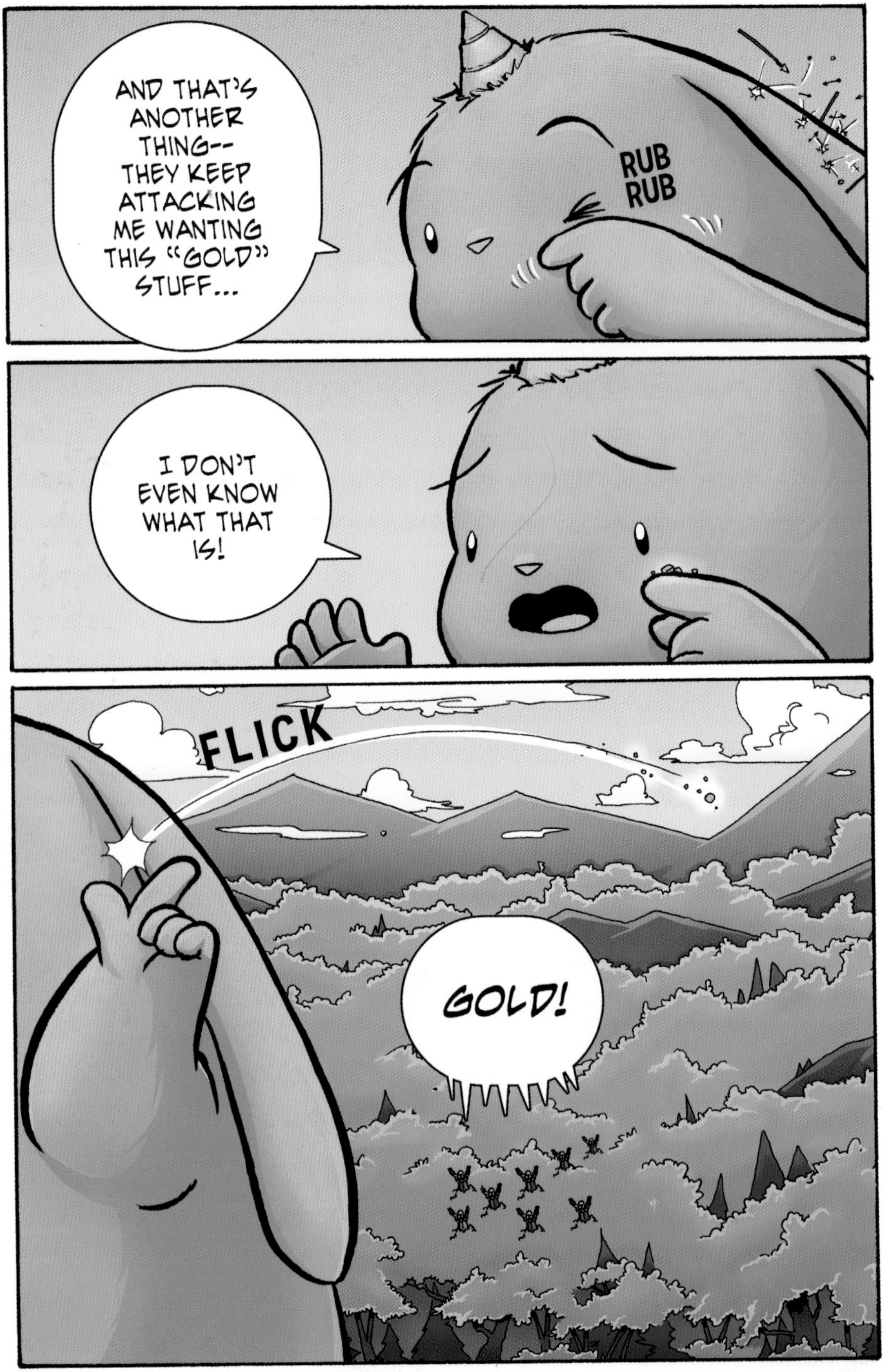
AND THAT'S ANOTHER THING-- THEY KEEP ATTACKING ME WANTING THIS "GOLD" STUFF...
RUB RUB
I DON'T EVEN KNOW WHAT THAT IS!
FLICK
GOLD!

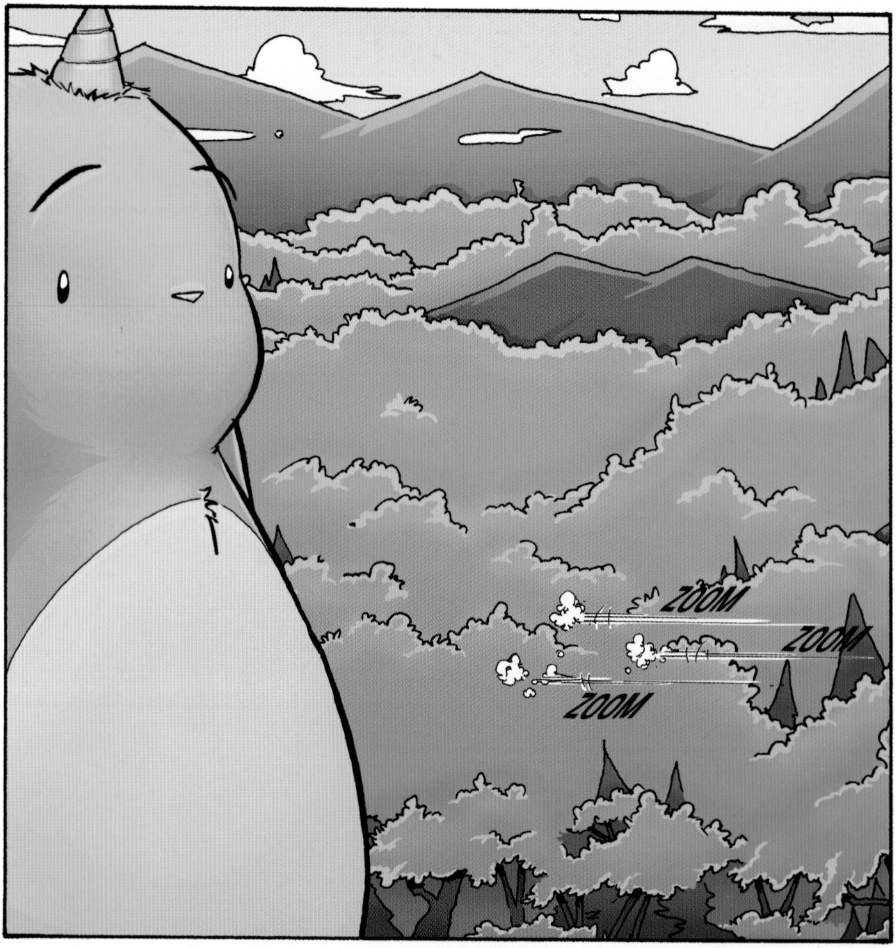
ZOOM
ZOOM
ZOOM

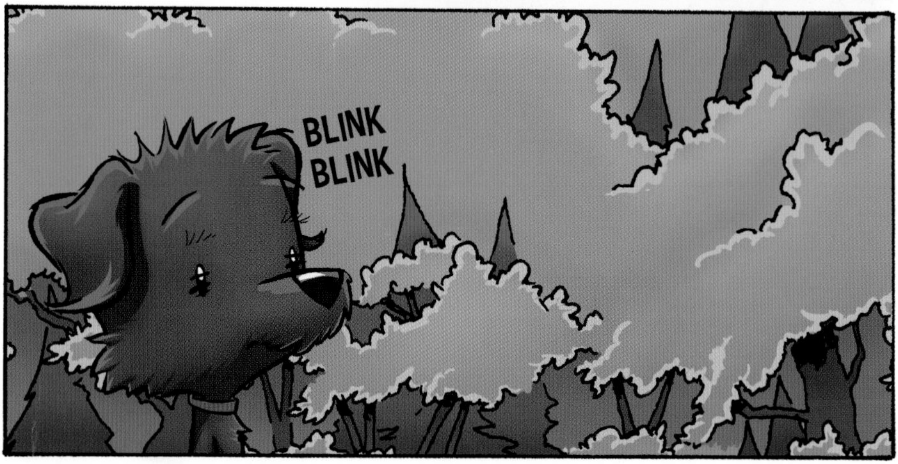
BLINK
BLINK

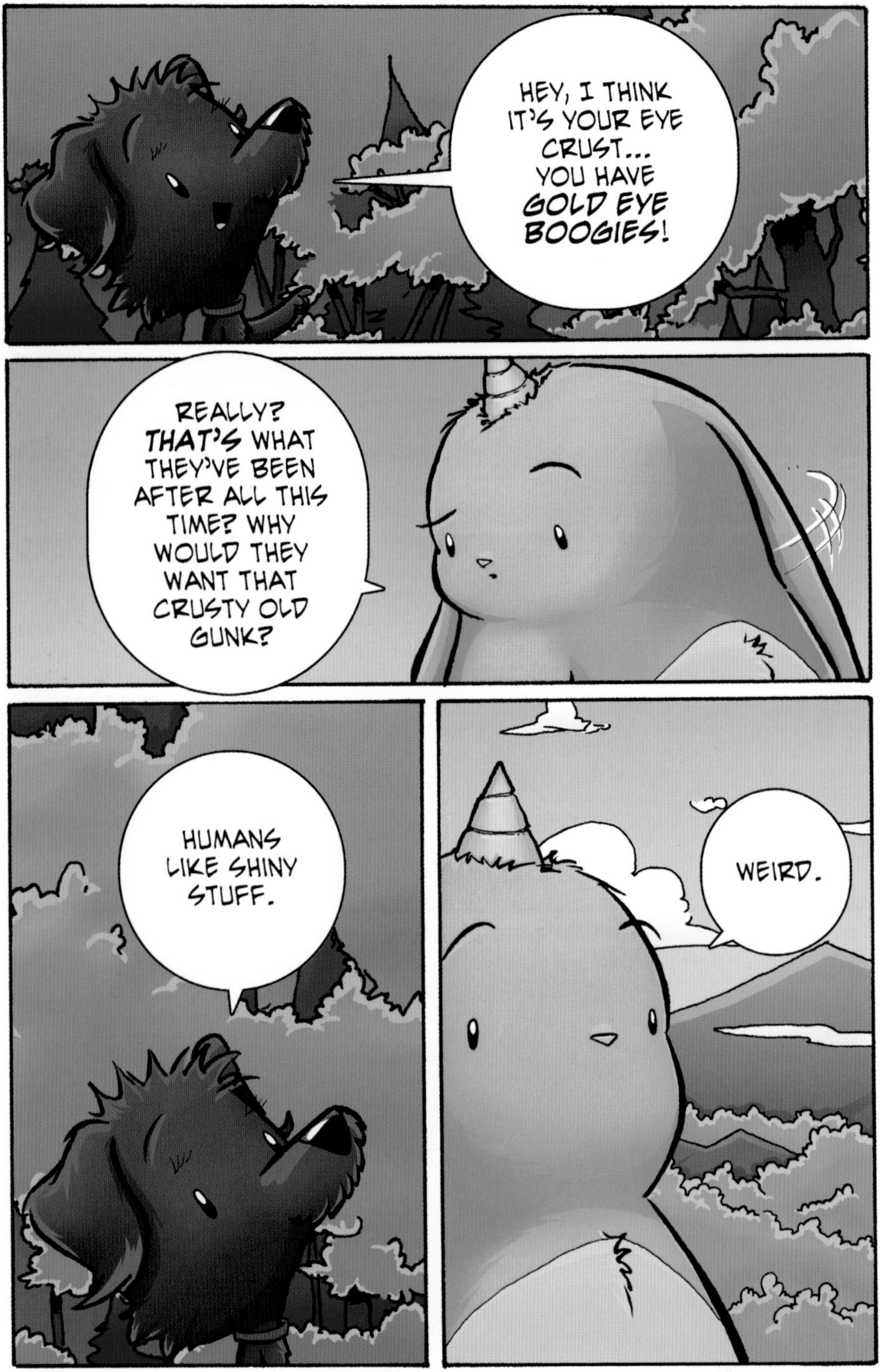
HEY, I THINK IT'S YOUR EYE CRUST... YOU HAVE ***GOLD EYE BOOGIES!***
REALLY? ***THAT'S*** WHAT THEY'VE BEEN AFTER ALL THIS TIME? WHY WOULD THEY WANT THAT CRUSTY OLD GUNK?
HUMANS LIKE SHINY STUFF.
WEIRD.

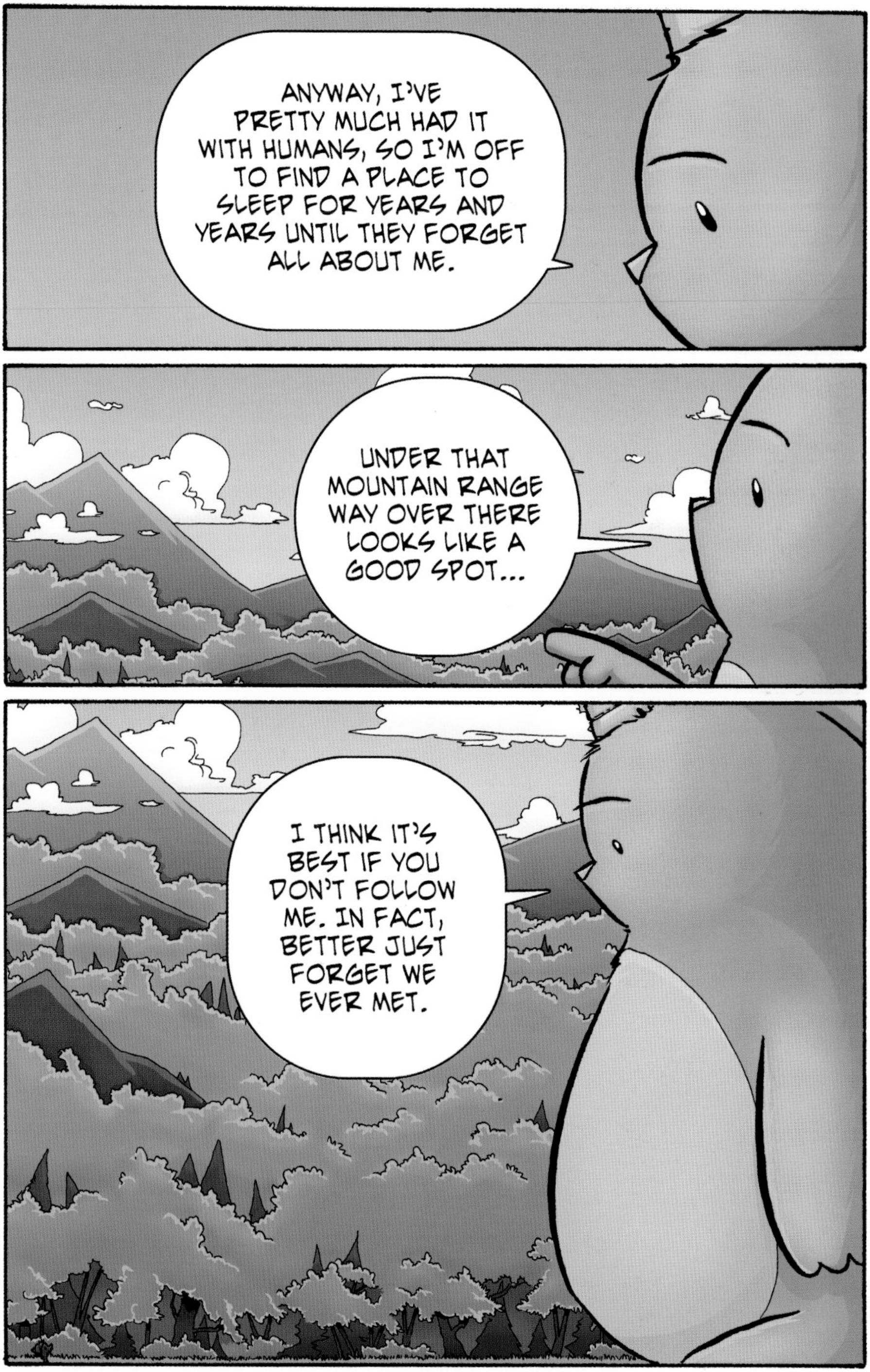
ANYWAY, I'VE PRETTY MUCH HAD IT WITH HUMANS, SO I'M OFF TO FIND A PLACE TO SLEEP FOR YEARS AND YEARS UNTIL THEY FORGET ALL ABOUT ME.
UNDER THAT MOUNTAIN RANGE WAY OVER THERE LOOKS LIKE A GOOD SPOT...
I THINK IT'S BEST IF YOU DON'T FOLLOW ME. IN FACT, BETTER JUST FORGET WE EVER MET.

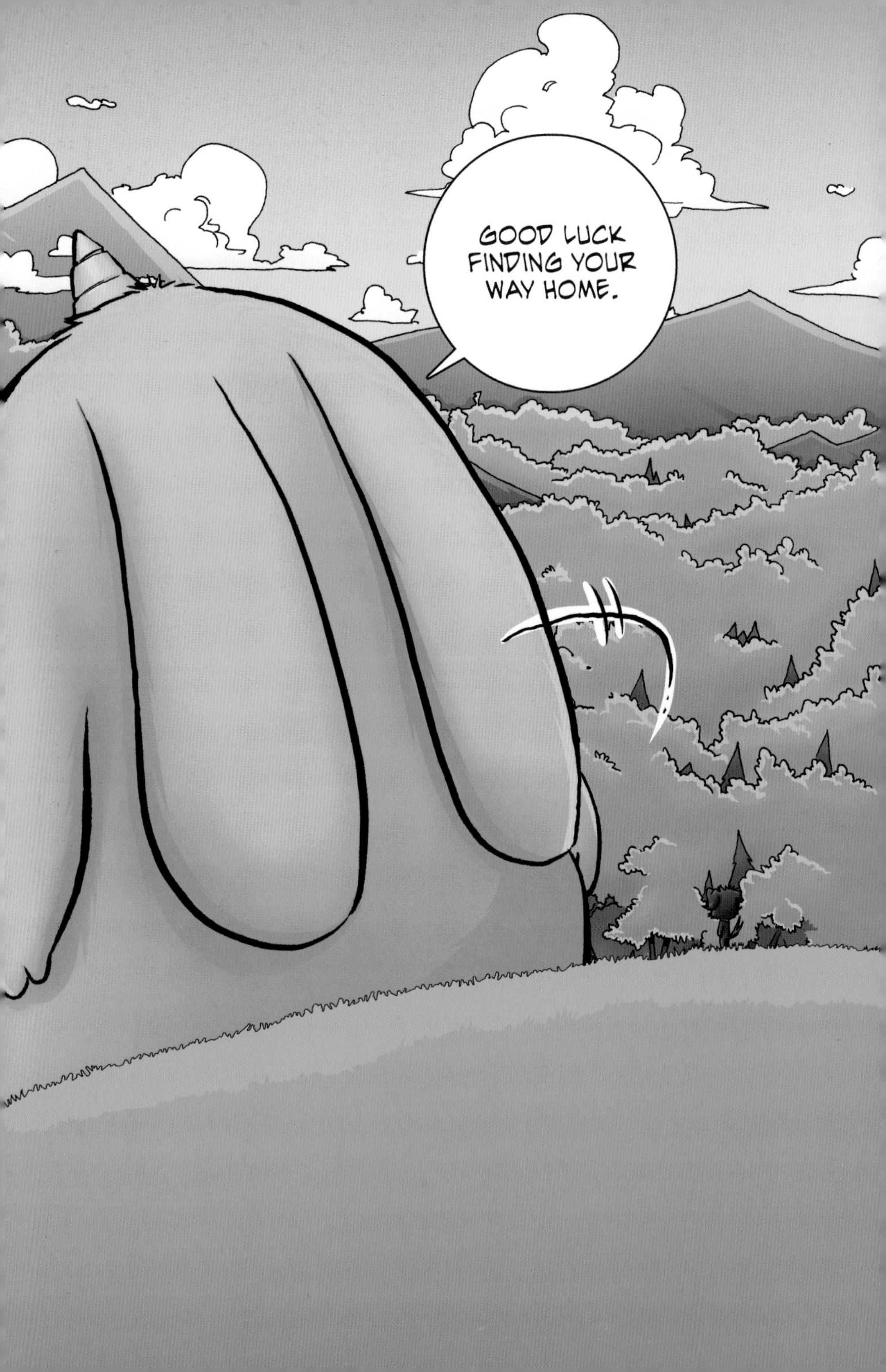
GOOD LUCK FINDING YOUR WAY HOME.

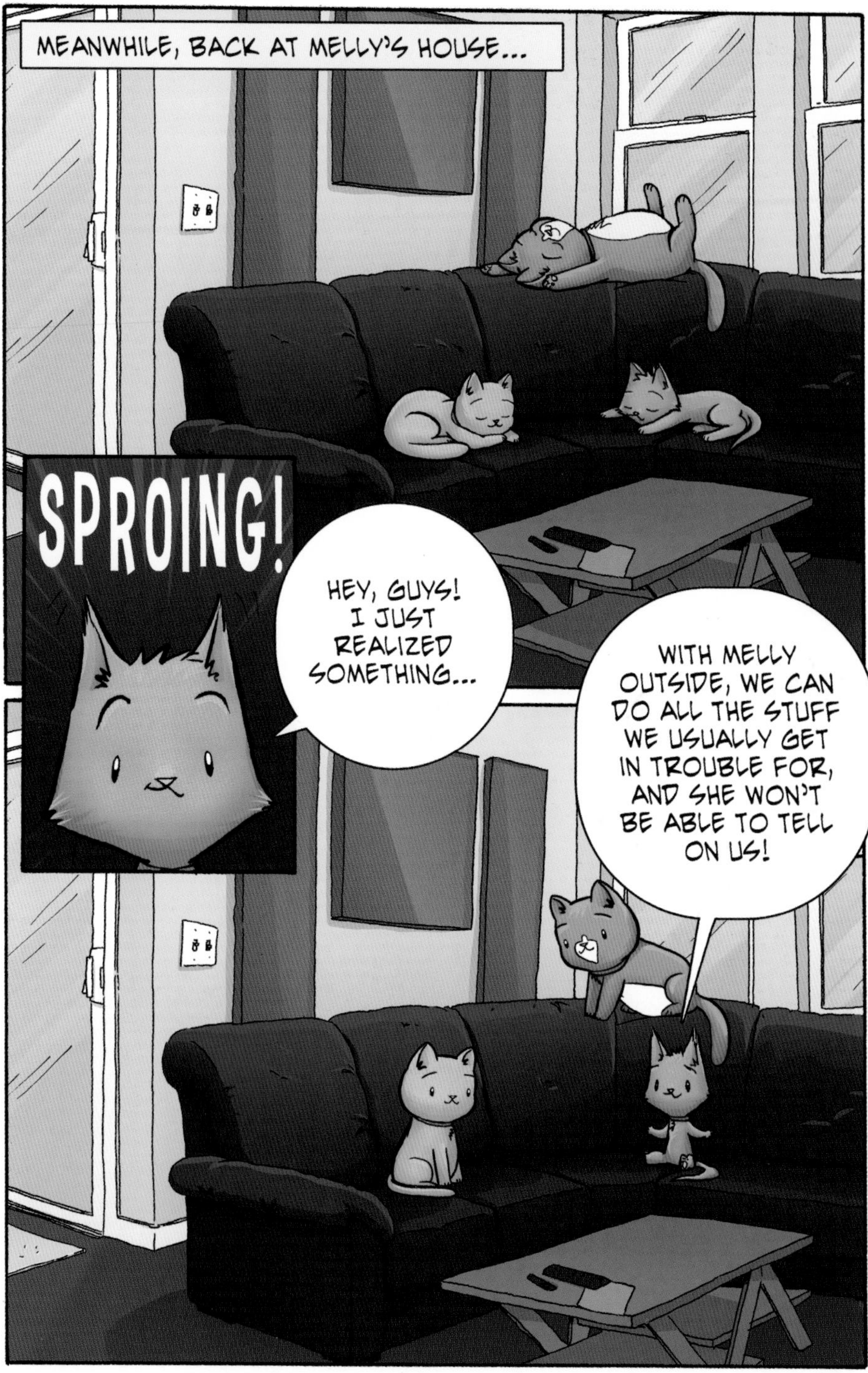

MEANWHILE, BACK AT MELLY'S HOUSE...
SPROING!
HEY, GUYS! I JUST REALIZED SOMETHING...
WITH MELLY OUTSIDE, WE CAN DO ALL THE STUFF WE USUALLY GET IN TROUBLE FOR, AND SHE WON'T BE ABLE TO TELL ON US!

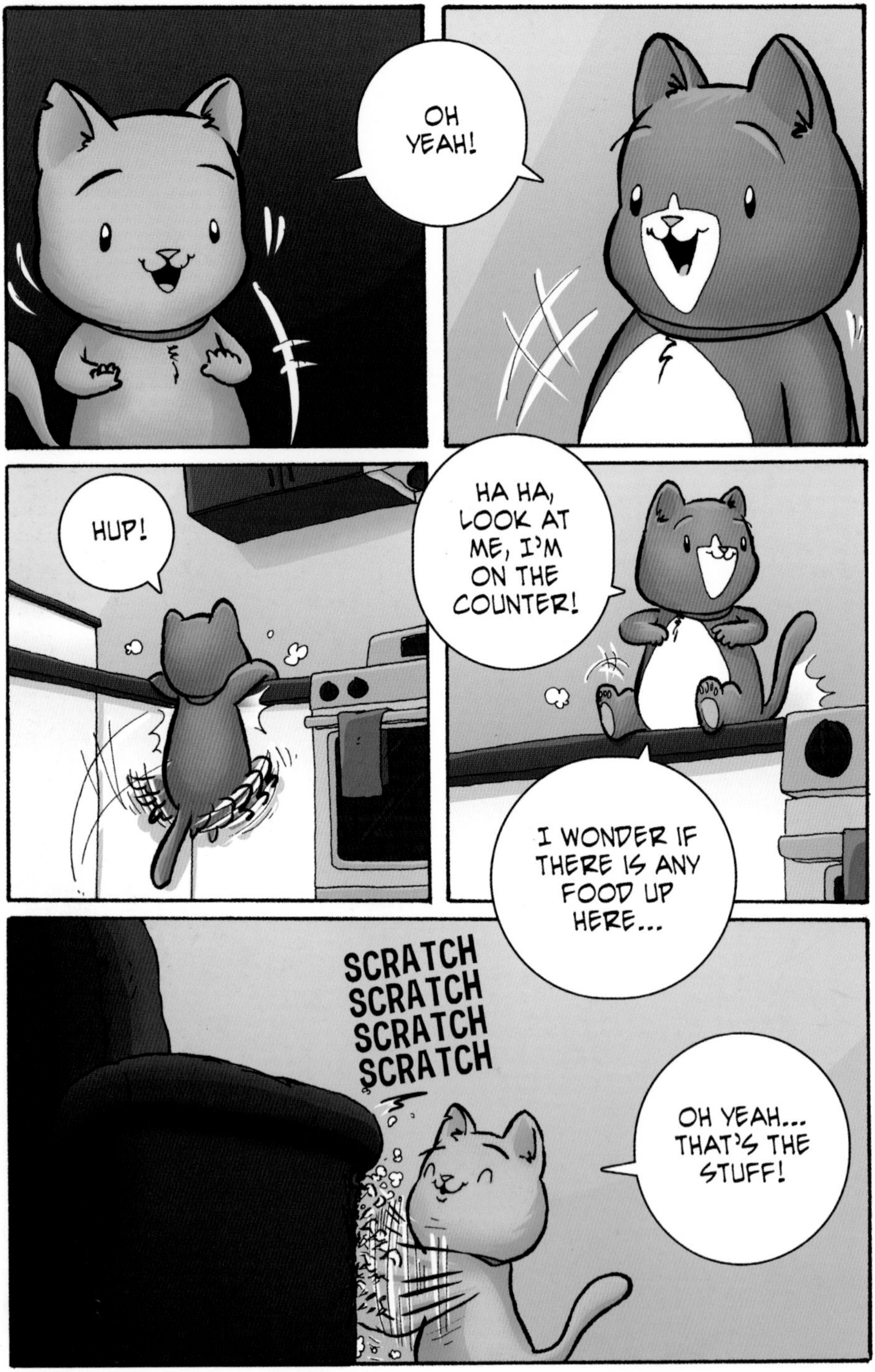
OH YEAH!
HUP!
HA HA, LOOK AT ME, I'M ON THE COUNTER!
I WONDER IF THERE IS ANY FOOD UP HERE...
SCRATCH SCRATCH SCRATCH SCRATCH
OH YEAH... THAT'S THE STUFF!

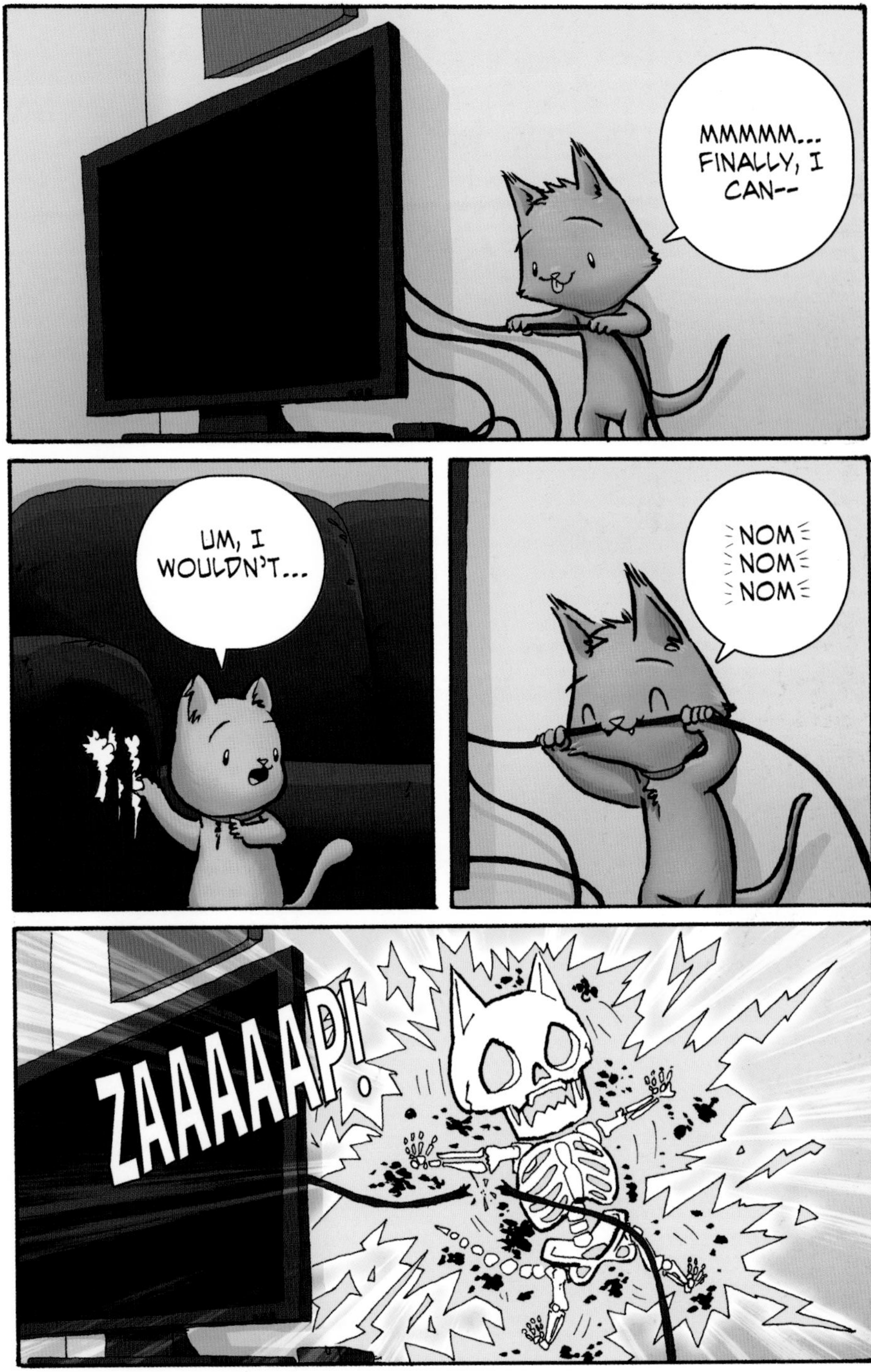
MMMMM...
FINALLY, I
CAN--
UM, I
WOULDN'T...
NOM
NOM
NOM
ZAAAAAP!

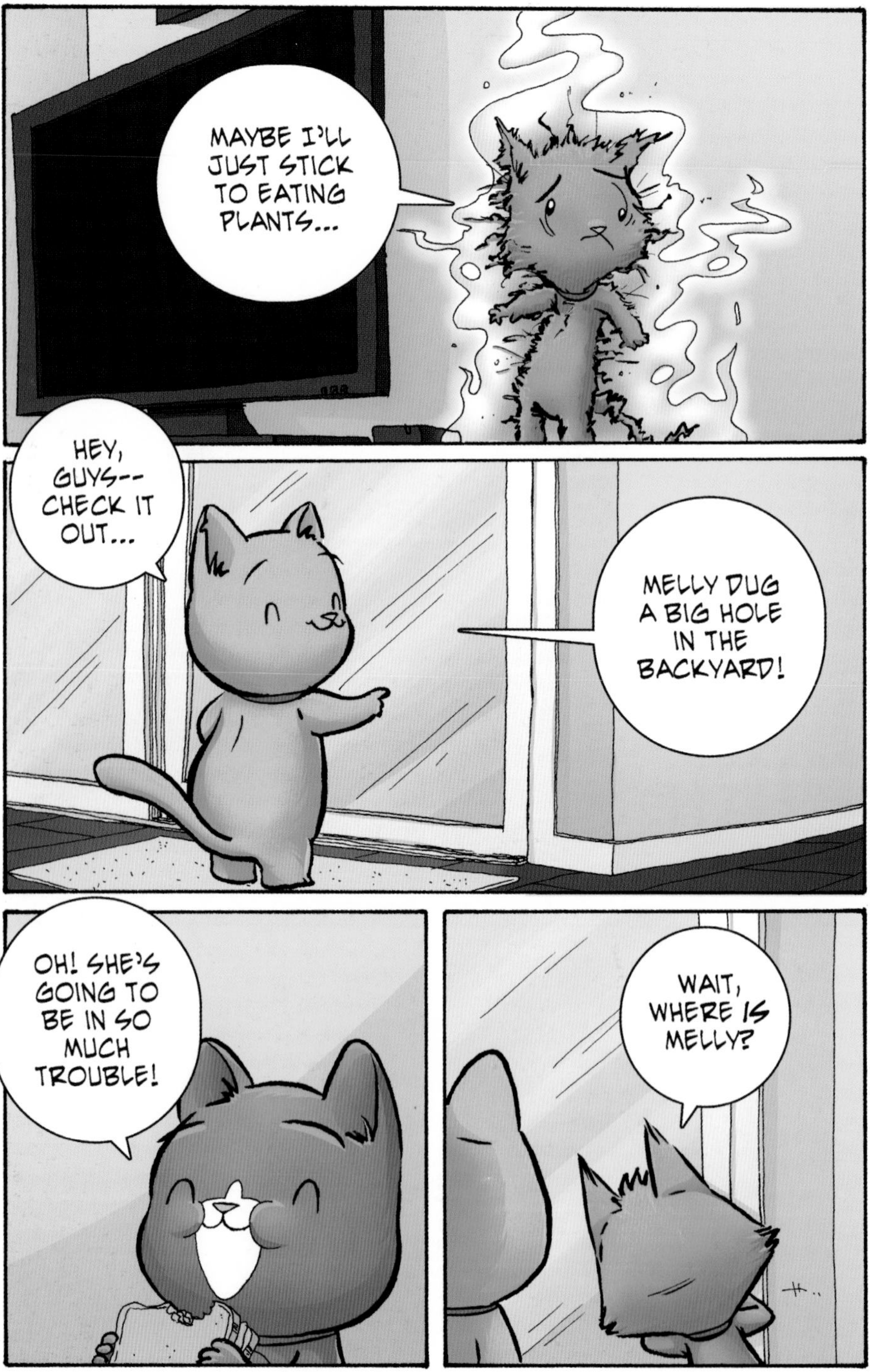
MAYBE I'LL JUST STICK TO EATING PLANTS...
HEY, GUYS--CHECK IT OUT...
MELLY DUG A BIG HOLE IN THE BACKYARD!
OH! SHE'S GOING TO BE IN SO MUCH TROUBLE!
WAIT, WHERE IS MELLY?

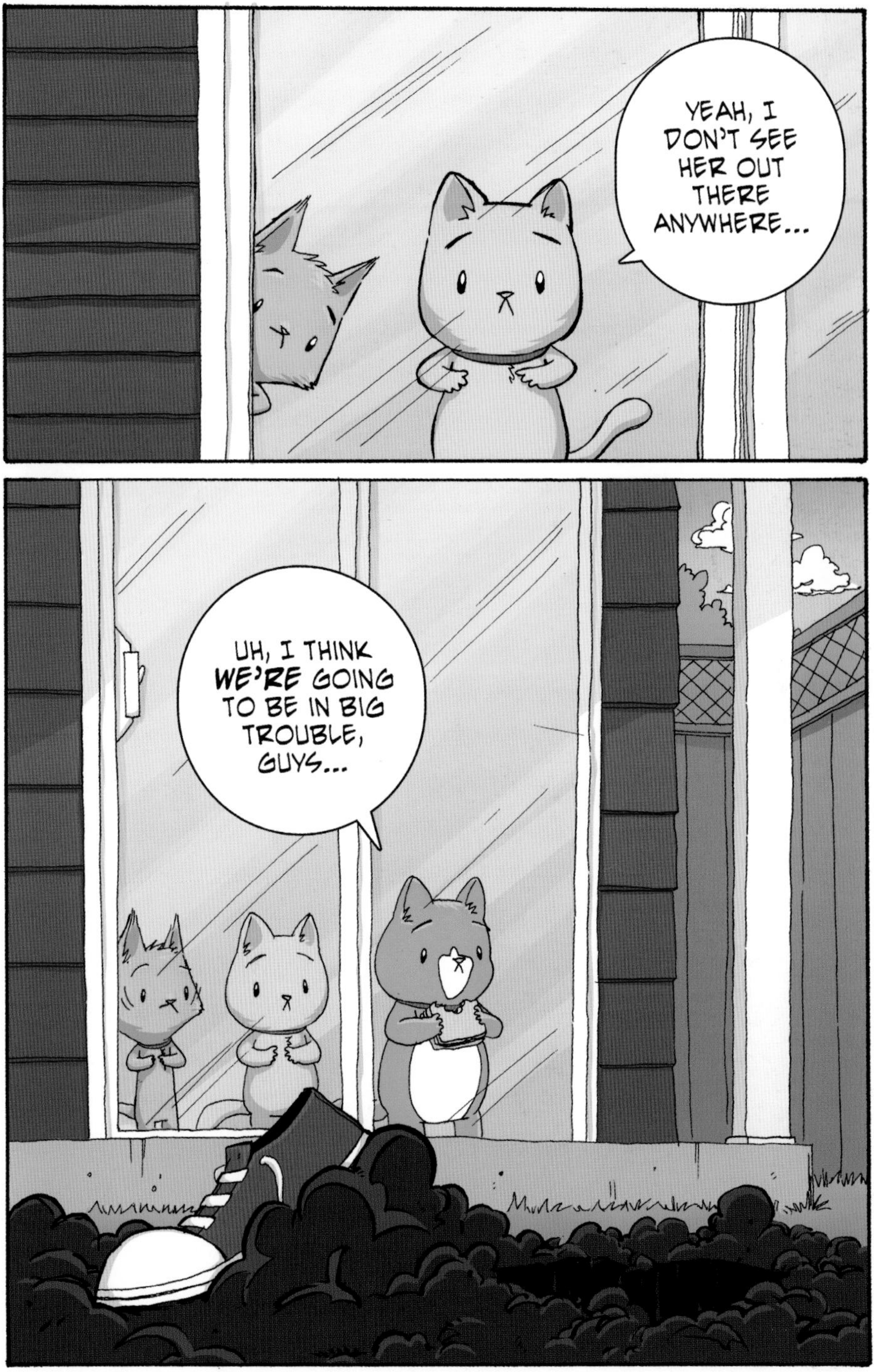
YEAH, I DON'T SEE HER OUT THERE ANYWHERE...
UH, I THINK **WE'RE** GOING TO BE IN BIG TROUBLE, GUYS...

CHAPTER 4
THE BAD KING

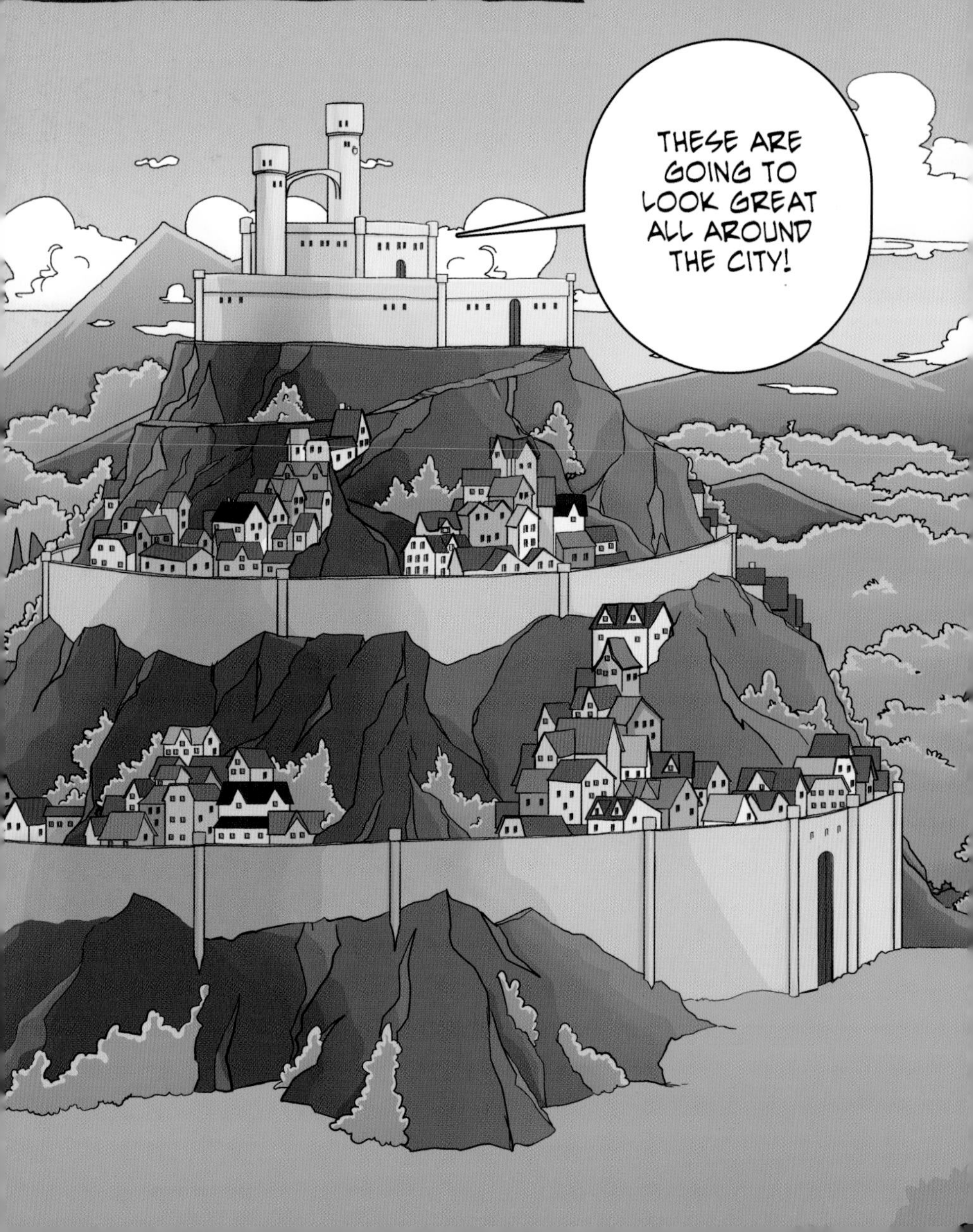
THESE ARE GOING TO LOOK GREAT ALL AROUND THE CITY!

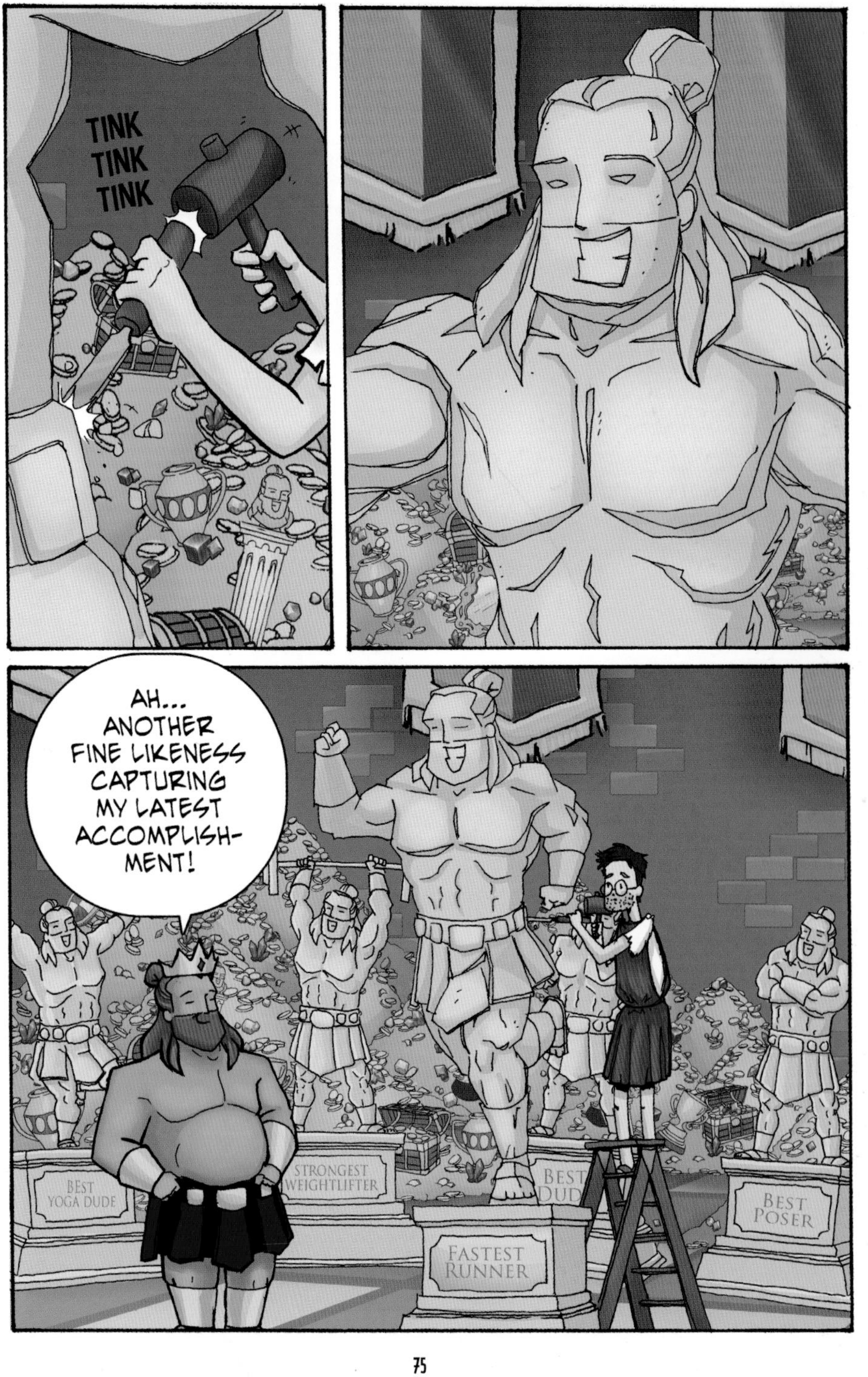
TINK
TINK
TINK
AH... ANOTHER FINE LIKENESS CAPTURING MY LATEST ACCOMPLISH-MENT!
BEST YOGA DUDE
STRONGEST WEIGHTLIFTER
BEST DUD
FASTEST RUNNER
BEST POSER

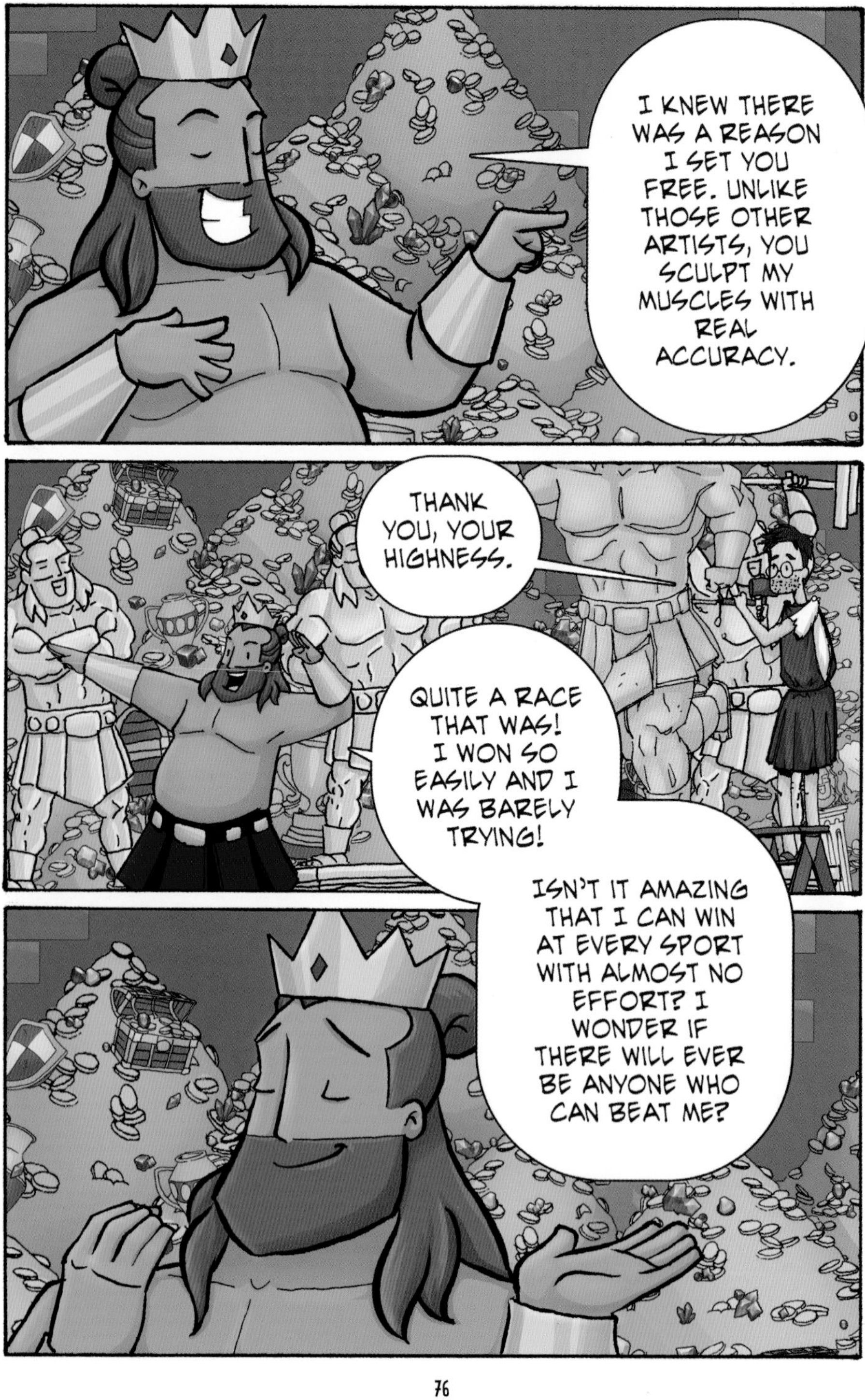
I KNEW THERE WAS A REASON I SET YOU FREE. UNLIKE THOSE OTHER ARTISTS, YOU SCULPT MY MUSCLES WITH REAL ACCURACY.
THANK YOU, YOUR HIGHNESS.
QUITE A RACE THAT WAS! I WON SO EASILY AND I WAS BARELY TRYING!
ISN'T IT AMAZING THAT I CAN WIN AT EVERY SPORT WITH ALMOST NO EFFORT? I WONDER IF THERE WILL EVER BE ANYONE WHO CAN BEAT ME?

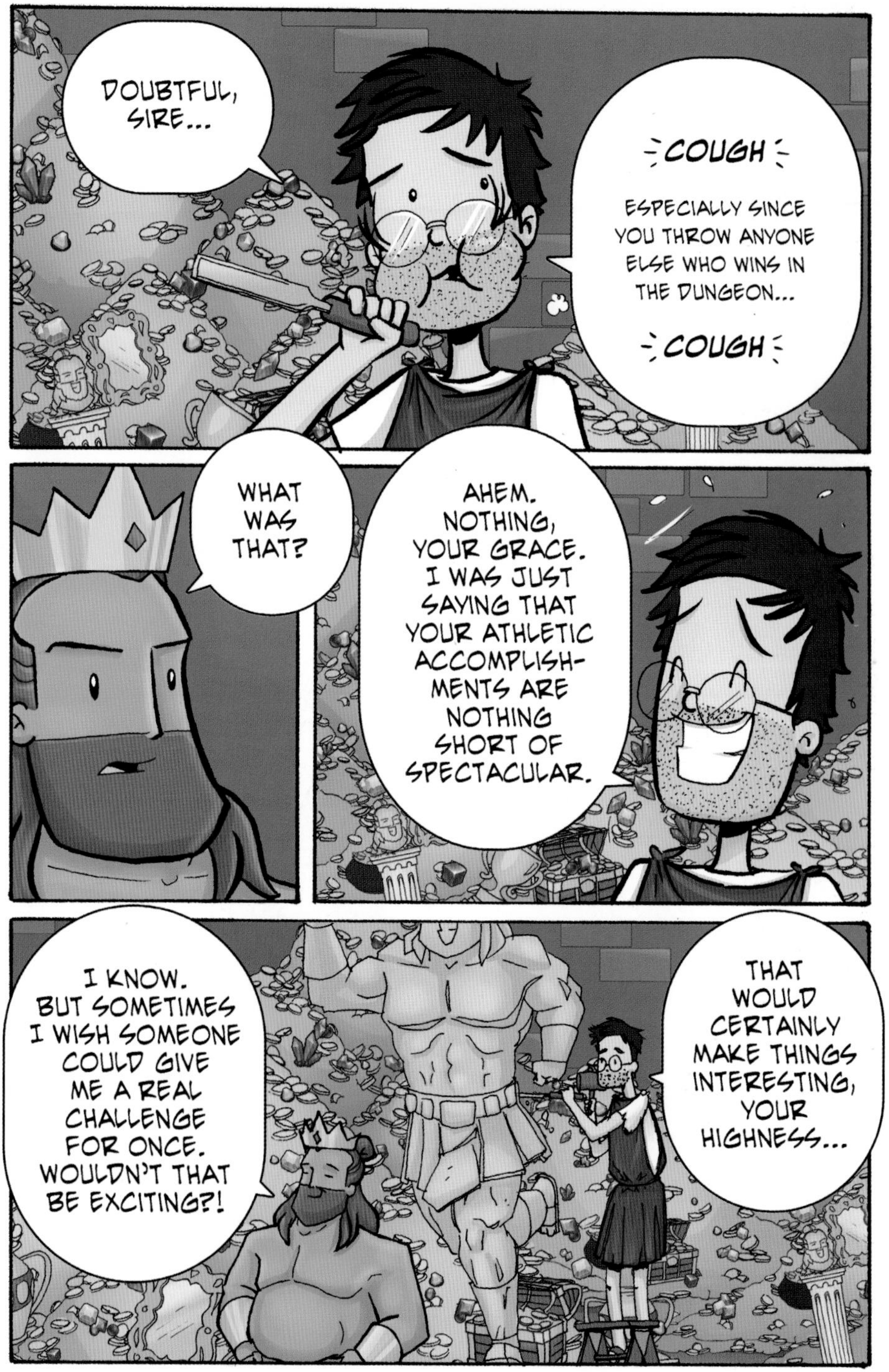

DOUBTFUL, SIRE...
COUGH
ESPECIALLY SINCE YOU THROW ANYONE ELSE WHO WINS IN THE DUNGEON...
COUGH
WHAT WAS THAT?
AHEM. NOTHING, YOUR GRACE. I WAS JUST SAYING THAT YOUR ATHLETIC ACCOMPLISH-MENTS ARE NOTHING SHORT OF SPECTACULAR.
I KNOW. BUT SOMETIMES I WISH SOMEONE COULD GIVE ME A REAL CHALLENGE FOR ONCE. WOULDN'T THAT BE EXCITING?!
THAT WOULD CERTAINLY MAKE THINGS INTERESTING, YOUR HIGHNESS...

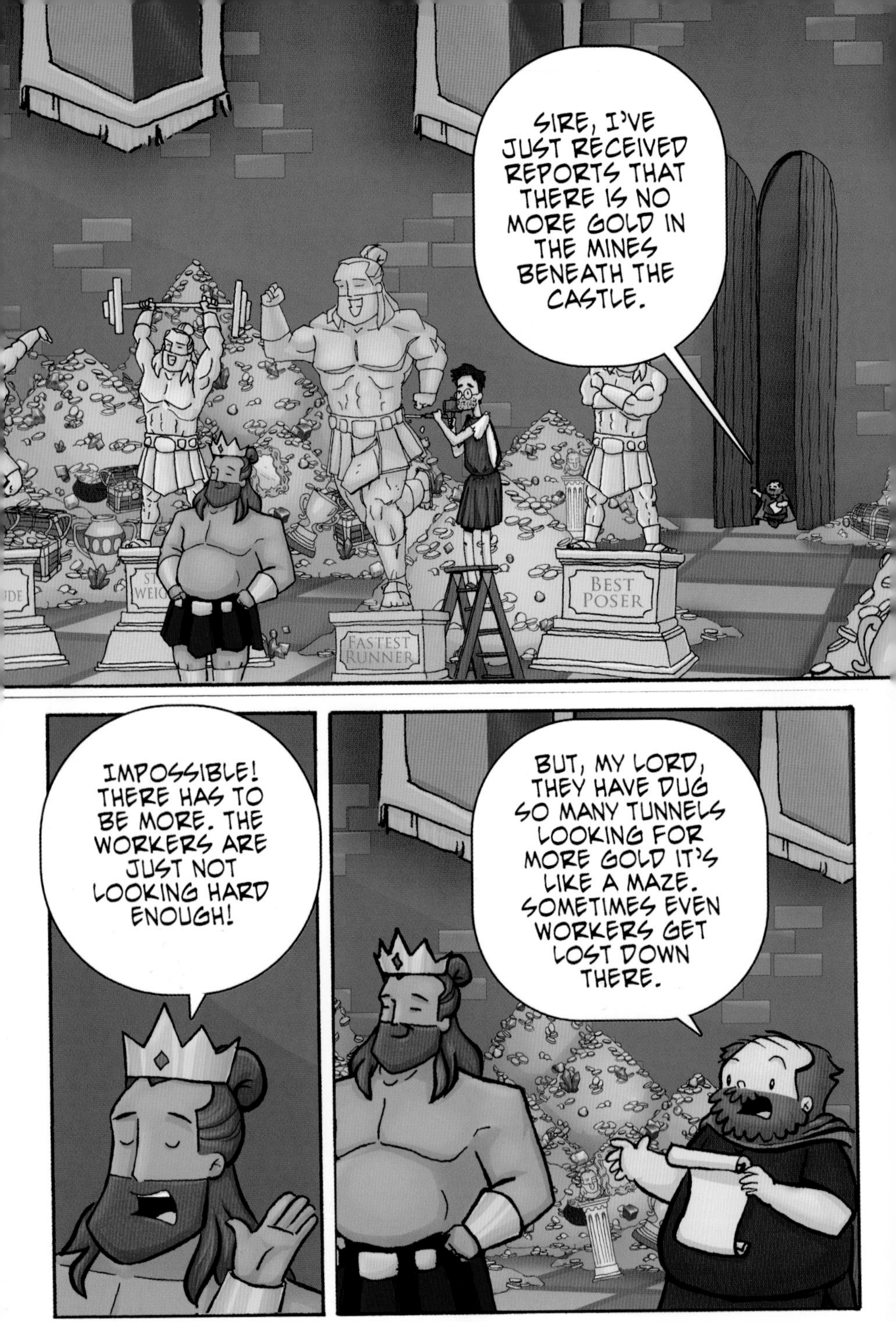
SIRE, I'VE JUST RECEIVED REPORTS THAT THERE IS NO MORE GOLD IN THE MINES BENEATH THE CASTLE.
FASTEST RUNNER
BEST POSER
IMPOSSIBLE! THERE HAS TO BE MORE. THE WORKERS ARE JUST NOT LOOKING HARD ENOUGH!
BUT, MY LORD, THEY HAVE DUG SO MANY TUNNELS LOOKING FOR MORE GOLD IT'S LIKE A MAZE. SOMETIMES EVEN WORKERS GET LOST DOWN THERE.

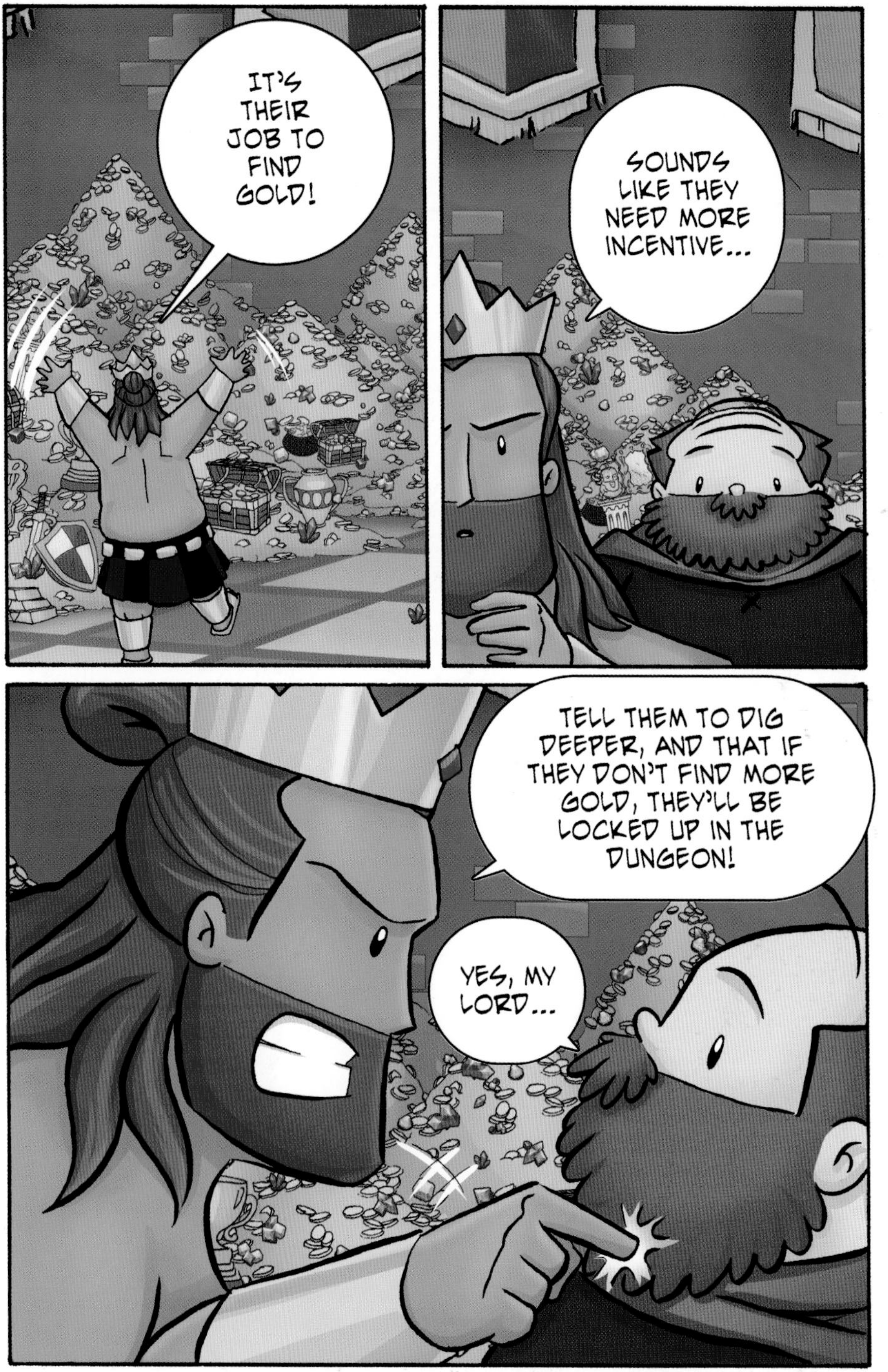
IT'S THEIR JOB TO FIND GOLD!
SOUNDS LIKE THEY NEED MORE INCENTIVE...
TELL THEM TO DIG DEEPER, AND THAT IF THEY DON'T FIND MORE GOLD, THEY'LL BE LOCKED UP IN THE DUNGEON!
YES, MY LORD...

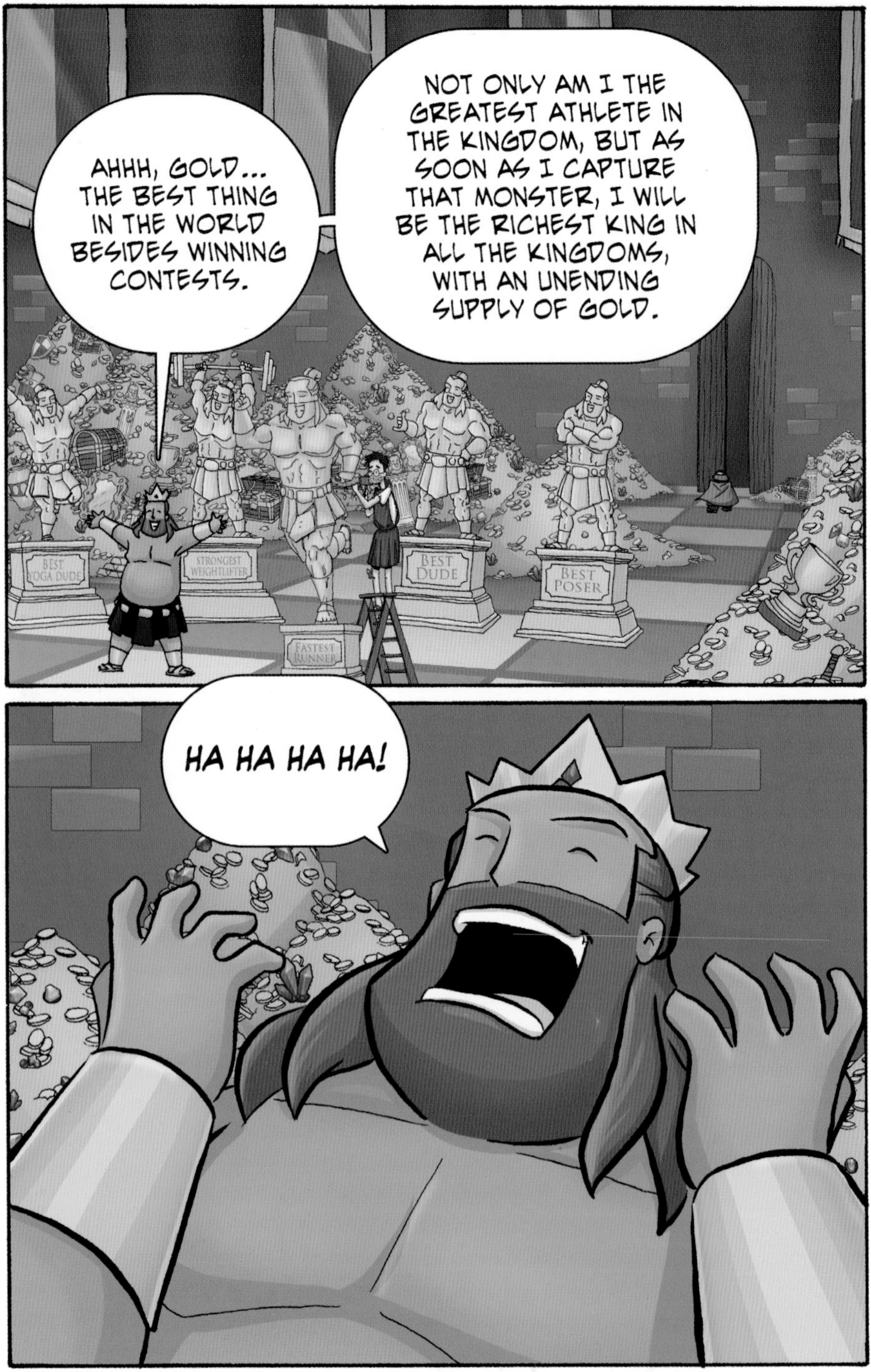
AHHH, GOLD... THE BEST THING IN THE WORLD BESIDES WINNING CONTESTS.
NOT ONLY AM I THE GREATEST ATHLETE IN THE KINGDOM, BUT AS SOON AS I CAPTURE THAT MONSTER, I WILL BE THE RICHEST KING IN ALL THE KINGDOMS, WITH AN UNENDING SUPPLY OF GOLD.
BEST YOGA DUDE
STRONGEST WEIGHTLIFTER
FASTEST RUNNER
BEST DUDE
BEST POSER
HA HA HA HA!

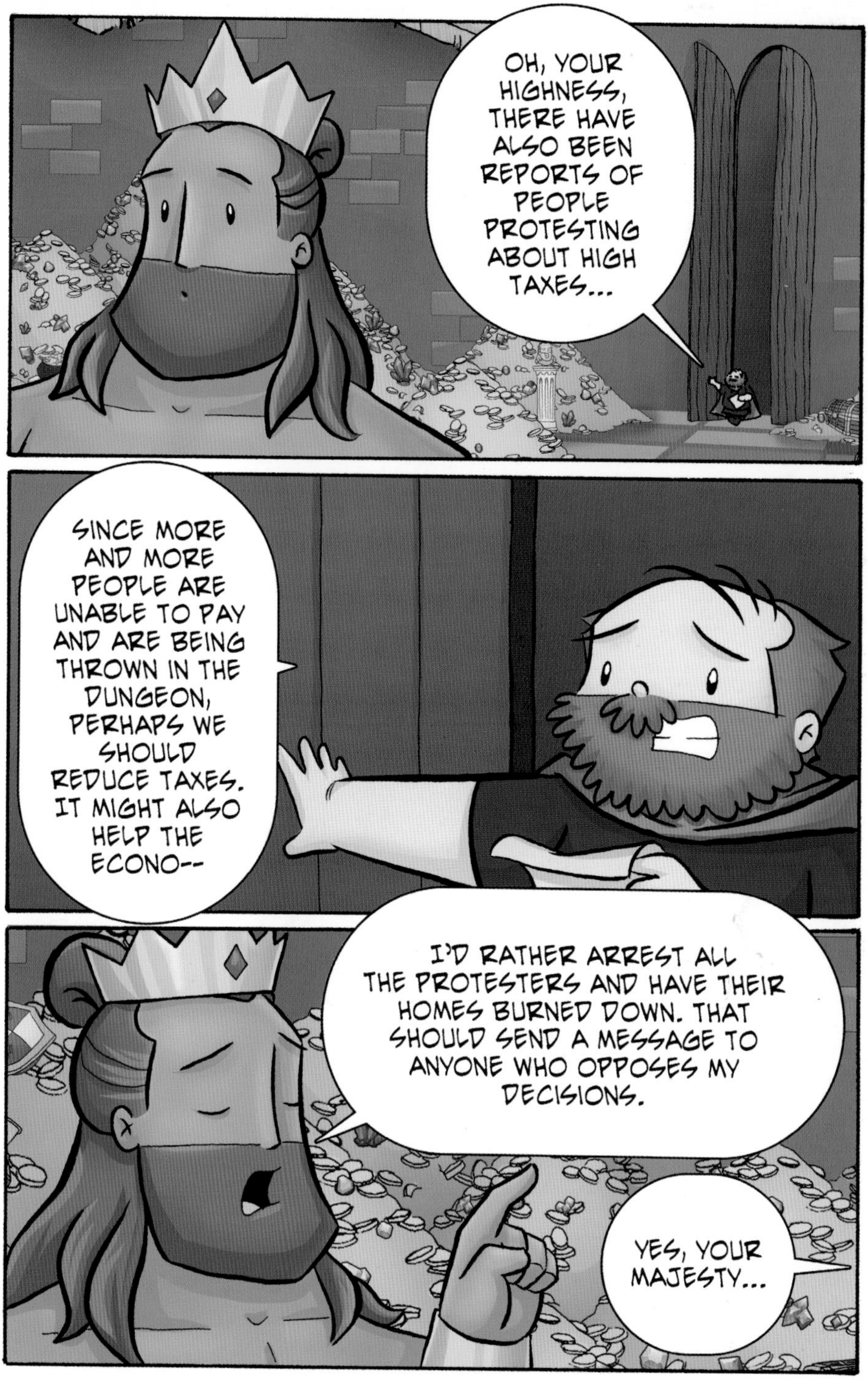
OH, YOUR HIGHNESS, THERE HAVE ALSO BEEN REPORTS OF PEOPLE PROTESTING ABOUT HIGH TAXES...
SINCE MORE AND MORE PEOPLE ARE UNABLE TO PAY AND ARE BEING THROWN IN THE DUNGEON, PERHAPS WE SHOULD REDUCE TAXES. IT MIGHT ALSO HELP THE ECONO--
I'D RATHER ARREST ALL THE PROTESTERS AND HAVE THEIR HOMES BURNED DOWN. THAT SHOULD SEND A MESSAGE TO ANYONE WHO OPPOSES MY DECISIONS.
YES, YOUR MAJESTY...

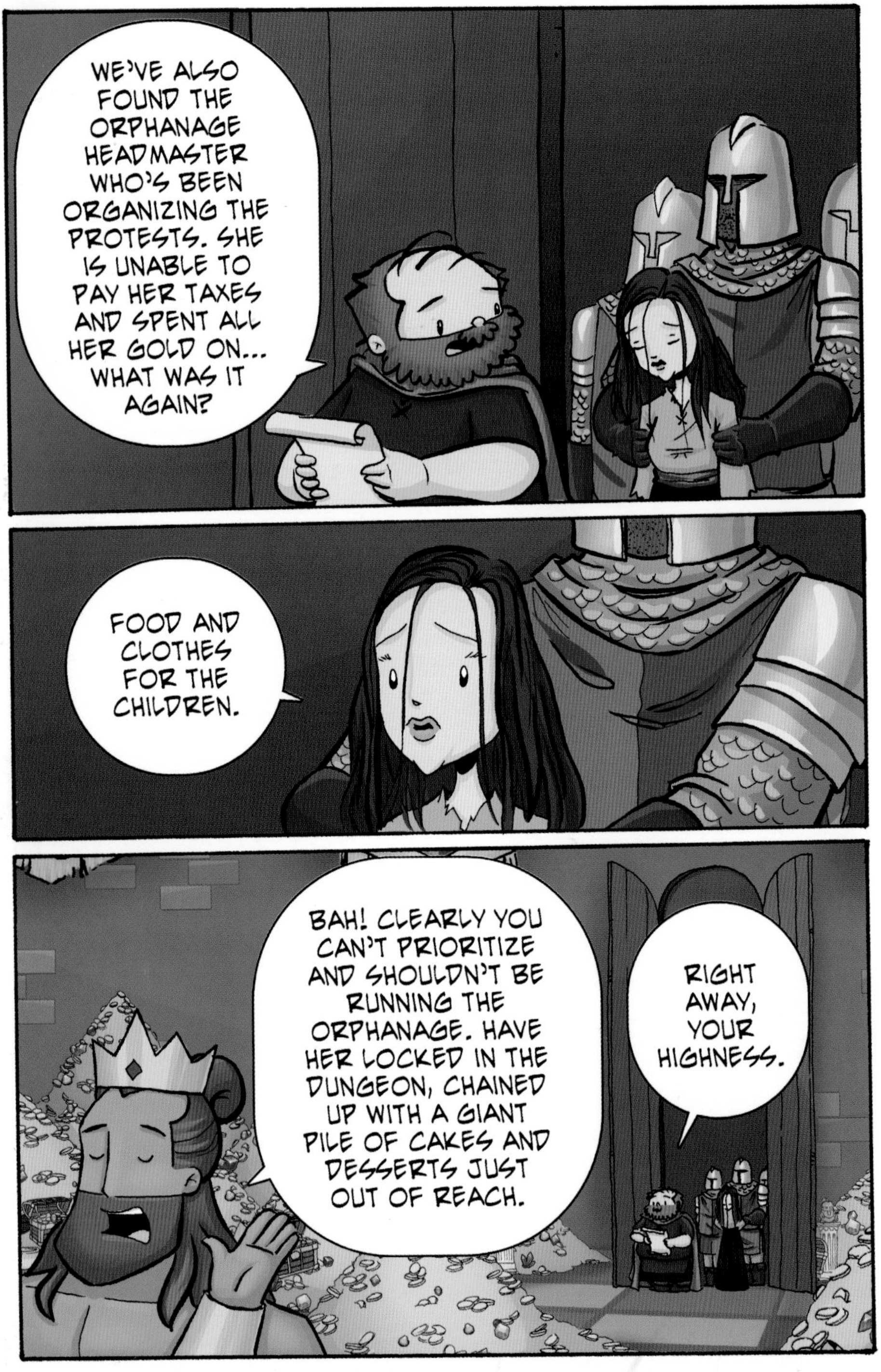
WE'VE ALSO FOUND THE ORPHANAGE HEADMASTER WHO'S BEEN ORGANIZING THE PROTESTS. SHE IS UNABLE TO PAY HER TAXES AND SPENT ALL HER GOLD ON... WHAT WAS IT AGAIN?
FOOD AND CLOTHES FOR THE CHILDREN.
BAH! CLEARLY YOU CAN'T PRIORITIZE AND SHOULDN'T BE RUNNING THE ORPHANAGE. HAVE HER LOCKED IN THE DUNGEON, CHAINED UP WITH A GIANT PILE OF CAKES AND DESSERTS JUST OUT OF REACH.
RIGHT AWAY, YOUR HIGHNESS.

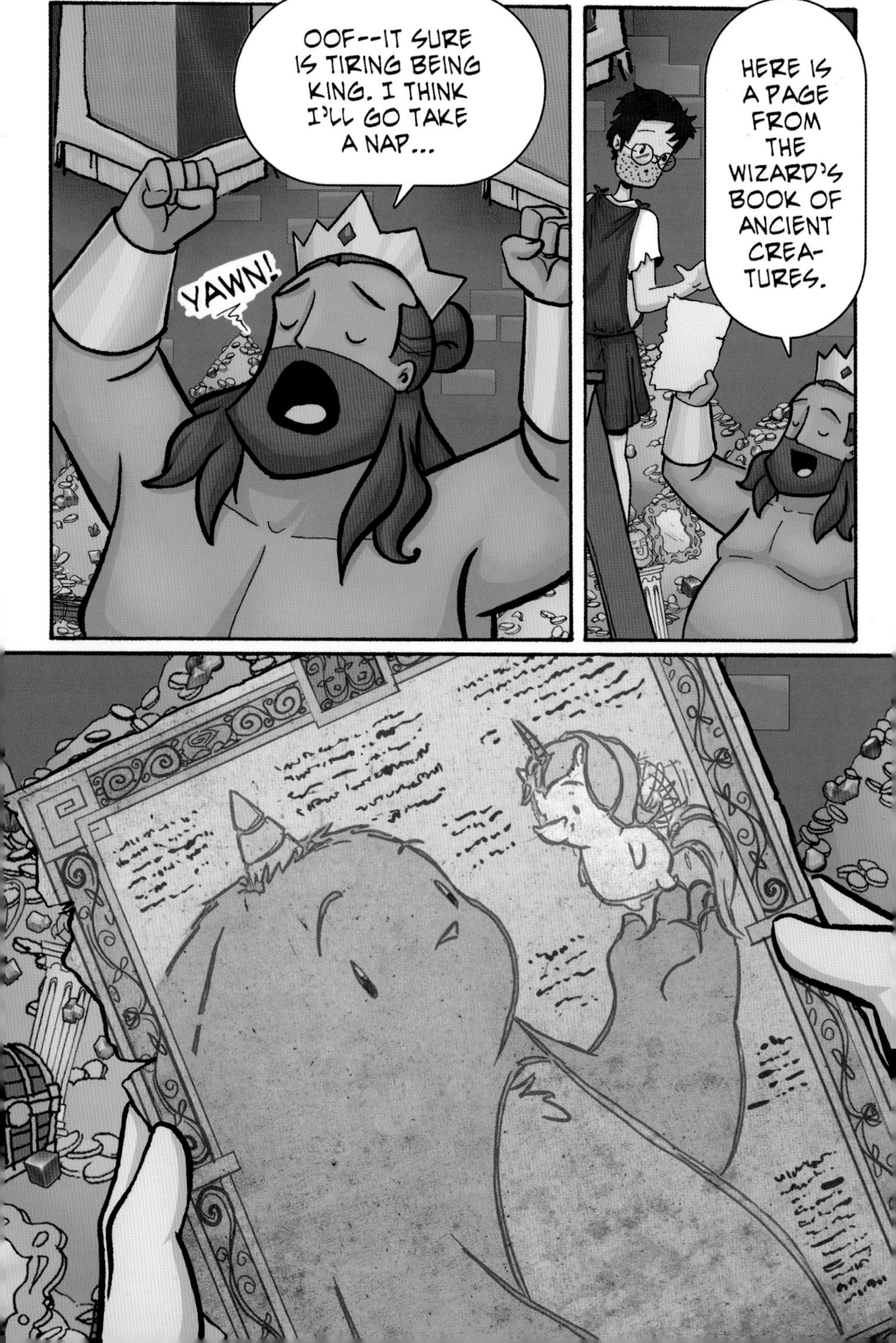
OOF--IT SURE IS TIRING BEING KING. I THINK I'LL GO TAKE A NAP...
YAWN!
HERE IS A PAGE FROM THE WIZARD'S BOOK OF ANCIENT CREA-TURES.

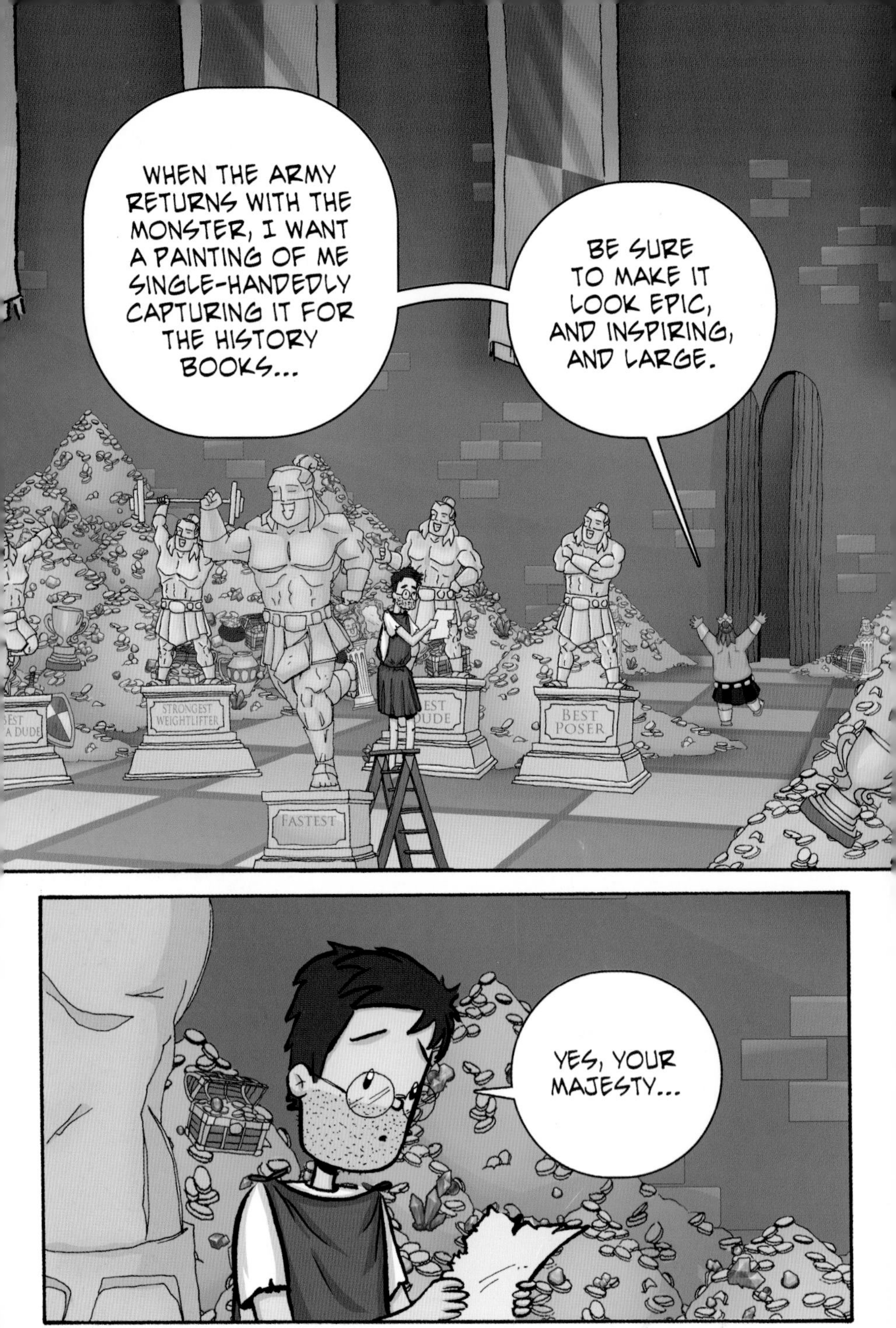
WHEN THE ARMY RETURNS WITH THE MONSTER, I WANT A PAINTING OF ME SINGLE-HANDEDLY CAPTURING IT FOR THE HISTORY BOOKS...
BE SURE TO MAKE IT LOOK EPIC, AND INSPIRING, AND LARGE.
STRONGEST WEIGHTLIFTER
BEST POSER
FASTEST
YES, YOUR MAJESTY...

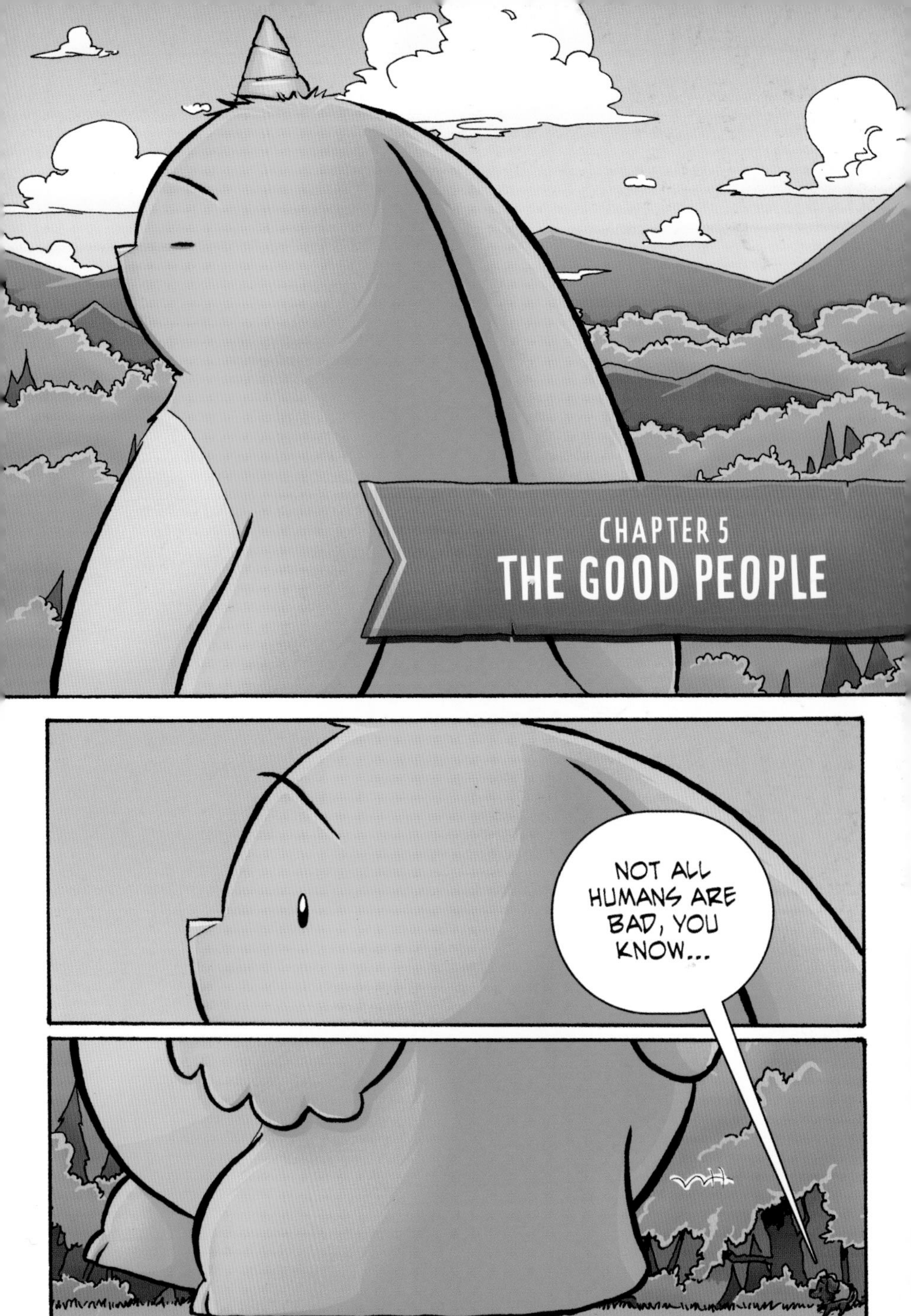
CHAPTER 5
THE GOOD PEOPLE
NOT ALL HUMANS ARE BAD, YOU KNOW...

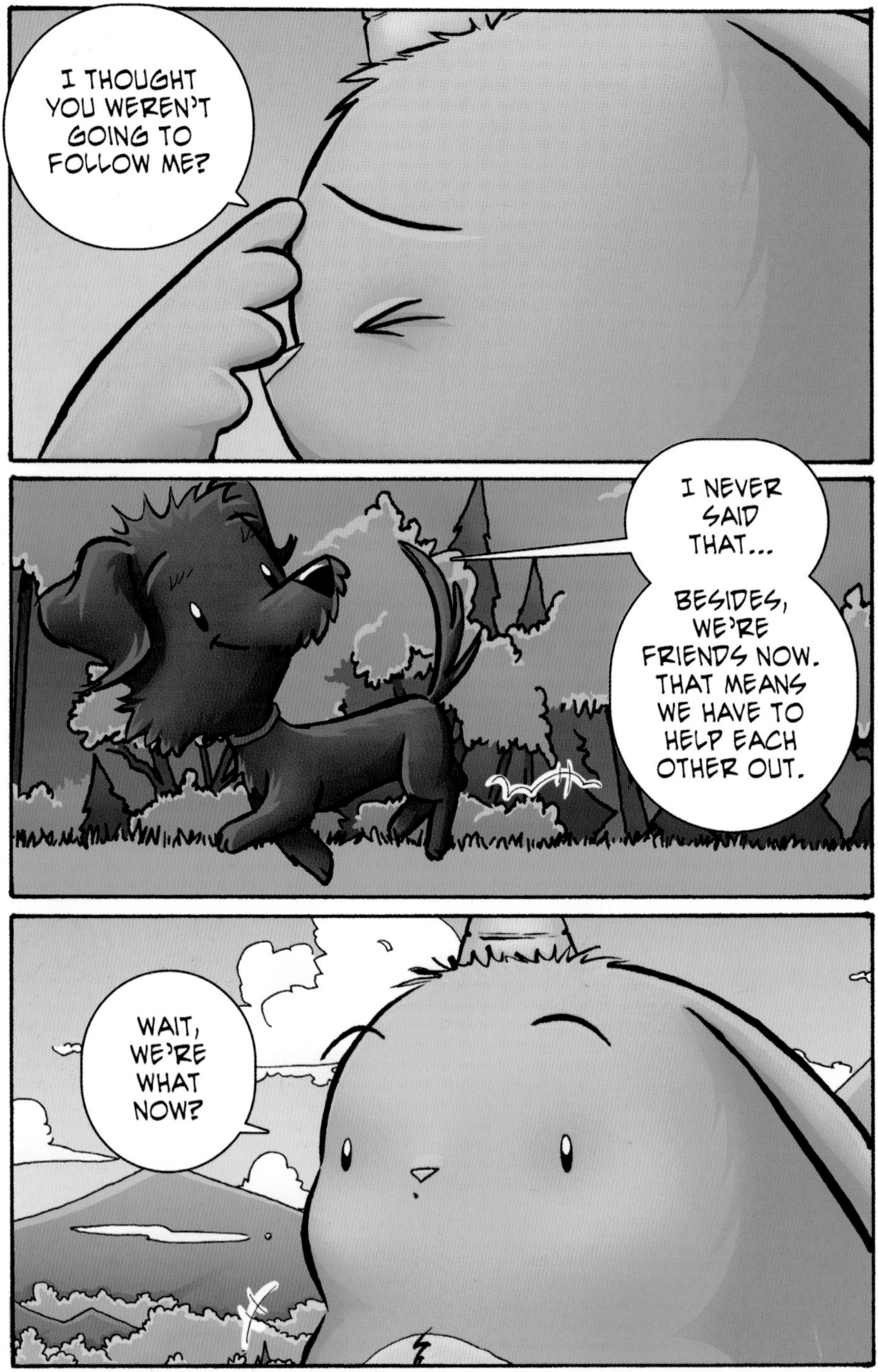
I THOUGHT YOU WEREN'T GOING TO FOLLOW ME?
I NEVER SAID THAT...
BESIDES, WE'RE FRIENDS NOW. THAT MEANS WE HAVE TO HELP EACH OTHER OUT.
WAIT, WE'RE WHAT NOW?

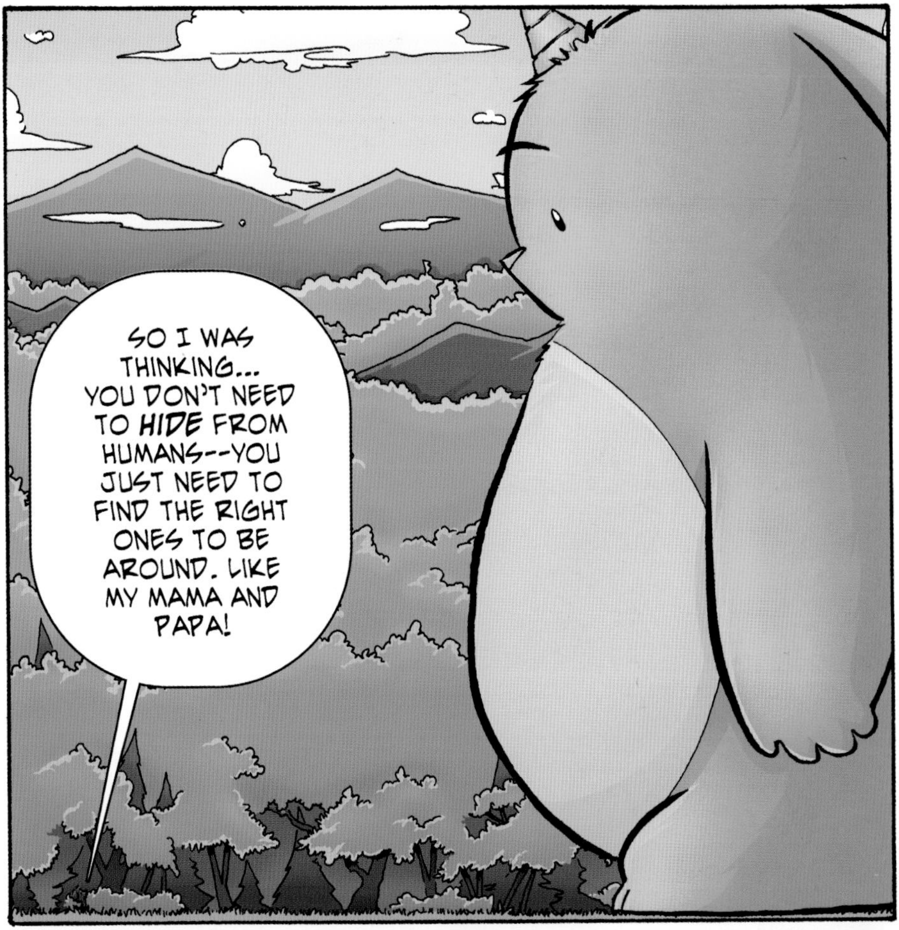
SO I WAS THINKING... YOU DON'T NEED TO *HIDE* FROM HUMANS--YOU JUST NEED TO FIND THE RIGHT ONES TO BE AROUND. LIKE MY MAMA AND PAPA!

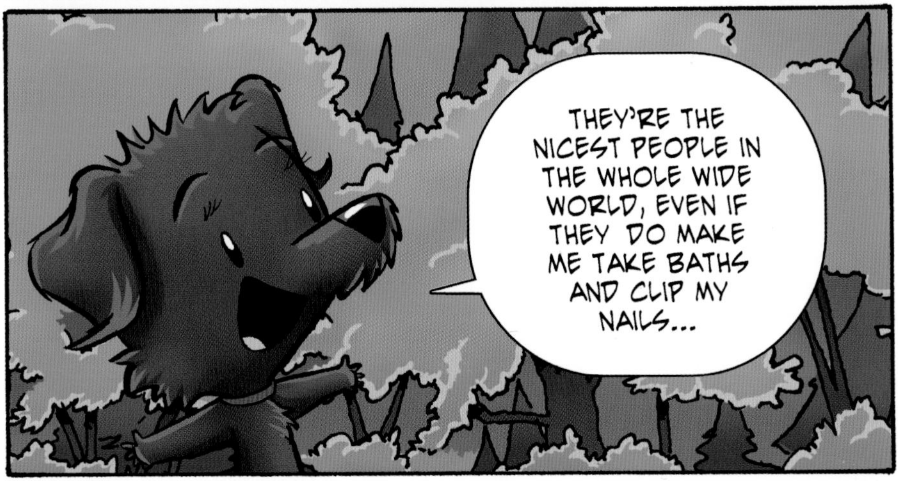
THEY'RE THE NICEST PEOPLE IN THE WHOLE WIDE WORLD, EVEN IF THEY DO MAKE ME TAKE BATHS AND CLIP MY NAILS...

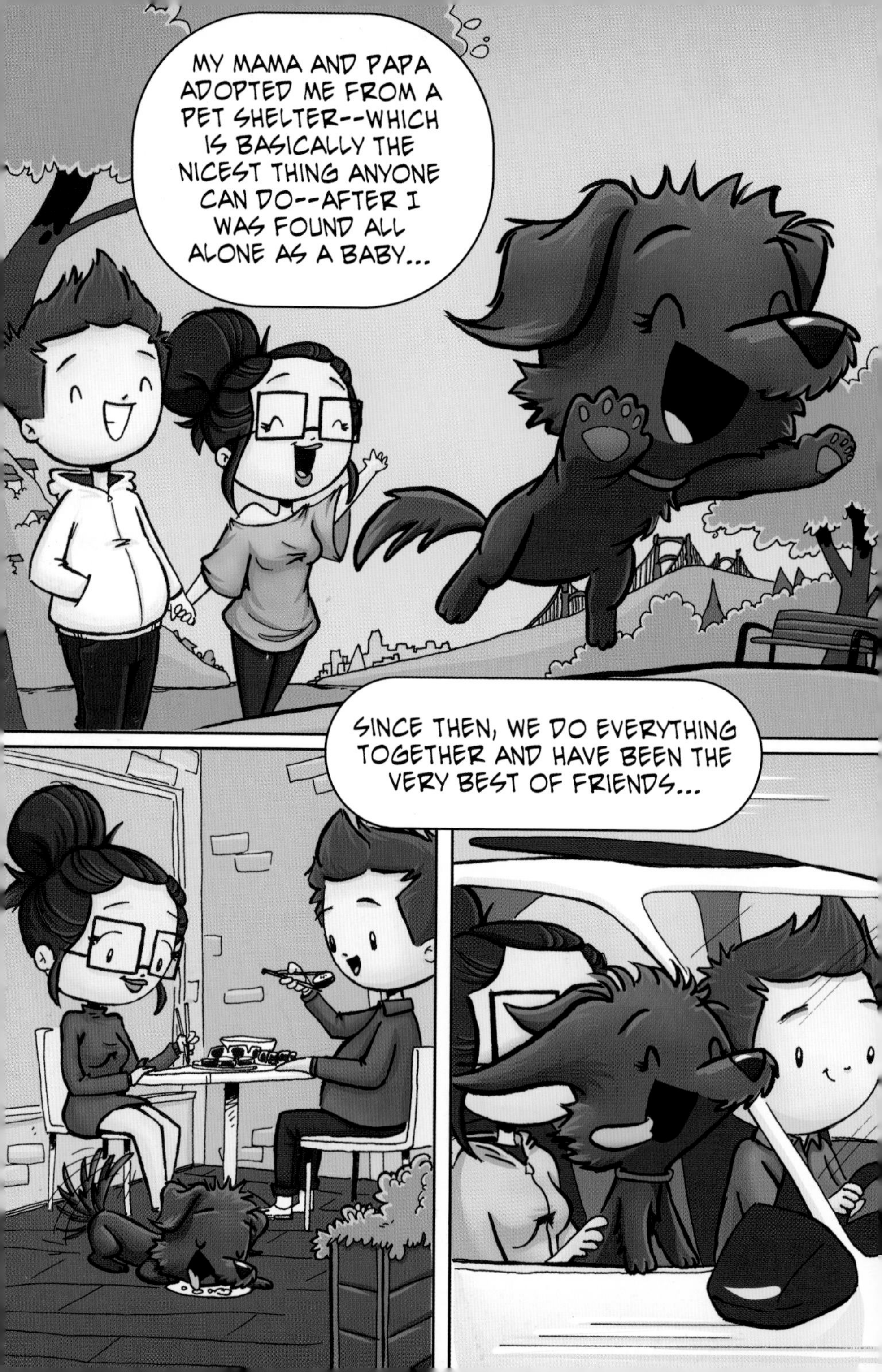
MY MAMA AND PAPA ADOPTED ME FROM A PET SHELTER--WHICH IS BASICALLY THE NICEST THING ANYONE CAN DO--AFTER I WAS FOUND ALL ALONE AS A BABY...
SINCE THEN, WE DO EVERYTHING TOGETHER AND HAVE BEEN THE VERY BEST OF FRIENDS...

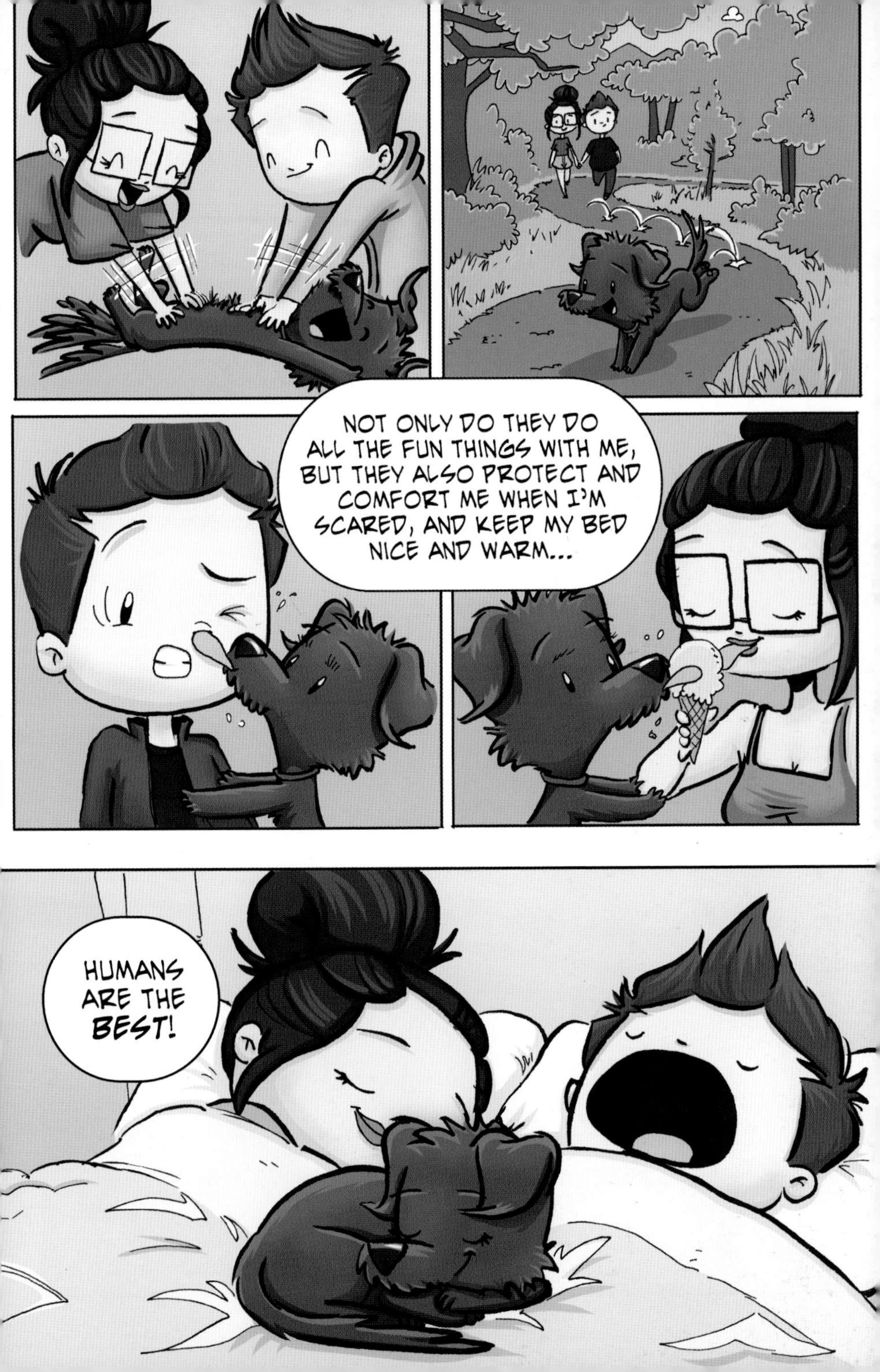
NOT ONLY DO THEY DO ALL THE FUN THINGS WITH ME, BUT THEY ALSO PROTECT AND COMFORT ME WHEN I'M SCARED, AND KEEP MY BED NICE AND WARM...
HUMANS ARE THE BEST!

EVEN STRANGERS ON THE STREET ARE NICE AND STOP TO GIVE ME PETS AND BELLY RUBS!

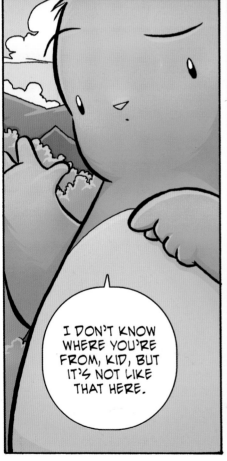

I DON'T KNOW WHERE YOU'RE FROM, KID, BUT IT'S NOT LIKE THAT HERE.

HEY, WHY DON'T YOU COME TO MY HOUSE? IF YOU HELP ME FIND IT, WE CAN HAVE A SLEEPOVER! WE DON'T HAVE ANY SOLDIERS OR WIZARDS, SO YOU WON'T BE BOTHERED ANYMORE. YOU CAN SLEEP ALL YOU WANT, JUST LIKE THE CATS!

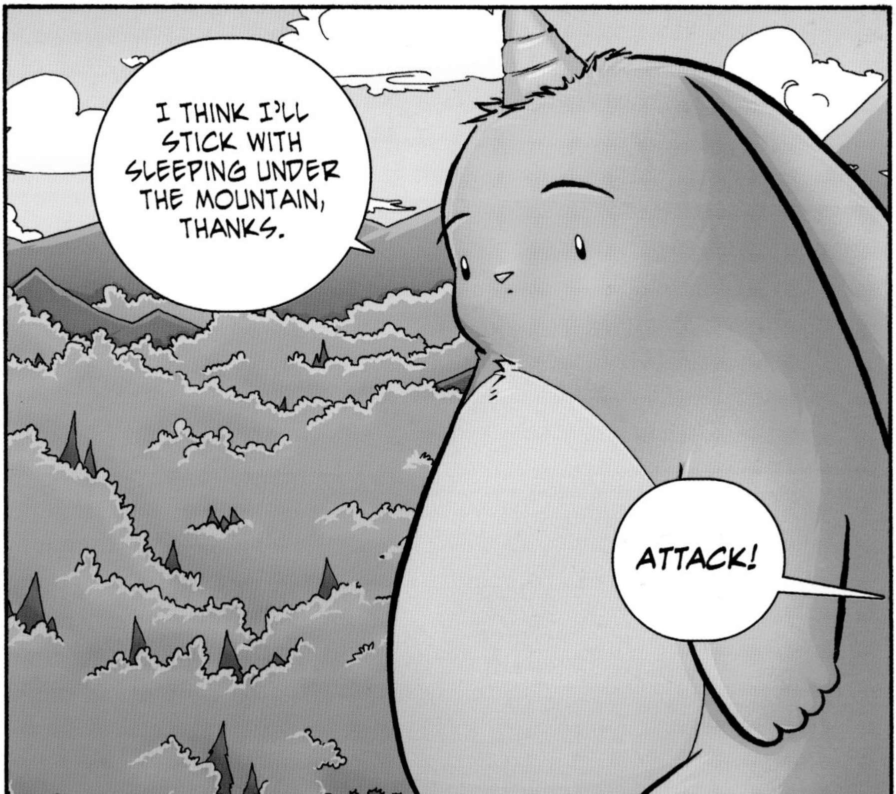
I THINK I'LL STICK WITH SLEEPING UNDER THE MOUNTAIN, THANKS.
ATTACK!

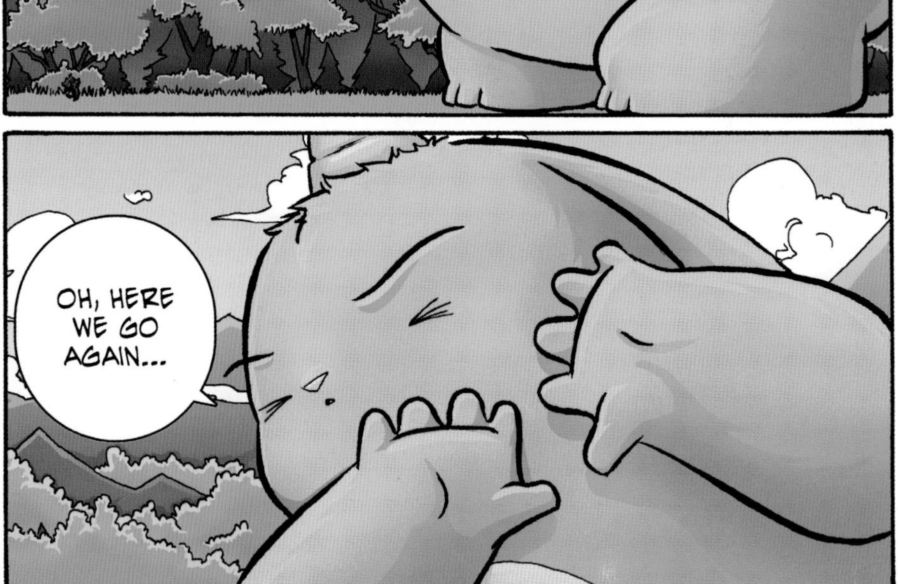
OH, HERE WE GO AGAIN...

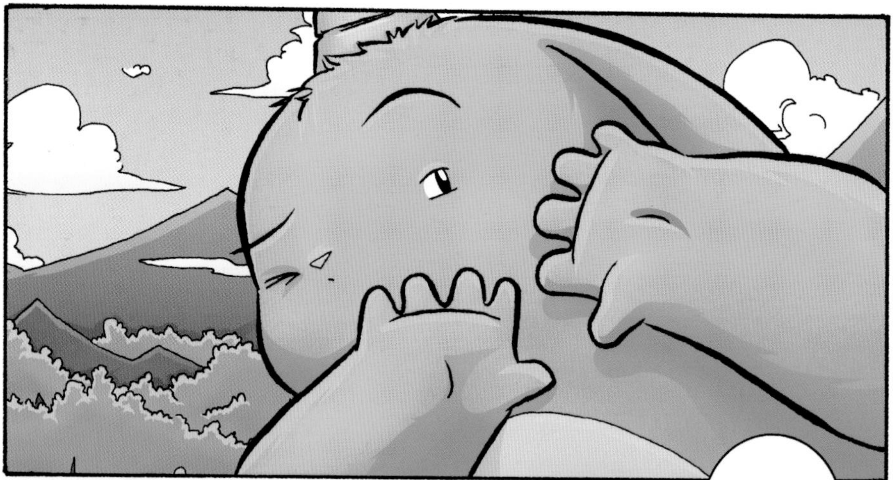

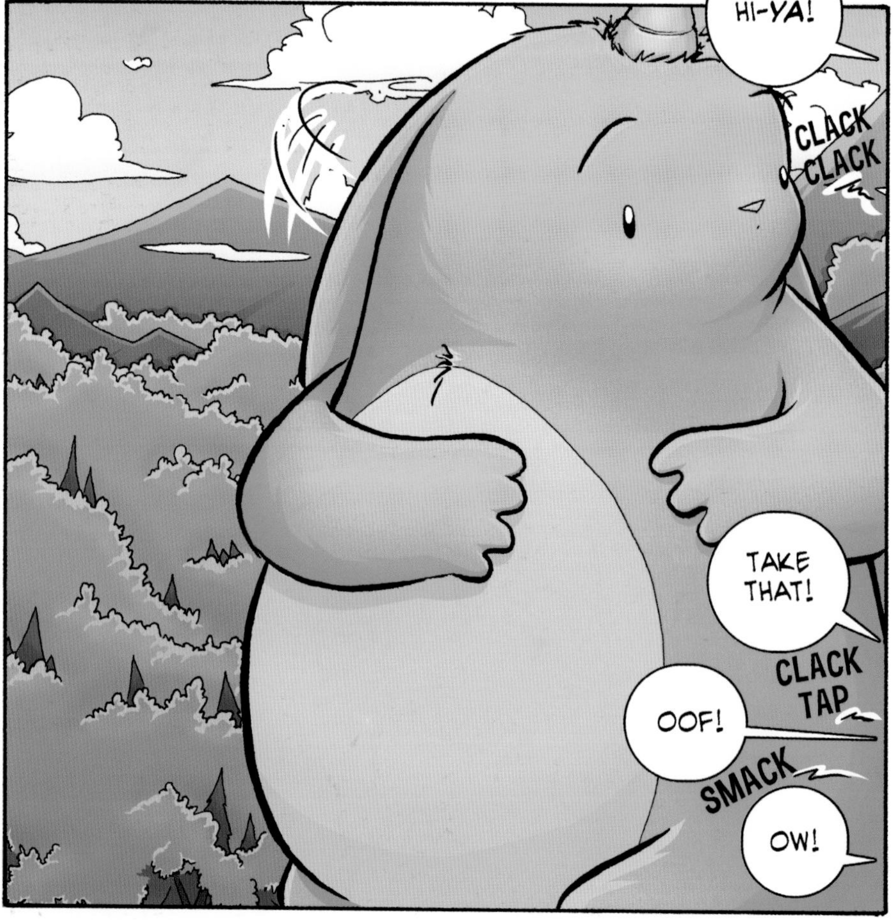
HI-YA!
CLACK
CLACK
TAKE THAT!
CLACK
TAP
OOF!
SMACK
OW!

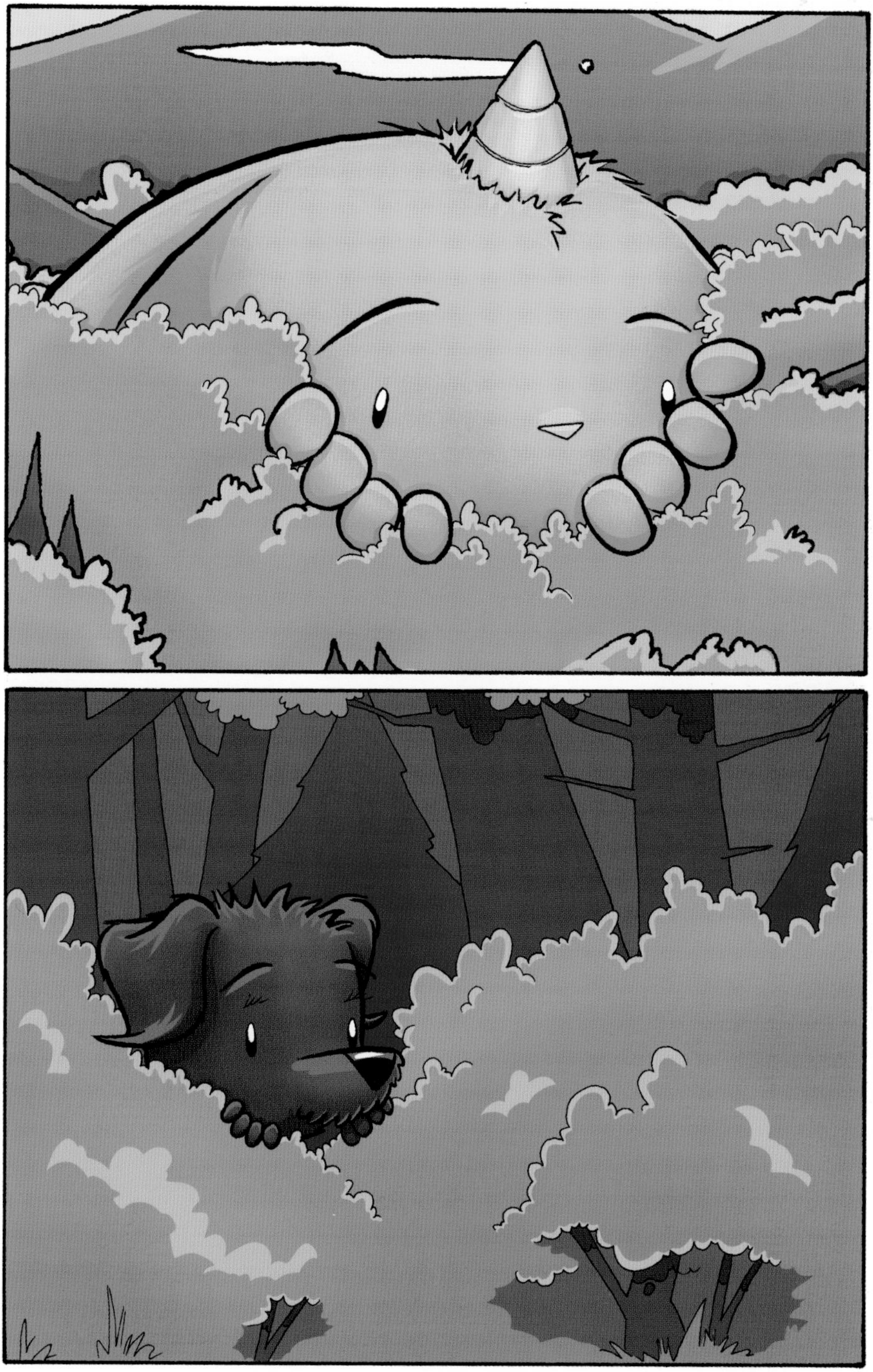

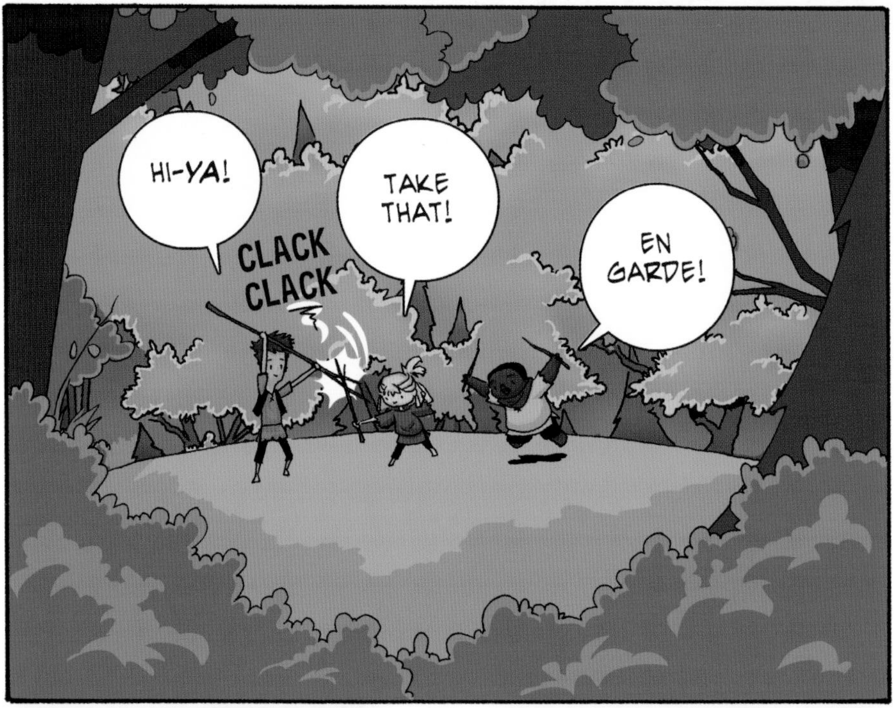
HI-YA!
CLACK CLACK
TAKE THAT!
EN GARDE!

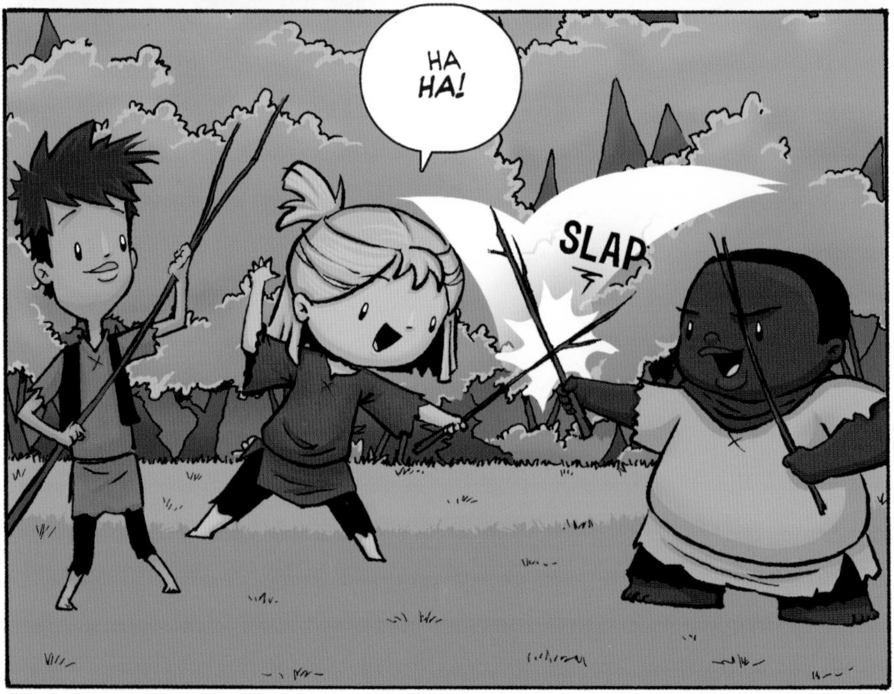
HA HA!
SLAP

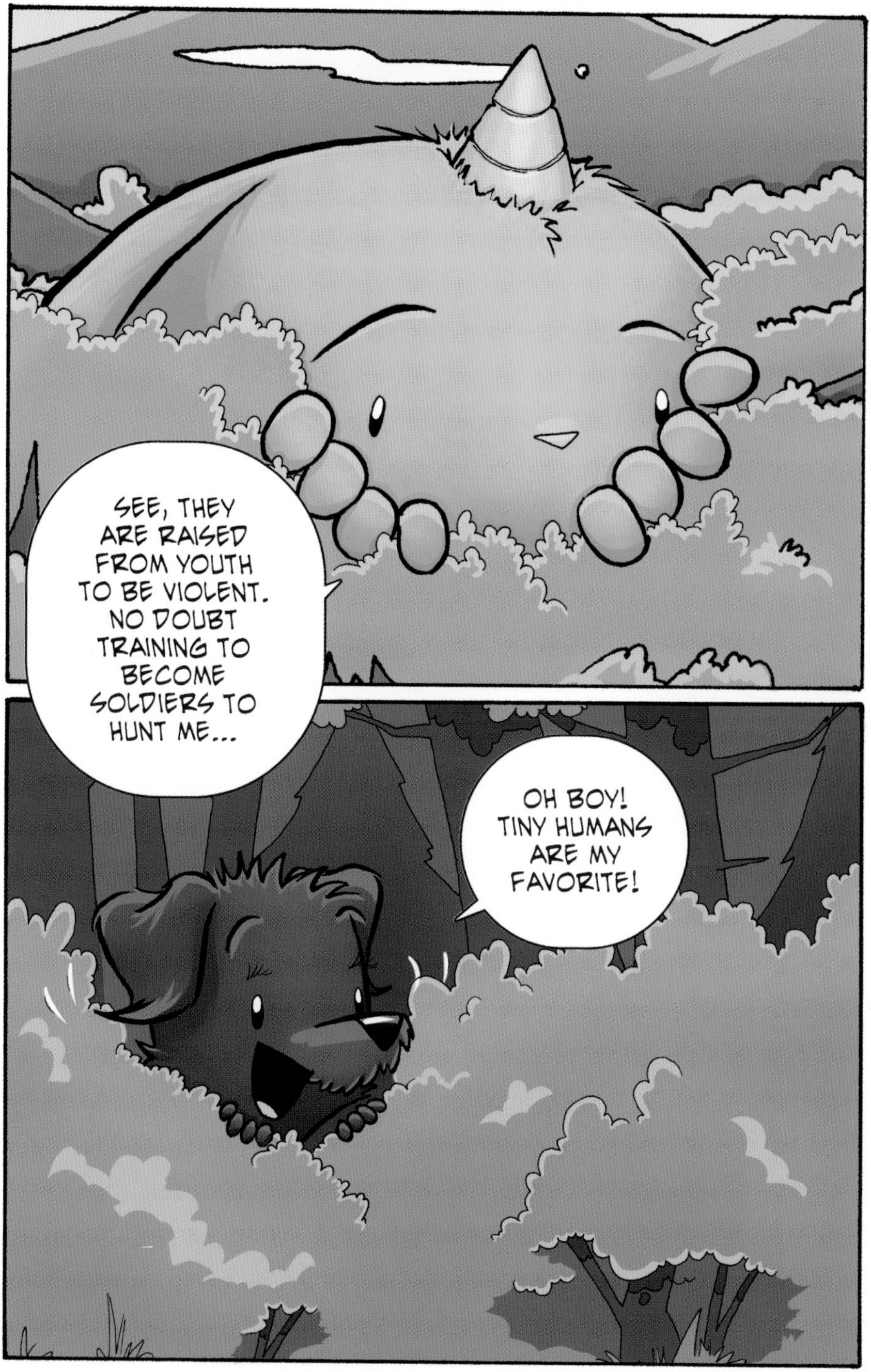
SEE, THEY ARE RAISED FROM YOUTH TO BE VIOLENT. NO DOUBT TRAINING TO BECOME SOLDIERS TO HUNT ME...
OH BOY! TINY HUMANS ARE MY FAVORITE!

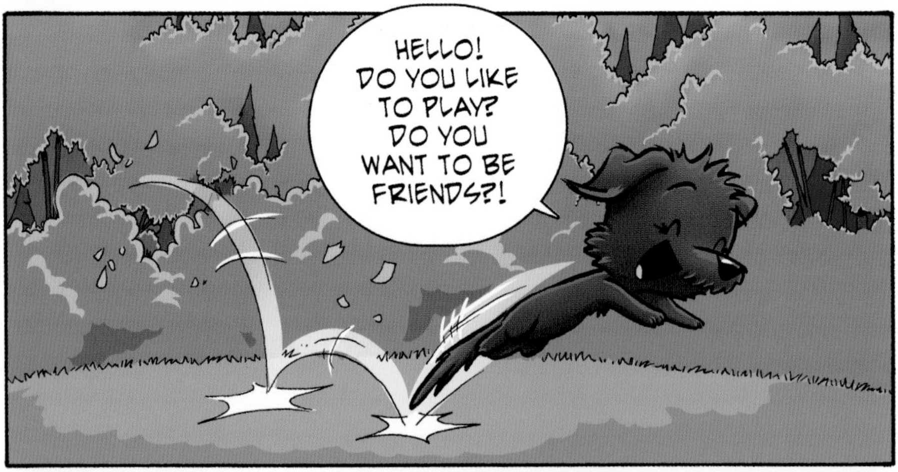
HELLO! DO YOU LIKE TO PLAY? DO YOU WANT TO BE FRIENDS?!

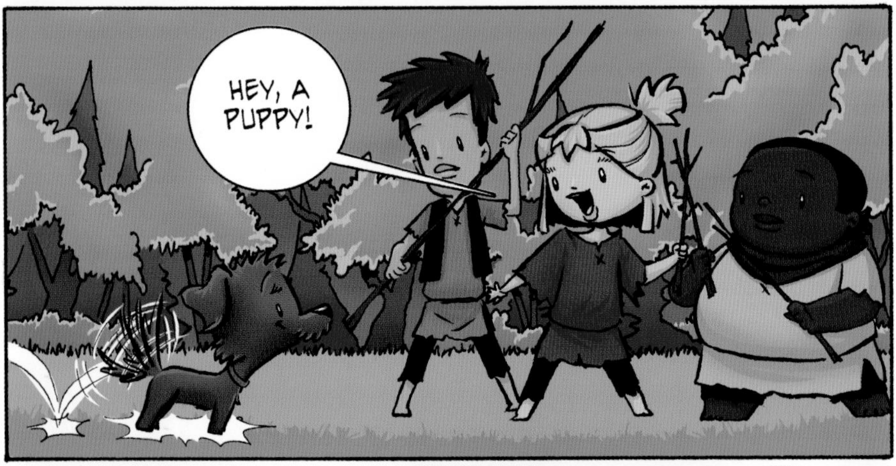
HEY, A PUPPY!

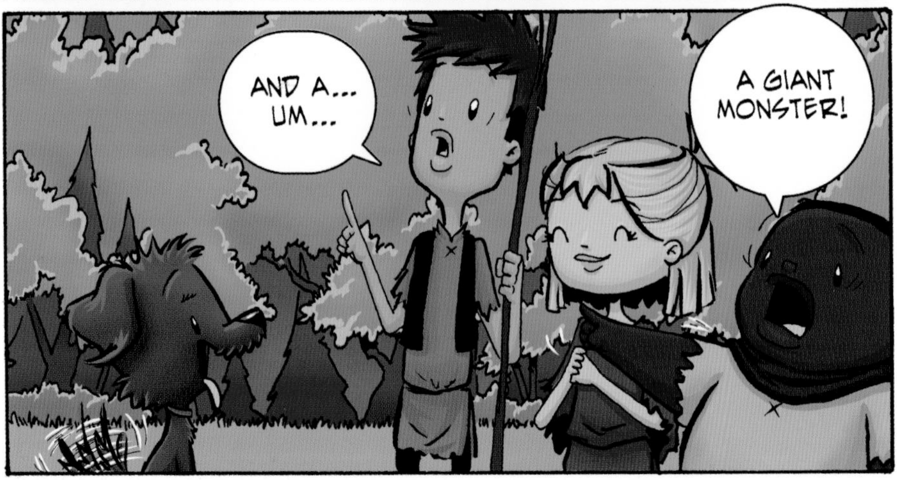
AND A... UM...
A GIANT MONSTER!

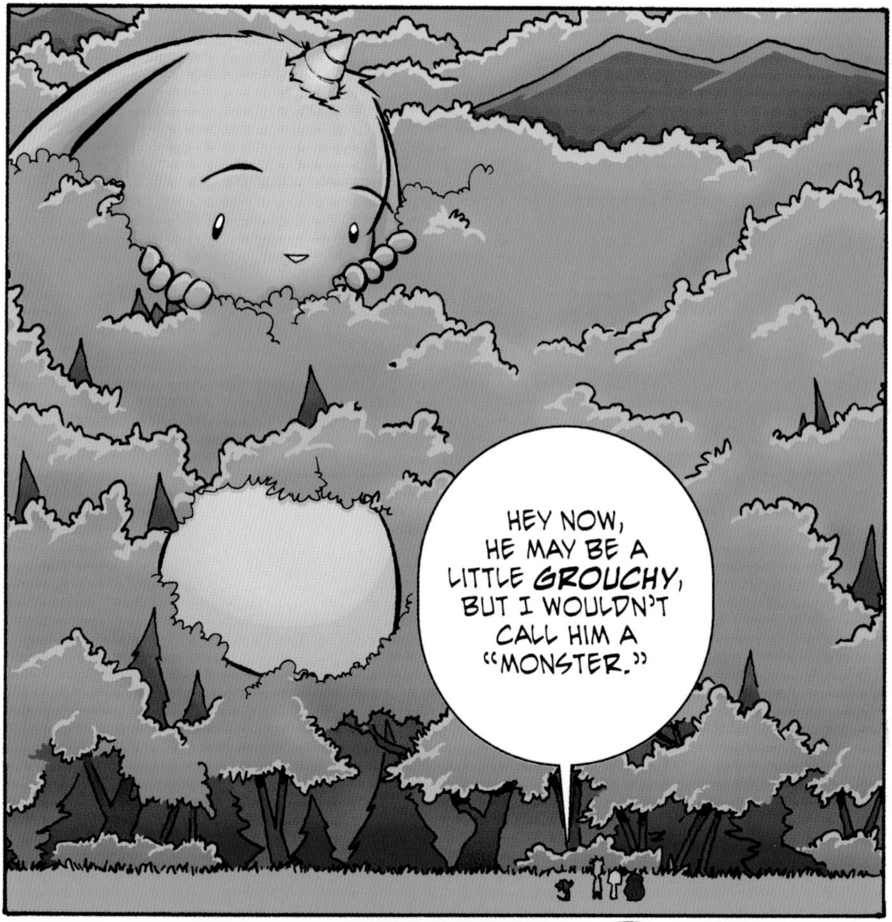
HEY NOW, HE MAY BE A LITTLE GROUCHY, BUT I WOULDN'T CALL HIM A "MONSTER."

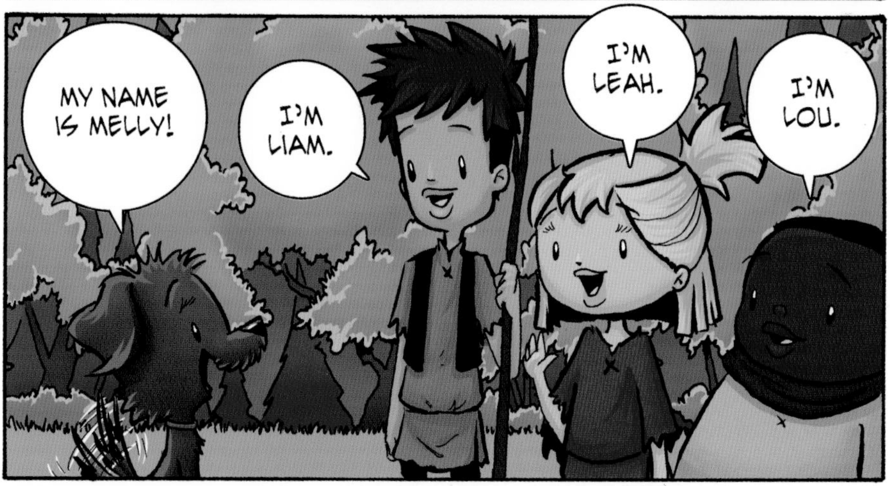
MY NAME IS MELLY!
I'M LIAM.
I'M LEAH.
I'M LOU.

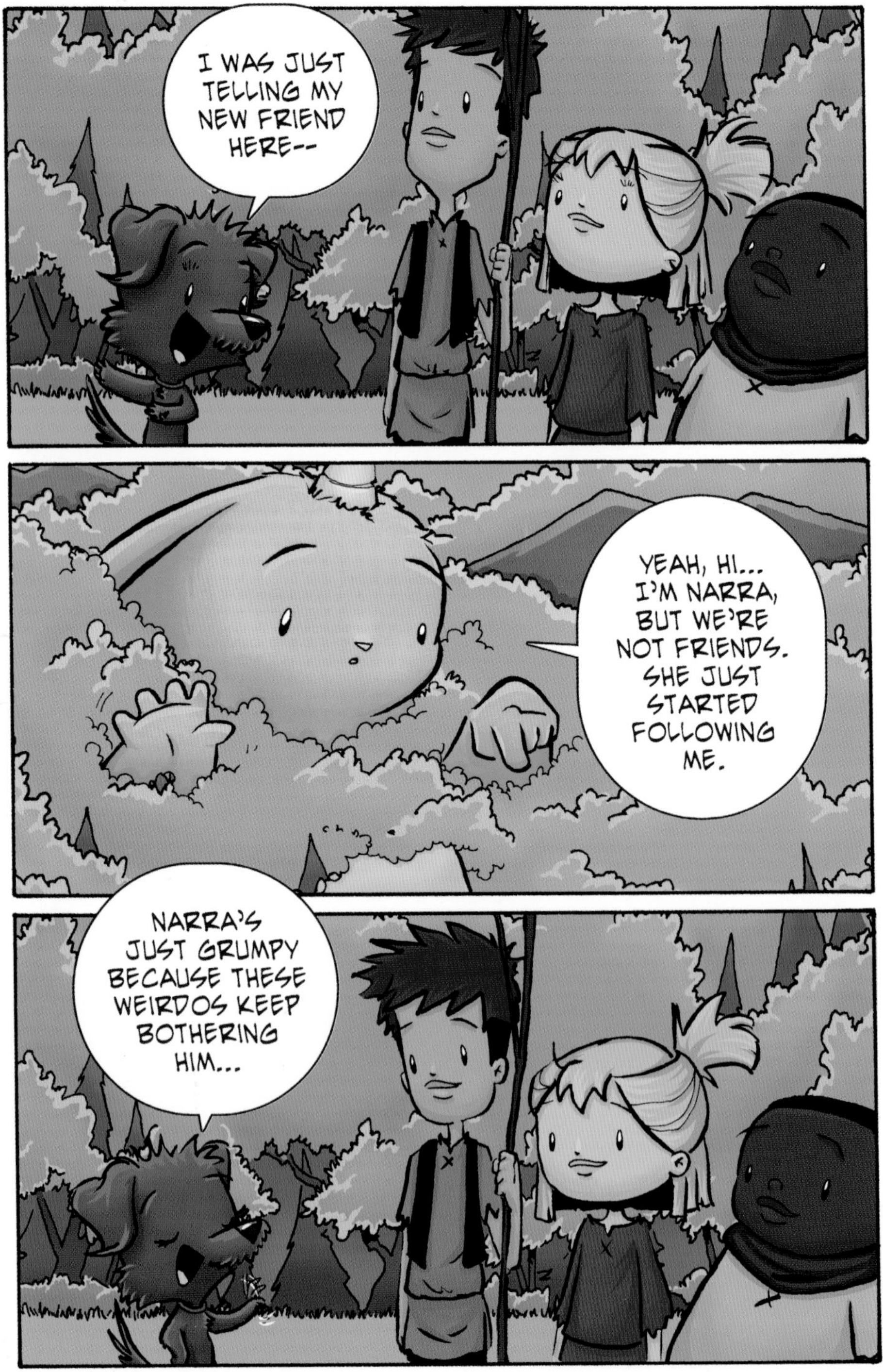
I WAS JUST TELLING MY NEW FRIEND HERE--
YEAH, HI... I'M NARRA, BUT WE'RE NOT FRIENDS. SHE JUST STARTED FOLLOWING ME.
NARRA'S JUST GRUMPY BECAUSE THESE WEIRDOS KEEP BOTHERING HIM...

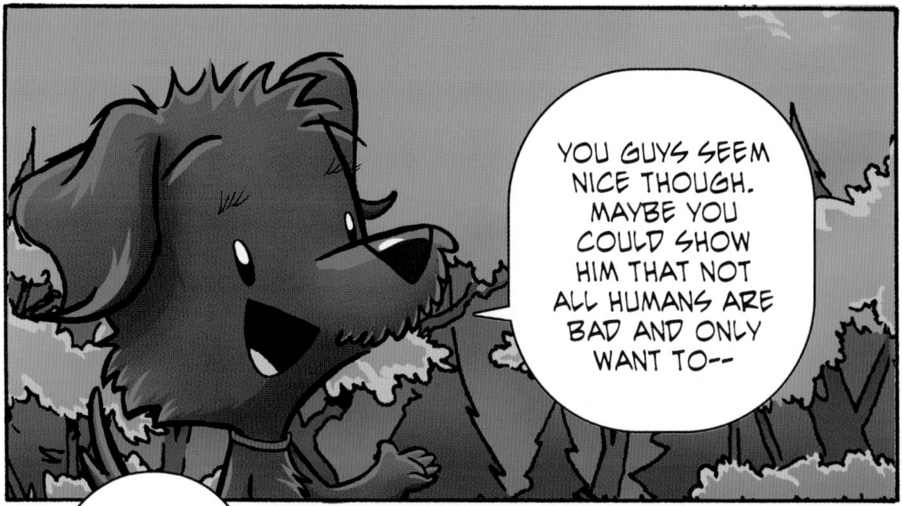
YOU GUYS SEEM NICE THOUGH. MAYBE YOU COULD SHOW HIM THAT NOT ALL HUMANS ARE BAD AND ONLY WANT TO--

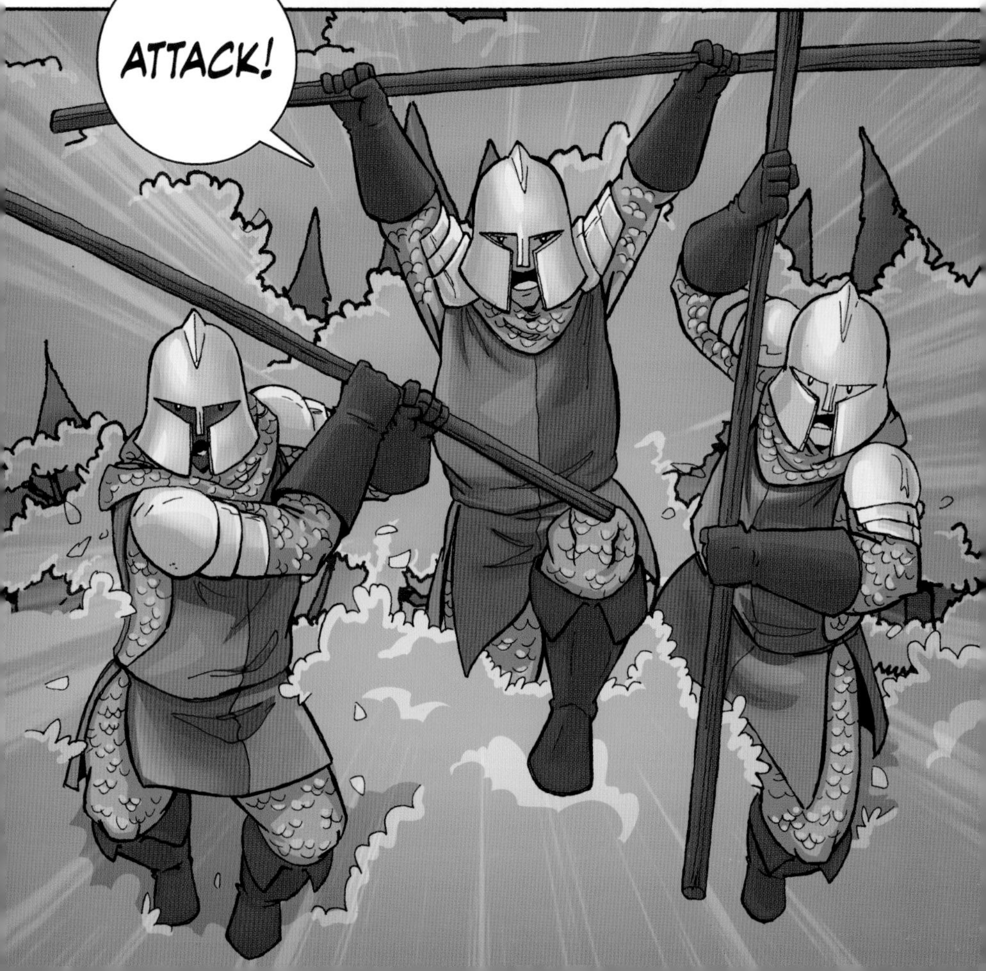
ATTACK!

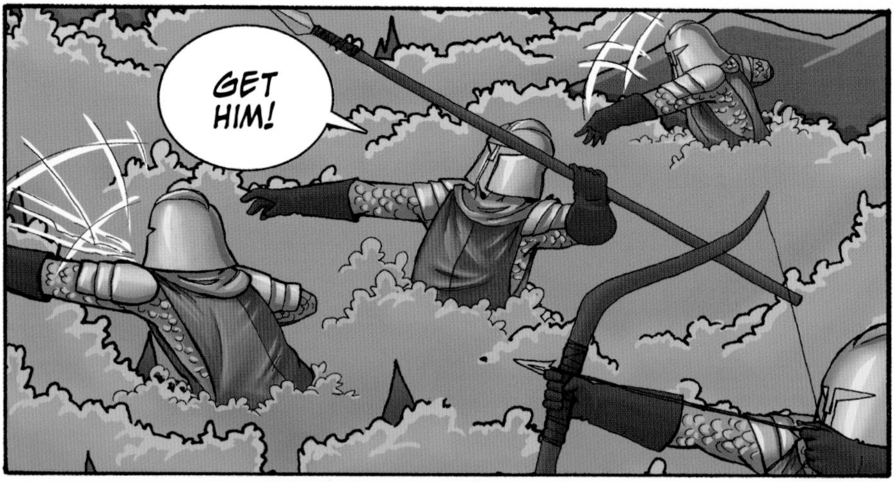
GET HIM!

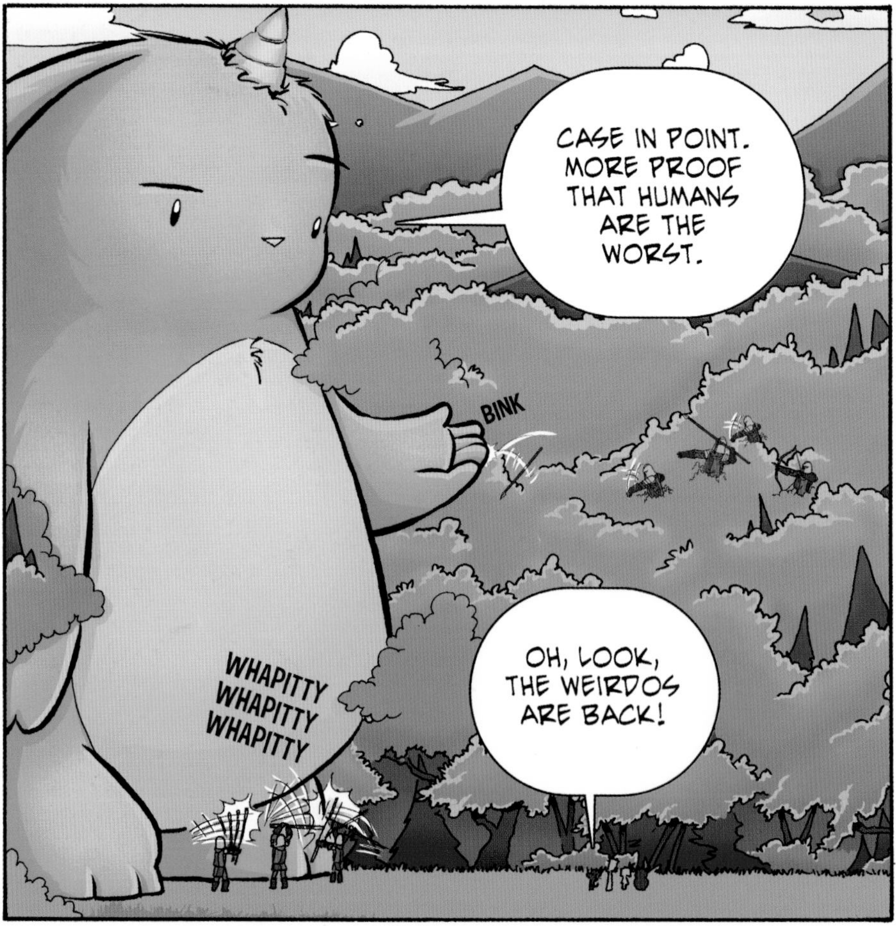
CASE IN POINT. MORE PROOF THAT HUMANS ARE THE WORST.
BINK
WHAPITTY WHAPITTY WHAPITTY
OH, LOOK, THE WEIRDOS ARE BACK!

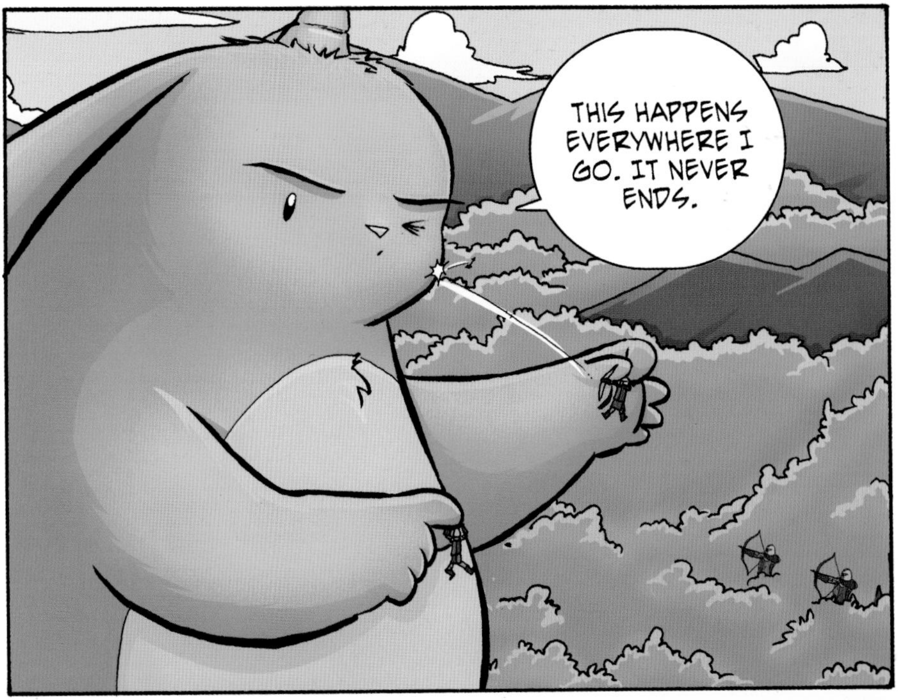
THIS HAPPENS EVERYWHERE I GO. IT NEVER ENDS.

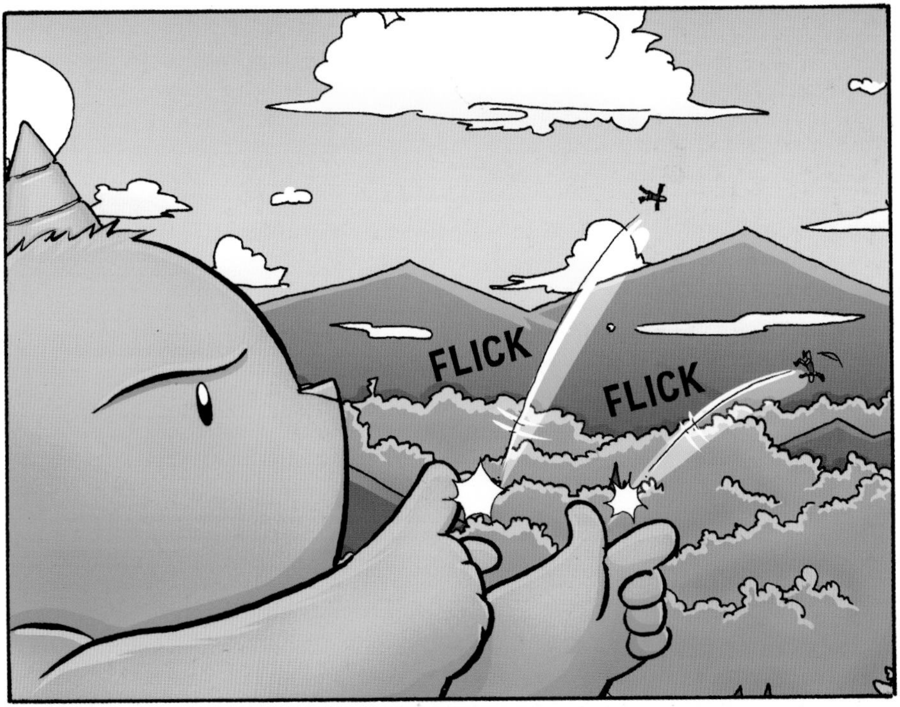
FLICK
FLICK

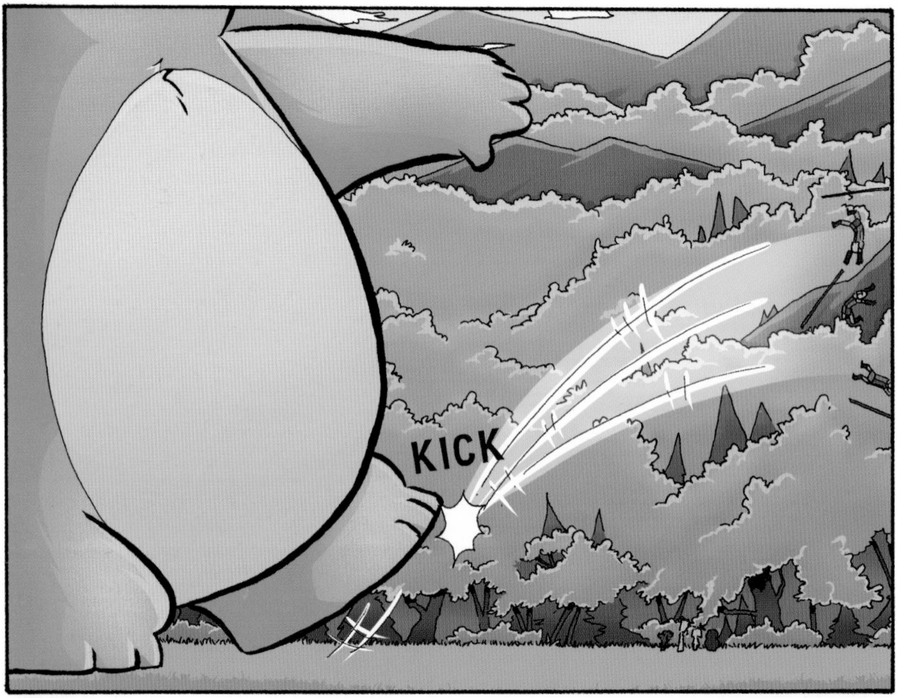
KICK

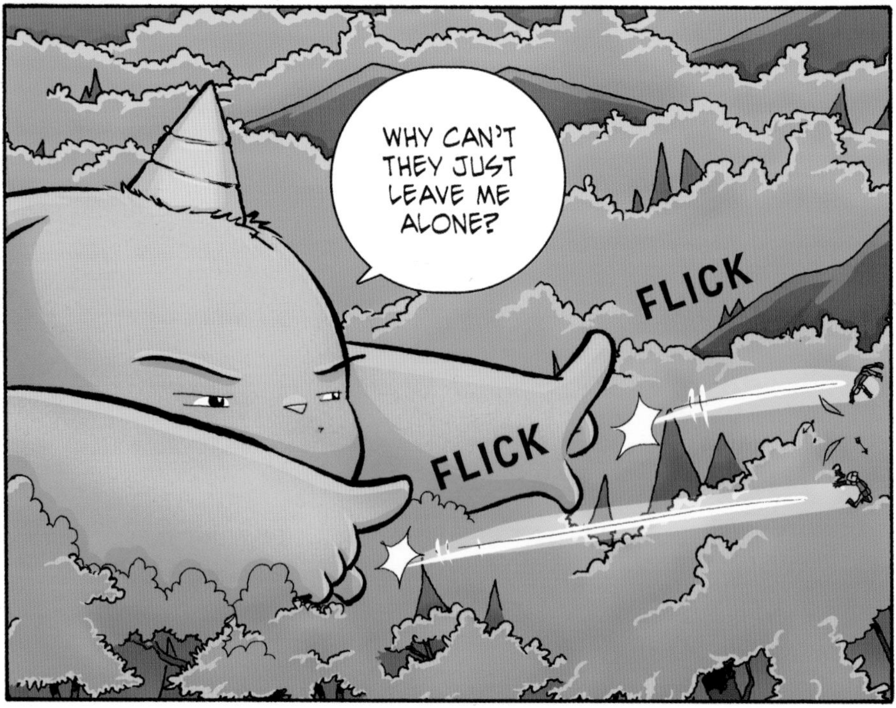
WHY CAN'T THEY JUST LEAVE ME ALONE?
FLICK
FLICK

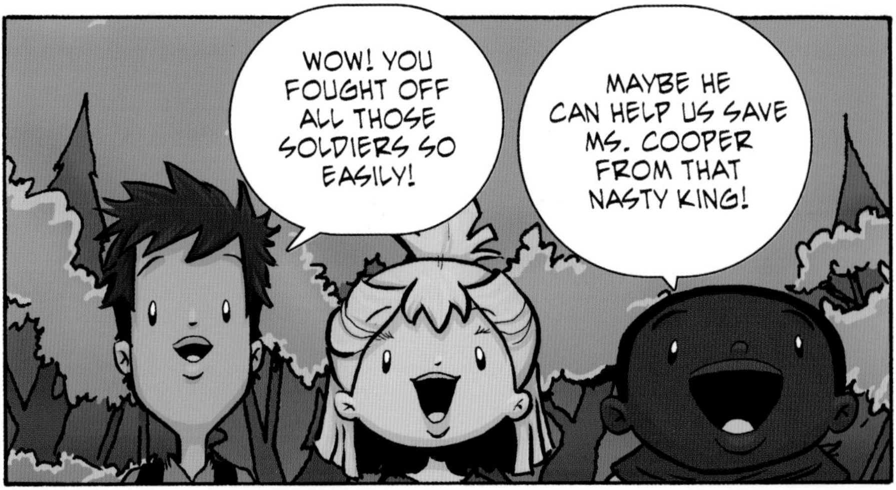
WOW! YOU FOUGHT OFF ALL THOSE SOLDIERS SO EASILY!
MAYBE HE CAN HELP US SAVE MS. COOPER FROM THAT NASTY KING!

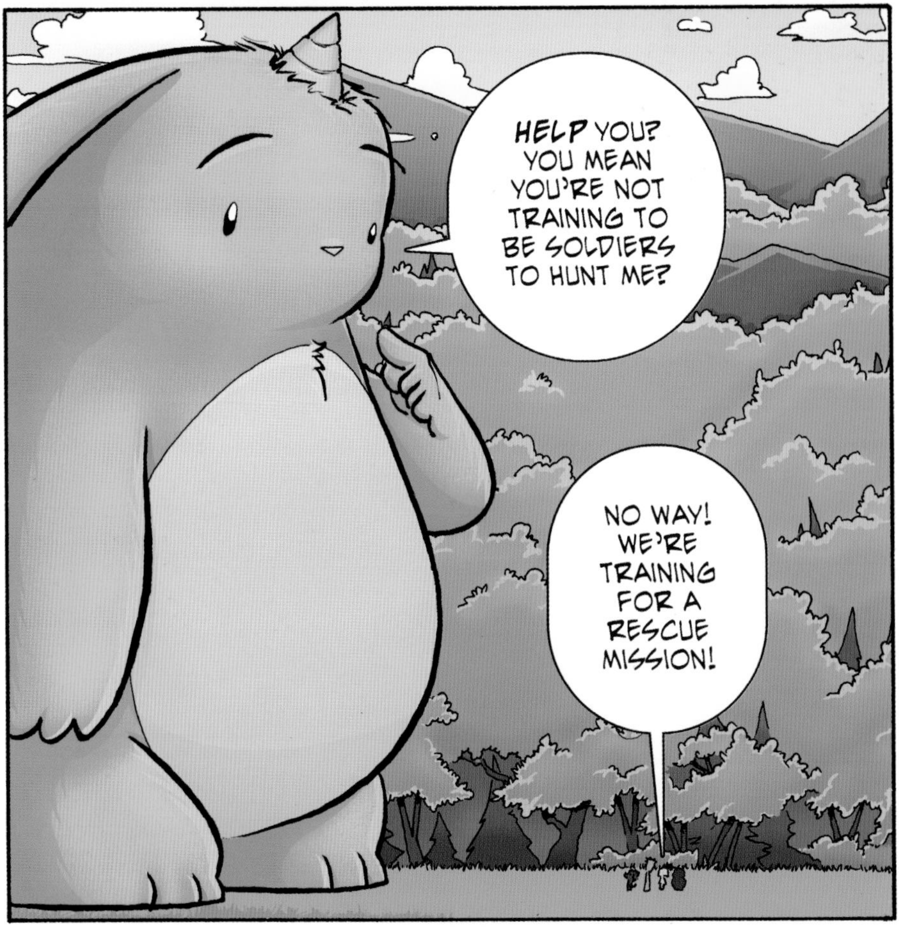
HELP YOU? YOU MEAN YOU'RE NOT TRAINING TO BE SOLDIERS TO HUNT ME?
NO WAY! WE'RE TRAINING FOR A RESCUE MISSION!

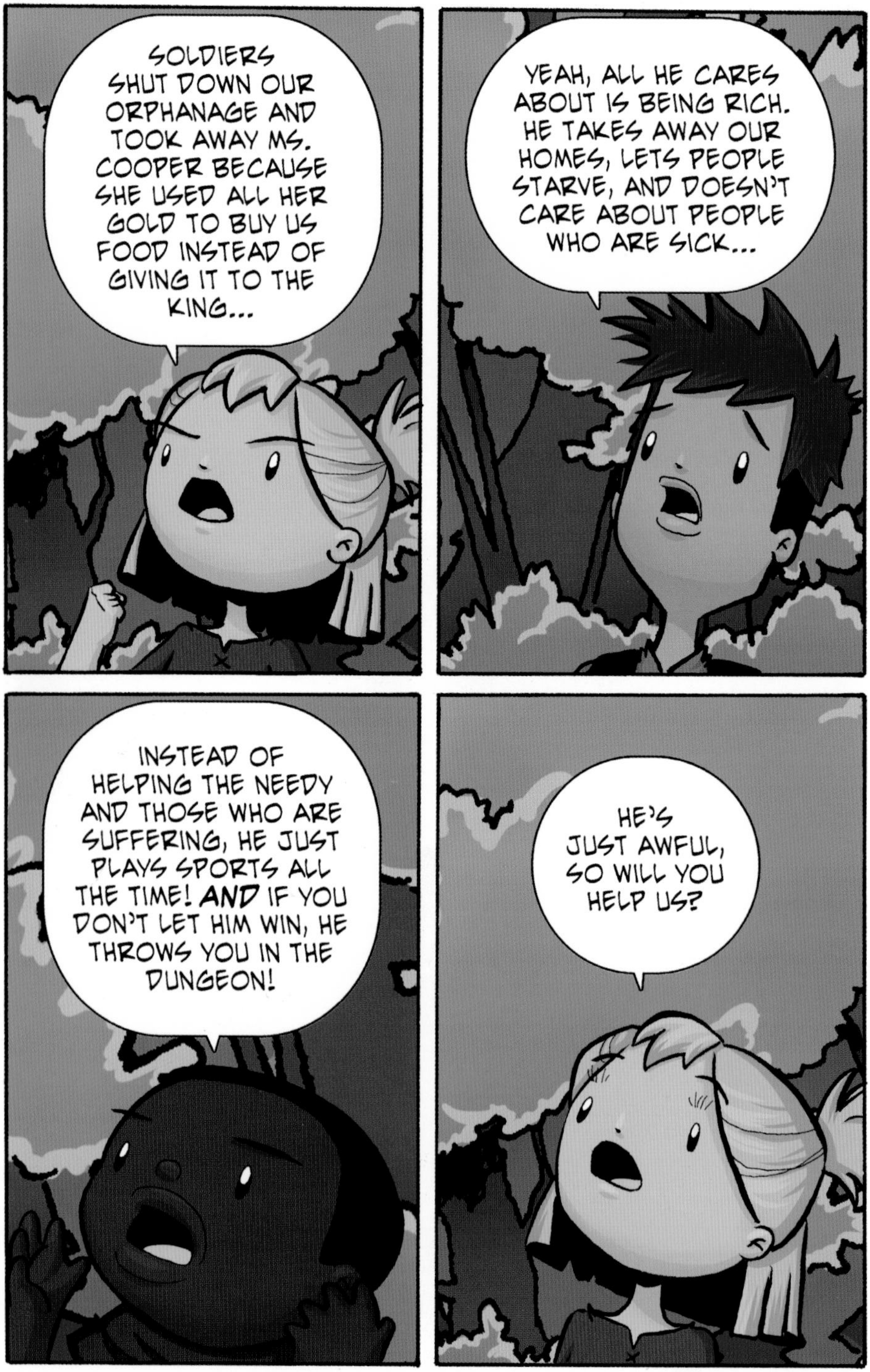
SOLDIERS SHUT DOWN OUR ORPHANAGE AND TOOK AWAY MS. COOPER BECAUSE SHE USED ALL HER GOLD TO BUY US FOOD INSTEAD OF GIVING IT TO THE KING...
YEAH, ALL HE CARES ABOUT IS BEING RICH. HE TAKES AWAY OUR HOMES, LETS PEOPLE STARVE, AND DOESN'T CARE ABOUT PEOPLE WHO ARE SICK...
INSTEAD OF HELPING THE NEEDY AND THOSE WHO ARE SUFFERING, HE JUST PLAYS SPORTS ALL THE TIME! **AND** IF YOU DON'T LET HIM WIN, HE THROWS YOU IN THE DUNGEON!
HE'S JUST AWFUL, SO WILL YOU HELP US?

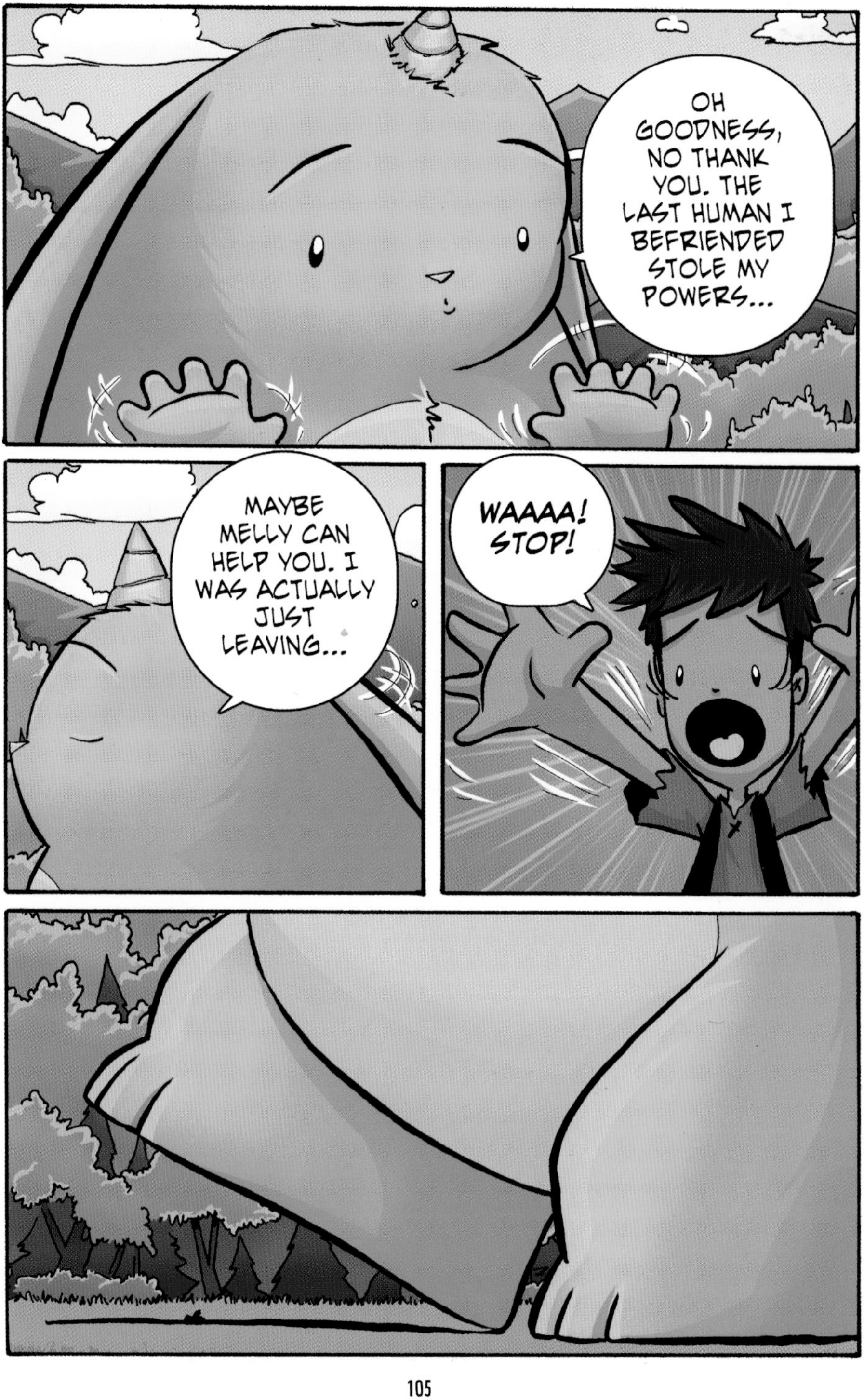
OH GOODNESS, NO THANK YOU. THE LAST HUMAN I BEFRIENDED STOLE MY POWERS...
MAYBE MELLY CAN HELP YOU. I WAS ACTUALLY JUST LEAVING...
WAAAA! STOP!

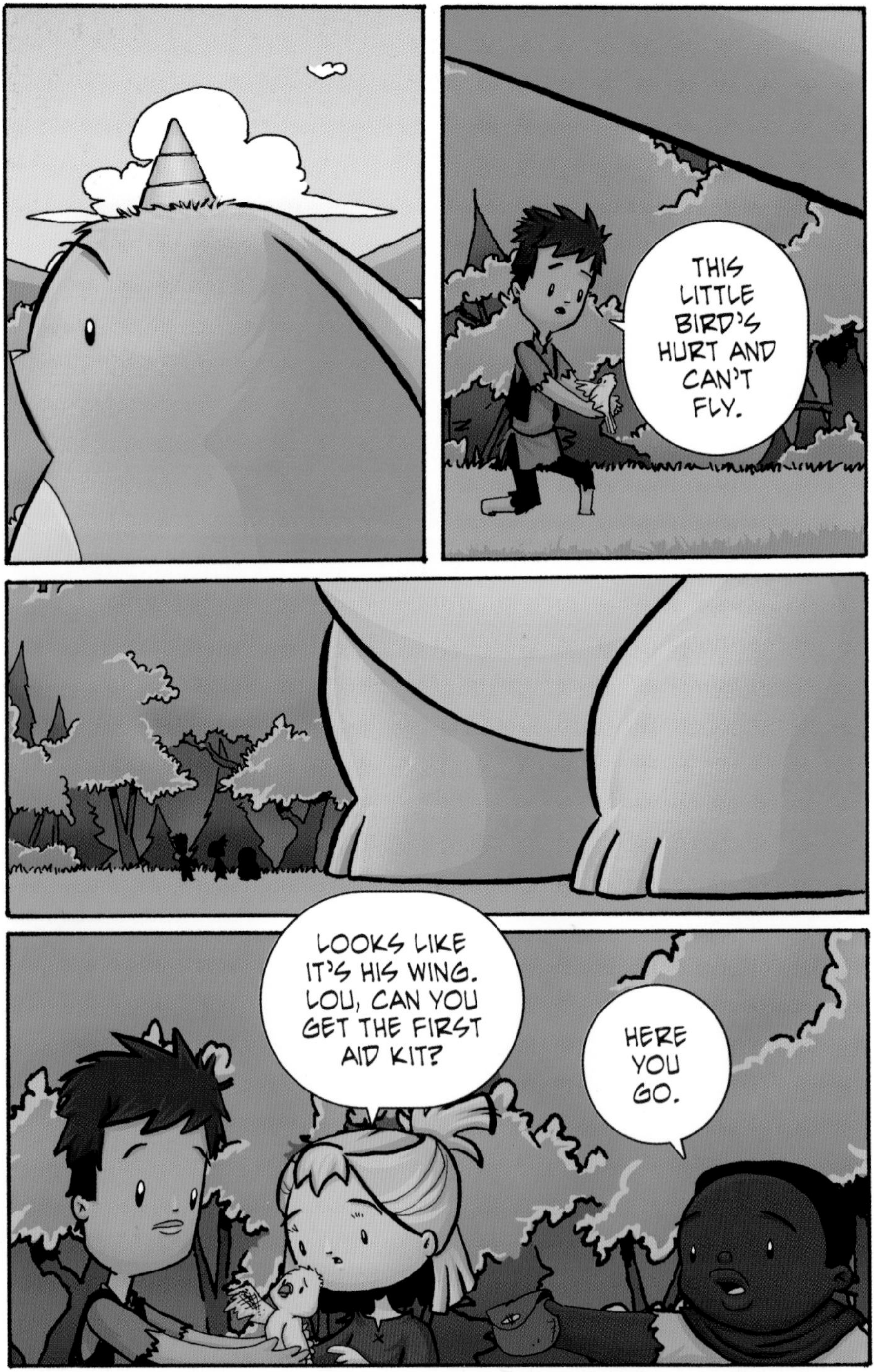
THIS LITTLE BIRD'S HURT AND CAN'T FLY.
LOOKS LIKE IT'S HIS WING. LOU, CAN YOU GET THE FIRST AID KIT?
HERE YOU GO.

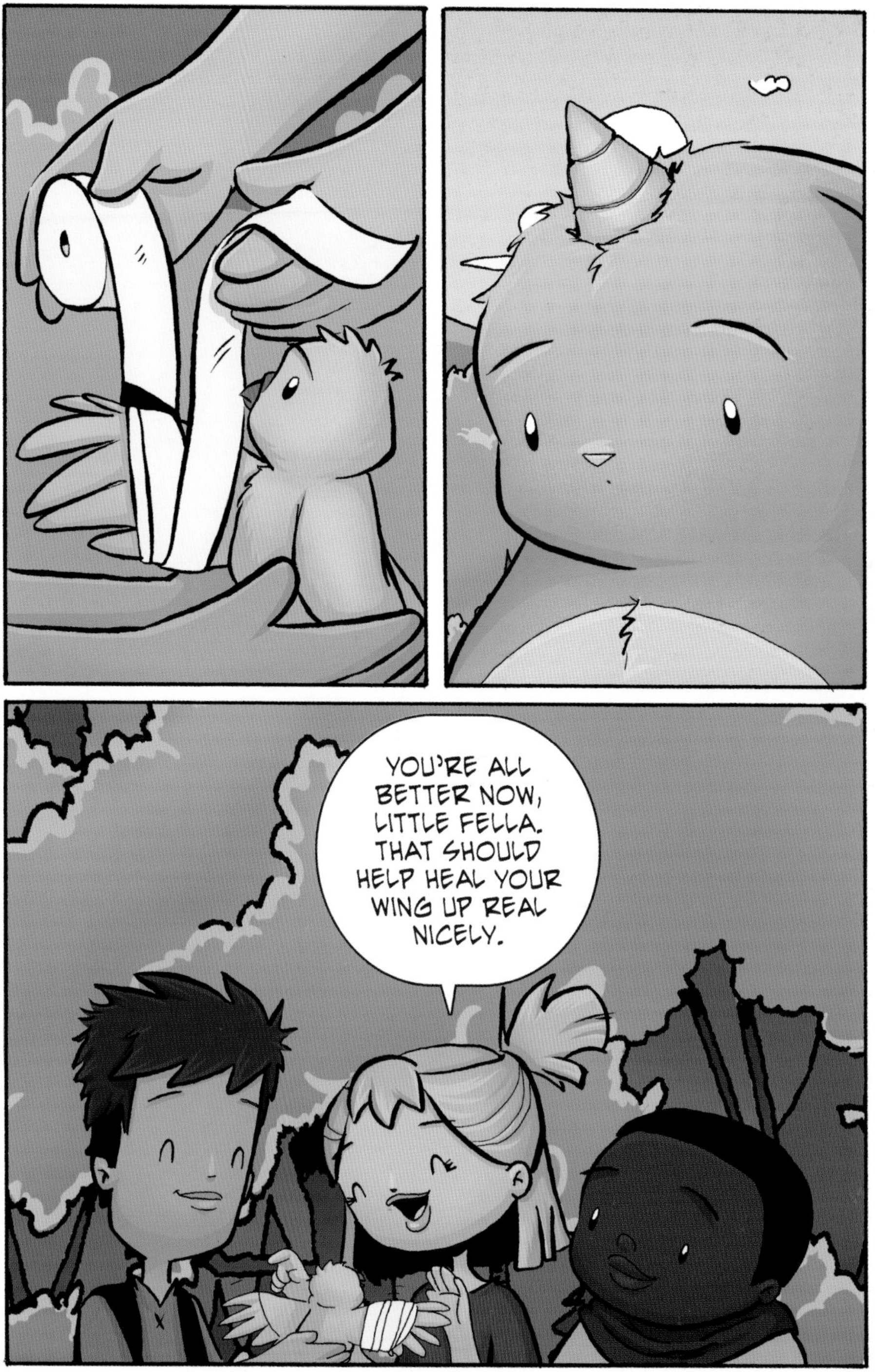
YOU'RE ALL BETTER NOW, LITTLE FELLA. THAT SHOULD HELP HEAL YOUR WING UP REAL NICELY.

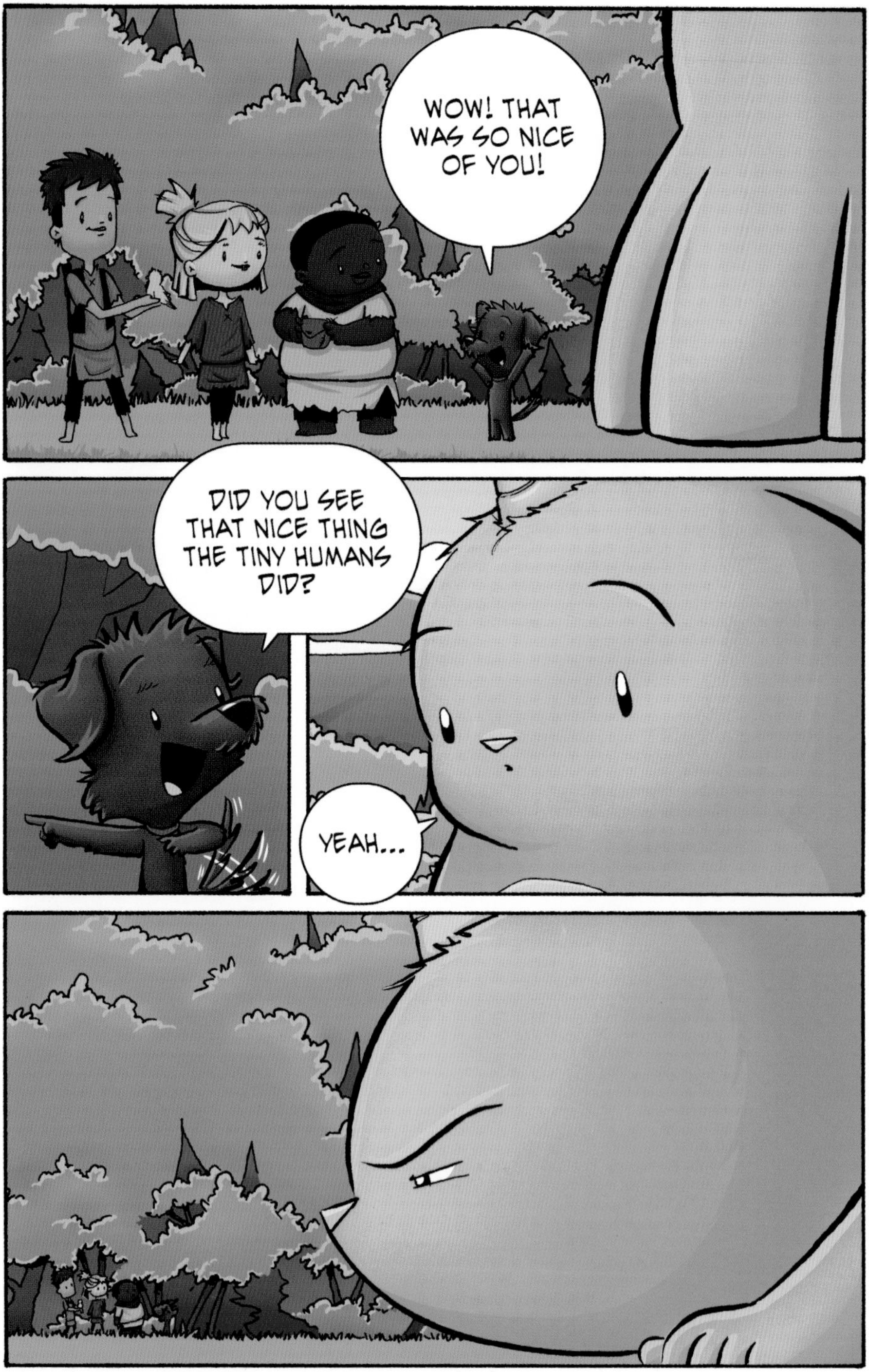
WOW! THAT WAS SO NICE OF YOU!
DID YOU SEE THAT NICE THING THE TINY HUMANS DID?
YEAH...

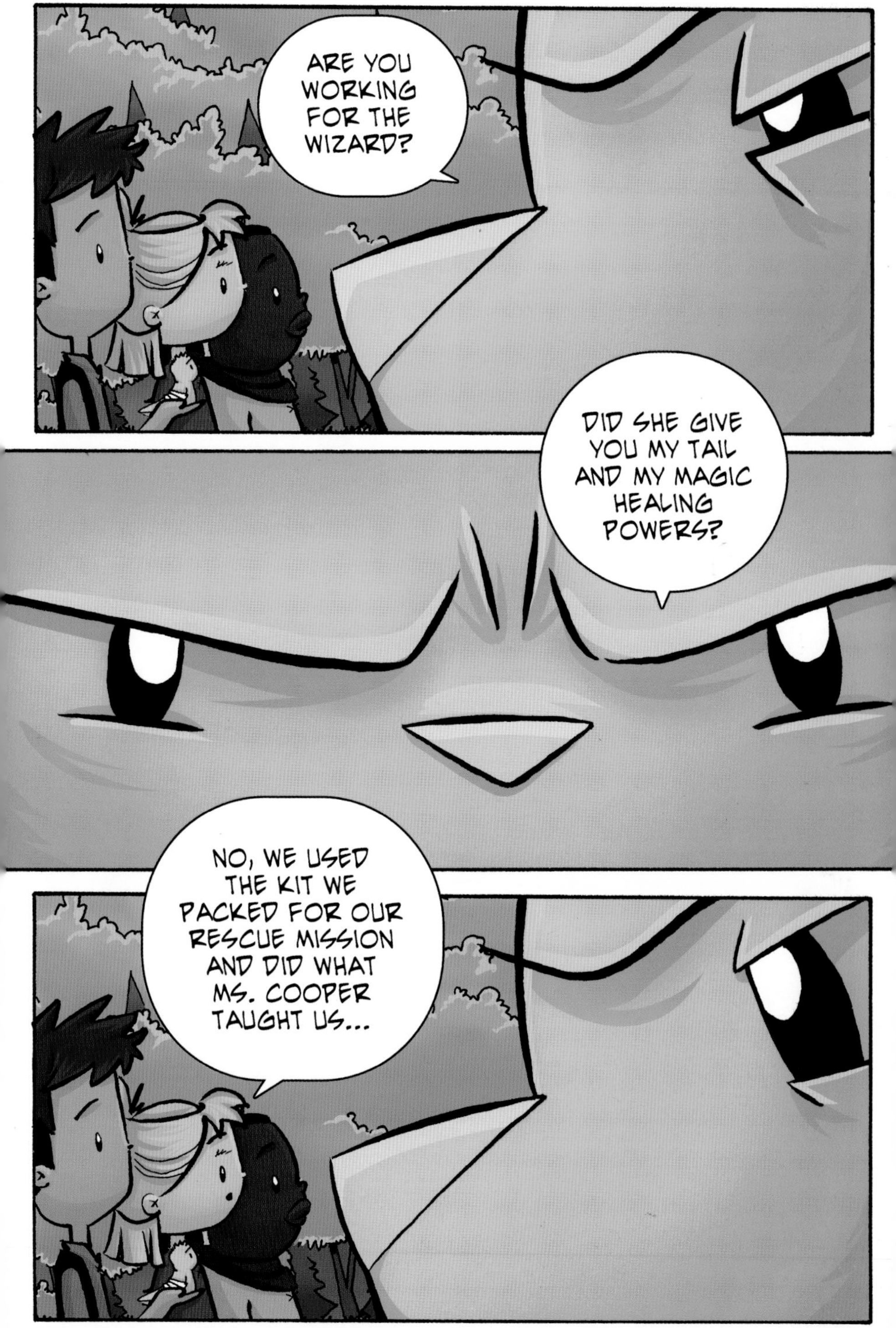
ARE YOU WORKING FOR THE WIZARD?
DID SHE GIVE YOU MY TAIL AND MY MAGIC HEALING POWERS?
NO, WE USED THE KIT WE PACKED FOR OUR RESCUE MISSION AND DID WHAT MS. COOPER TAUGHT US...

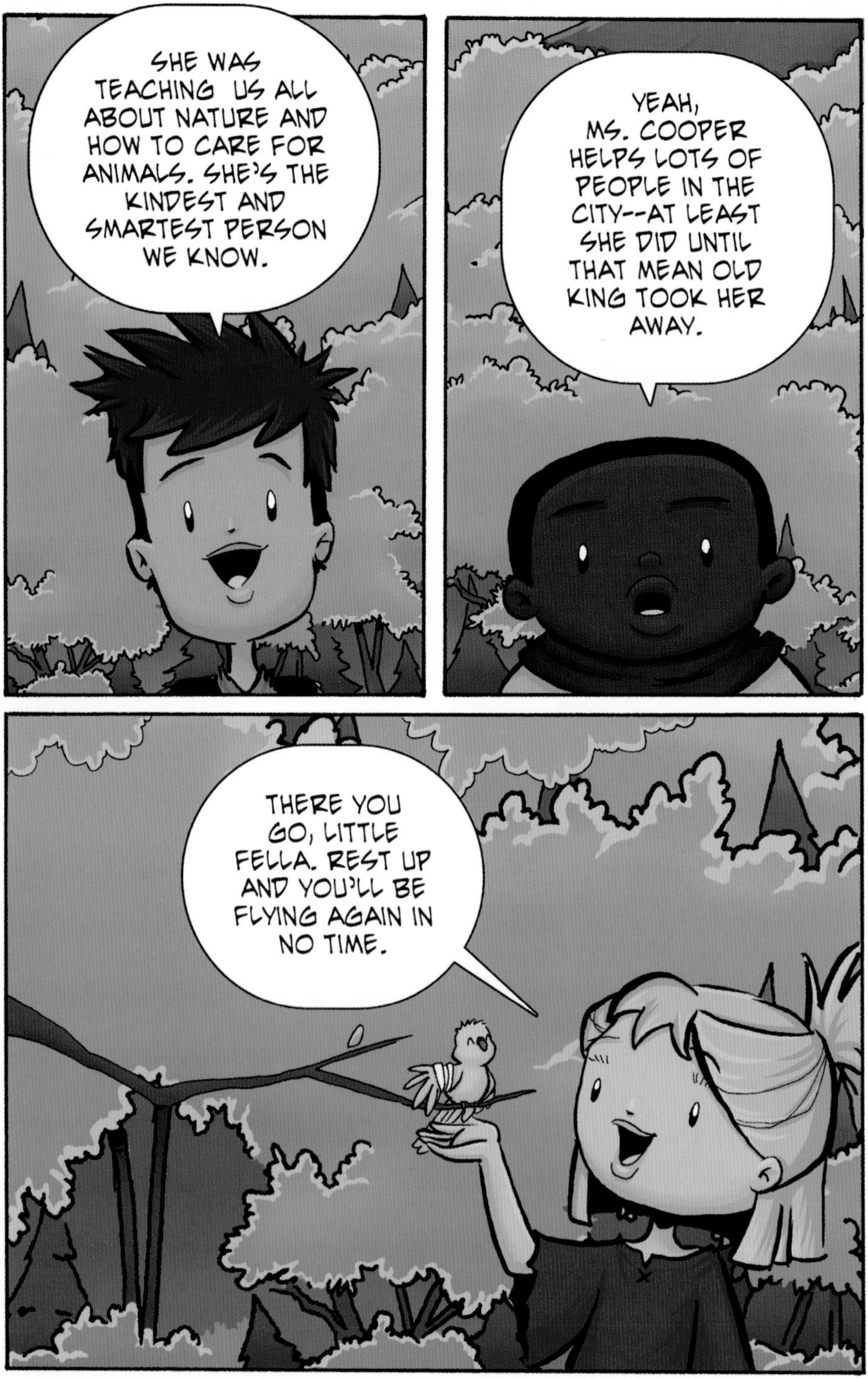
SHE WAS TEACHING US ALL ABOUT NATURE AND HOW TO CARE FOR ANIMALS. SHE'S THE KINDEST AND SMARTEST PERSON WE KNOW.
YEAH, MS. COOPER HELPS LOTS OF PEOPLE IN THE CITY--AT LEAST SHE DID UNTIL THAT MEAN OLD KING TOOK HER AWAY.
THERE YOU GO, LITTLE FELLA. REST UP AND YOU'LL BE FLYING AGAIN IN NO TIME.

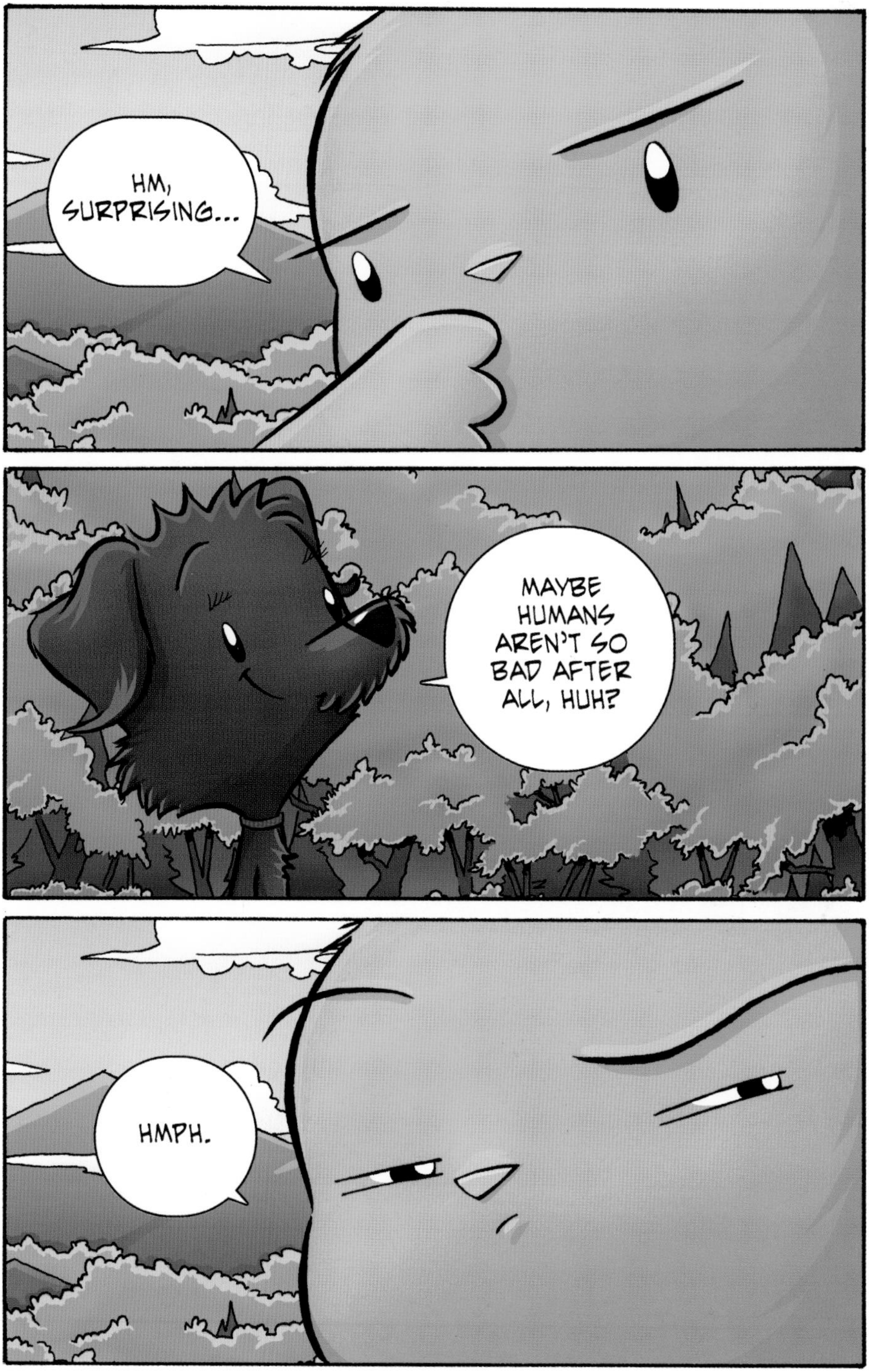
HM, SURPRISING...
MAYBE HUMANS AREN'T SO BAD AFTER ALL, HUH?
HMPH.

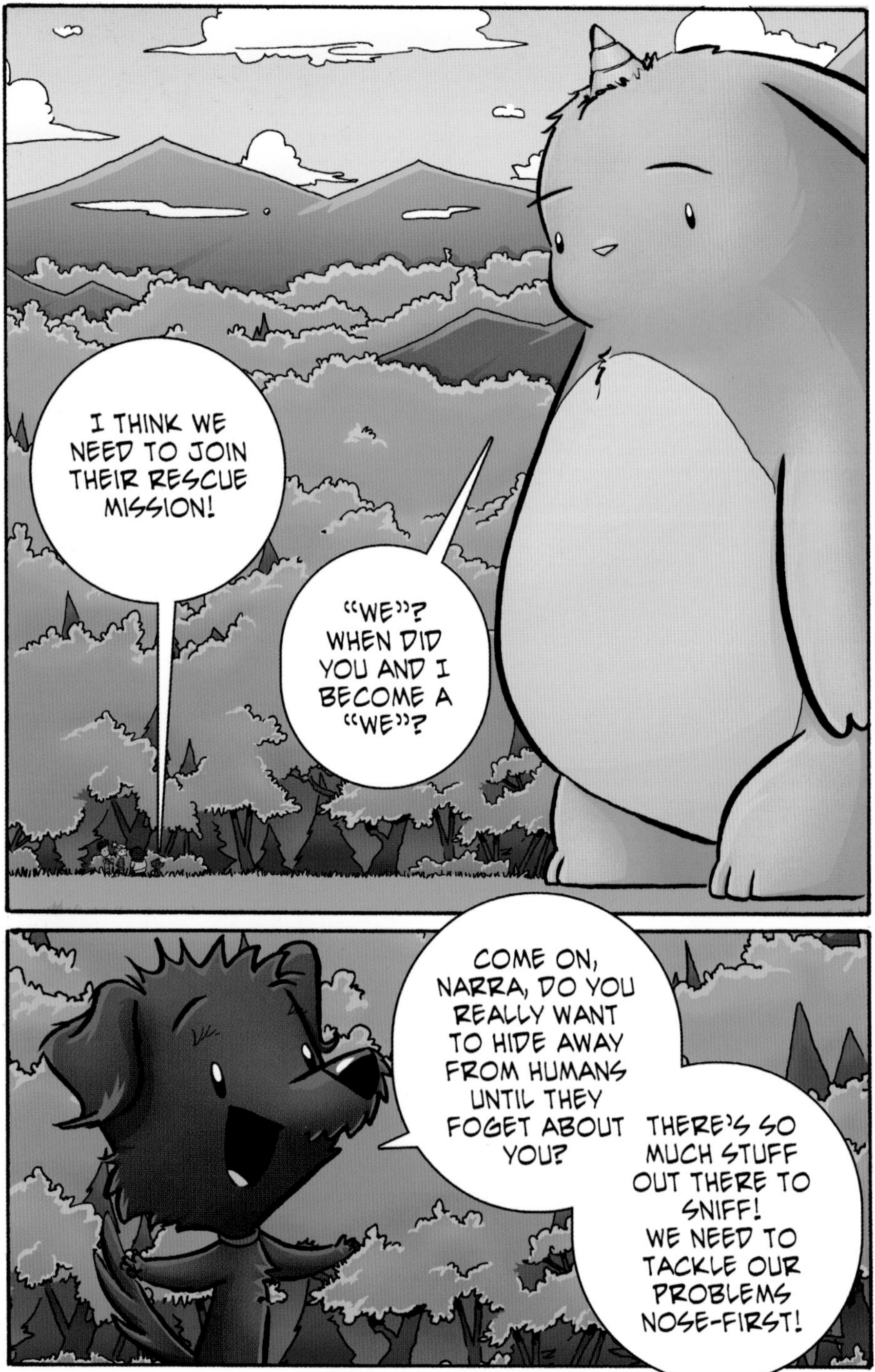
I THINK WE NEED TO JOIN THEIR RESCUE MISSION!
"WE"? WHEN DID YOU AND I BECOME A "WE"?
COME ON, NARRA, DO YOU REALLY WANT TO HIDE AWAY FROM HUMANS UNTIL THEY FOGET ABOUT YOU?
THERE'S SO MUCH STUFF OUT THERE TO SNIFF! WE NEED TO TACKLE OUR PROBLEMS NOSE-FIRST!

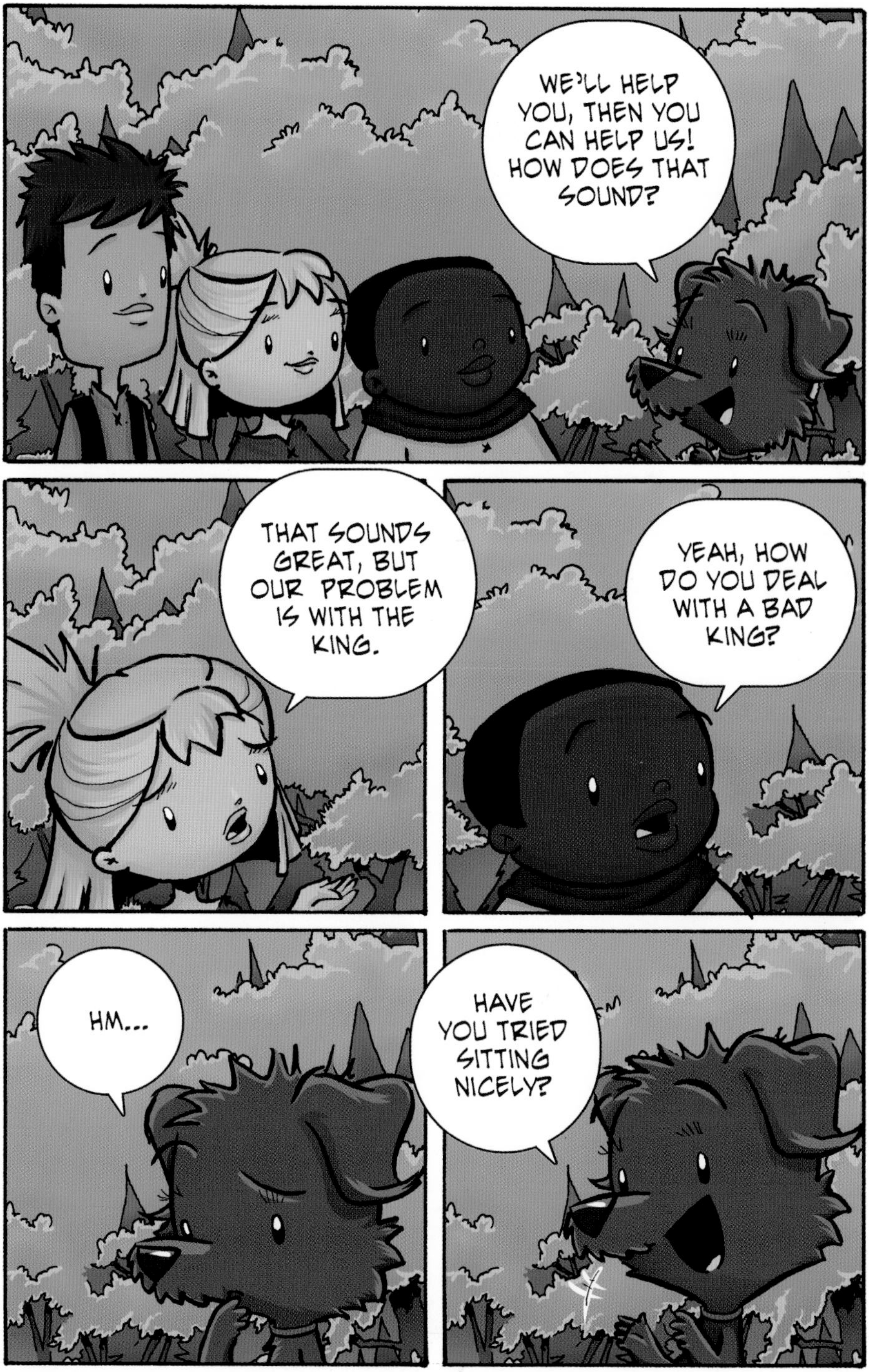
WE'LL HELP YOU, THEN YOU CAN HELP US! HOW DOES THAT SOUND?
THAT SOUNDS GREAT, BUT OUR PROBLEM IS WITH THE KING.
YEAH, HOW DO YOU DEAL WITH A BAD KING?
HM...
HAVE YOU TRIED SITTING NICELY?

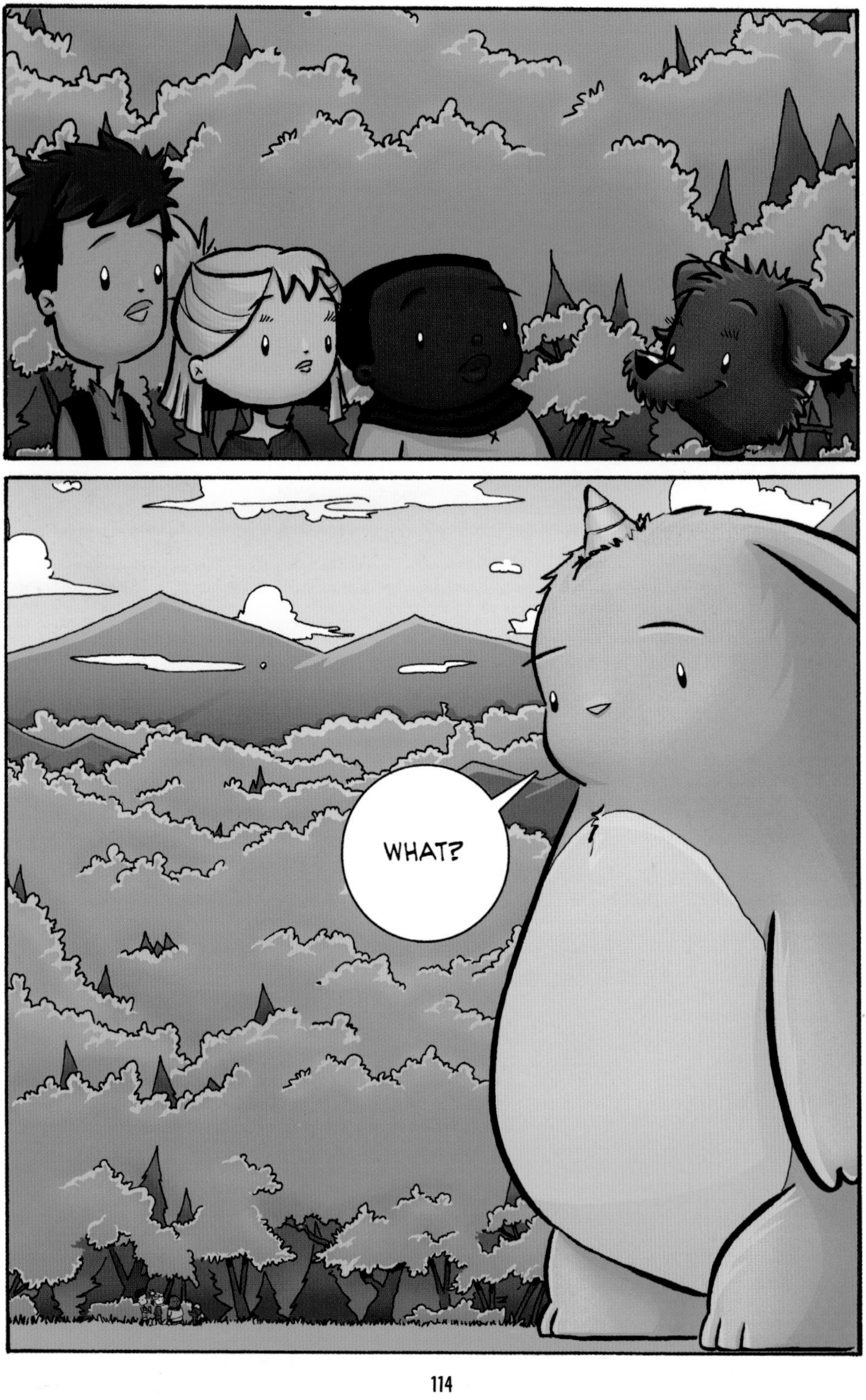
WHAT?

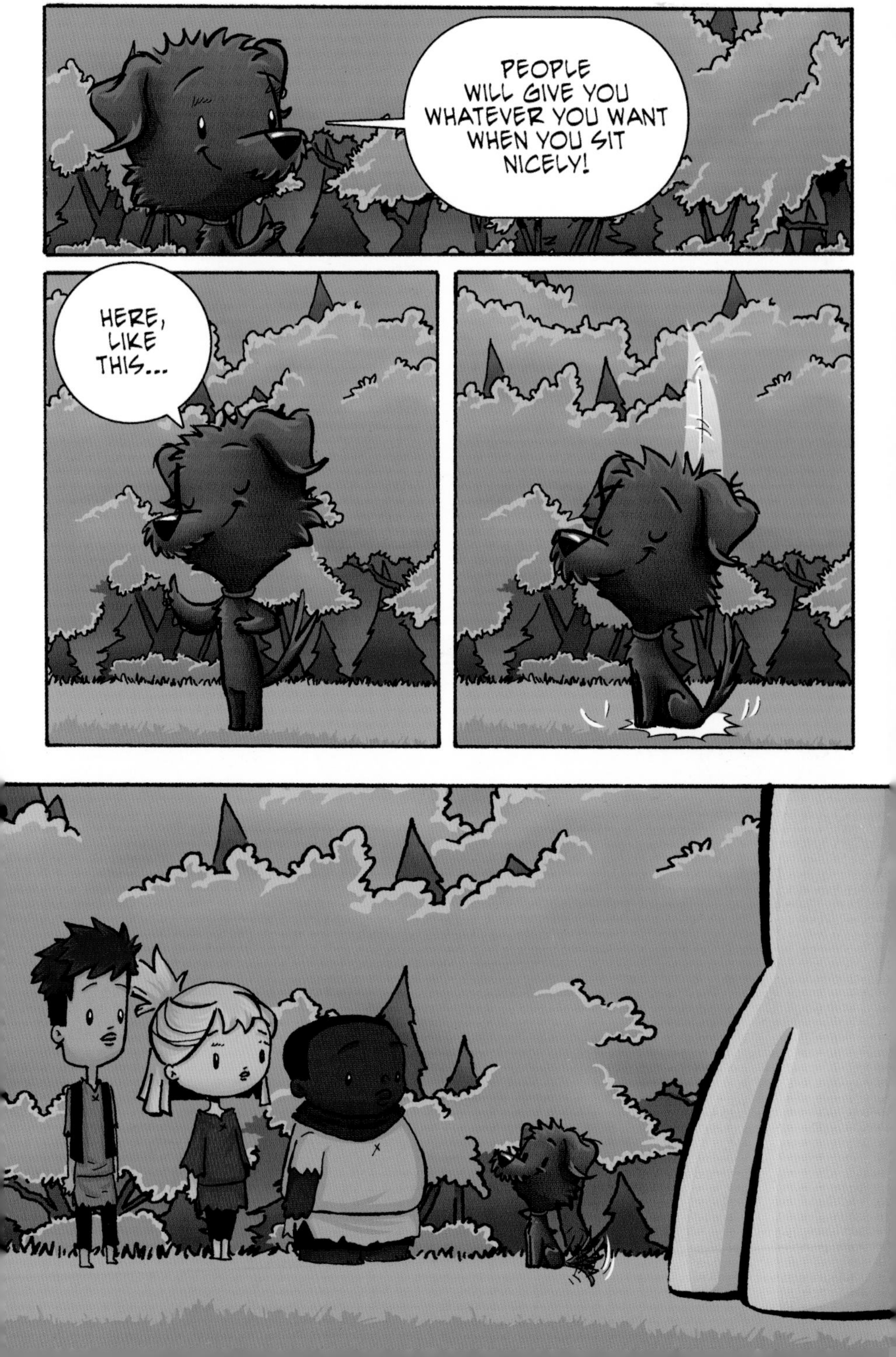
PEOPLE WILL GIVE YOU WHATEVER YOU WANT WHEN YOU SIT NICELY!
HERE, LIKE THIS...

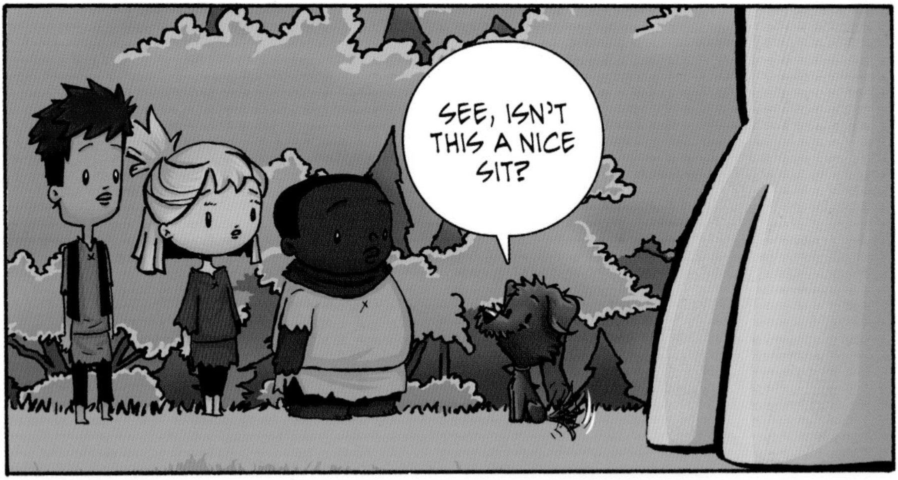
SEE, ISN'T THIS A NICE SIT?

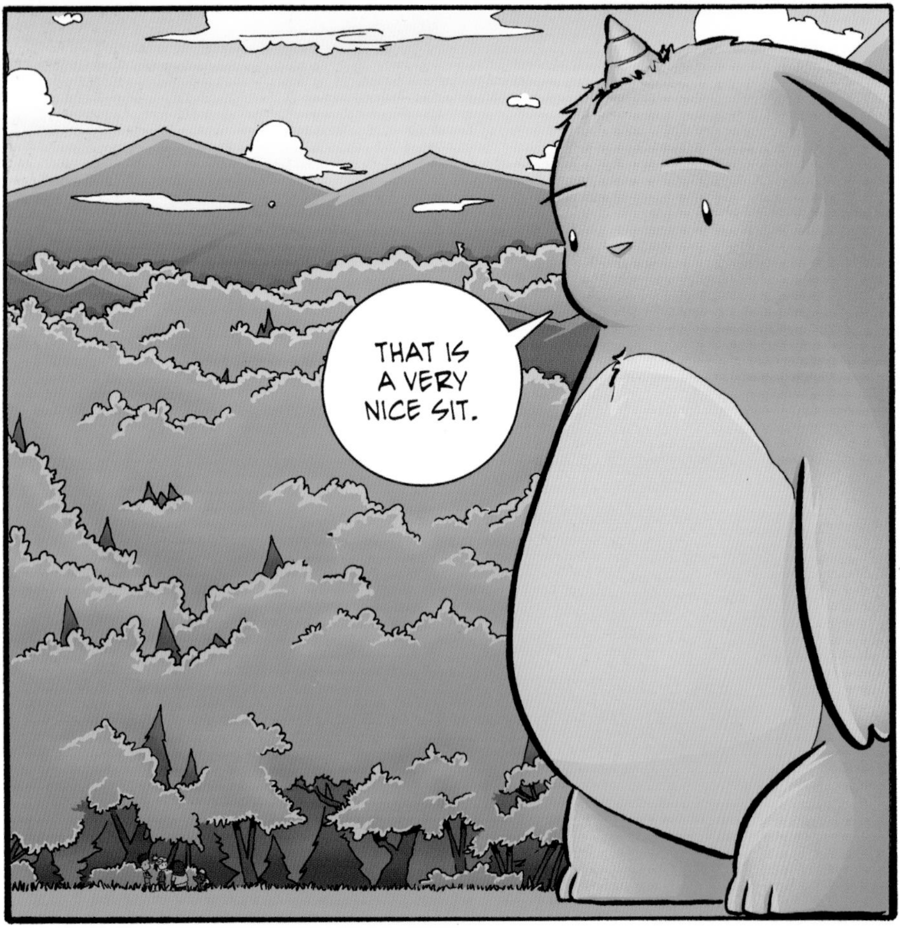
THAT IS A VERY NICE SIT.

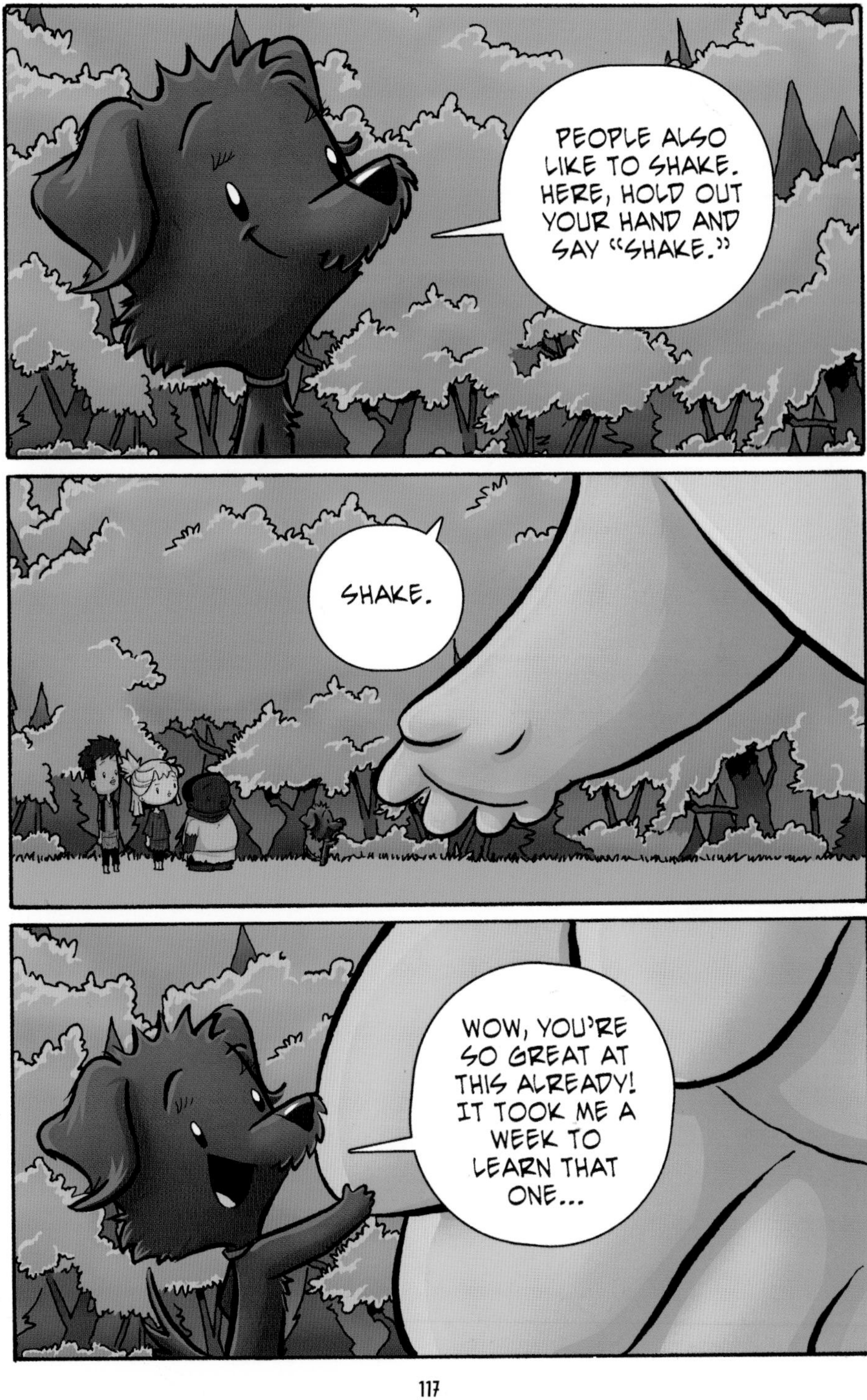
PEOPLE ALSO LIKE TO SHAKE. HERE, HOLD OUT YOUR HAND AND SAY "SHAKE."
SHAKE.
WOW, YOU'RE SO GREAT AT THIS ALREADY! IT TOOK ME A WEEK TO LEARN THAT ONE...

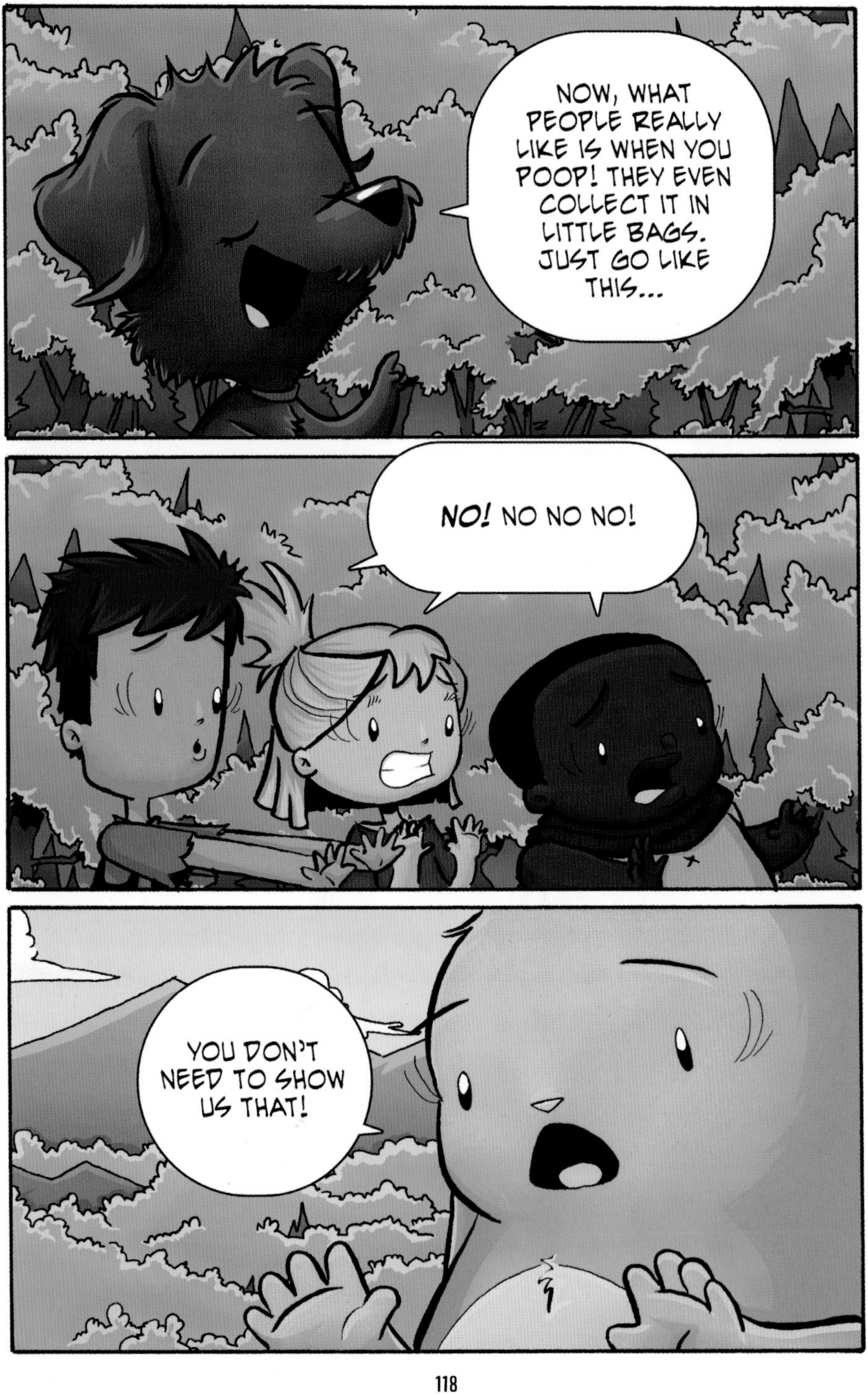
NOW, WHAT PEOPLE REALLY LIKE IS WHEN YOU POOP! THEY EVEN COLLECT IT IN LITTLE BAGS. JUST GO LIKE THIS...
NO! NO NO NO!
YOU DON'T NEED TO SHOW US THAT!

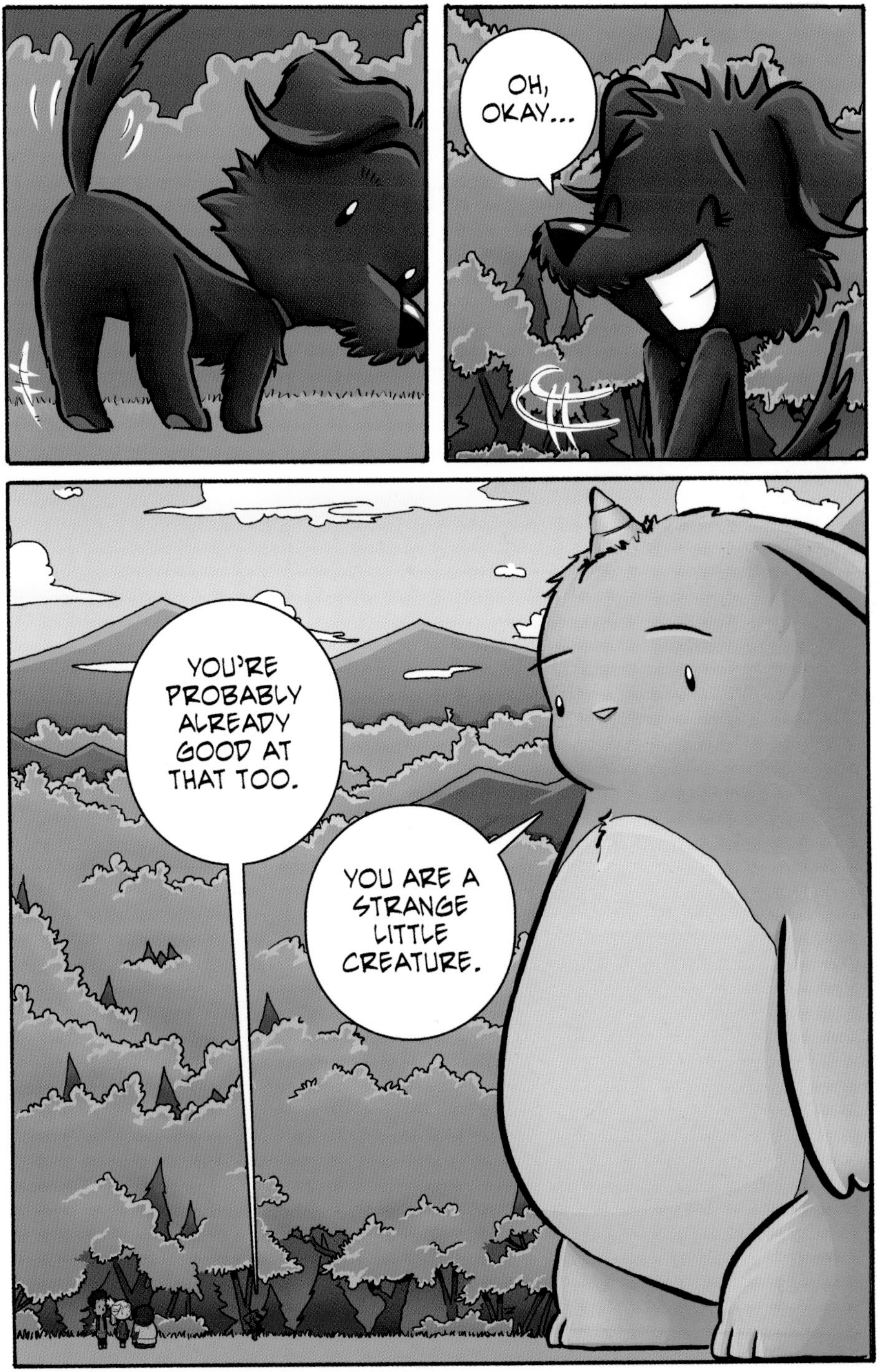
OH, OKAY...
YOU'RE PROBABLY ALREADY GOOD AT THAT TOO.
YOU ARE A STRANGE LITTLE CREATURE.

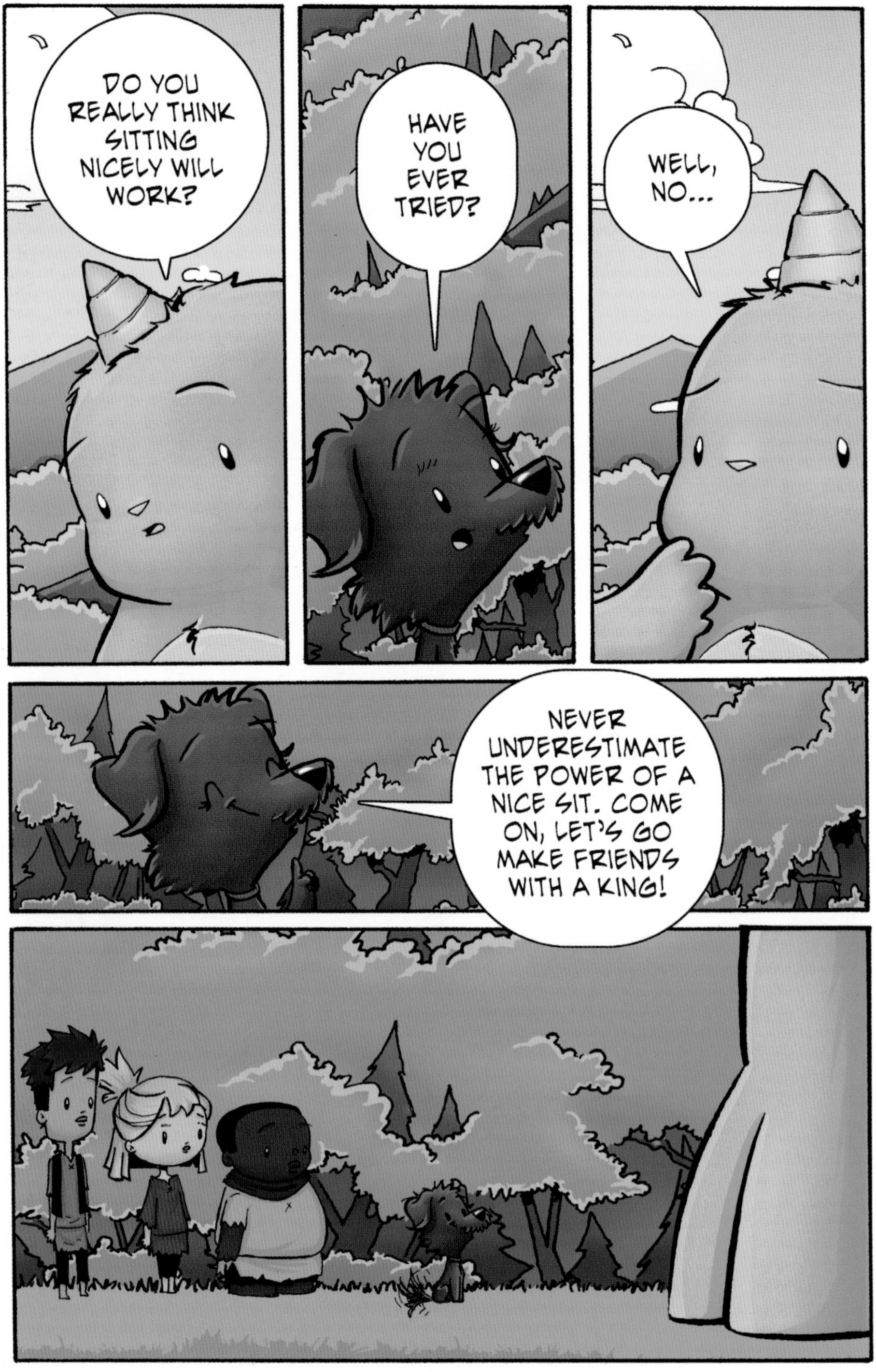
DO YOU REALLY THINK SITTING NICELY WILL WORK?
HAVE YOU EVER TRIED?
WELL, NO...
NEVER UNDERESTIMATE THE POWER OF A NICE SIT. COME ON, LET'S GO MAKE FRIENDS WITH A KING!

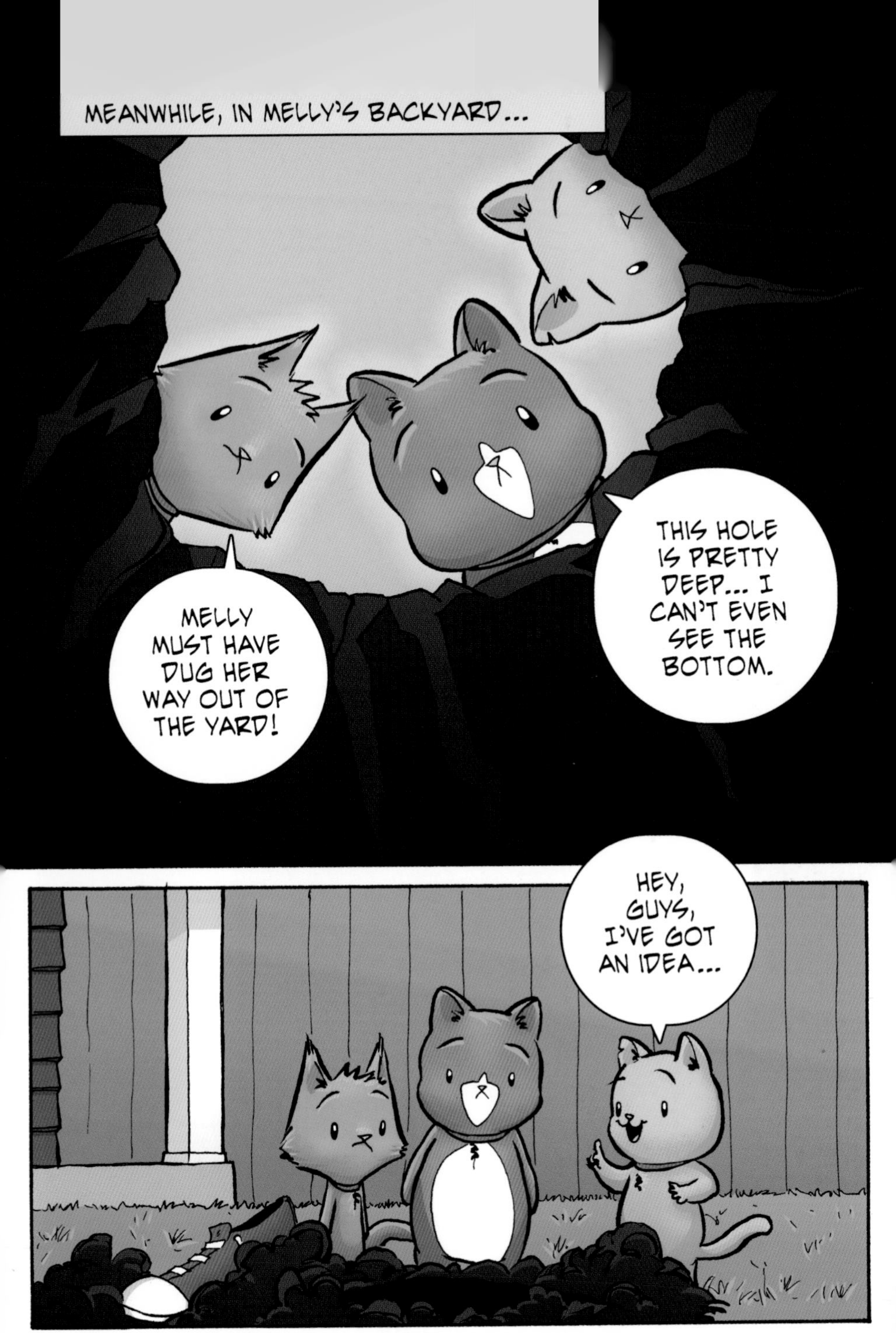
MEANWHILE, IN MELLY'S BACKYARD...
MELLY MUST HAVE DUG HER WAY OUT OF THE YARD!
THIS HOLE IS PRETTY DEEP... I CAN'T EVEN SEE THE BOTTOM.
HEY, GUYS, I'VE GOT AN IDEA...

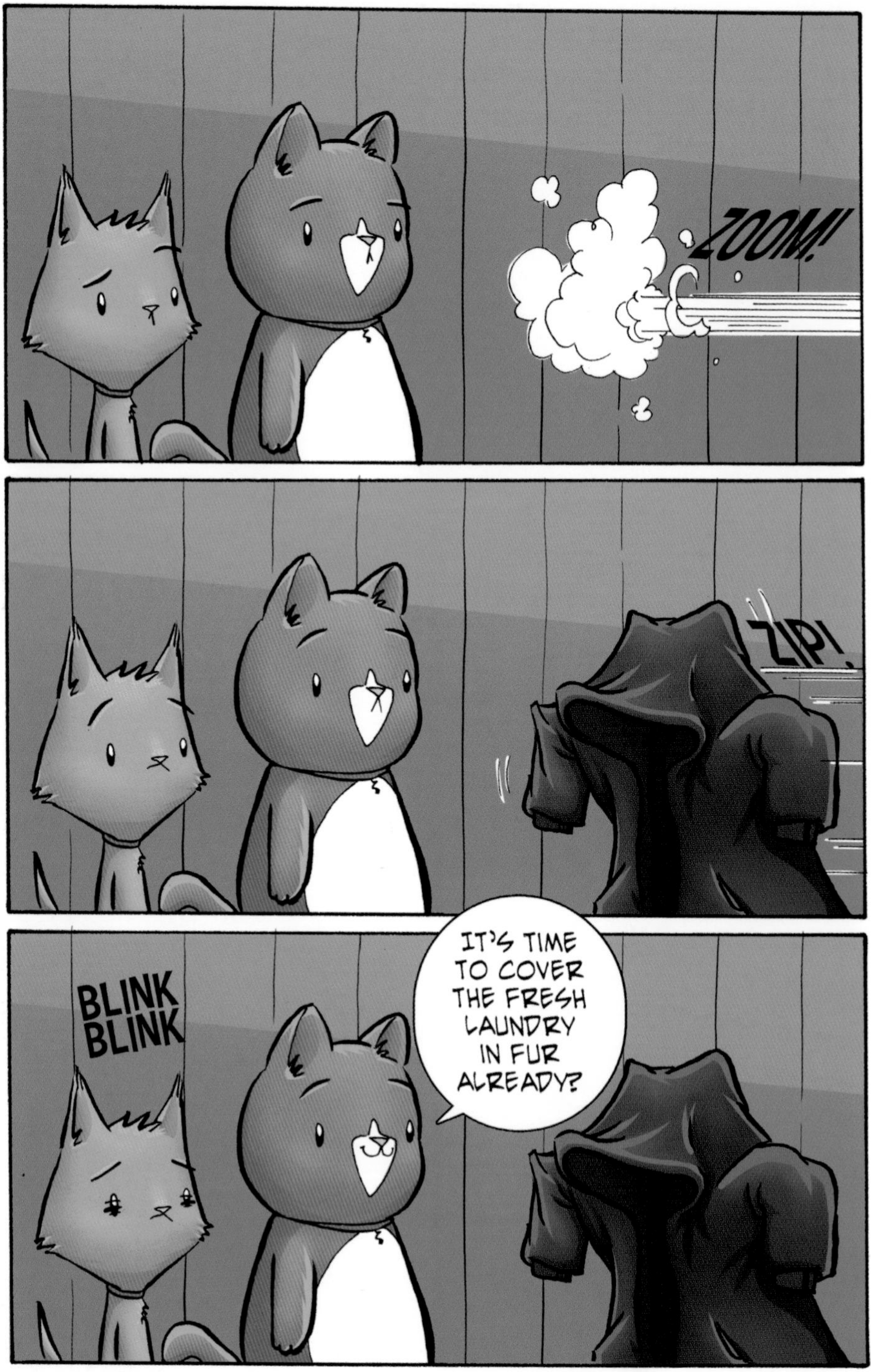
ZOOM!
ZIP!
BLINK BLINK
IT'S TIME TO COVER THE FRESH LAUNDRY IN FUR ALREADY?

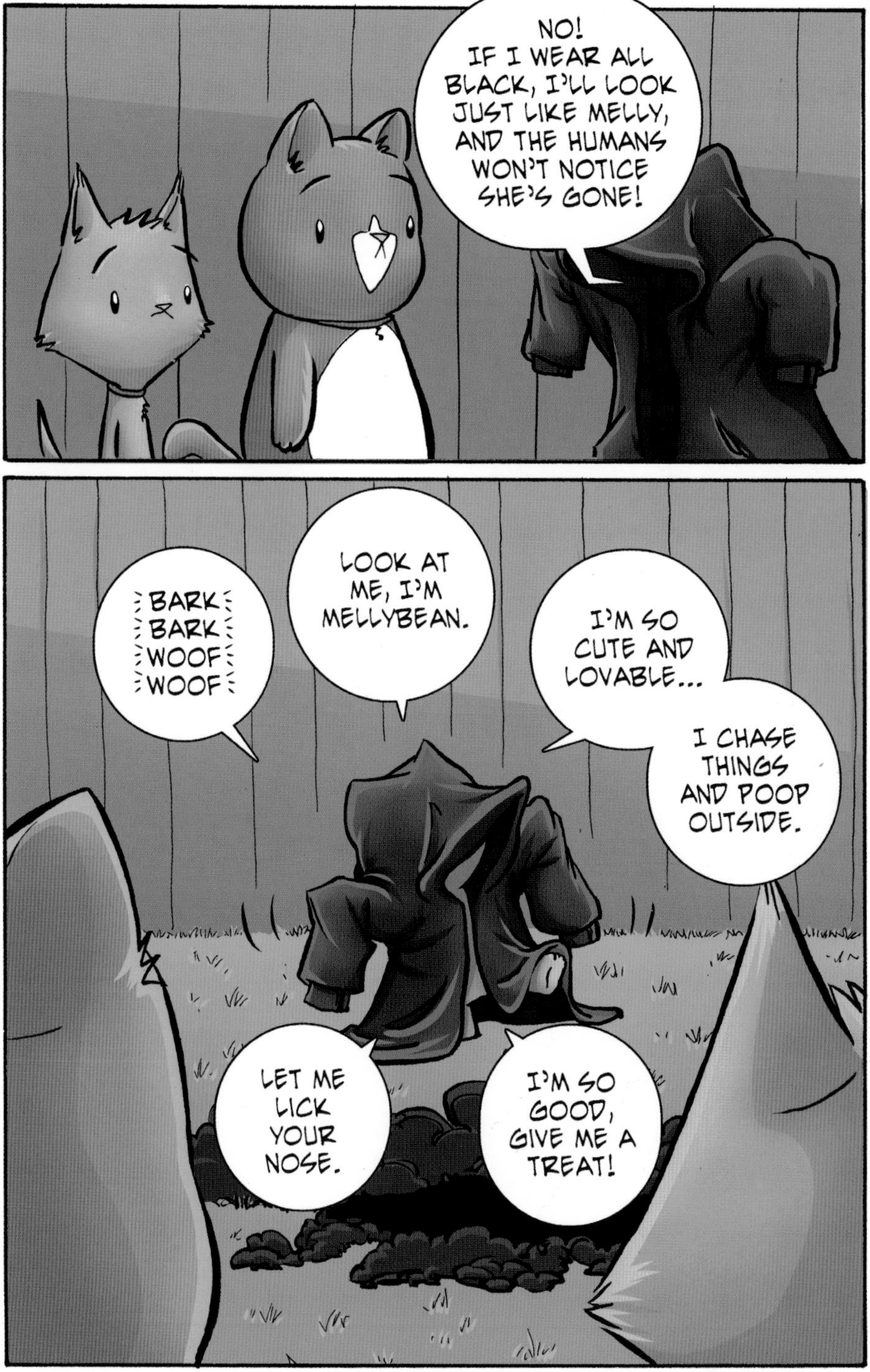
NO!
IF I WEAR ALL BLACK, I'LL LOOK JUST LIKE MELLY, AND THE HUMANS WON'T NOTICE SHE'S GONE!
BARK BARK WOOF WOOF
LOOK AT ME, I'M MELLYBEAN.
I'M SO CUTE AND LOVABLE...
I CHASE THINGS AND POOP OUTSIDE.
LET ME LICK YOUR NOSE.
I'M SO GOOD, GIVE ME A TREAT!

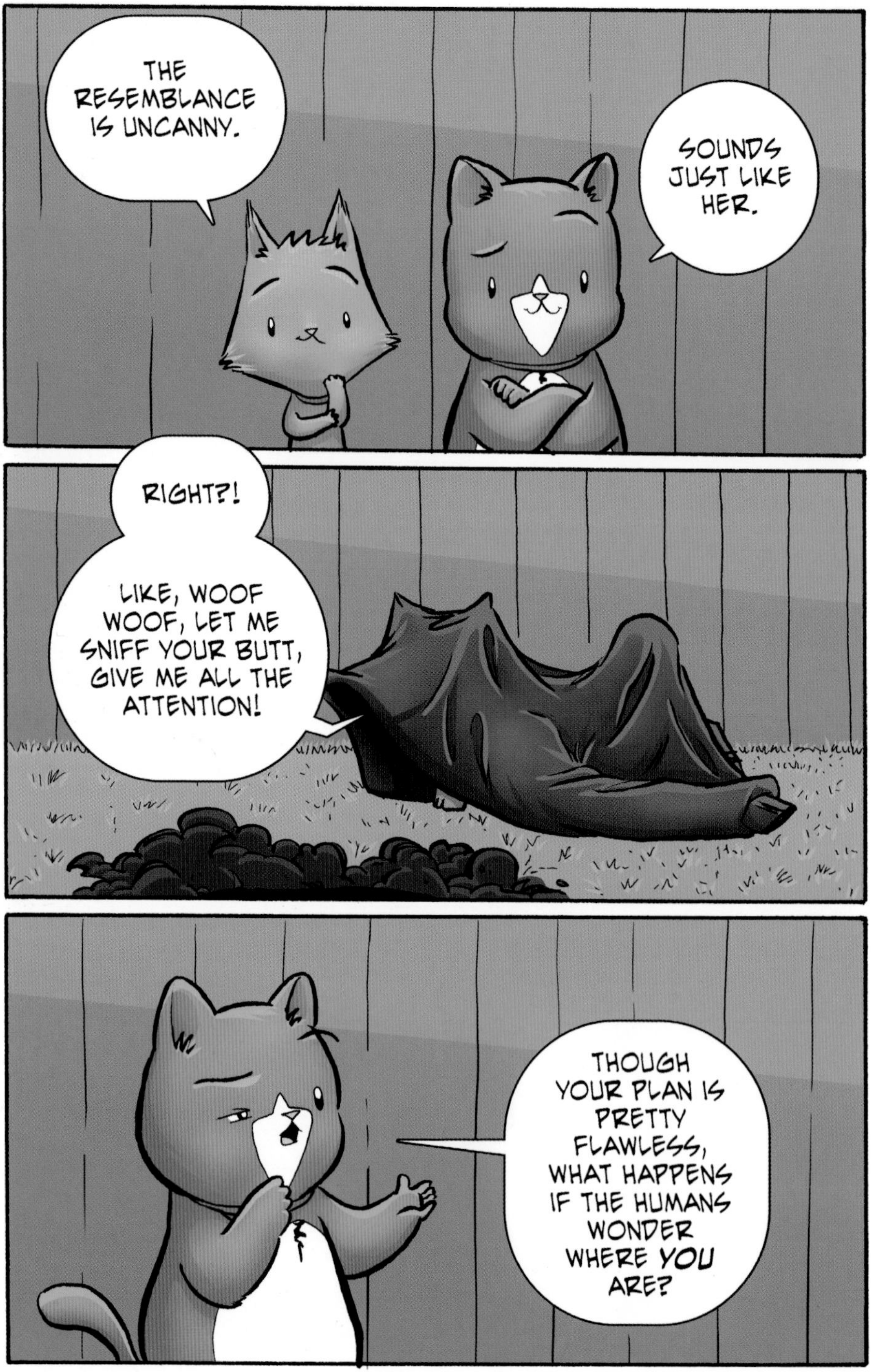
THE RESEMBLANCE IS UNCANNY.
SOUNDS JUST LIKE HER.
RIGHT?!
LIKE, WOOF WOOF, LET ME SNIFF YOUR BUTT, GIVE ME ALL THE ATTENTION!
THOUGH YOUR PLAN IS PRETTY FLAWLESS, WHAT HAPPENS IF THE HUMANS WONDER WHERE *YOU* ARE?

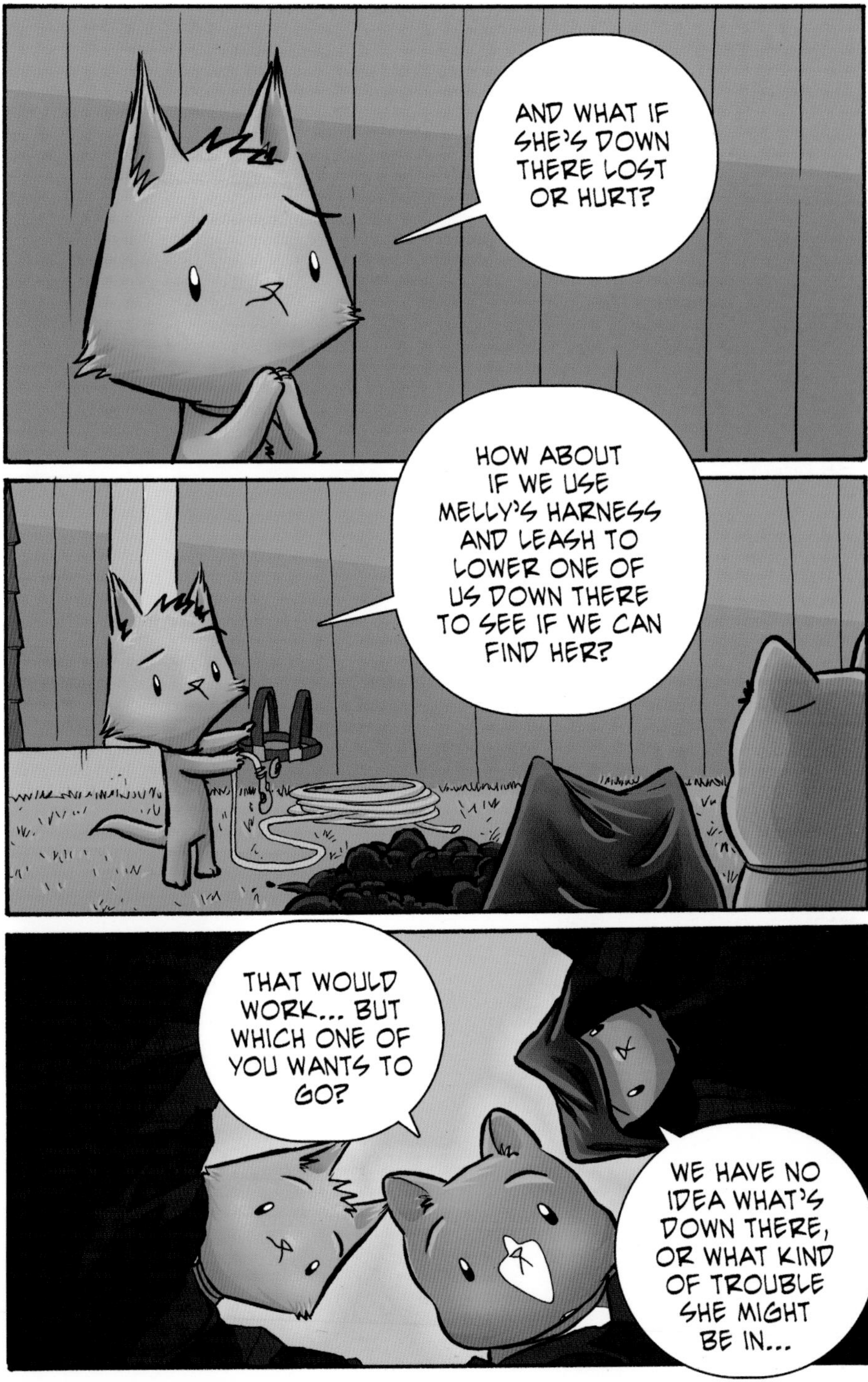

AND WHAT IF SHE'S DOWN THERE LOST OR HURT?
HOW ABOUT IF WE USE MELLY'S HARNESS AND LEASH TO LOWER ONE OF US DOWN THERE TO SEE IF WE CAN FIND HER?
THAT WOULD WORK... BUT WHICH ONE OF YOU WANTS TO GO?
WE HAVE NO IDEA WHAT'S DOWN THERE, OR WHAT KIND OF TROUBLE SHE MIGHT BE IN...

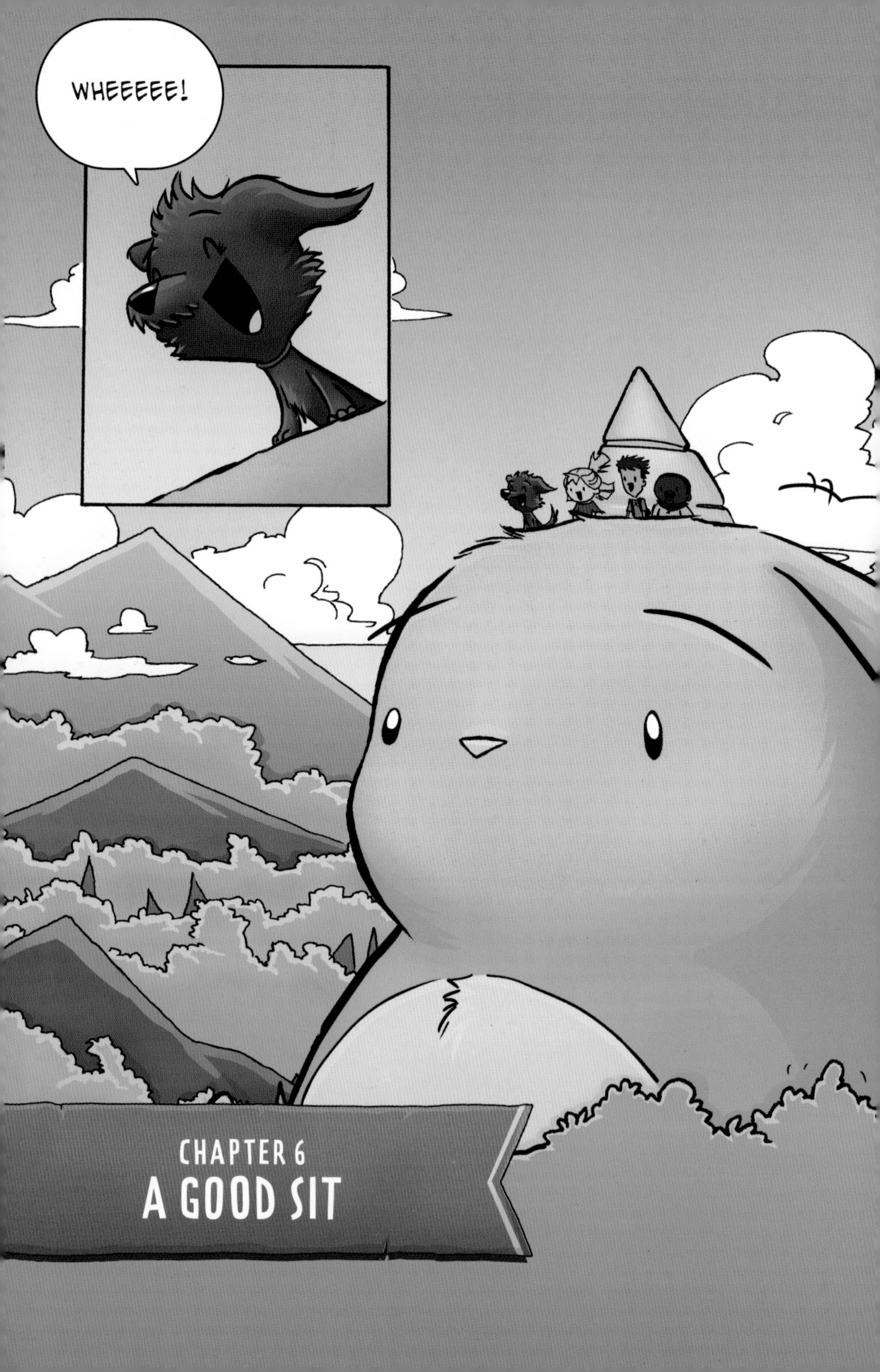
WHEEEEEE!

CHAPTER 6
A GOOD SIT

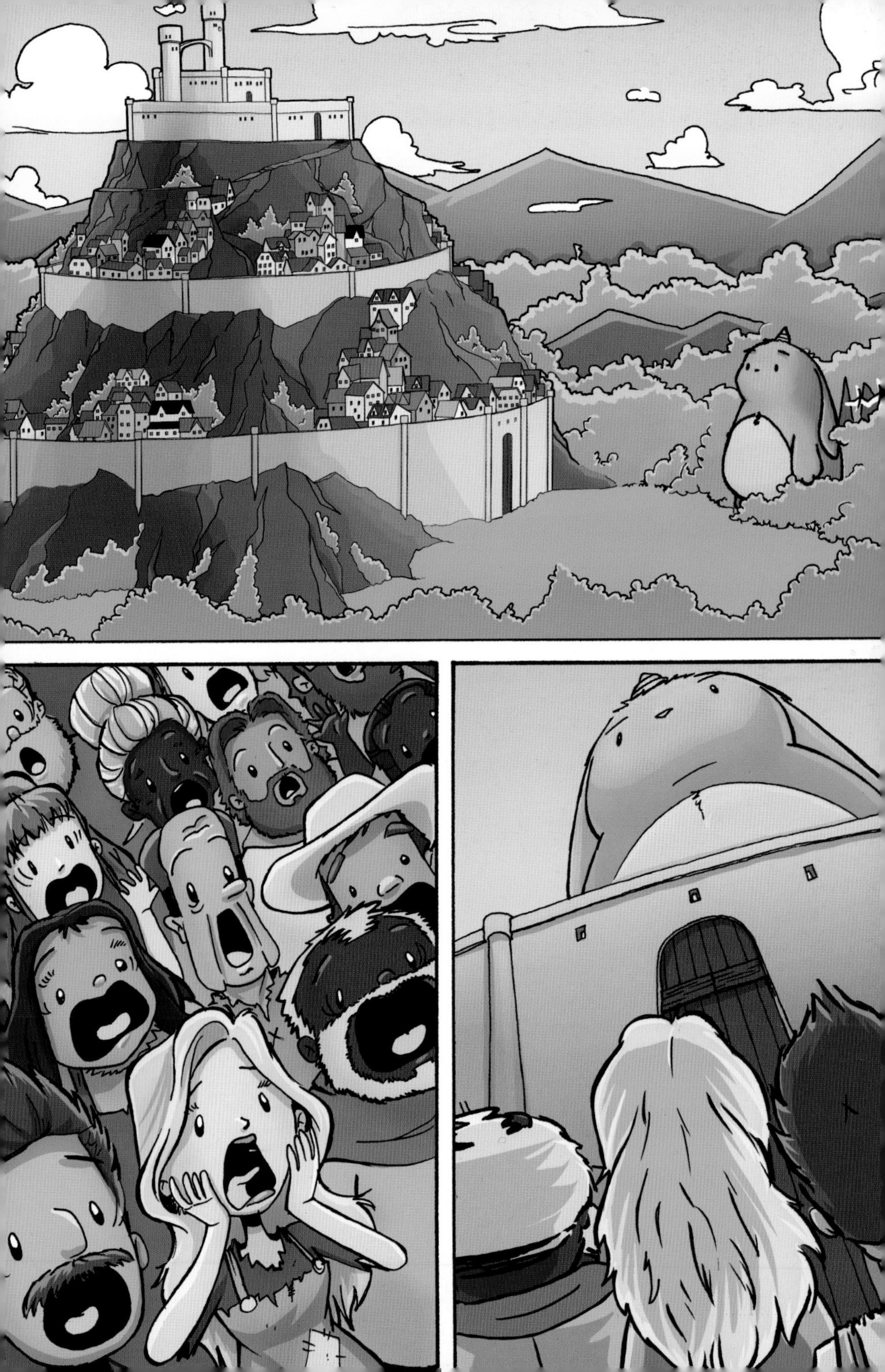

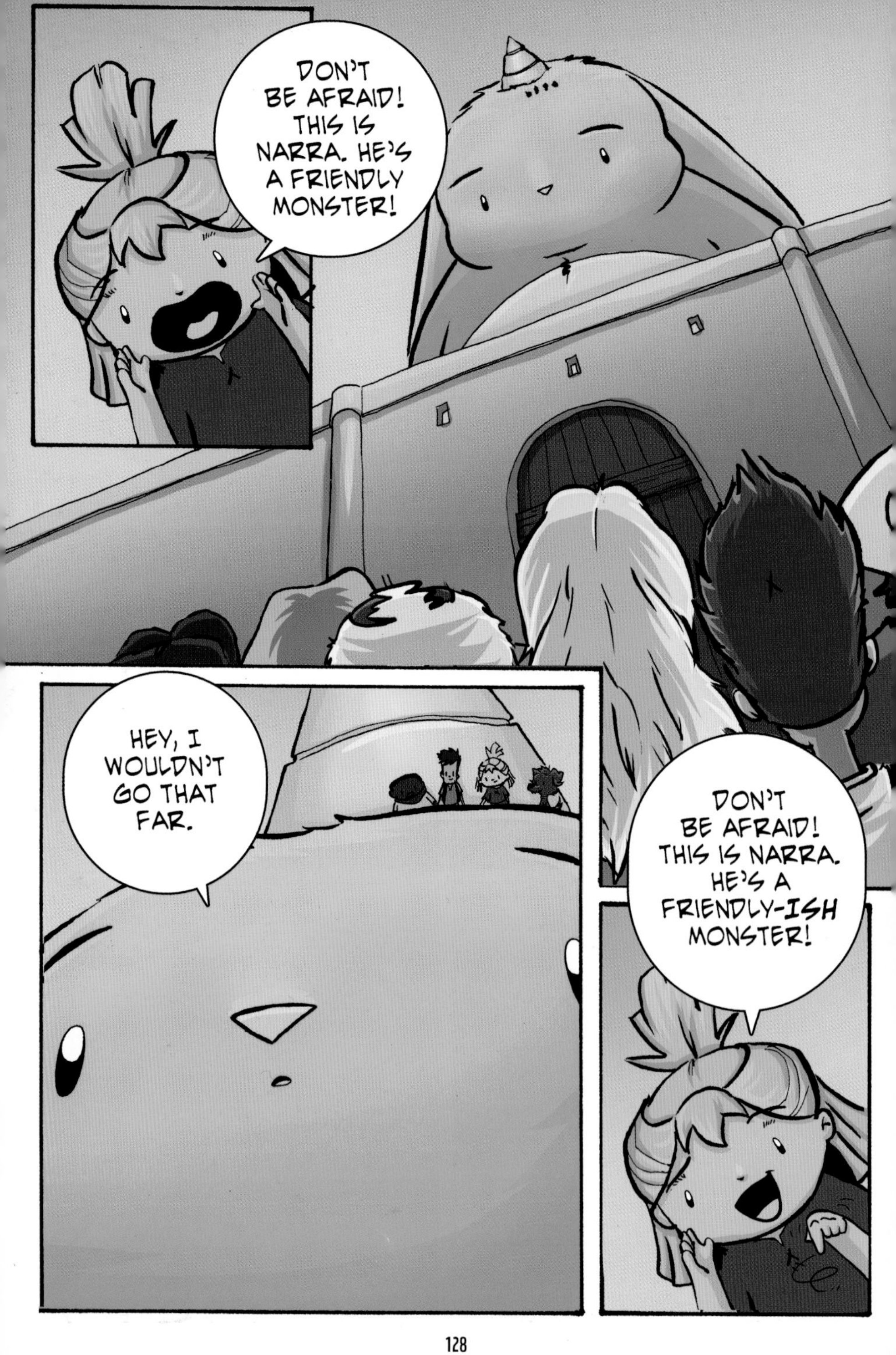
DON'T BE AFRAID! THIS IS NARRA. HE'S A FRIENDLY MONSTER!
HEY, I WOULDN'T GO THAT FAR.
DON'T BE AFRAID! THIS IS NARRA. HE'S A FRIENDLY-ISH MONSTER!

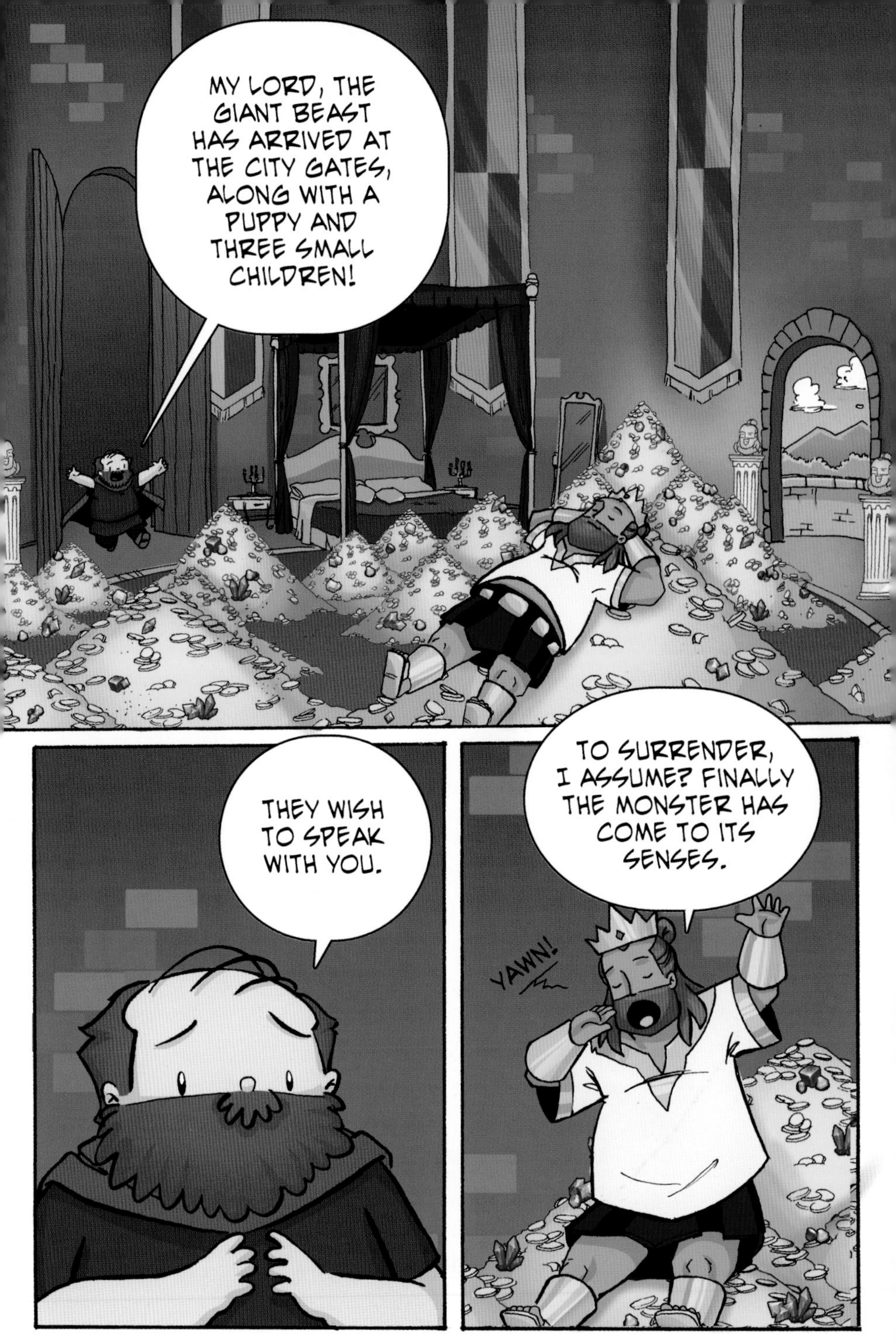
MY LORD, THE GIANT BEAST HAS ARRIVED AT THE CITY GATES, ALONG WITH A PUPPY AND THREE SMALL CHILDREN!
THEY WISH TO SPEAK WITH YOU.
TO SURRENDER, I ASSUME? FINALLY THE MONSTER HAS COME TO ITS SENSES.
YAWN!

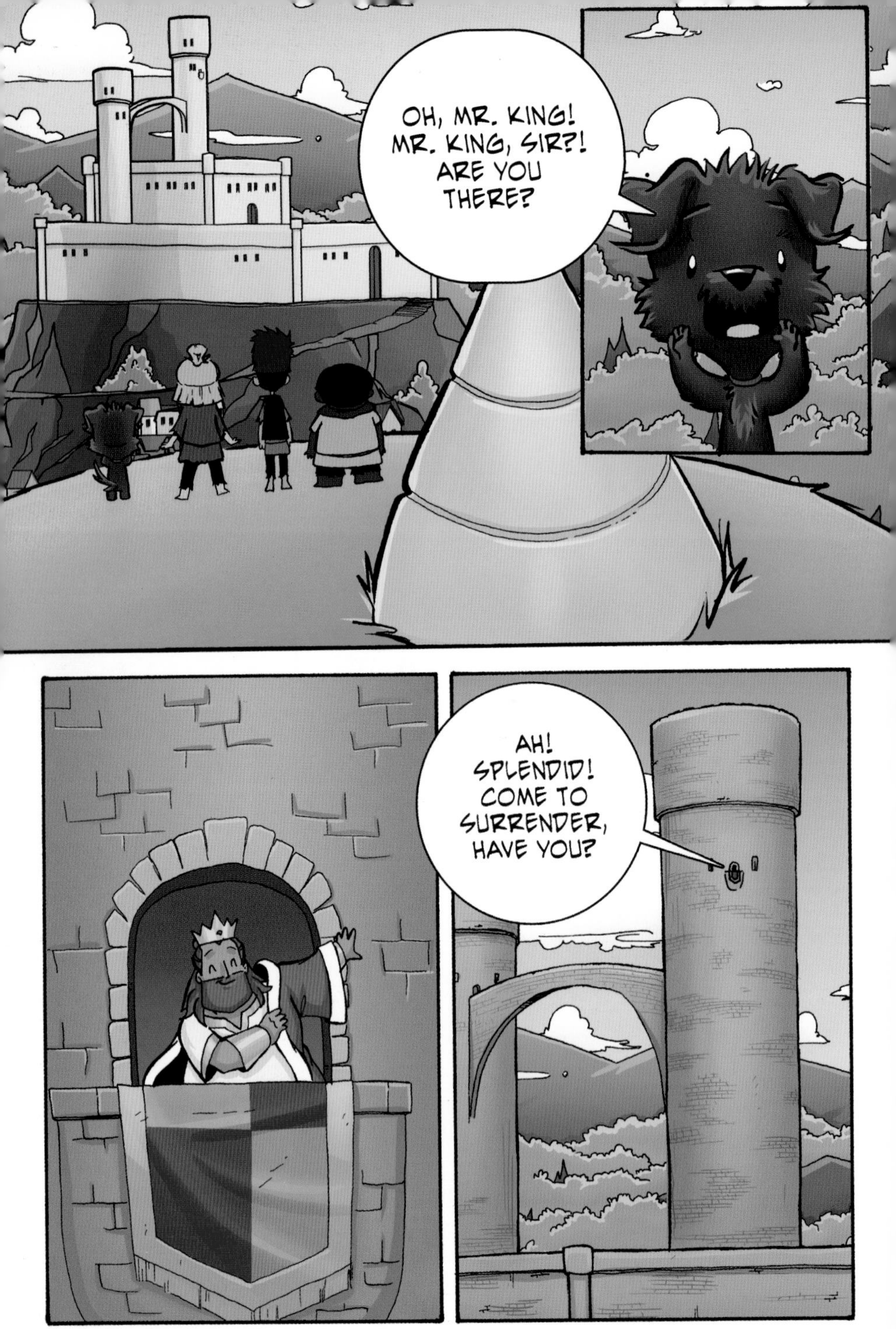

OH, MR. KING! MR. KING, SIR?! ARE YOU THERE?
AH! SPLENDID! COME TO SURRENDER, HAVE YOU?

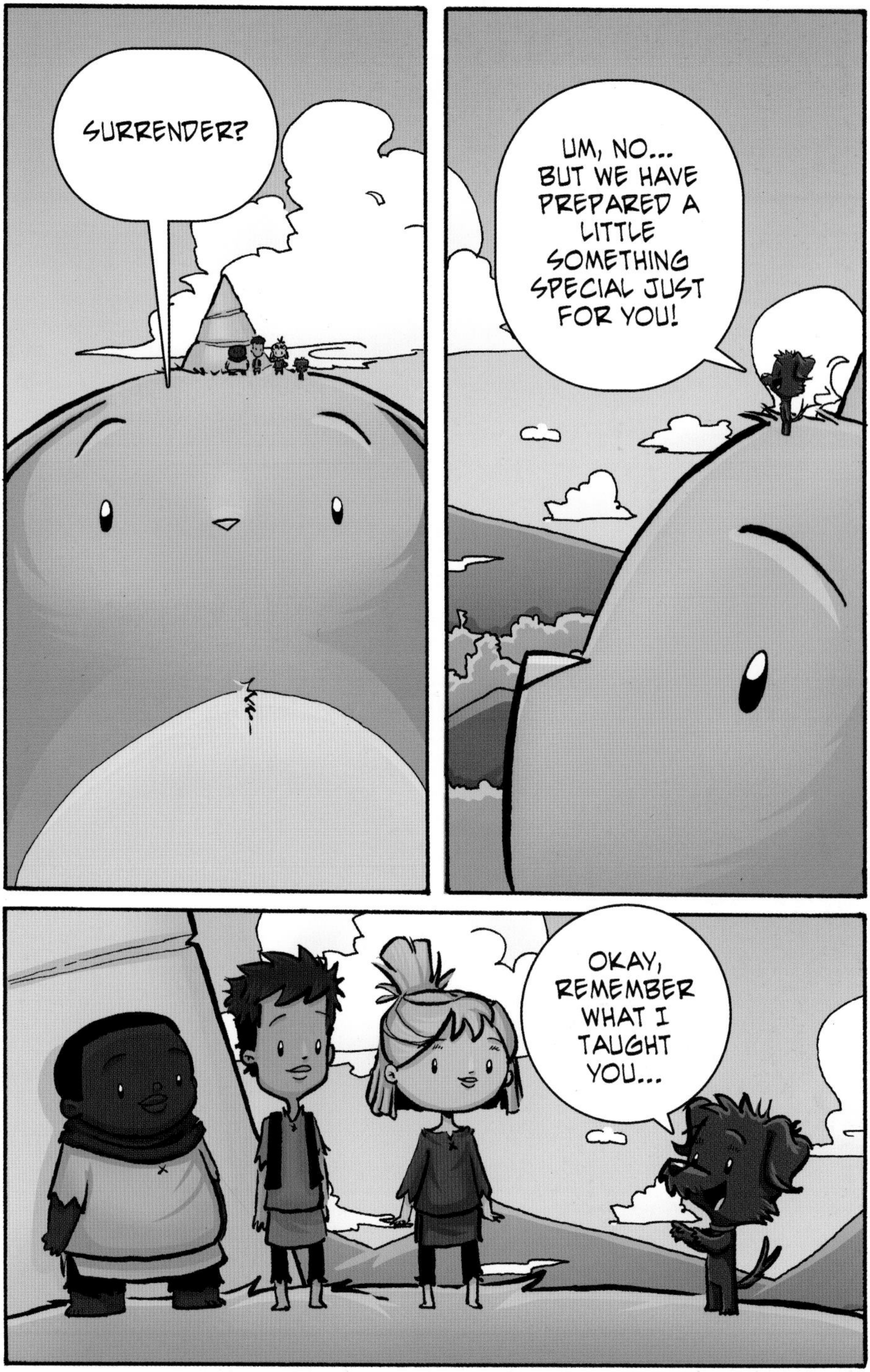
SURRENDER?
UM, NO... BUT WE HAVE PREPARED A LITTLE SOMETHING SPECIAL JUST FOR YOU!
OKAY, REMEMBER WHAT I TAUGHT YOU...

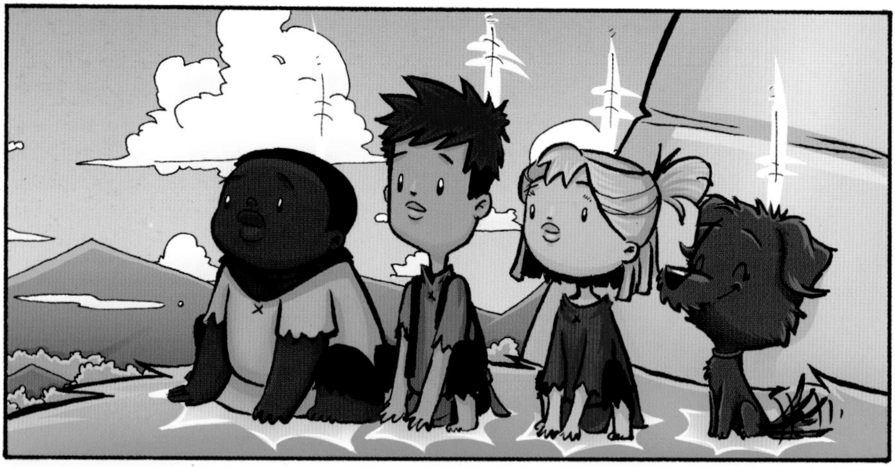
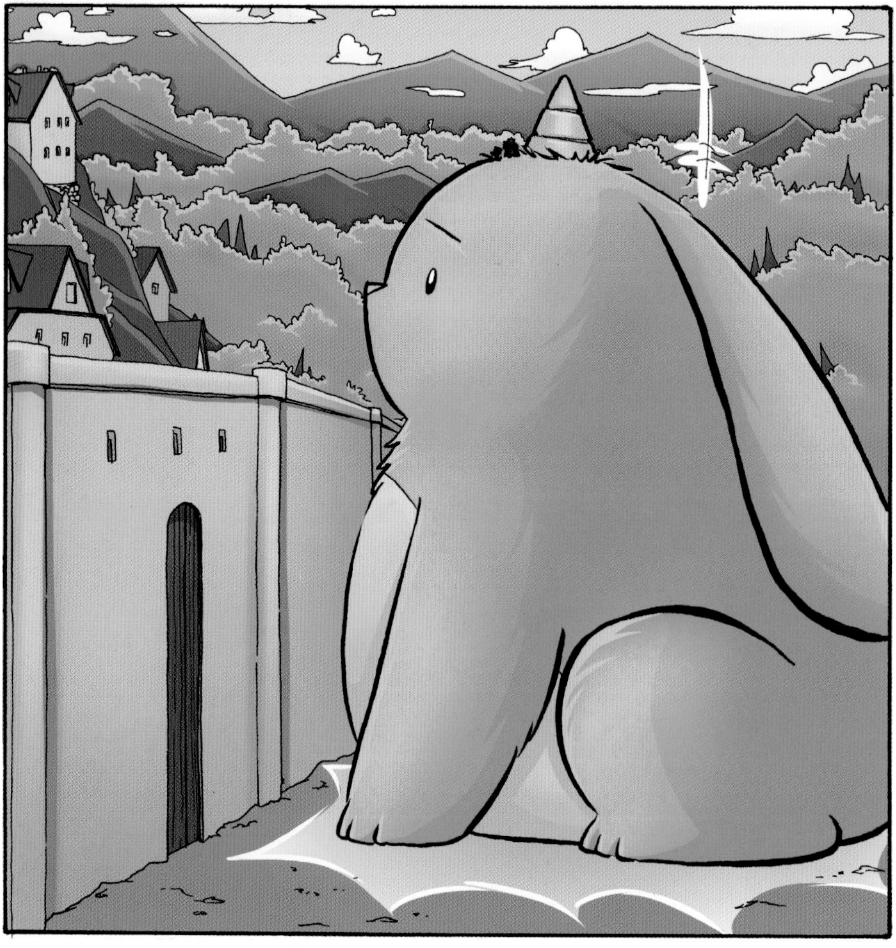

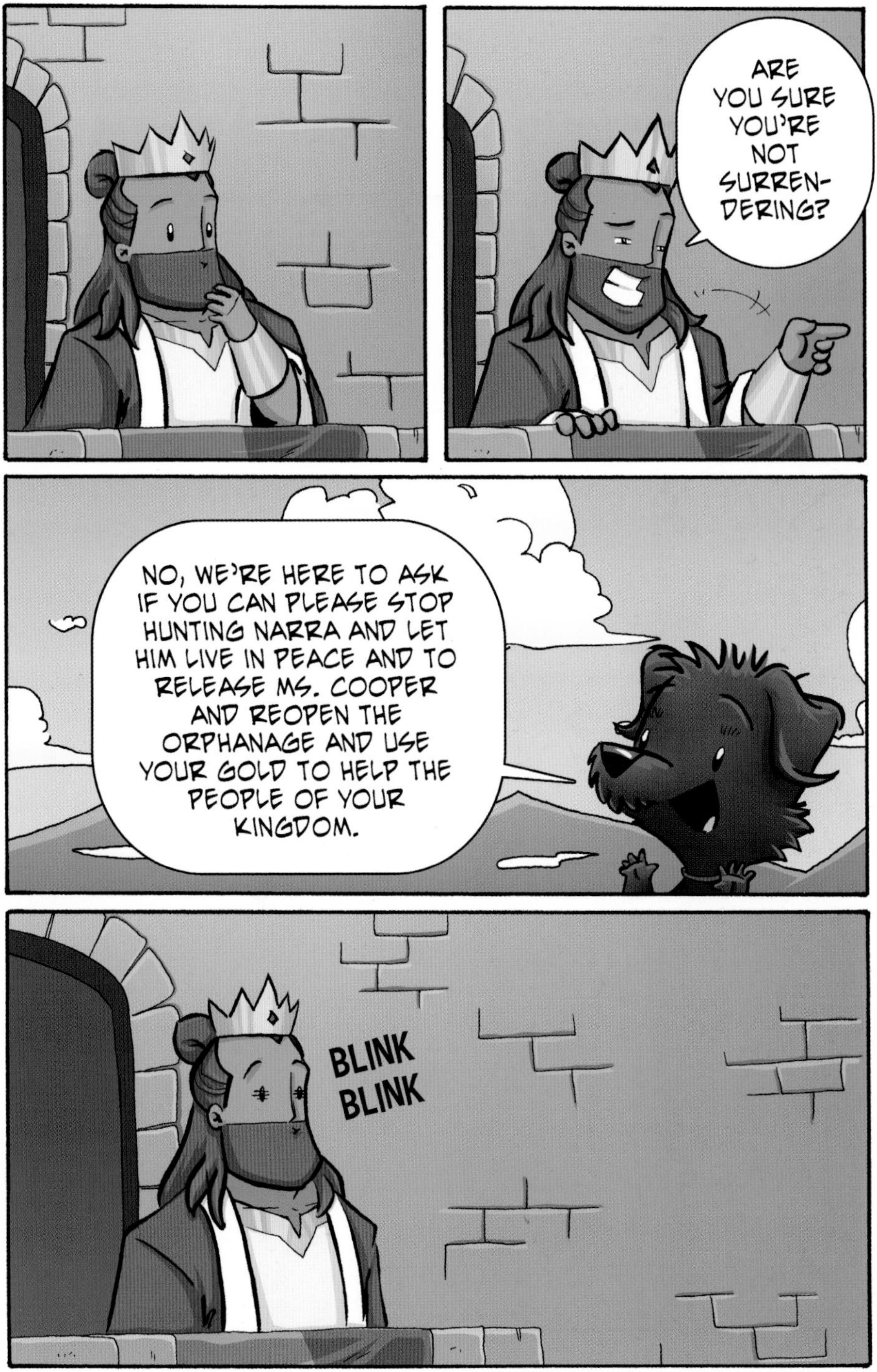
ARE YOU SURE YOU'RE NOT SURREN-DERING?
NO, WE'RE HERE TO ASK IF YOU CAN PLEASE STOP HUNTING NARRA AND LET HIM LIVE IN PEACE AND TO RELEASE MS. COOPER AND REOPEN THE ORPHANAGE AND USE YOUR GOLD TO HELP THE PEOPLE OF YOUR KINGDOM.
BLINK BLINK

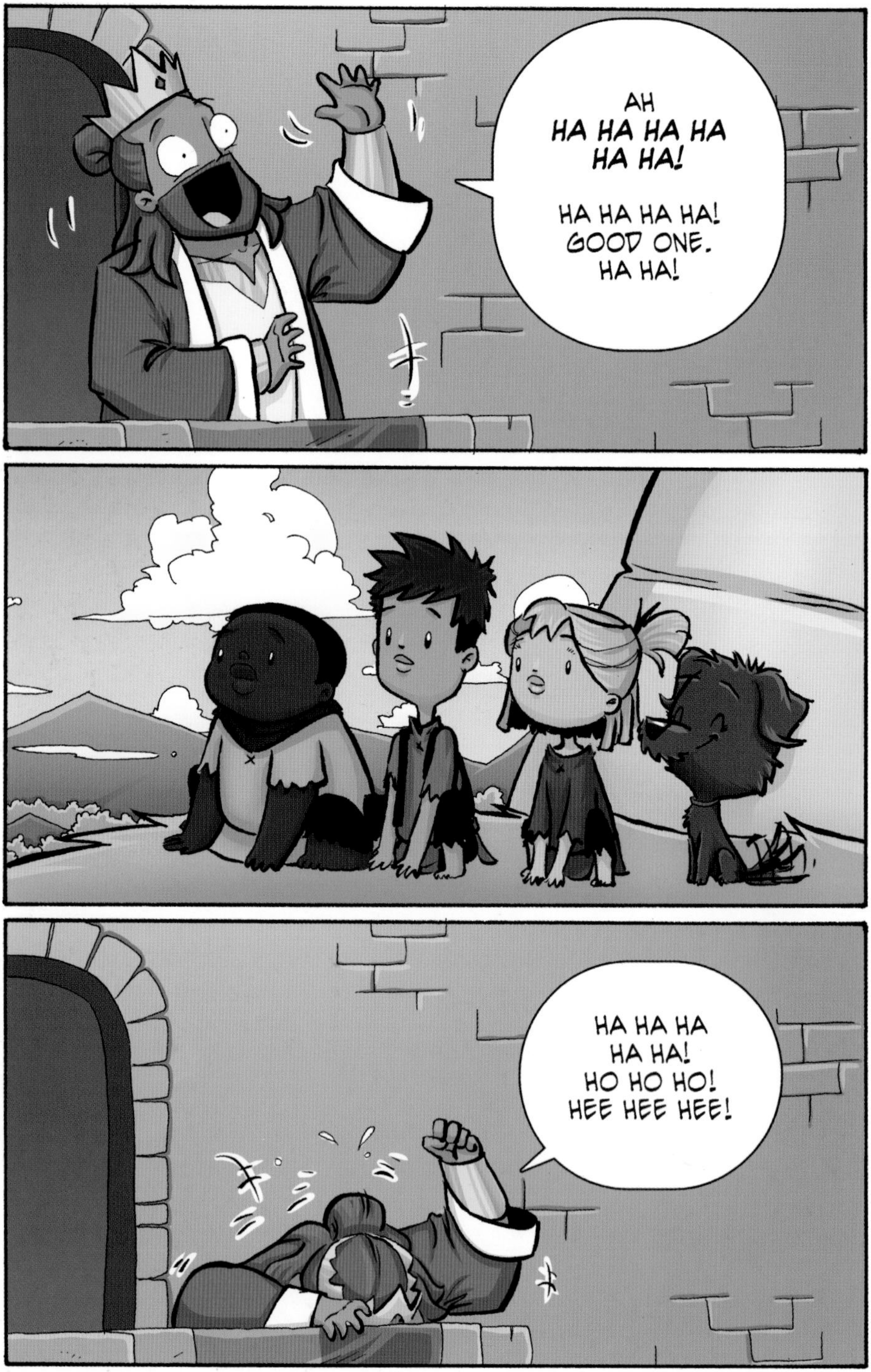
AH
HA HA HA HA
HA HA!
HA HA HA HA!
GOOD ONE.
HA HA!
HA HA HA
HA HA!
HO HO HO!
HEE HEE HEE!

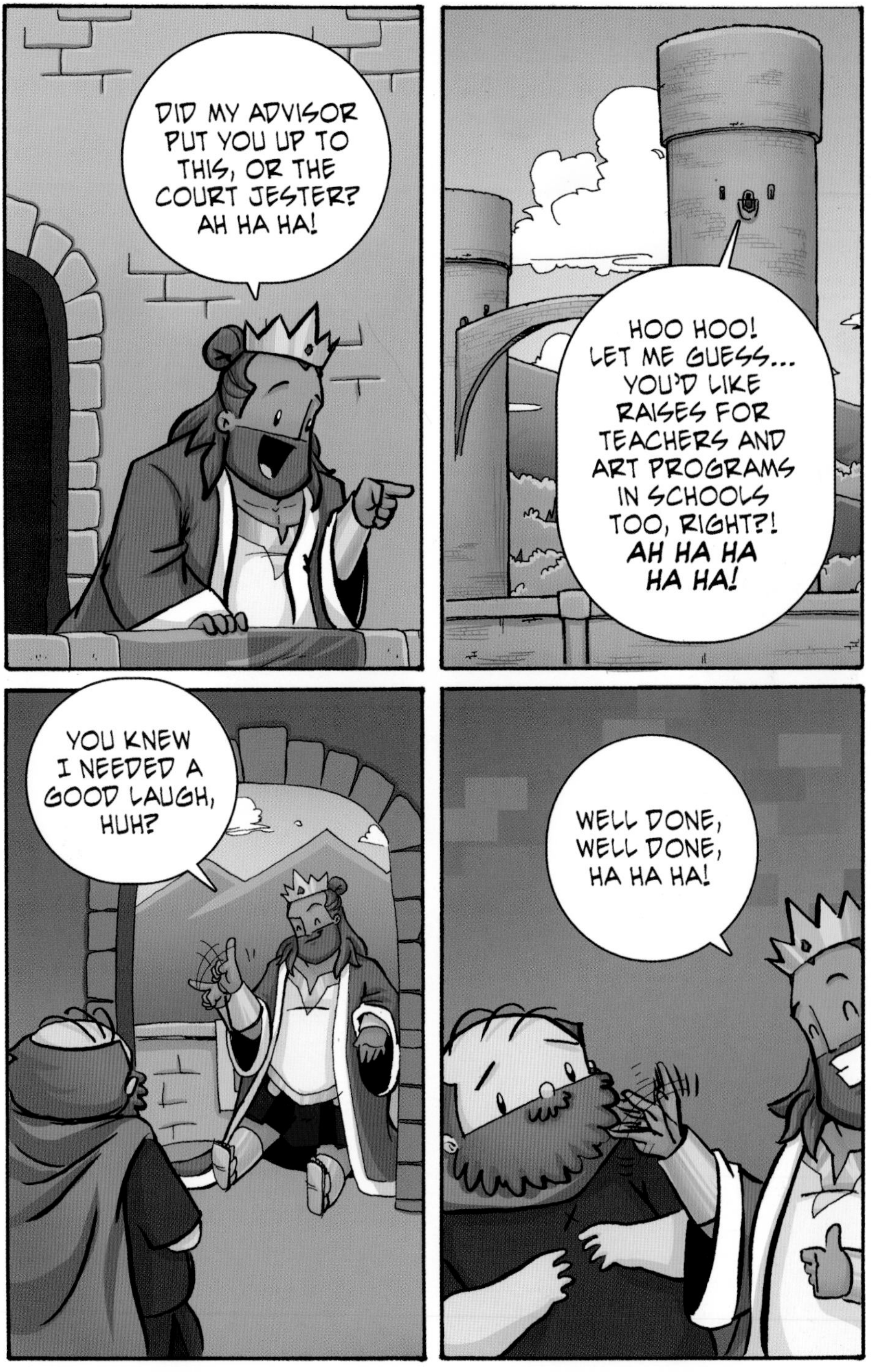
DID MY ADVISOR PUT YOU UP TO THIS, OR THE COURT JESTER? AH HA HA!
HOO HOO! LET ME GUESS... YOU'D LIKE RAISES FOR TEACHERS AND ART PROGRAMS IN SCHOOLS TOO, RIGHT?! AH HA HA HA HA!
YOU KNEW I NEEDED A GOOD LAUGH, HUH?
WELL DONE, WELL DONE, HA HA HA!

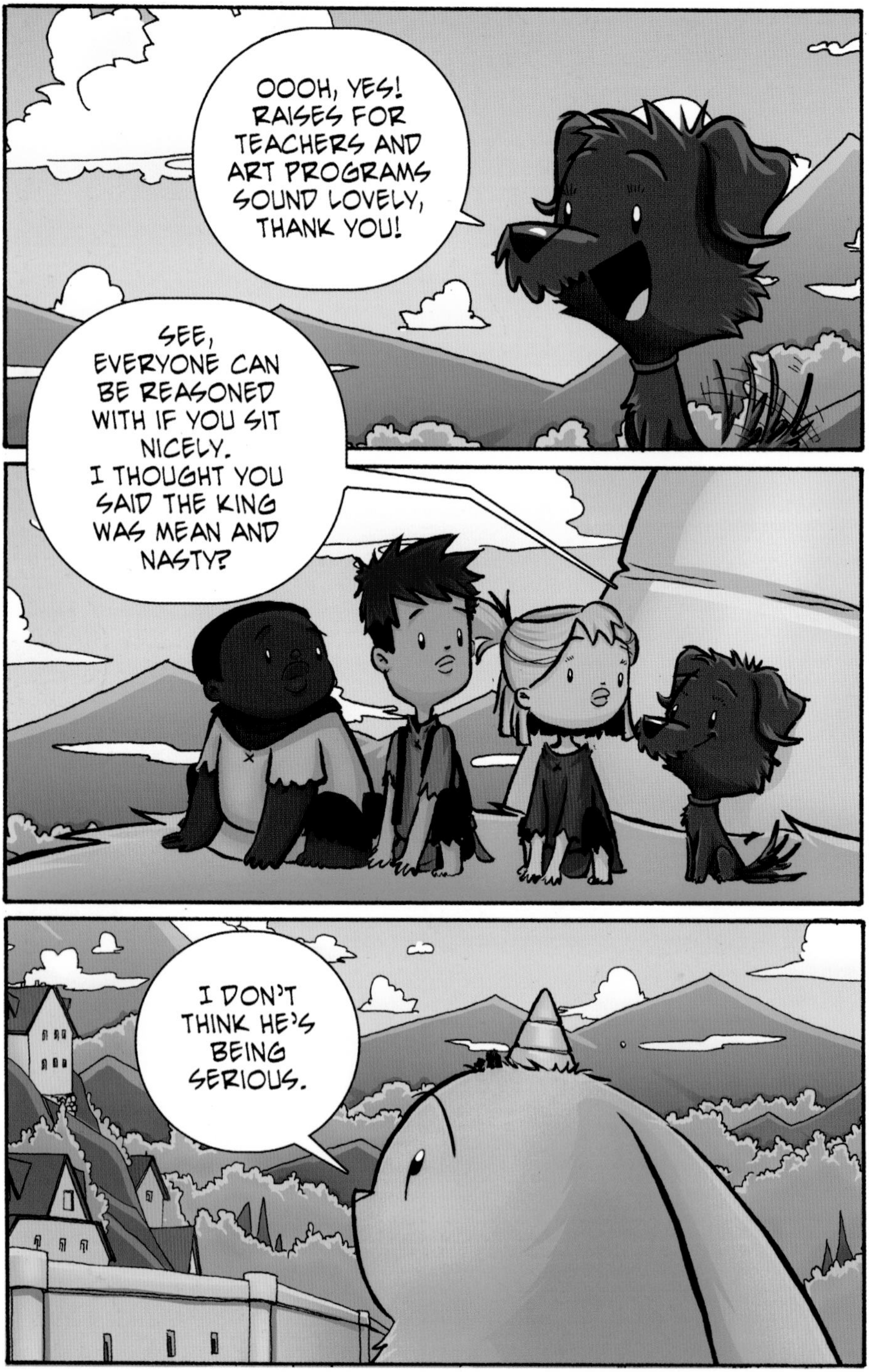
OOOH, YES! RAISES FOR TEACHERS AND ART PROGRAMS SOUND LOVELY, THANK YOU!
SEE, EVERYONE CAN BE REASONED WITH IF YOU SIT NICELY. I THOUGHT YOU SAID THE KING WAS MEAN AND NASTY?
I DON'T THINK HE'S BEING SERIOUS.

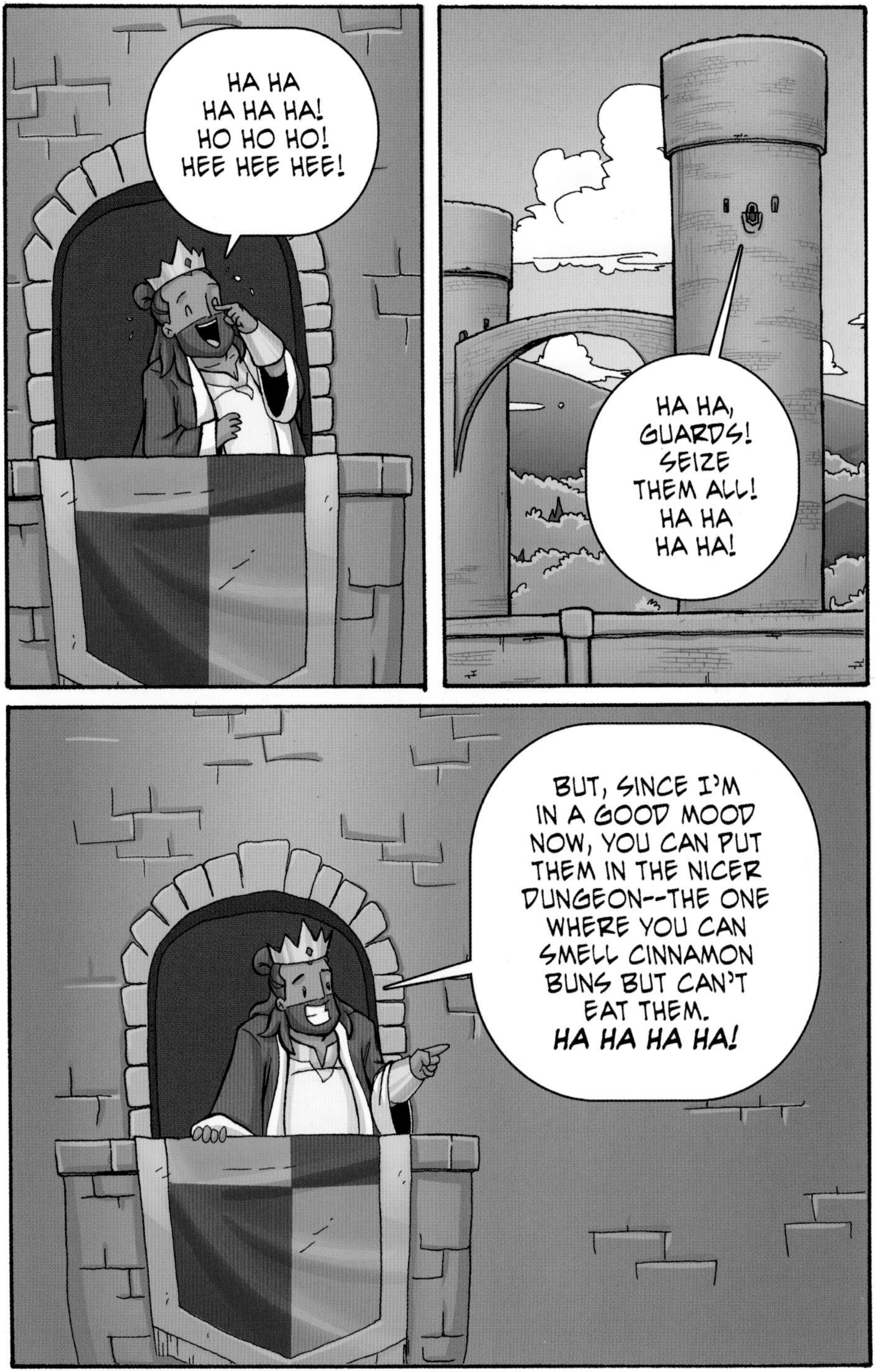
HA HA
HA HA HA!
HO HO HO!
HEE HEE HEE!
HA HA,
GUARDS!
SEIZE
THEM ALL!
HA HA
HA HA!
BUT, SINCE I'M IN A GOOD MOOD NOW, YOU CAN PUT THEM IN THE NICER DUNGEON--THE ONE WHERE YOU CAN SMELL CINNAMON BUNS BUT CAN'T EAT THEM.
HA HA HA HA!

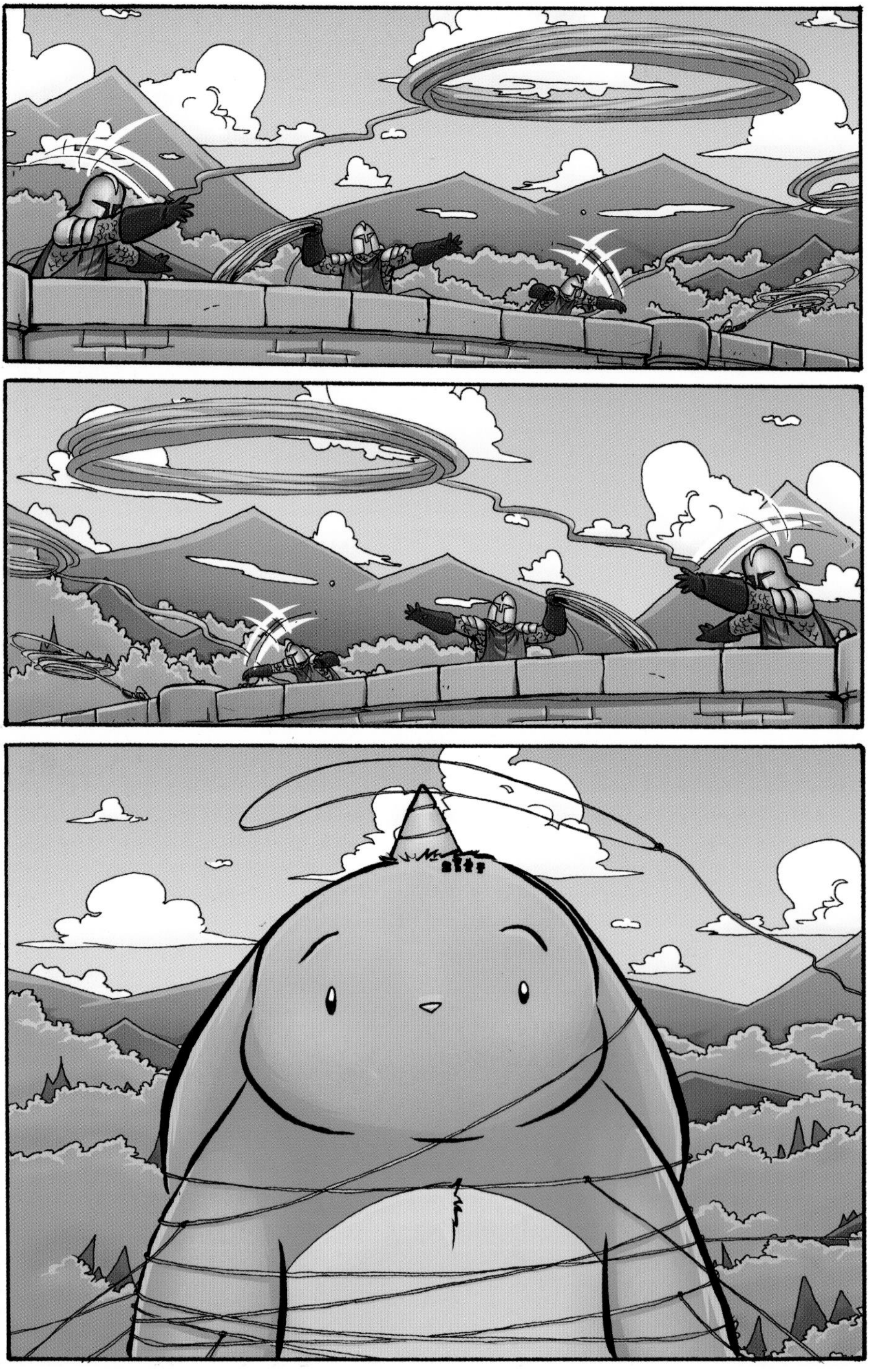

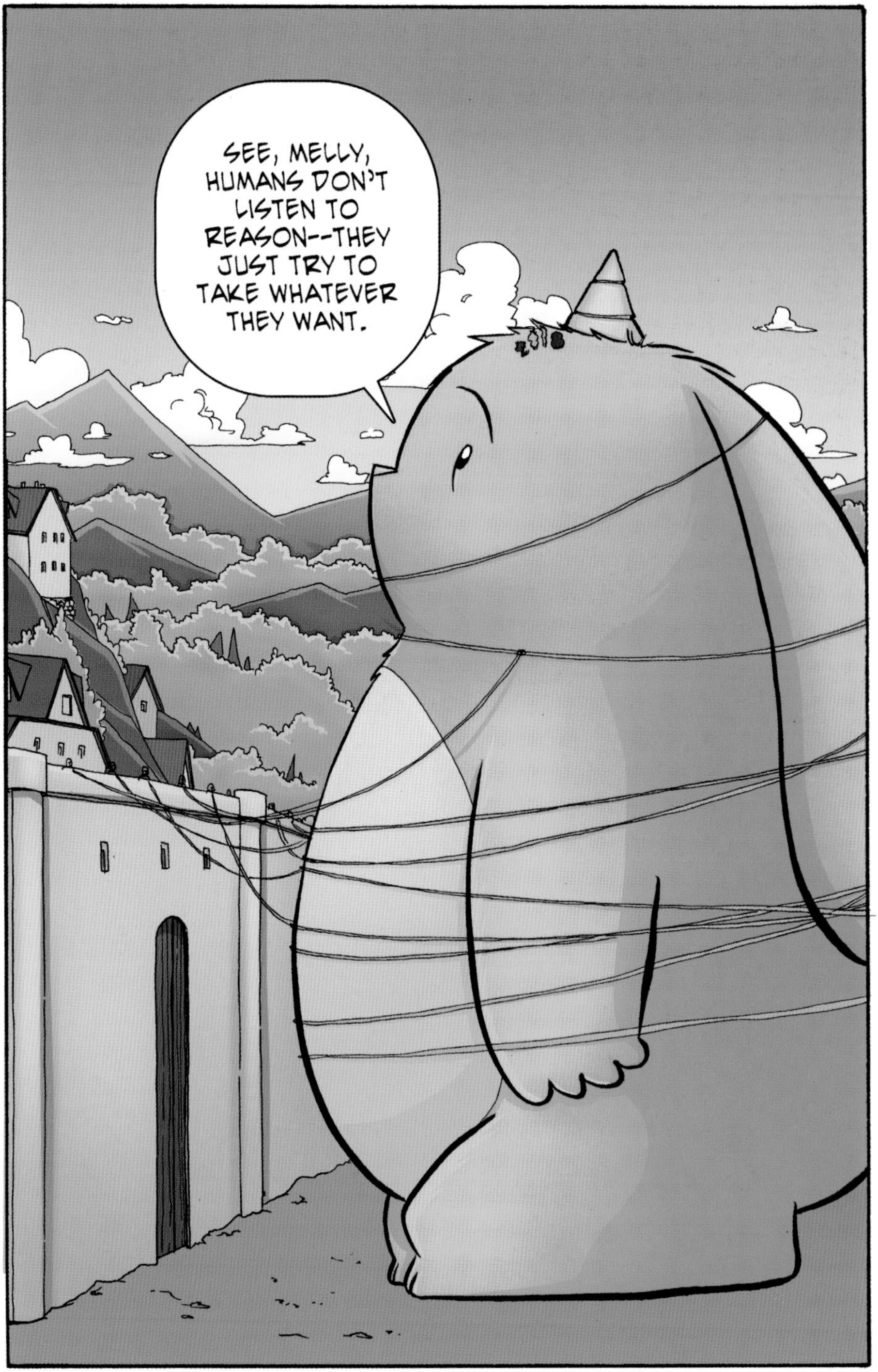
SEE, MELLY, HUMANS DON'T LISTEN TO REASON--THEY JUST TRY TO TAKE WHATEVER THEY WANT.

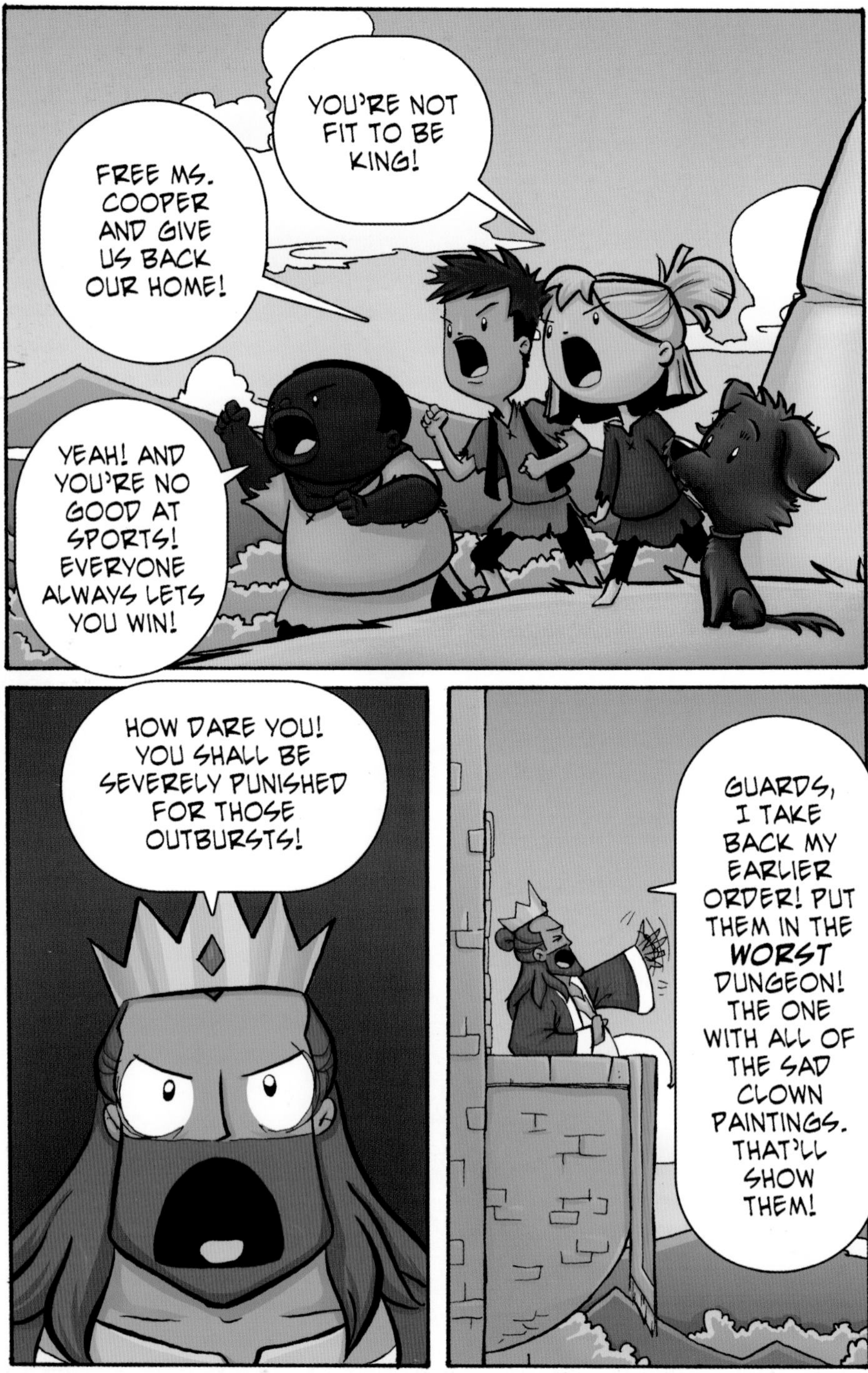
FREE MS. COOPER AND GIVE US BACK OUR HOME!
YOU'RE NOT FIT TO BE KING!
YEAH! AND YOU'RE NO GOOD AT SPORTS! EVERYONE ALWAYS LETS YOU WIN!
HOW DARE YOU! YOU SHALL BE SEVERELY PUNISHED FOR THOSE OUTBURSTS!
GUARDS, I TAKE BACK MY EARLIER ORDER! PUT THEM IN THE **WORST** DUNGEON! THE ONE WITH ALL OF THE SAD CLOWN PAINTINGS. THAT'LL SHOW THEM!

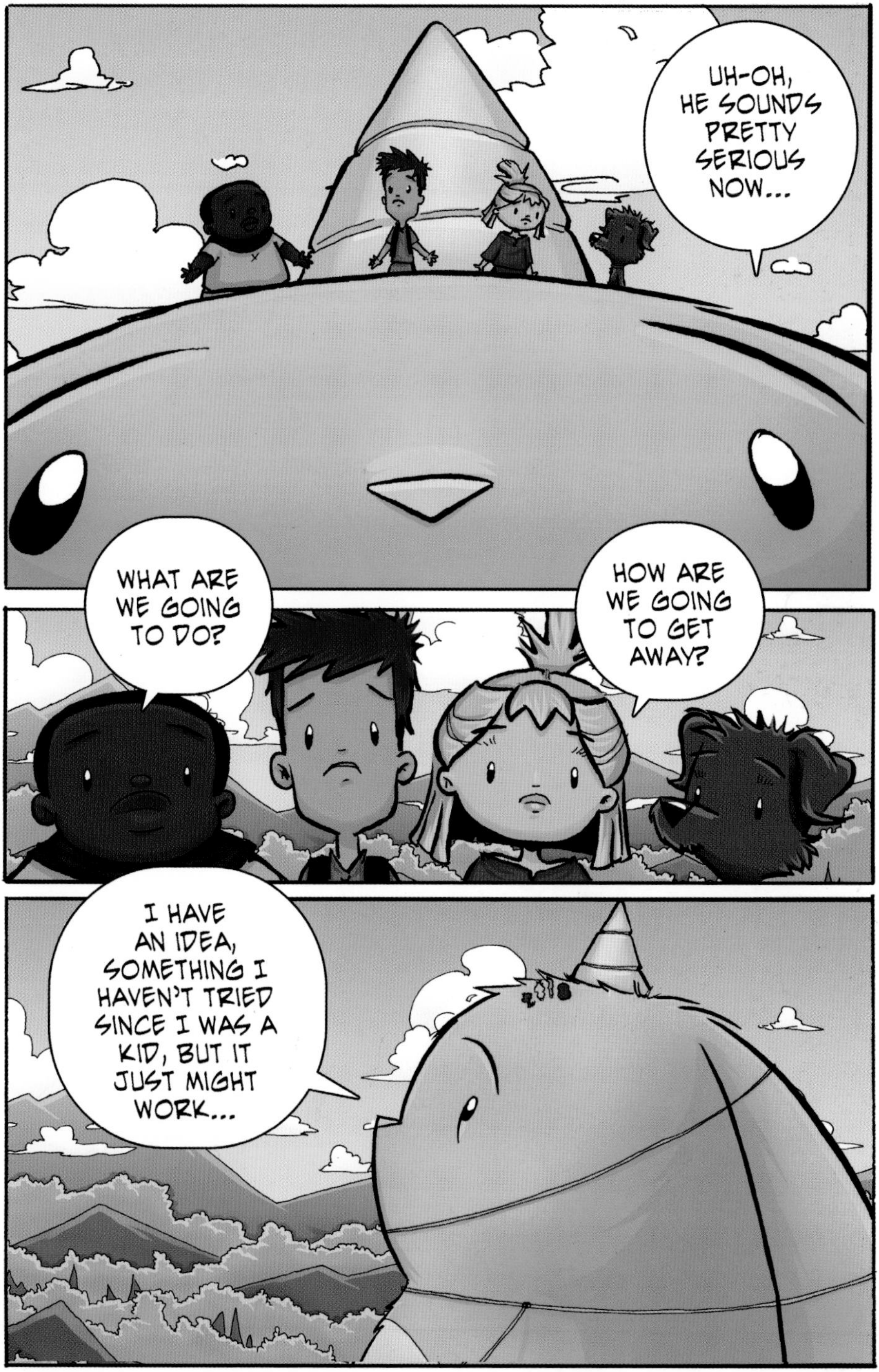
UH-OH, HE SOUNDS PRETTY SERIOUS NOW...
WHAT ARE WE GOING TO DO?
HOW ARE WE GOING TO GET AWAY?
I HAVE AN IDEA, SOMETHING I HAVEN'T TRIED SINCE I WAS A KID, BUT IT JUST MIGHT WORK...

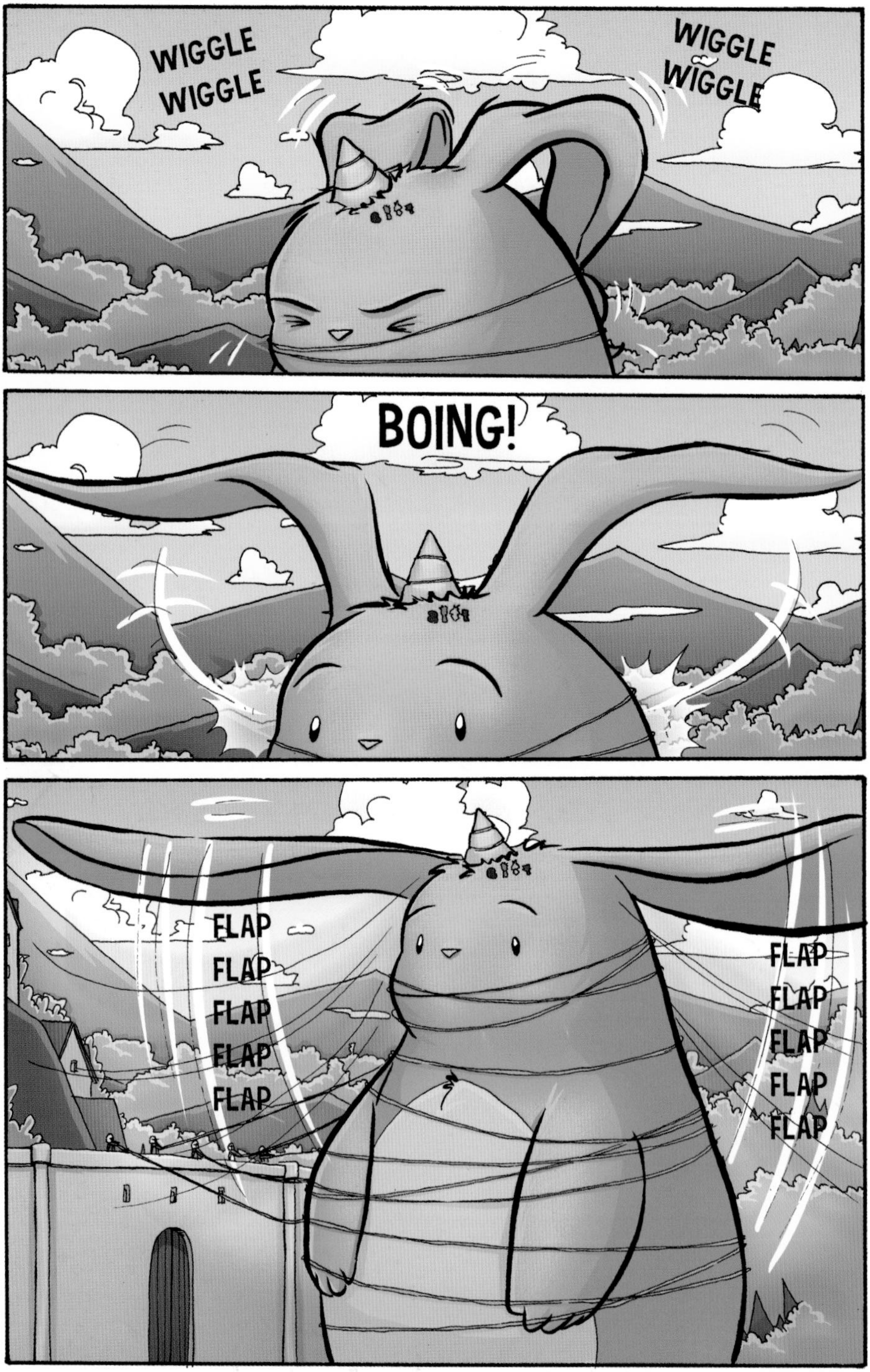
WIGGLE
WIGGLE
WIGGLE
WIGGLE
BOING!
FLAP
FLAP
FLAP
FLAP
FLAP
FLAP
FLAP
FLAP
FLAP
FLAP

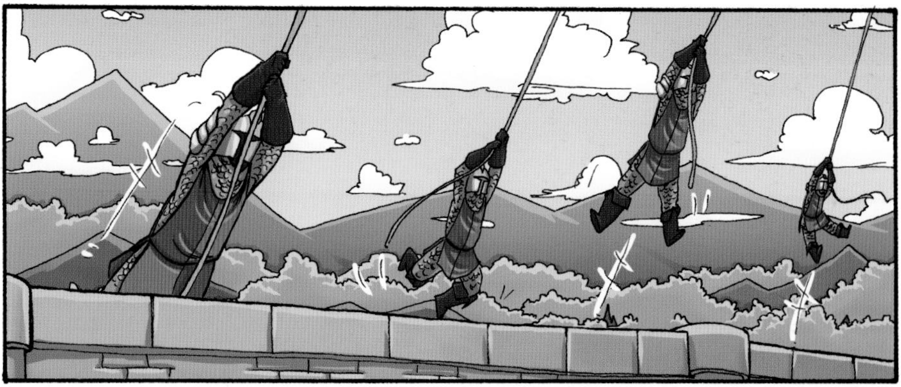

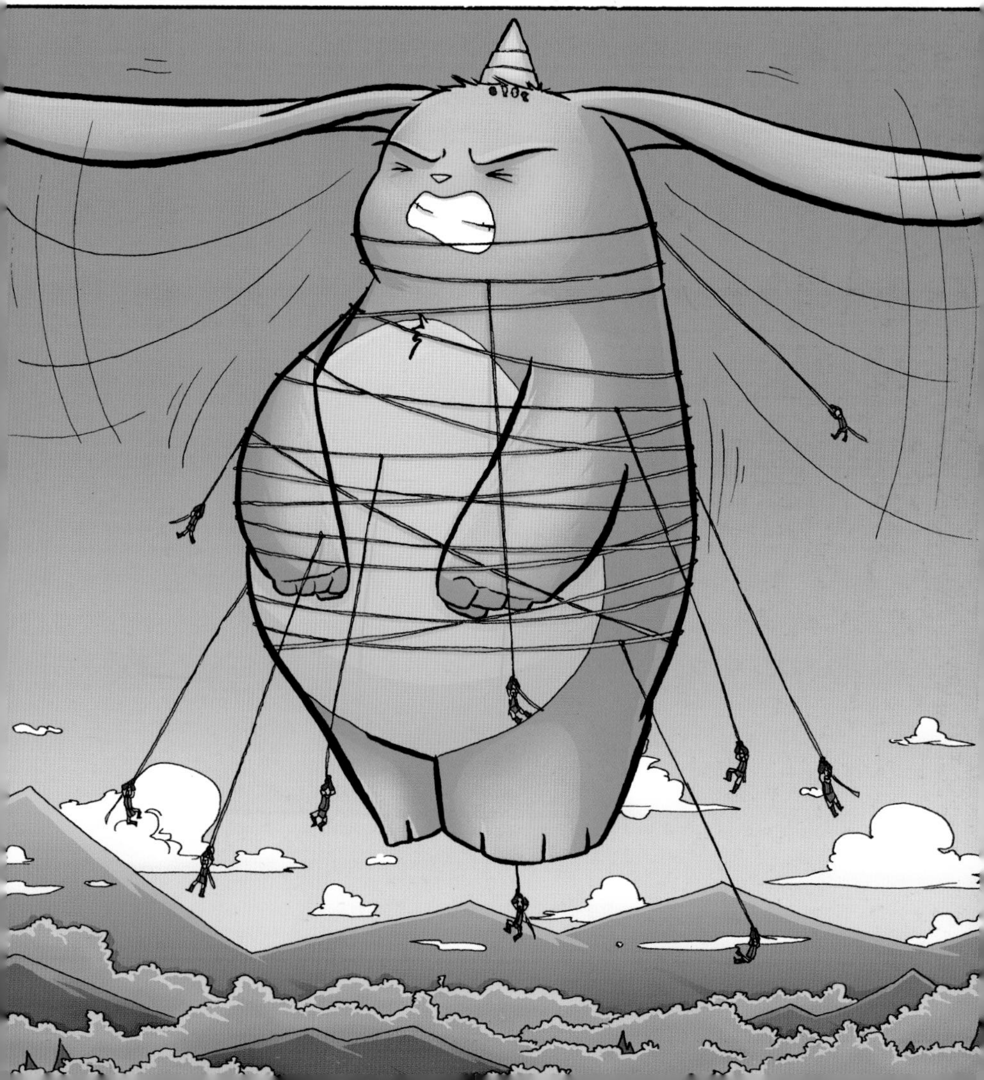

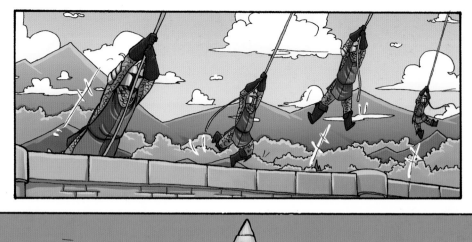

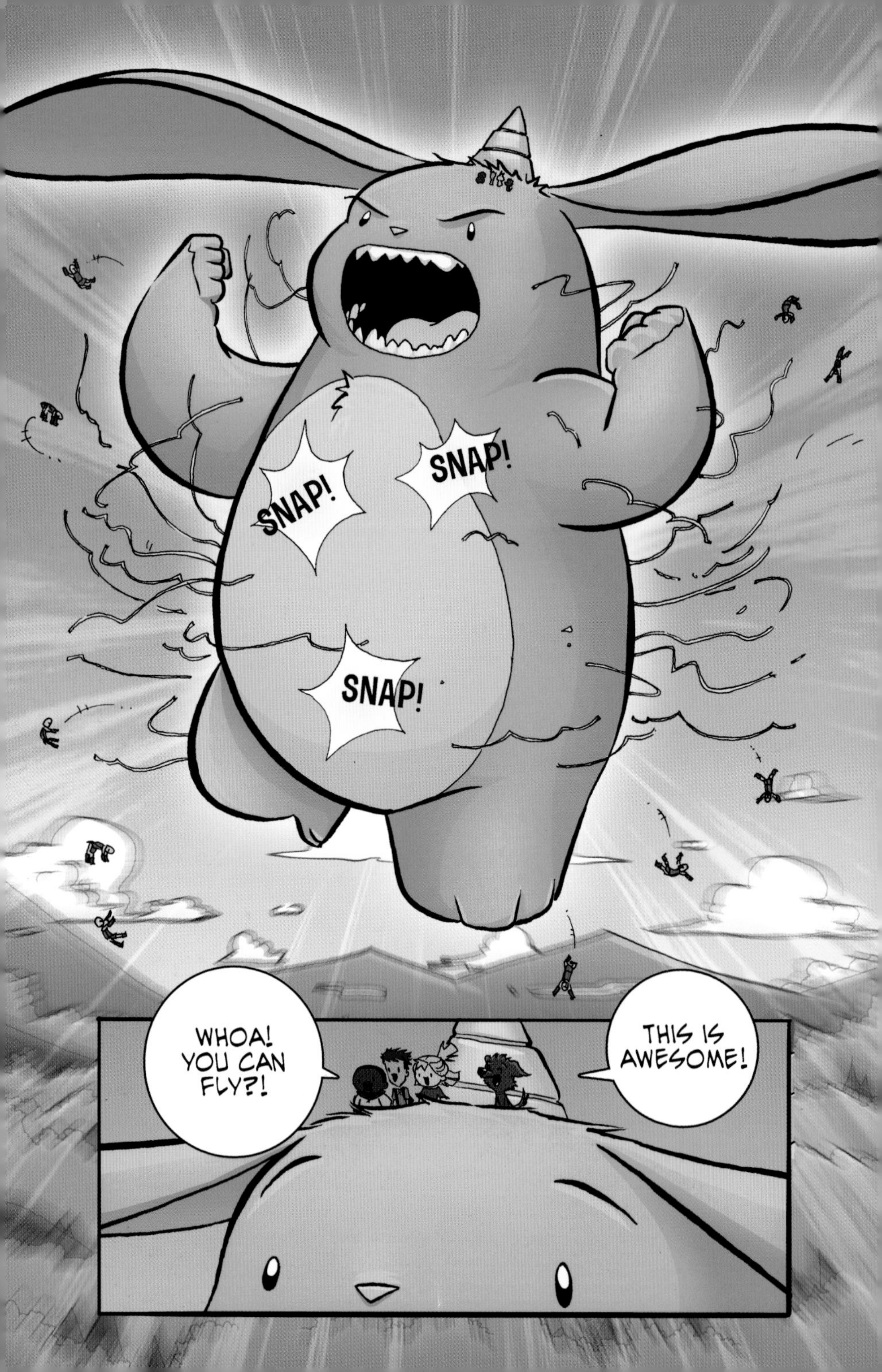
SNAP!
SNAP!
SNAP!
WHOA! YOU CAN FLY?!
THIS IS AWESOME!

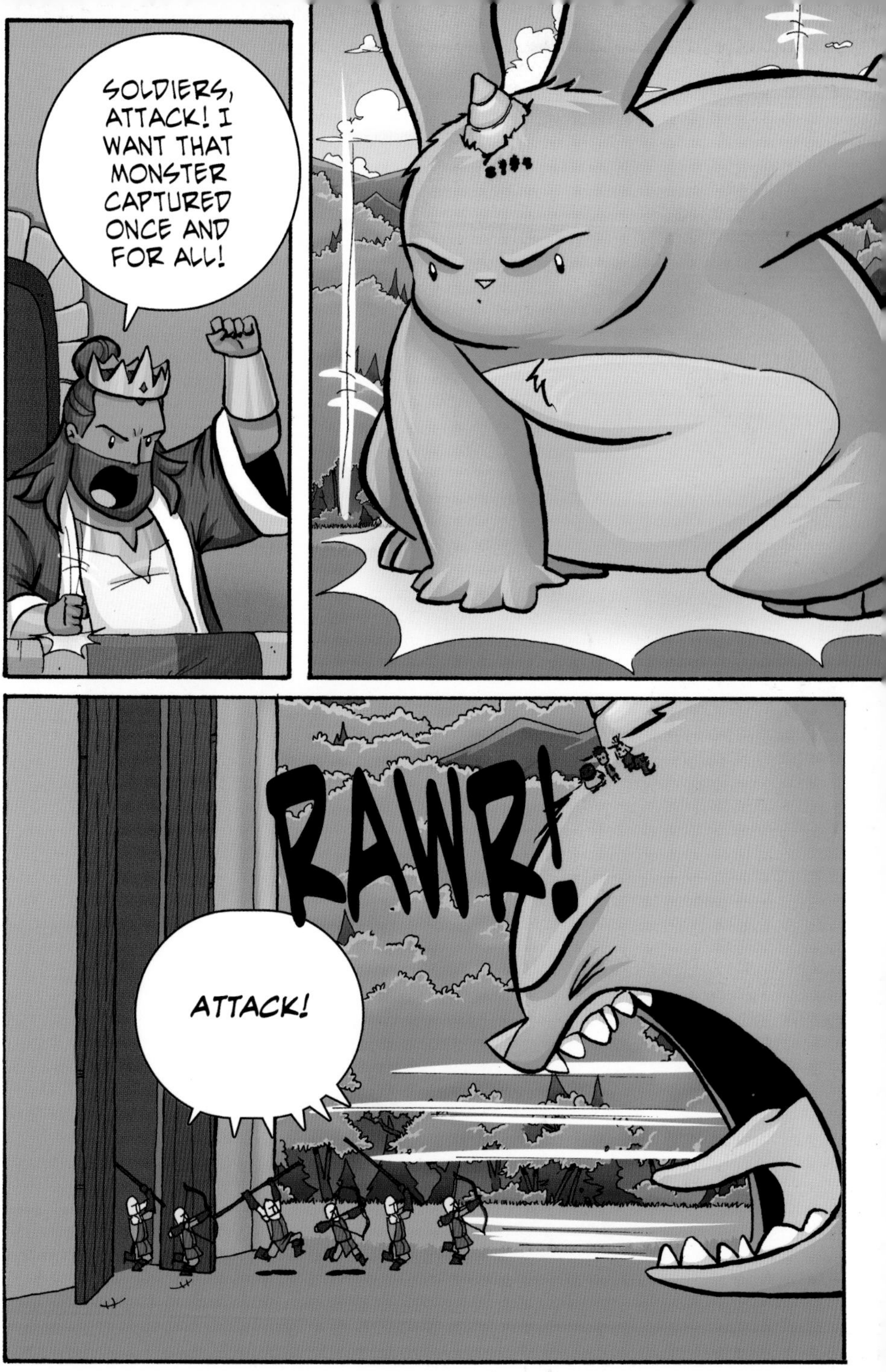
SOLDIERS, ATTACK! I WANT THAT MONSTER CAPTURED ONCE AND FOR ALL!
RAWR!
ATTACK!

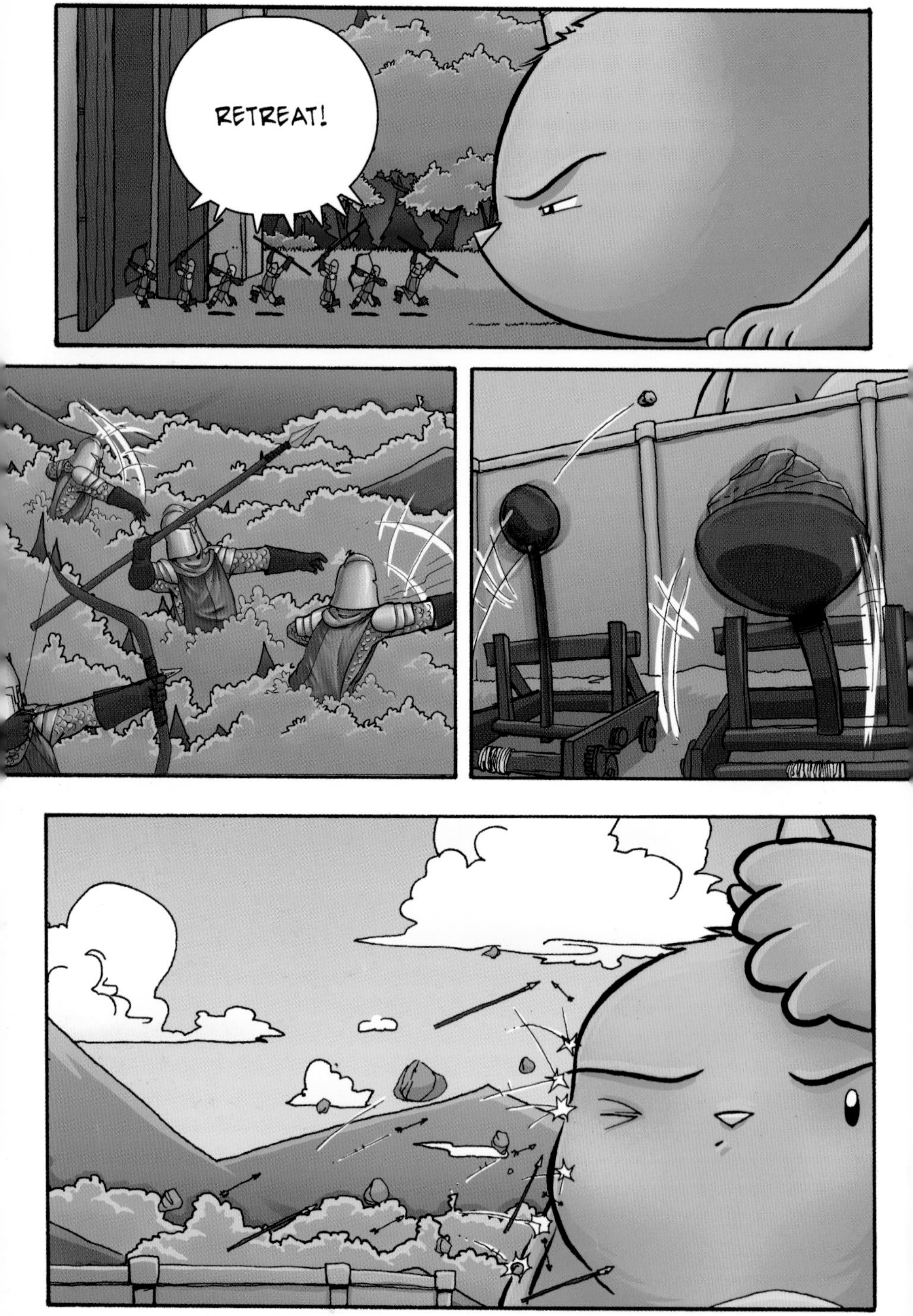
RETREAT!

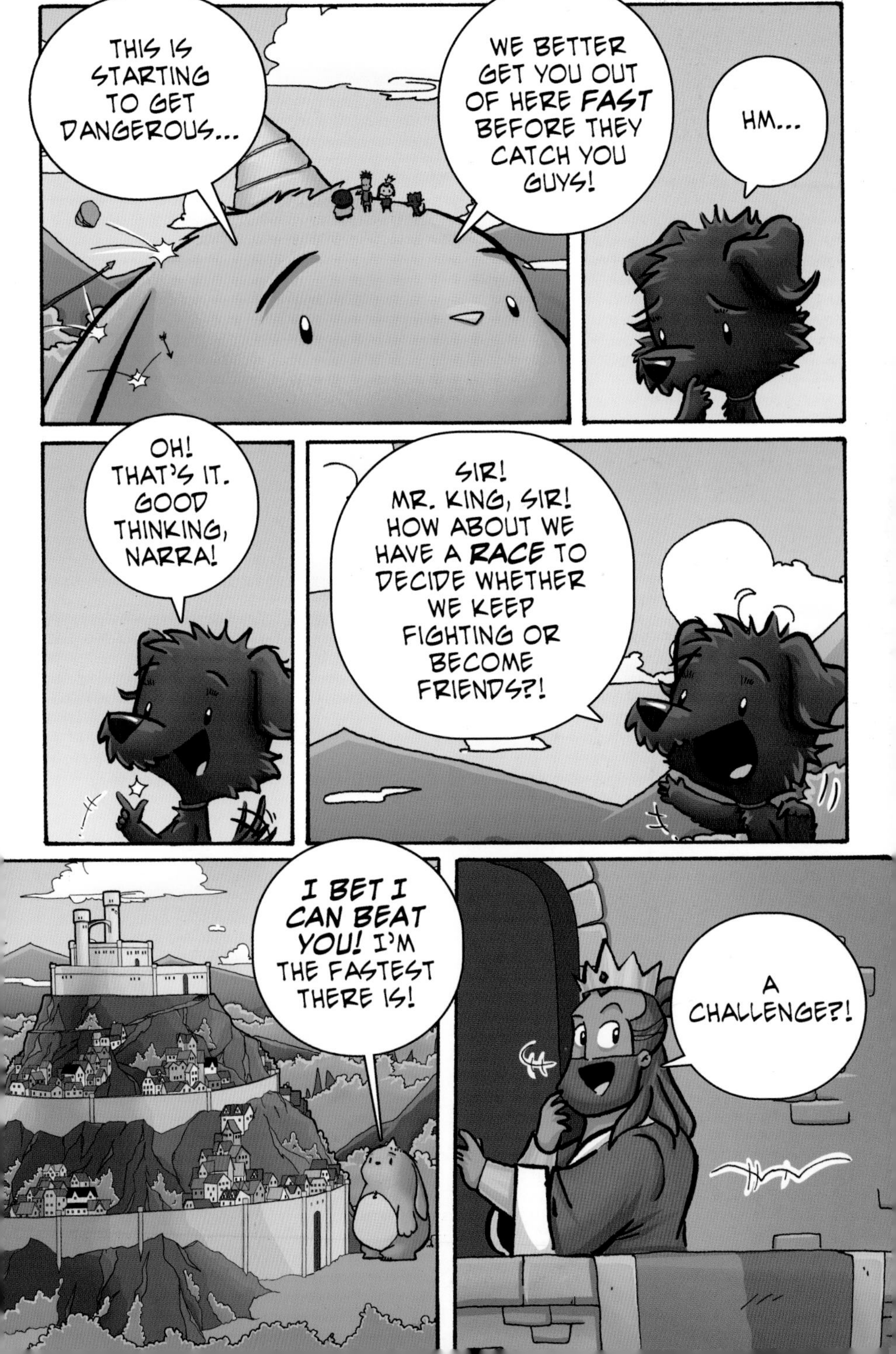
THIS IS STARTING TO GET DANGEROUS...
WE BETTER GET YOU OUT OF HERE FAST BEFORE THEY CATCH YOU GUYS!
HM...
OH! THAT'S IT. GOOD THINKING, NARRA!
SIR! MR. KING, SIR! HOW ABOUT WE HAVE A RACE TO DECIDE WHETHER WE KEEP FIGHTING OR BECOME FRIENDS?!
I BET I CAN BEAT YOU! I'M THE FASTEST THERE IS!
A CHALLENGE?!

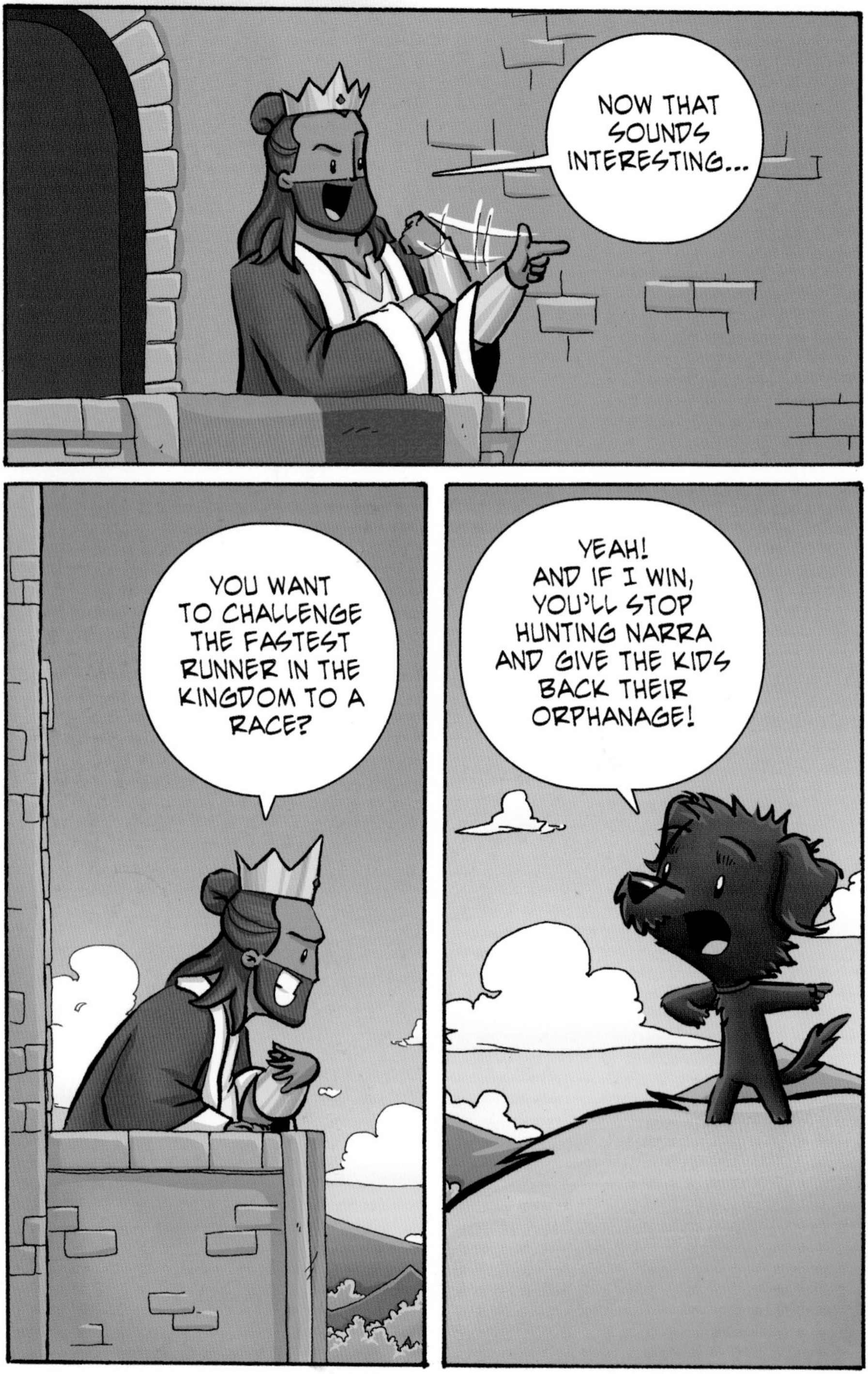
NOW THAT SOUNDS INTERESTING...
YOU WANT TO CHALLENGE THE FASTEST RUNNER IN THE KINGDOM TO A RACE?
YEAH! AND IF I WIN, YOU'LL STOP HUNTING NARRA AND GIVE THE KIDS BACK THEIR ORPHANAGE!

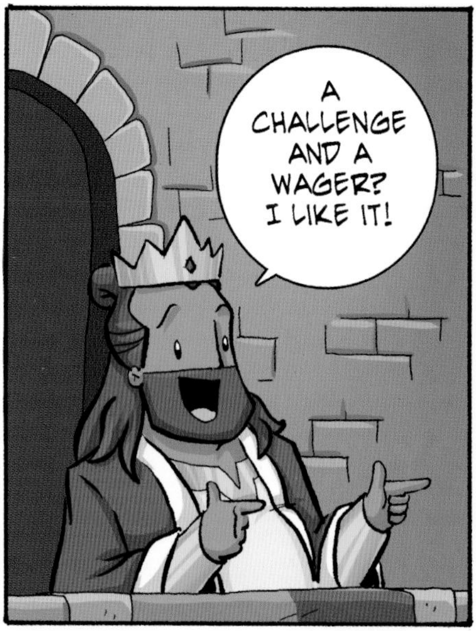
A CHALLENGE AND A WAGER? I LIKE IT!

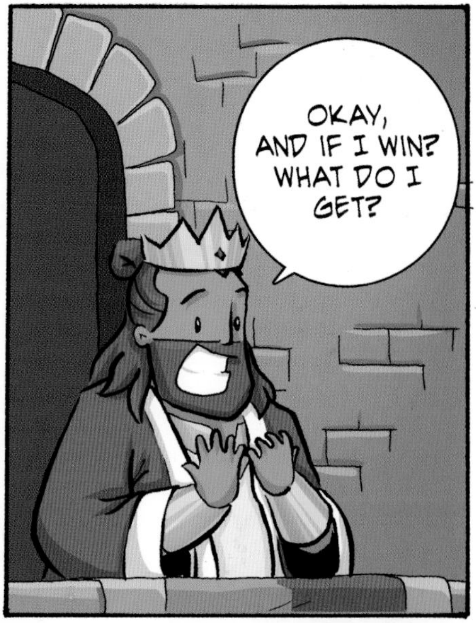
OKAY, AND IF I WIN? WHAT DO I GET?

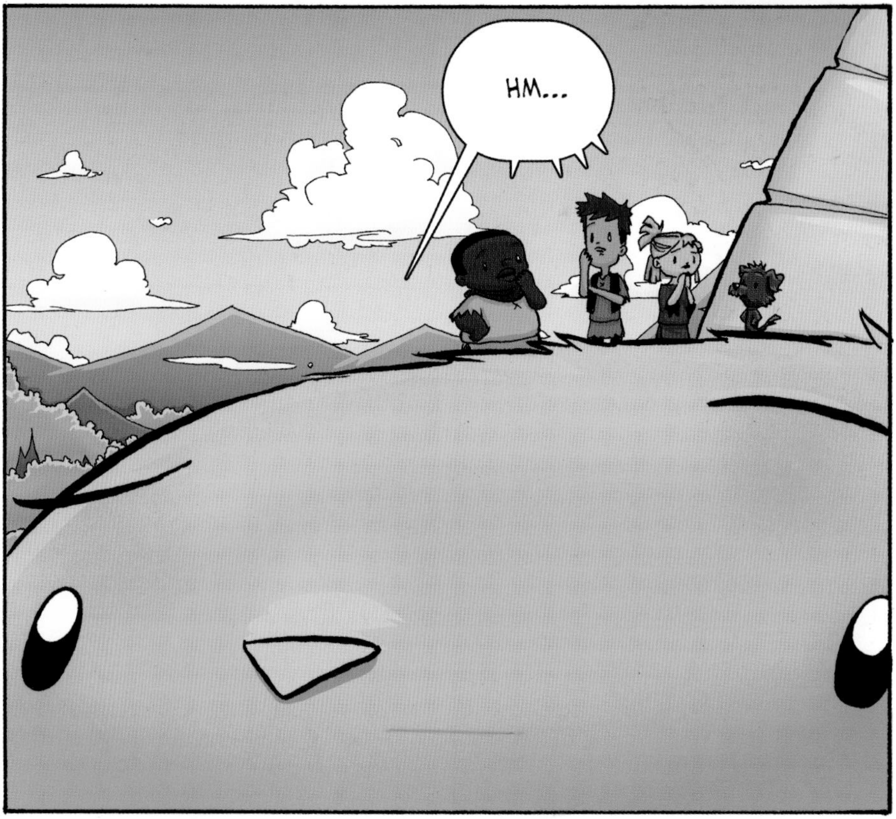
HM...

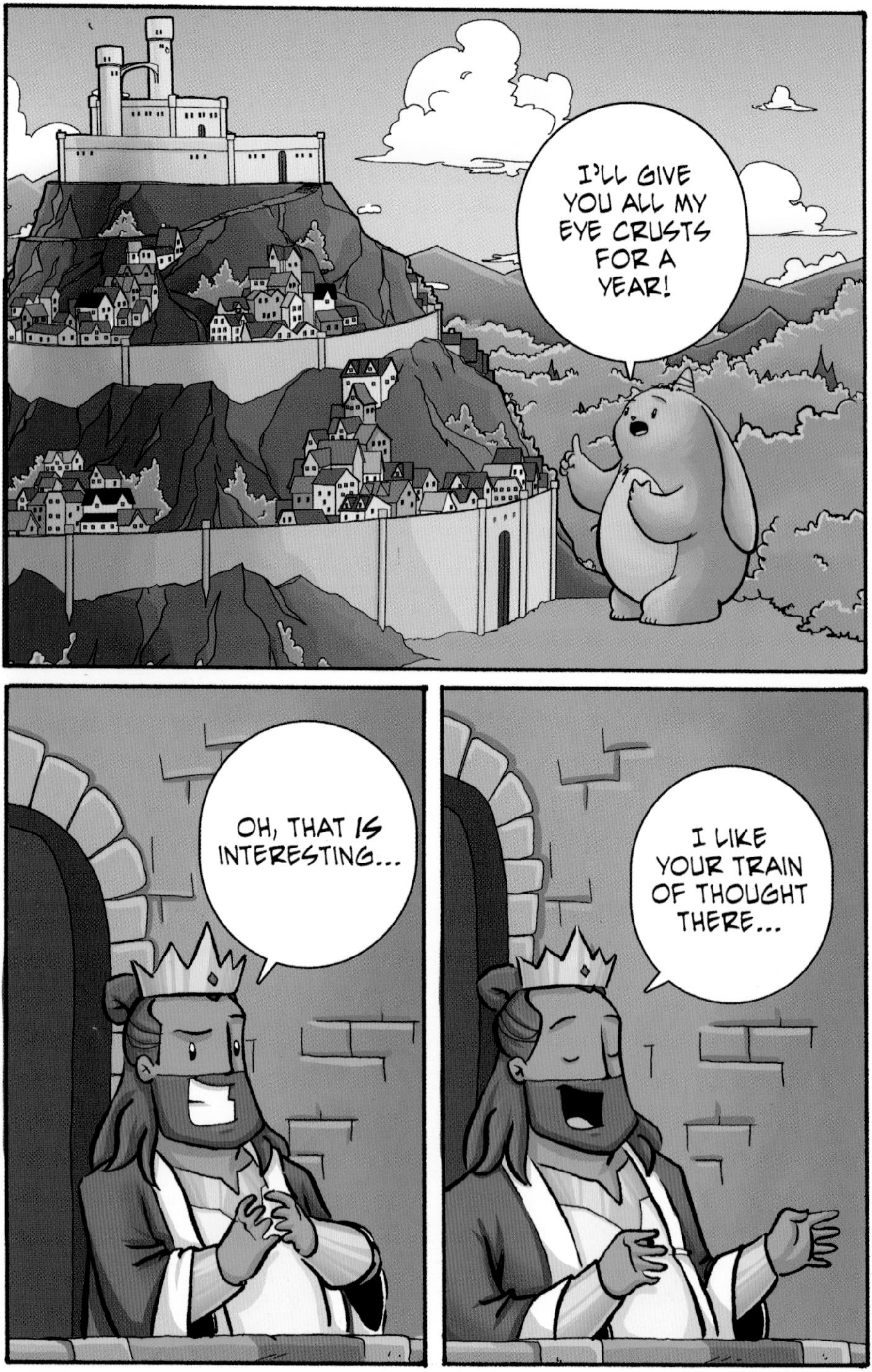
I'LL GIVE YOU ALL MY EYE CRUSTS FOR A YEAR!
OH, THAT IS INTERESTING...
I LIKE YOUR TRAIN OF THOUGHT THERE...

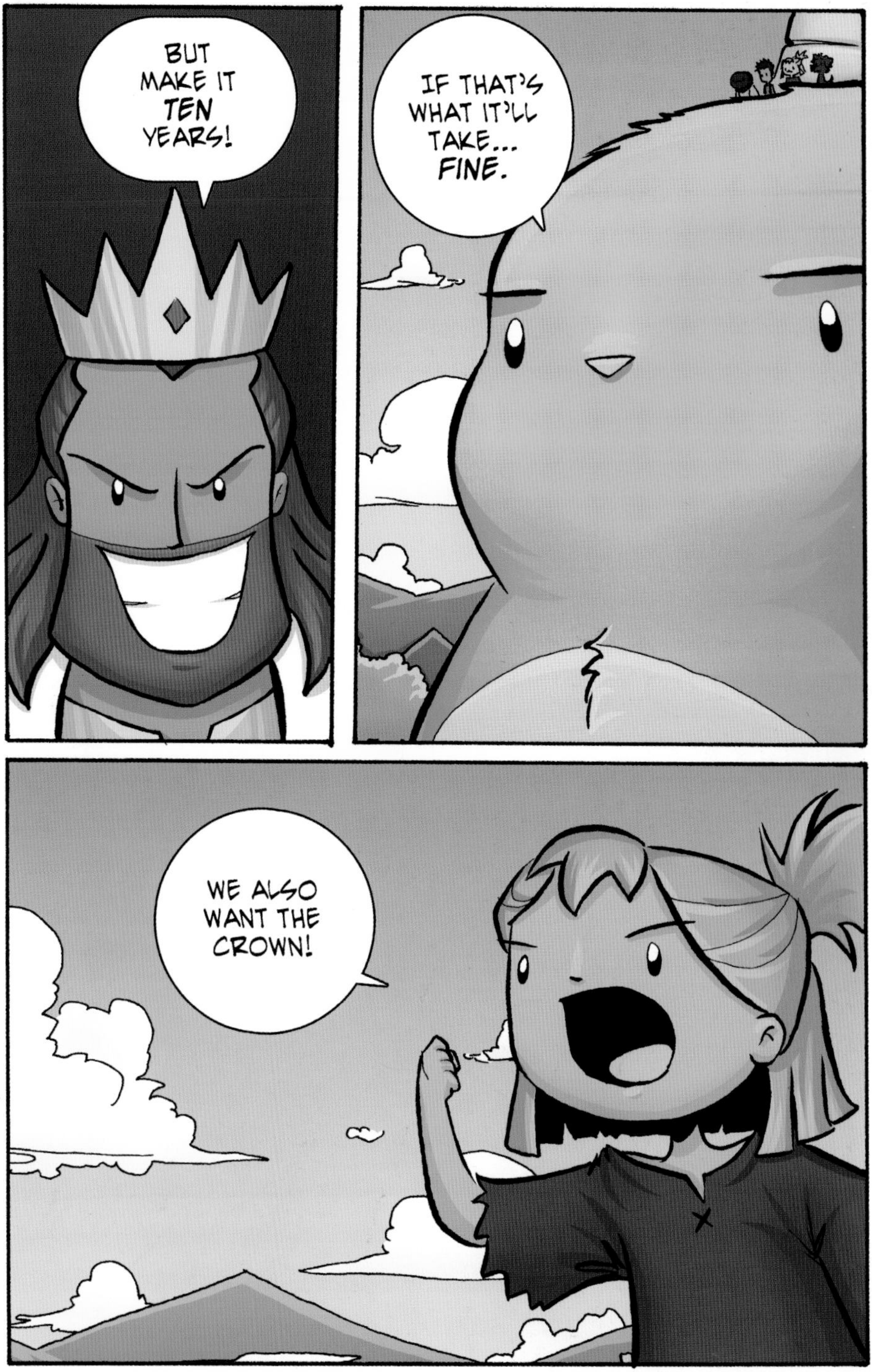
BUT MAKE IT TEN YEARS!
IF THAT'S WHAT IT'LL TAKE... FINE.
WE ALSO WANT THE CROWN!

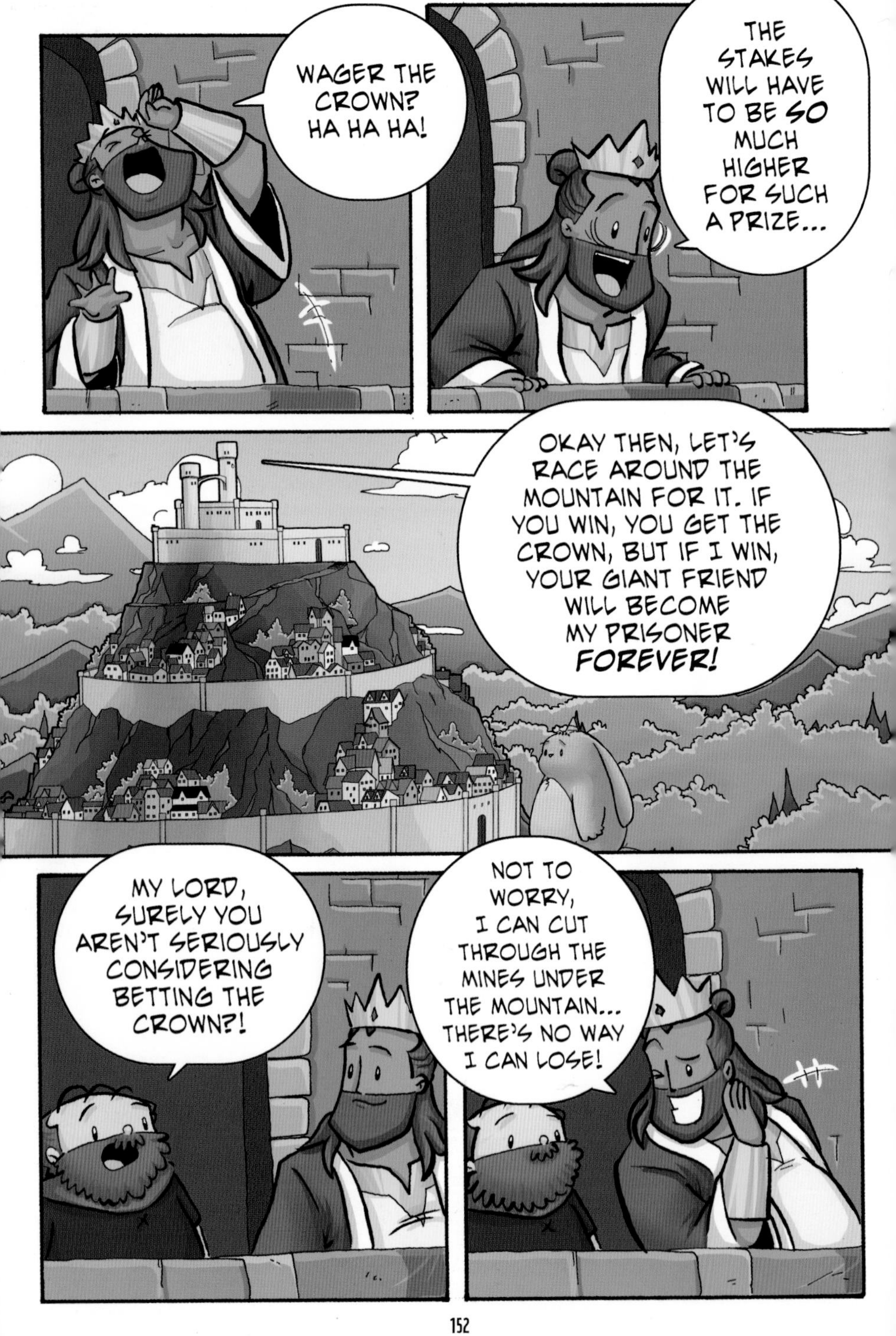
WAGER THE CROWN? HA HA HA!
THE STAKES WILL HAVE TO BE **SO** MUCH HIGHER FOR SUCH A PRIZE...
OKAY THEN, LET'S RACE AROUND THE MOUNTAIN FOR IT. IF YOU WIN, YOU GET THE CROWN, BUT IF I WIN, YOUR GIANT FRIEND WILL BECOME MY PRISONER ***FOREVER!***
MY LORD, SURELY YOU AREN'T SERIOUSLY CONSIDERING BETTING THE CROWN?!
NOT TO WORRY, I CAN CUT THROUGH THE MINES UNDER THE MOUNTAIN... THERE'S NO WAY I CAN LOSE!

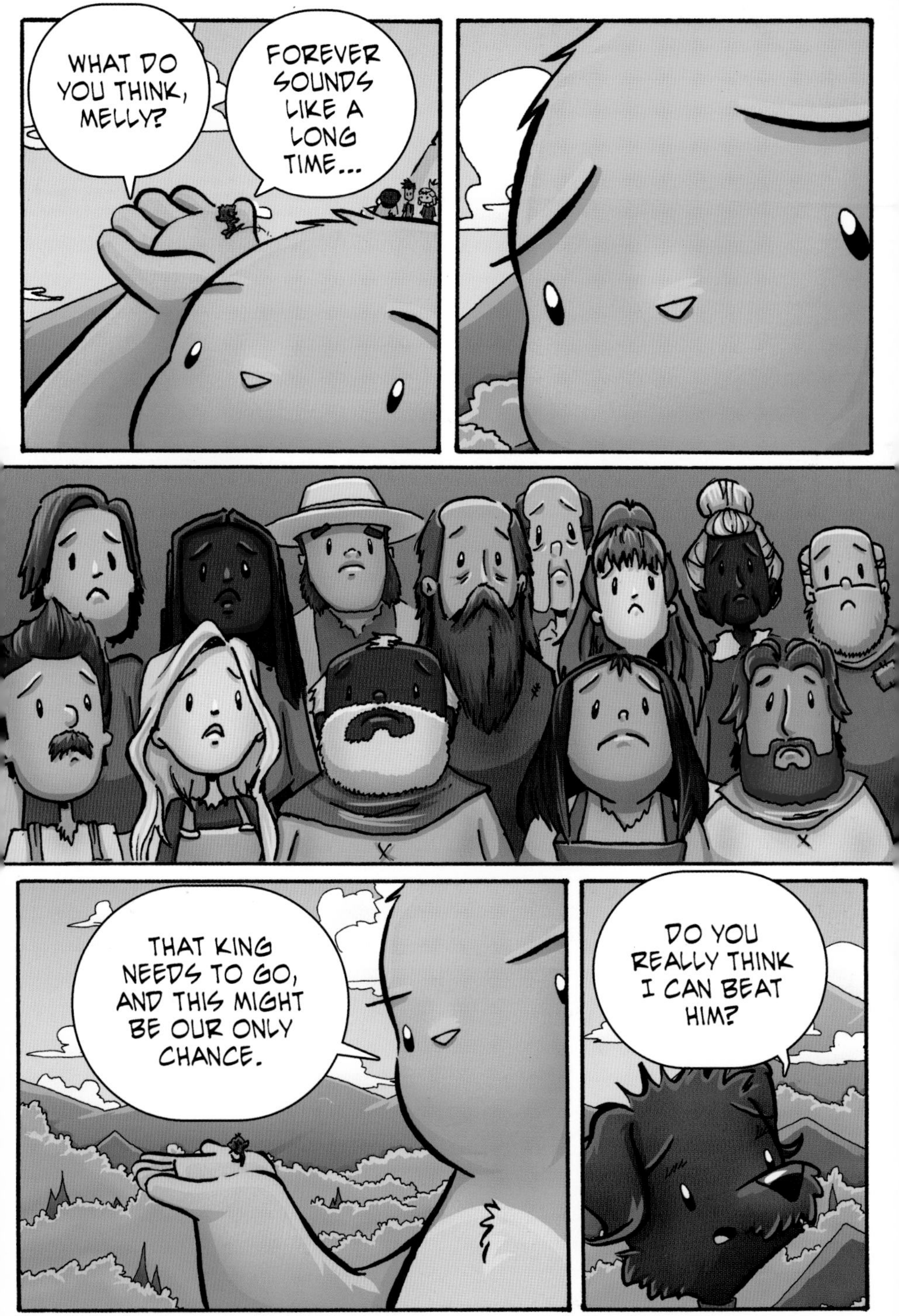
WHAT DO YOU THINK, MELLY?
FOREVER SOUNDS LIKE A LONG TIME...
THAT KING NEEDS TO GO, AND THIS MIGHT BE OUR ONLY CHANCE.
DO YOU REALLY THINK I CAN BEAT HIM?

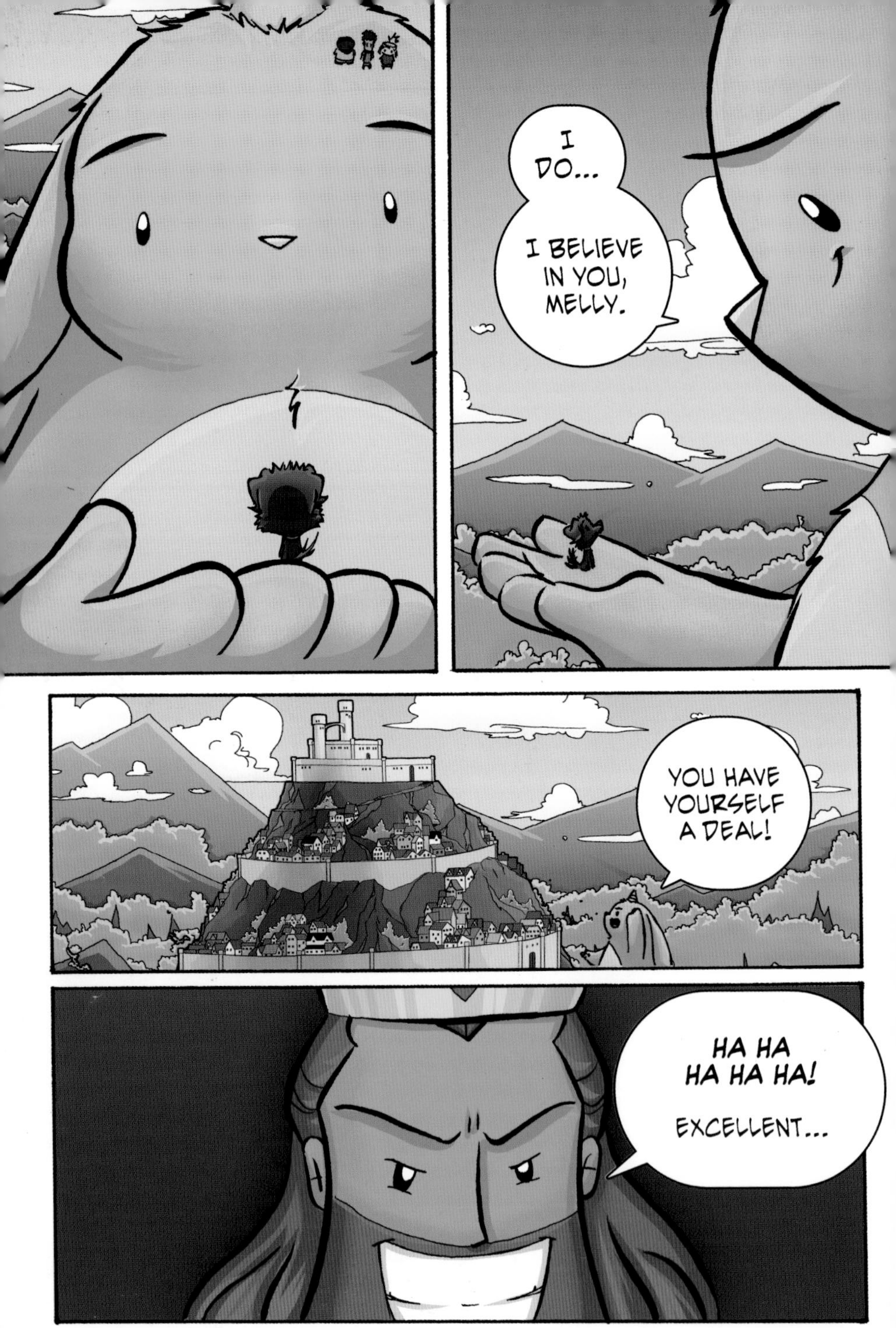
I DO...
I BELIEVE IN YOU, MELLY.
YOU HAVE YOURSELF A DEAL!
HA HA HA HA HA!
EXCELLENT...

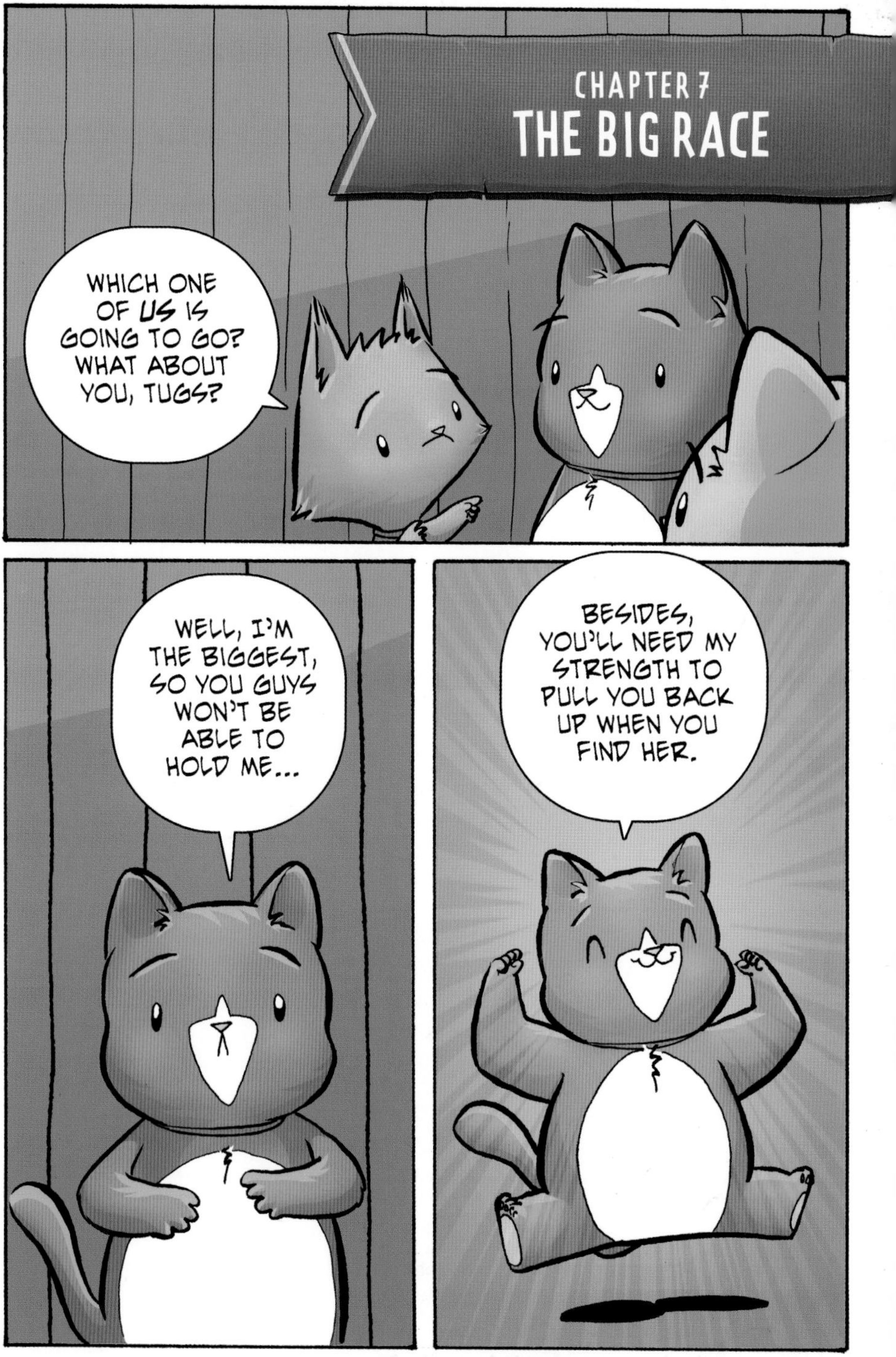
CHAPTER 7
THE BIG RACE
WHICH ONE OF US IS GOING TO GO? WHAT ABOUT YOU, TUGS?
WELL, I'M THE BIGGEST, SO YOU GUYS WON'T BE ABLE TO HOLD ME...
BESIDES, YOU'LL NEED MY STRENGTH TO PULL YOU BACK UP WHEN YOU FIND HER.

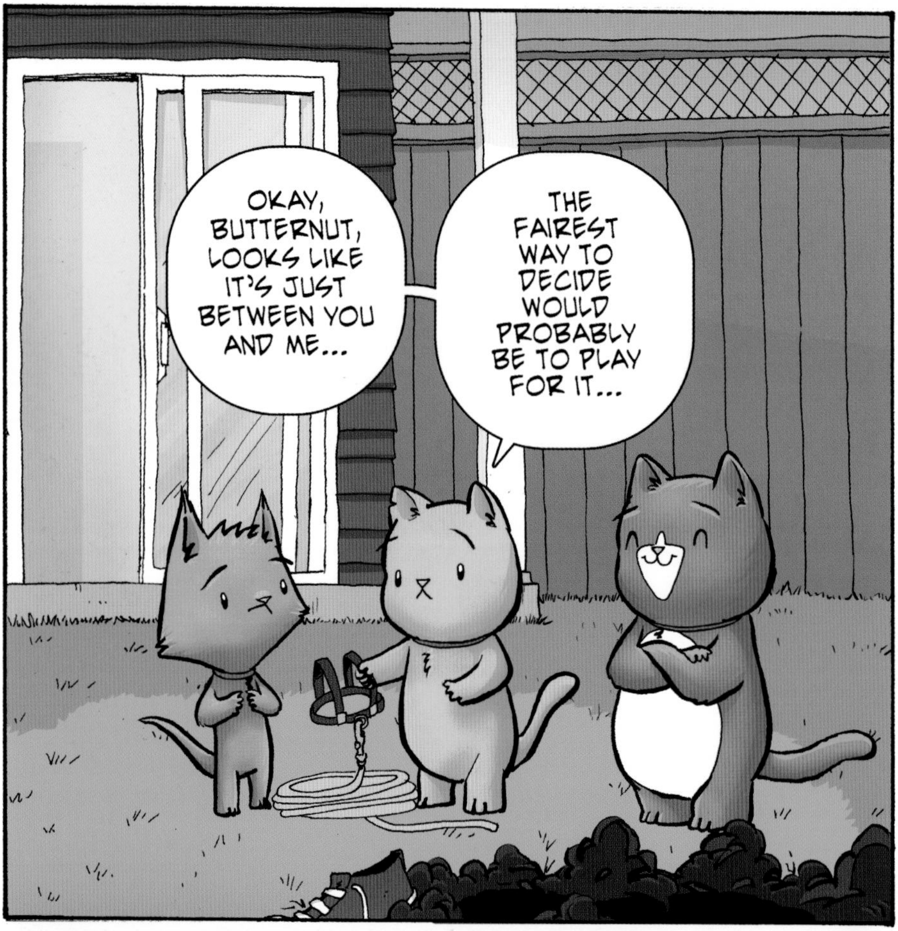
OKAY, BUTTERNUT, LOOKS LIKE IT'S JUST BETWEEN YOU AND ME...
THE FAIREST WAY TO DECIDE WOULD PROBABLY BE TO PLAY FOR IT...

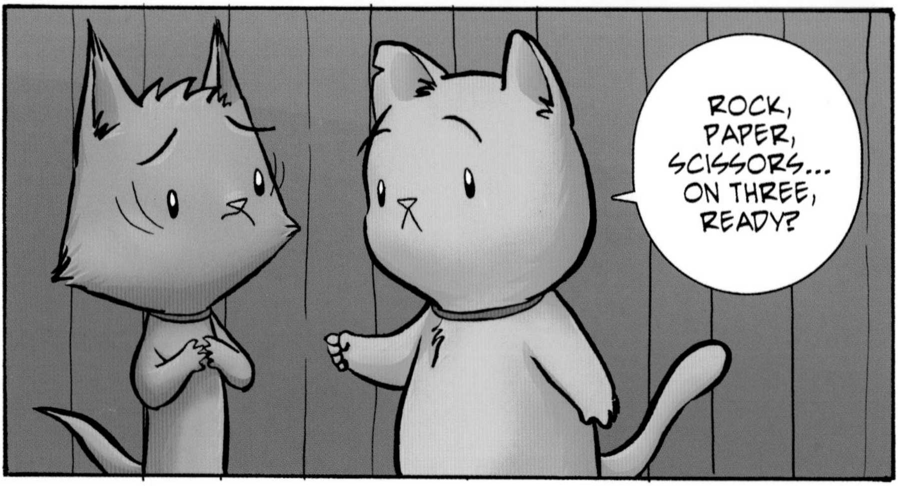
ROCK, PAPER, SCISSORS... ON THREE, READY?

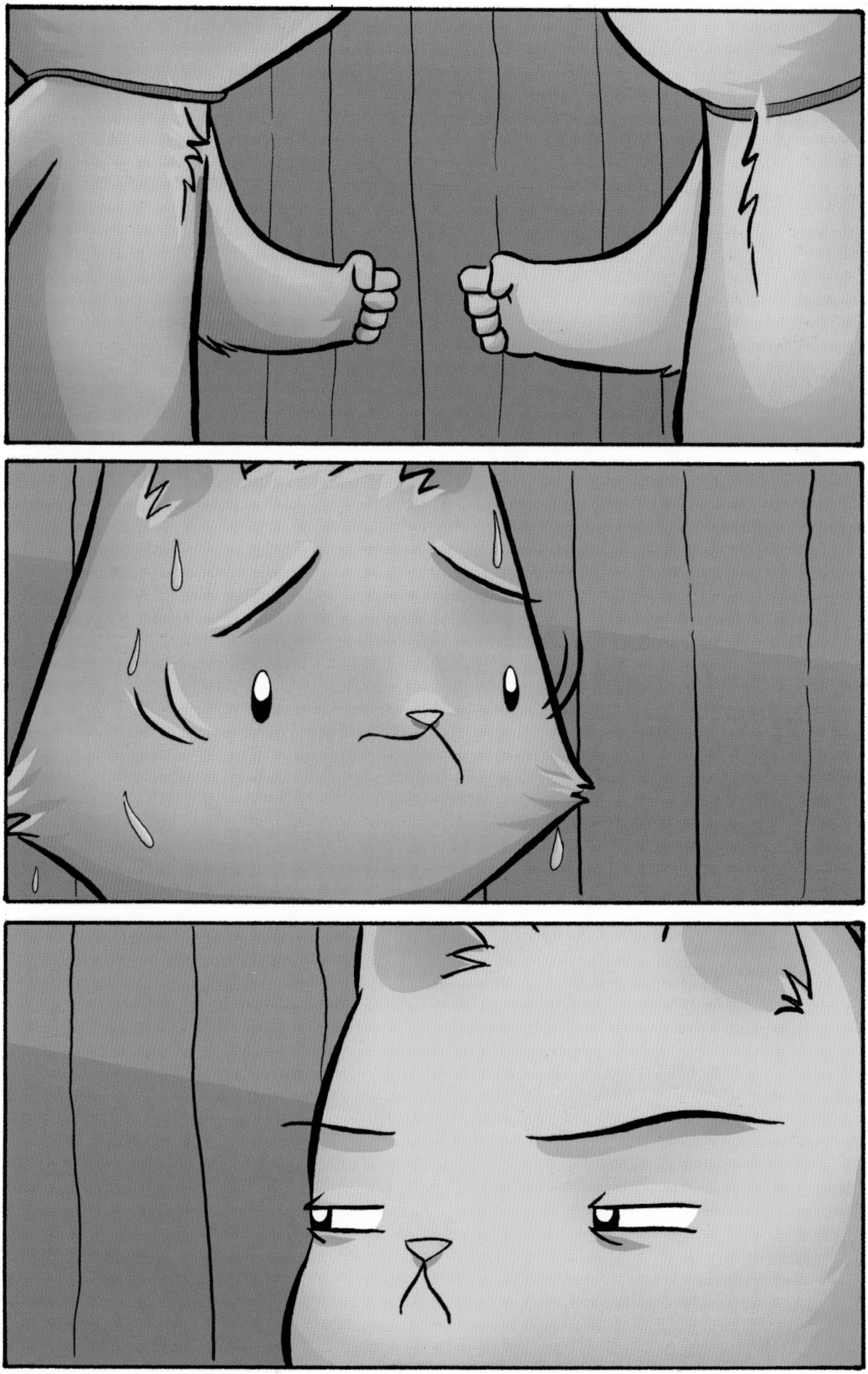

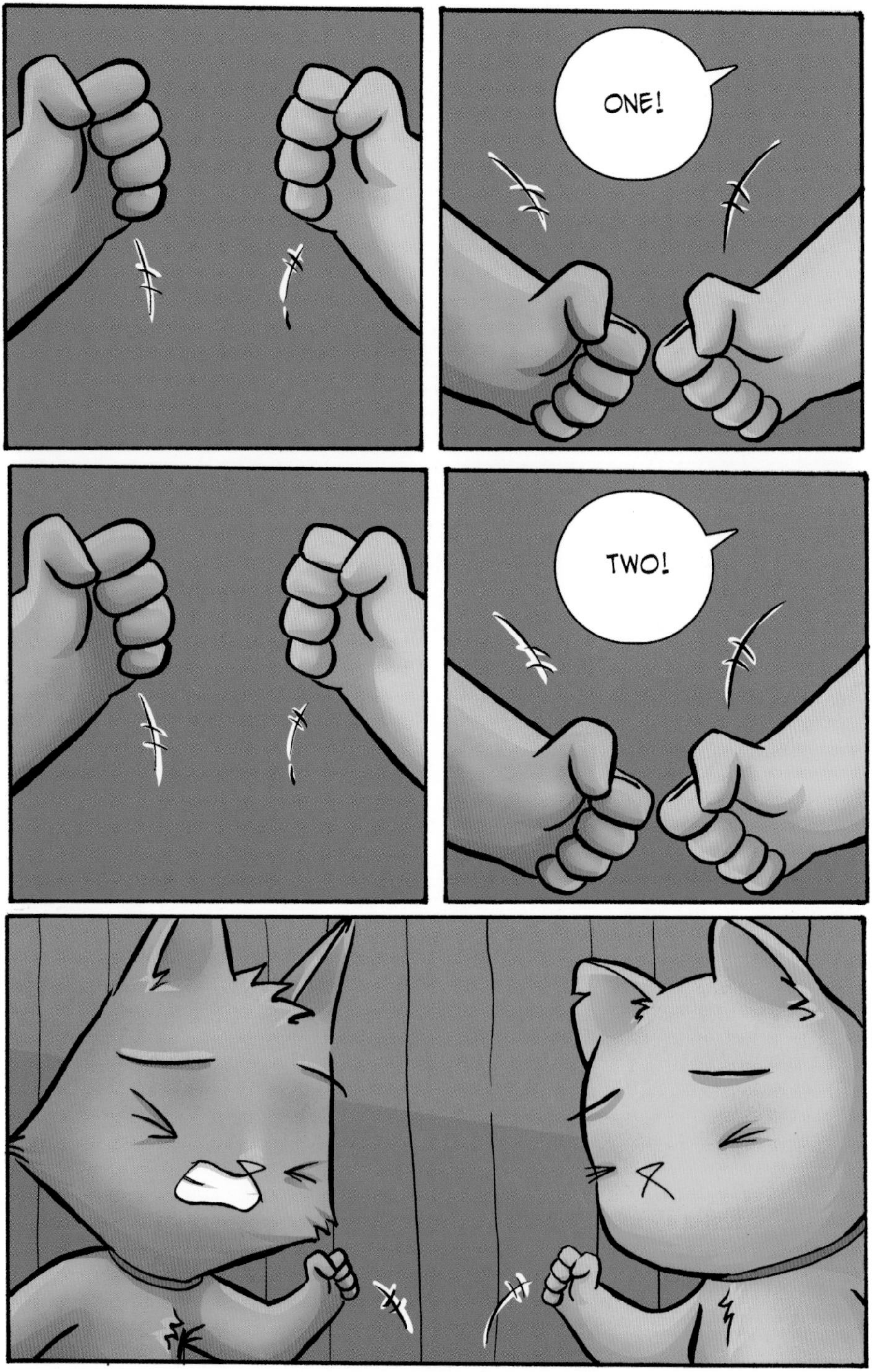
ONE!
TWO!

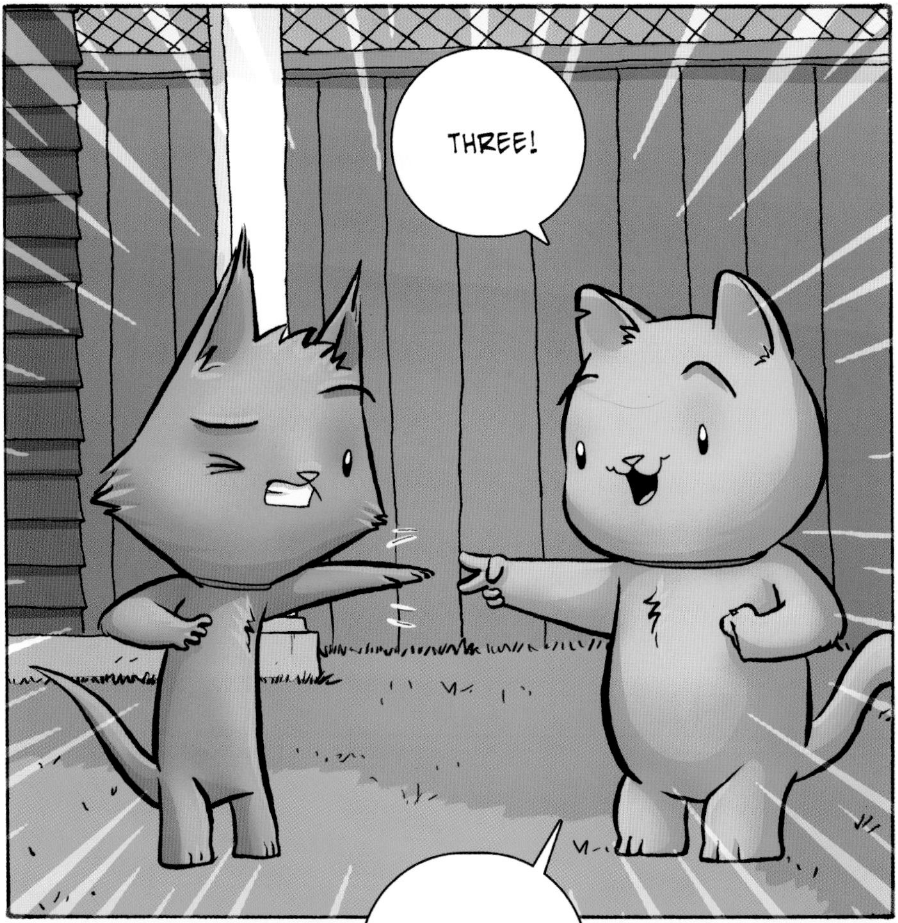
THREE!

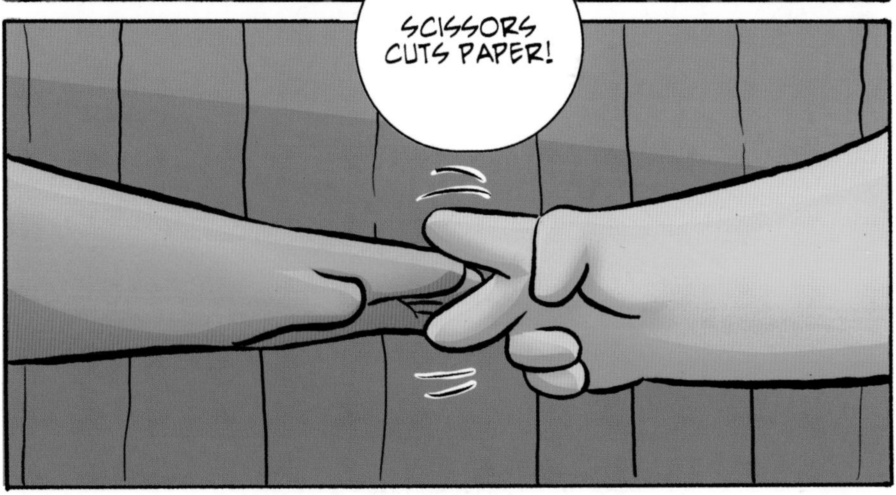
SCISSORS CUTS PAPER!

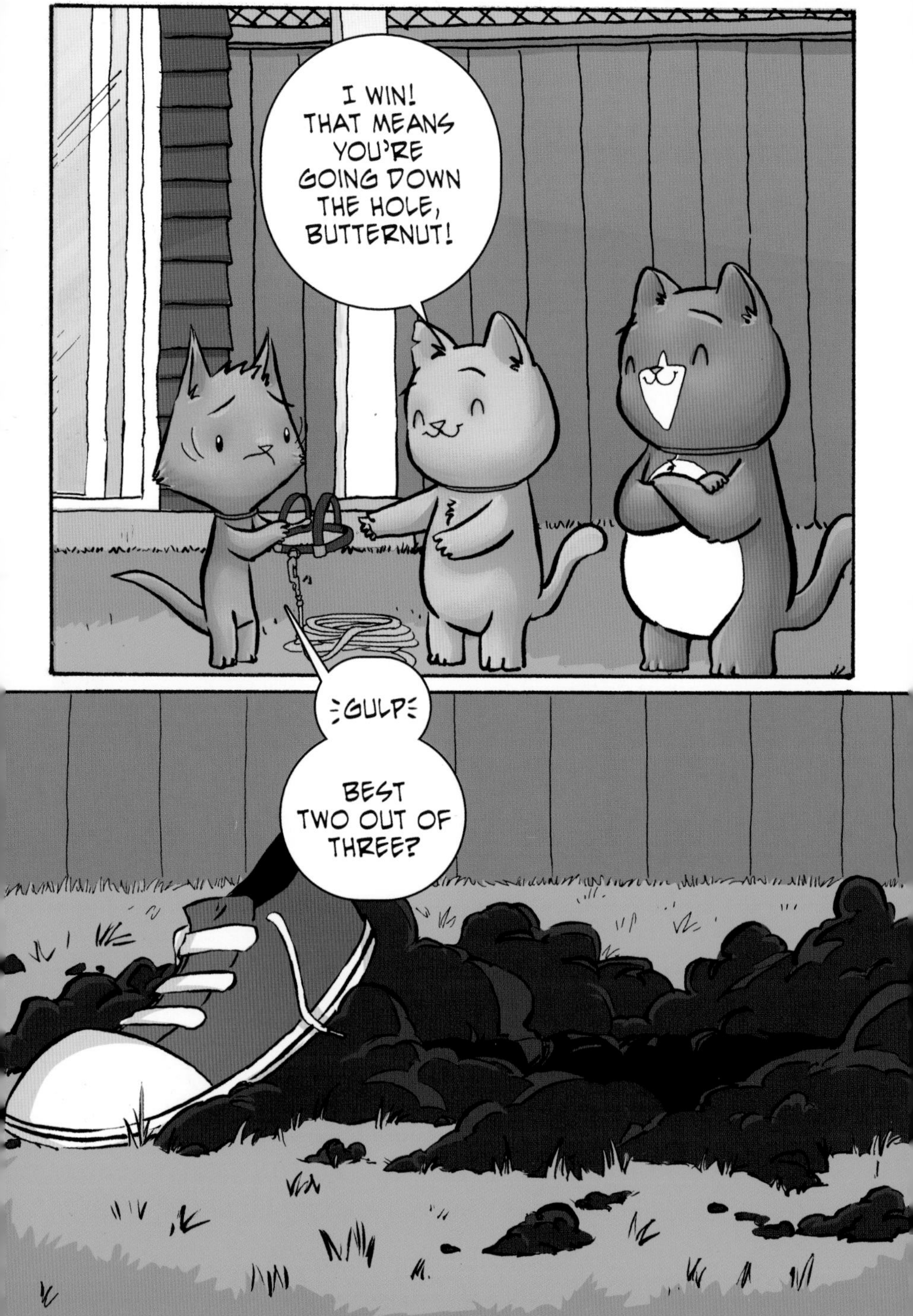
I WIN! THAT MEANS YOU'RE GOING DOWN THE HOLE, BUTTERNUT!
GULP
BEST TWO OUT OF THREE?

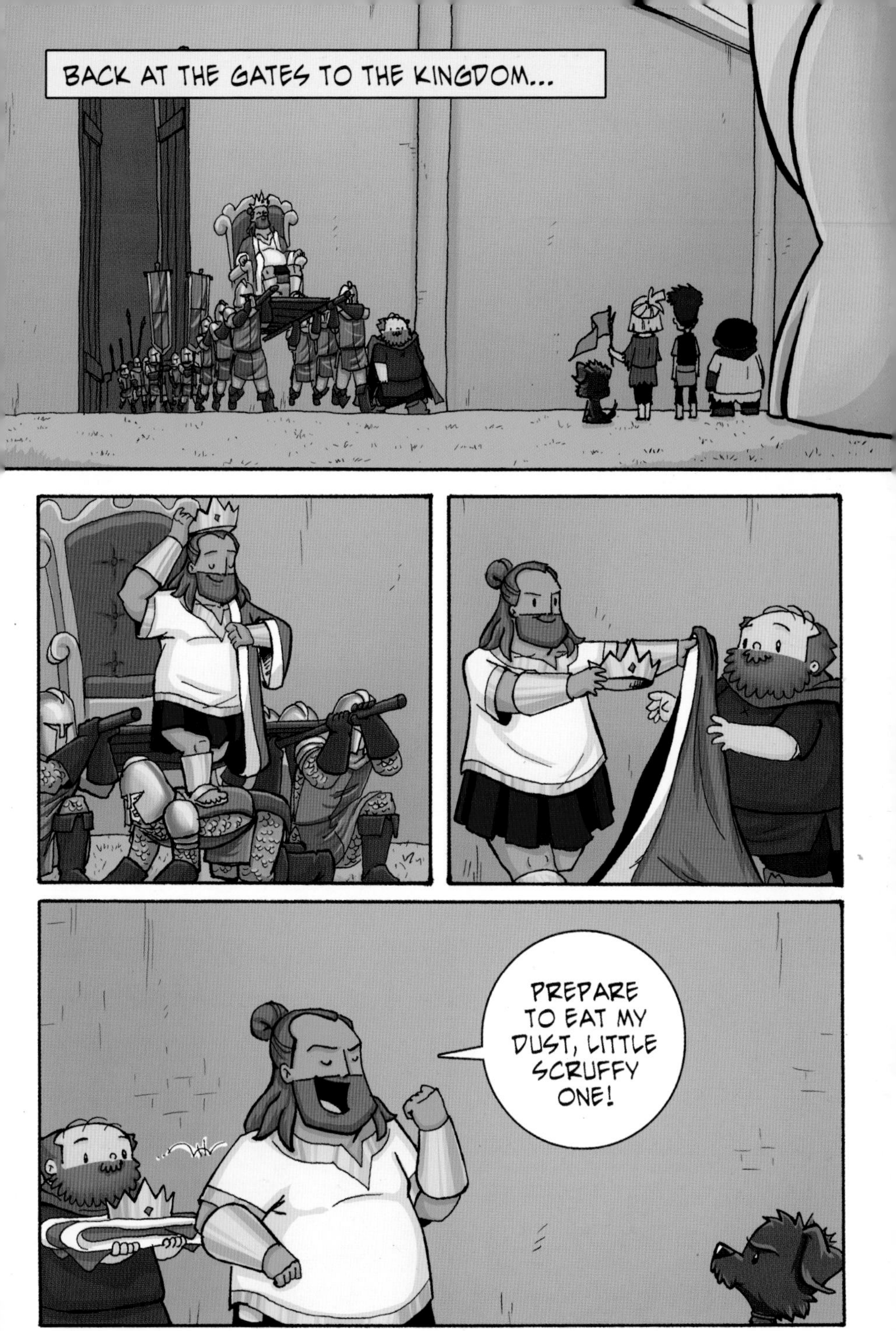
BACK AT THE GATES TO THE KINGDOM...
PREPARE TO EAT MY DUST, LITTLE SCRUFFY ONE!

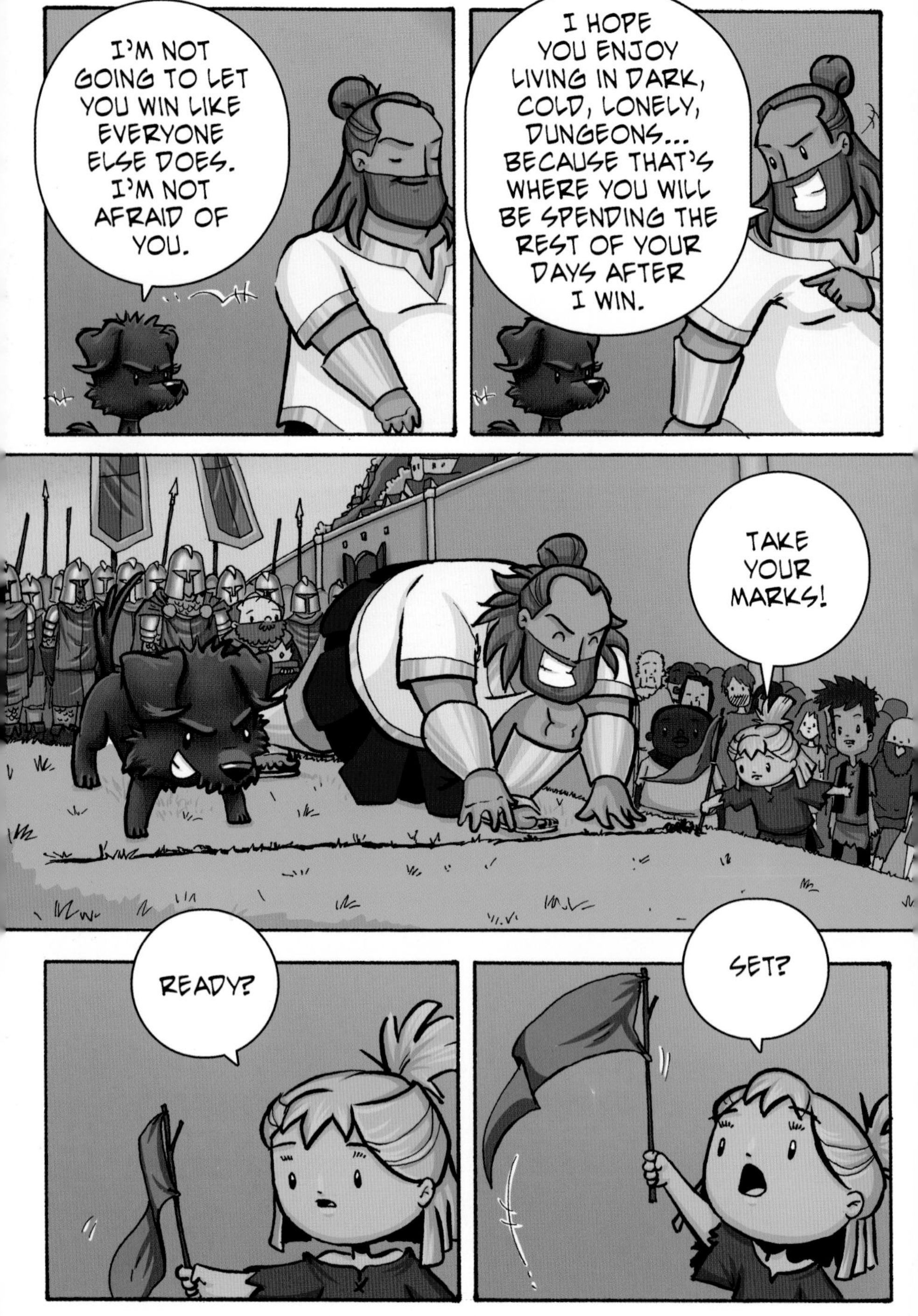
I'M NOT GOING TO LET YOU WIN LIKE EVERYONE ELSE DOES. I'M NOT AFRAID OF YOU.
I HOPE YOU ENJOY LIVING IN DARK, COLD, LONELY, DUNGEONS... BECAUSE THAT'S WHERE YOU WILL BE SPENDING THE REST OF YOUR DAYS AFTER I WIN.
TAKE YOUR MARKS!
READY?
SET?

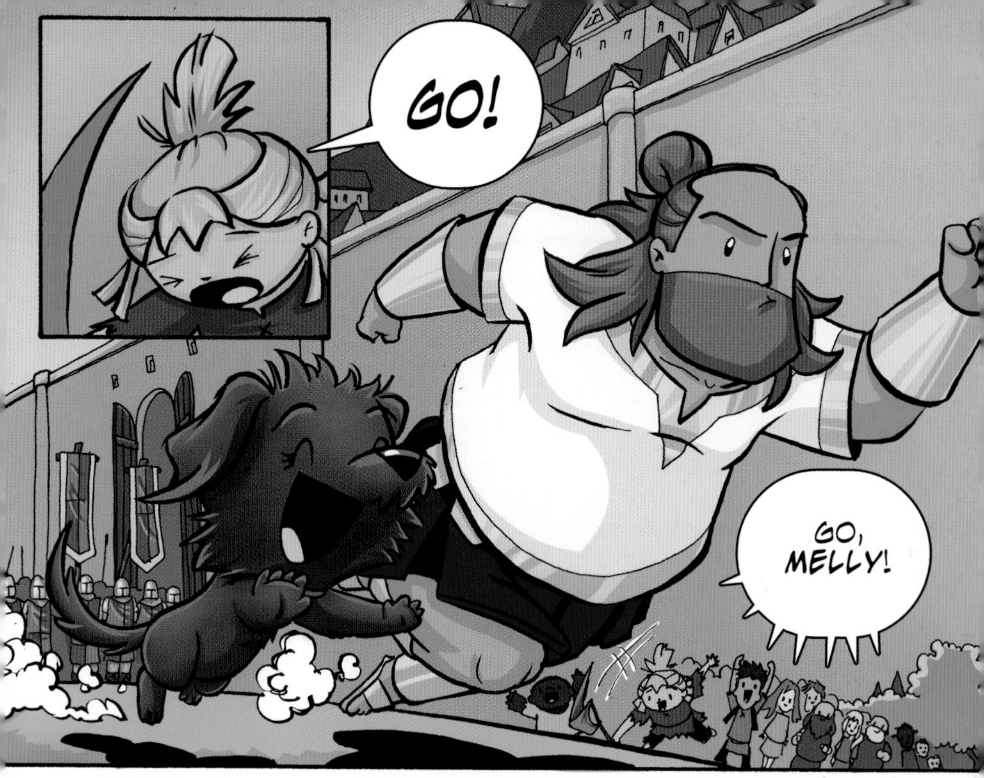
GO!
GO, MELLY!

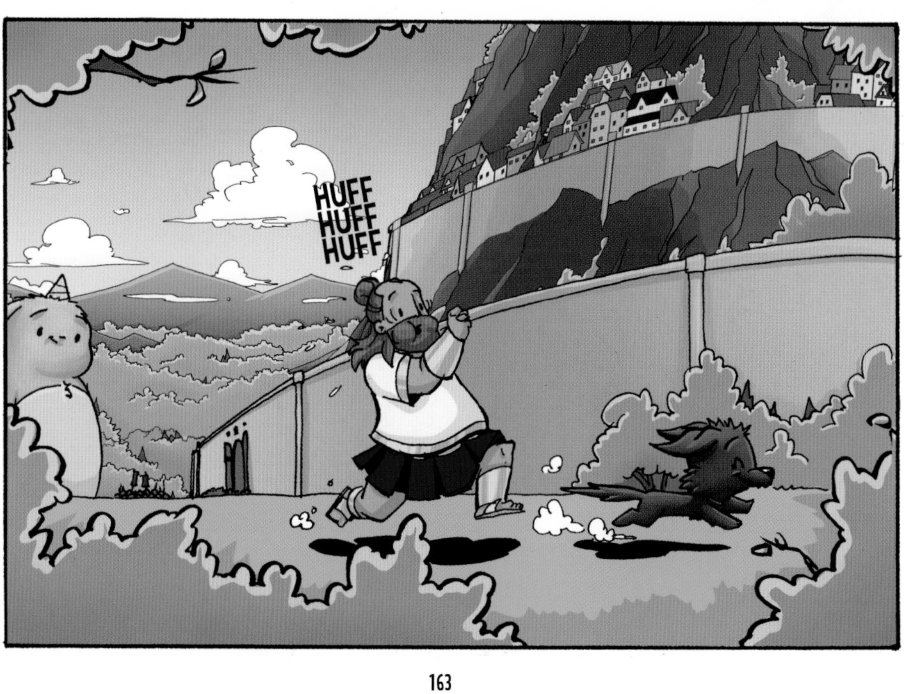
HUFF
HUFF
HUFF

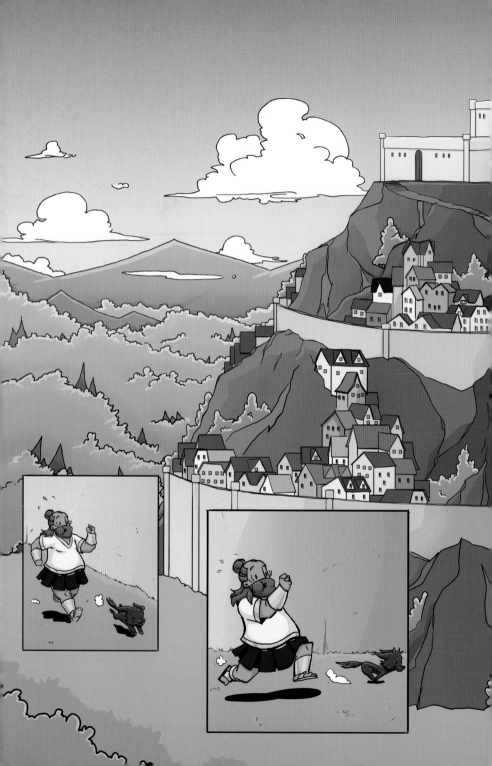

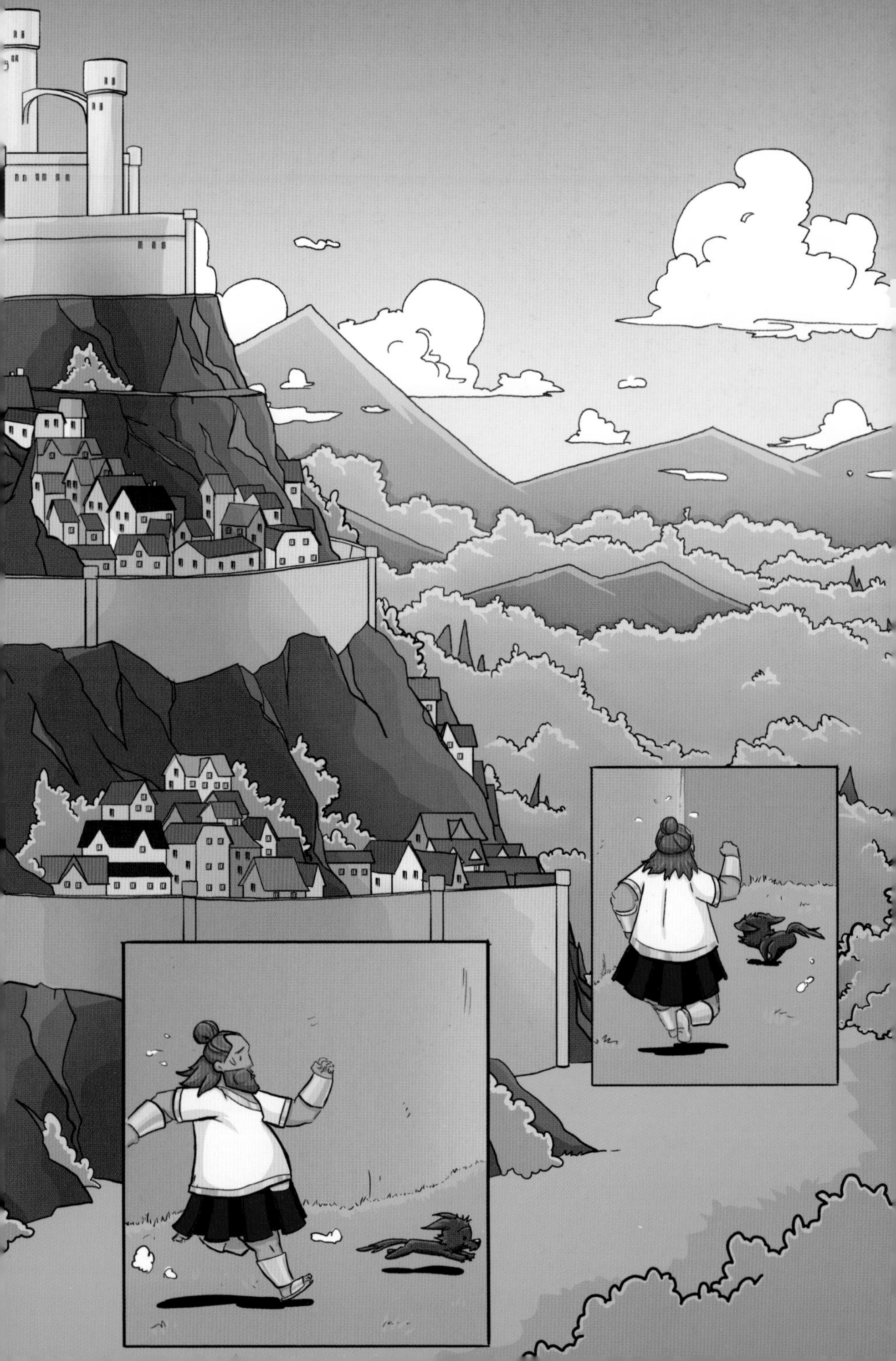

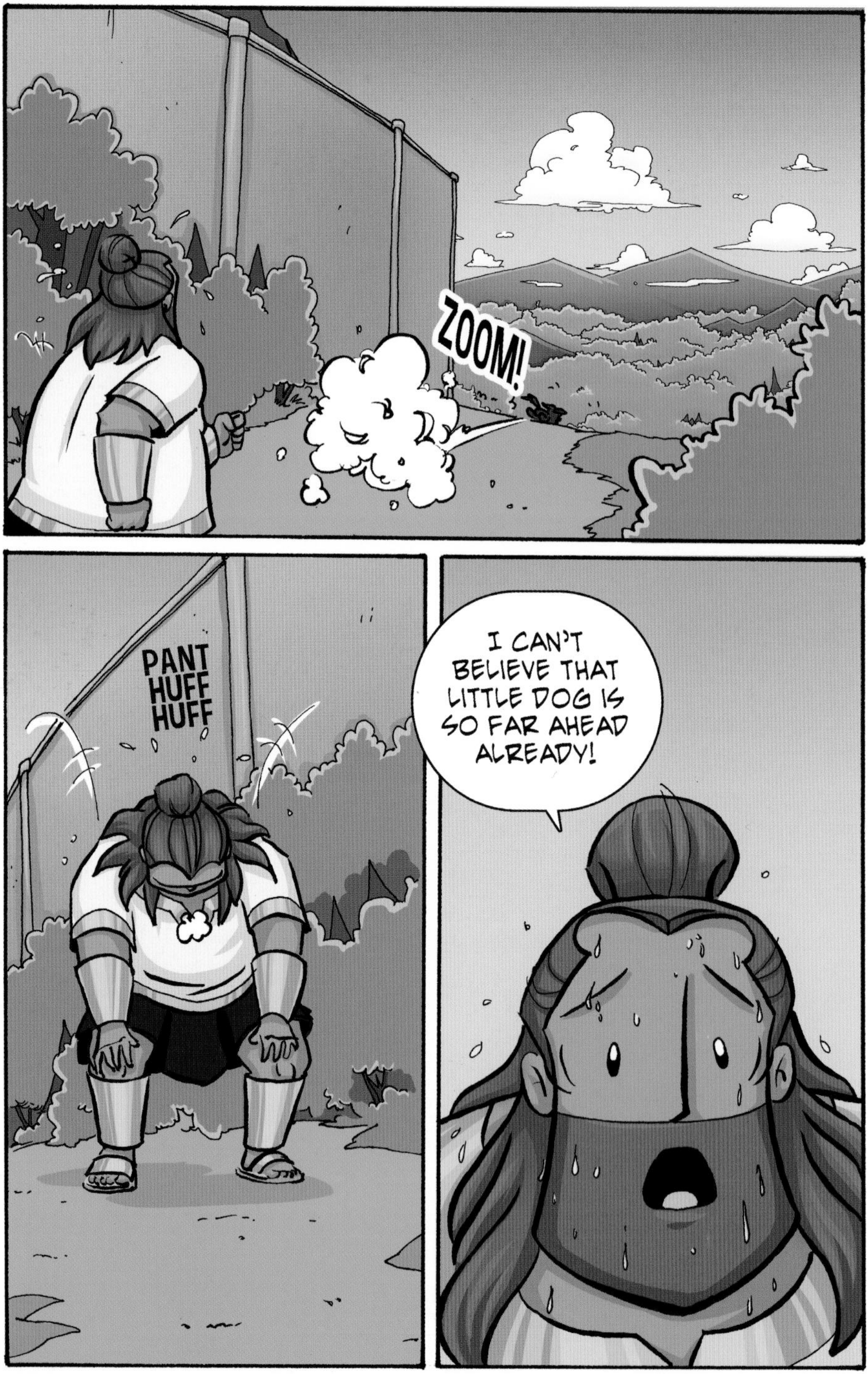
ZOOM!
PANT
HUFF
HUFF
I CAN'T BELIEVE THAT LITTLE DOG IS SO FAR AHEAD ALREADY!

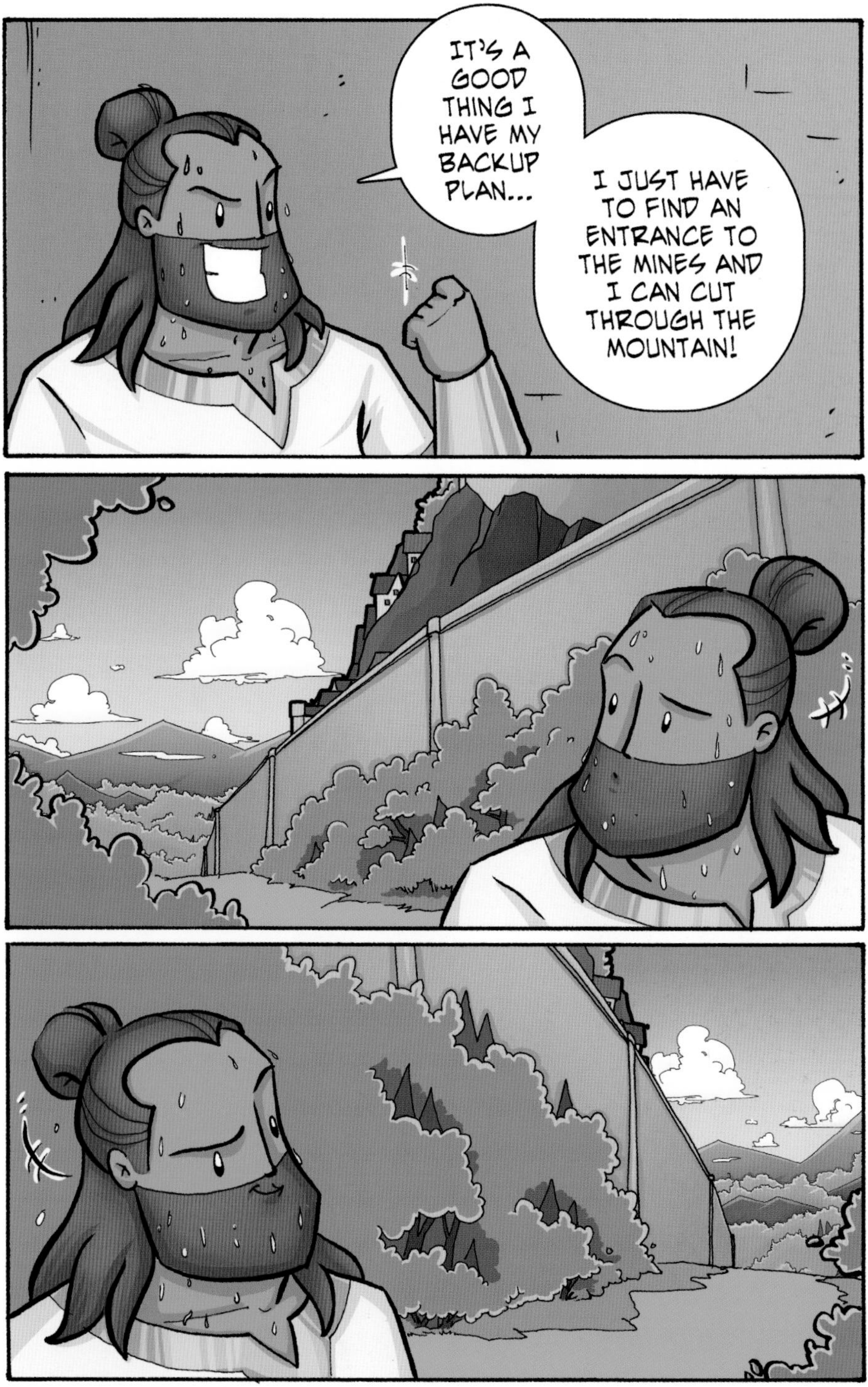
IT'S A GOOD THING I HAVE MY BACKUP PLAN...
I JUST HAVE TO FIND AN ENTRANCE TO THE MINES AND I CAN CUT THROUGH THE MOUNTAIN!

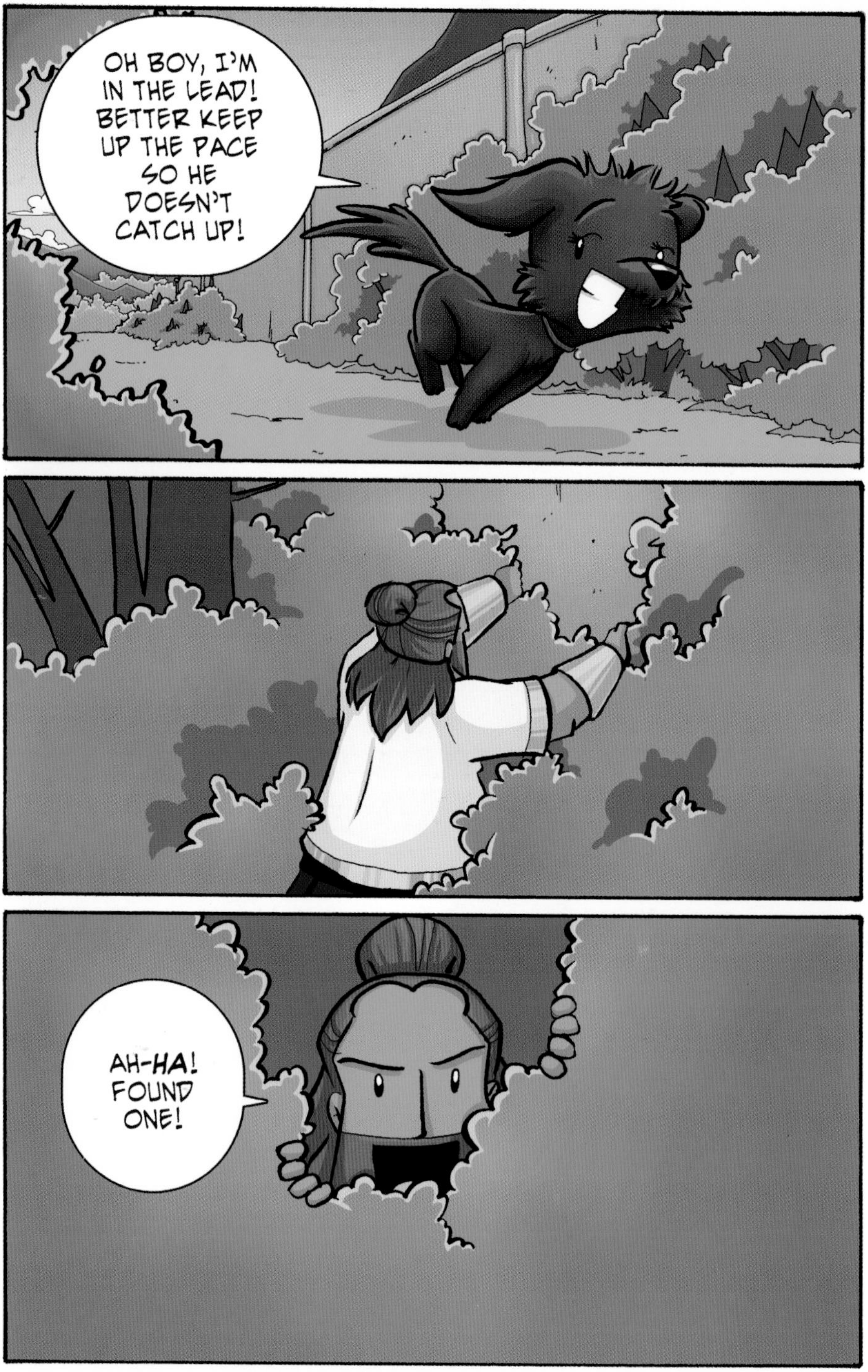
OH BOY, I'M IN THE LEAD! BETTER KEEP UP THE PACE SO HE DOESN'T CATCH UP!
AH-HA! FOUND ONE!

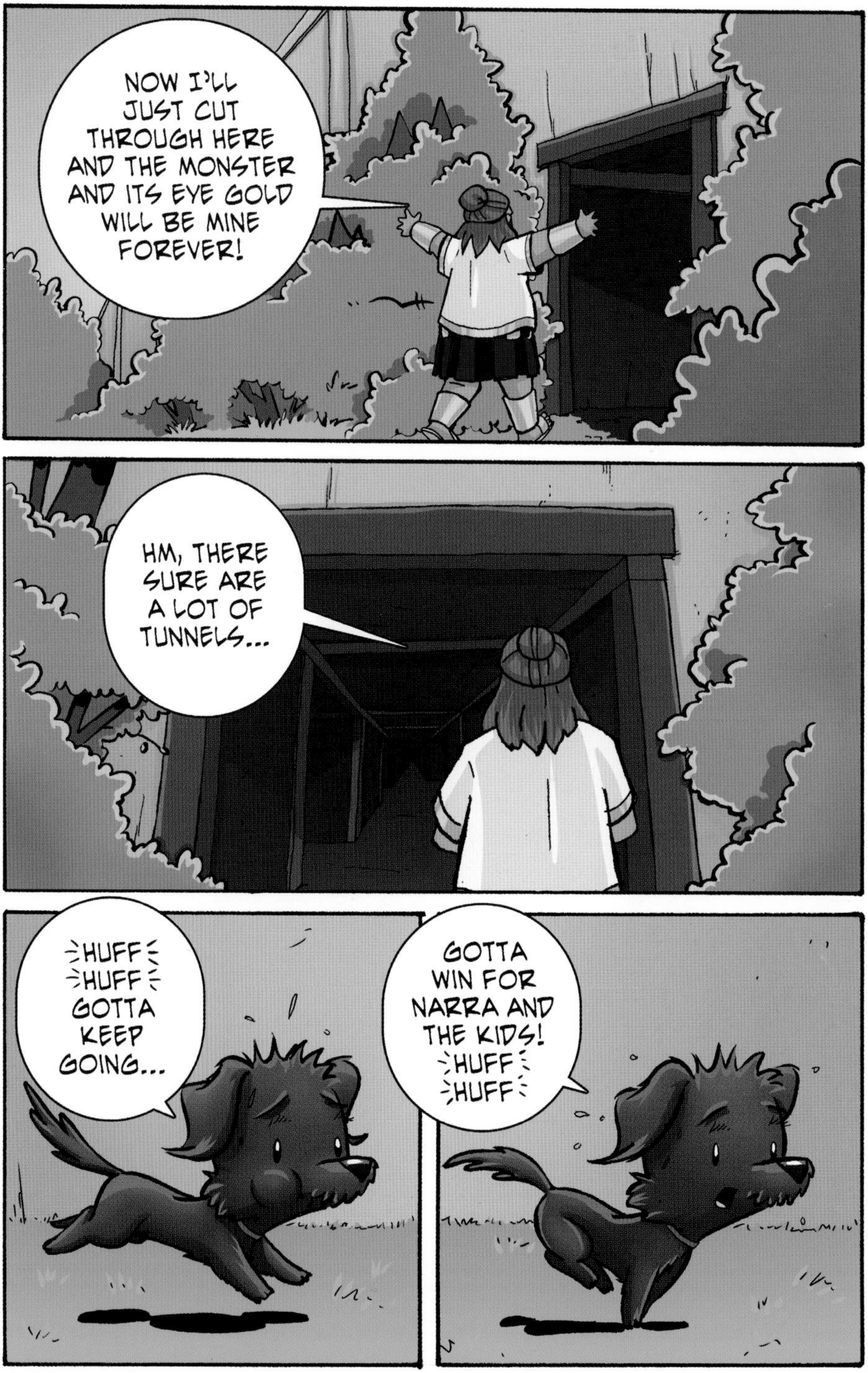
NOW I'LL JUST CUT THROUGH HERE AND THE MONSTER AND ITS EYE GOLD WILL BE MINE FOREVER!
HM, THERE SURE ARE A LOT OF TUNNELS...
HUFF HUFF GOTTA KEEP GOING...
GOTTA WIN FOR NARRA AND THE KIDS! HUFF HUFF

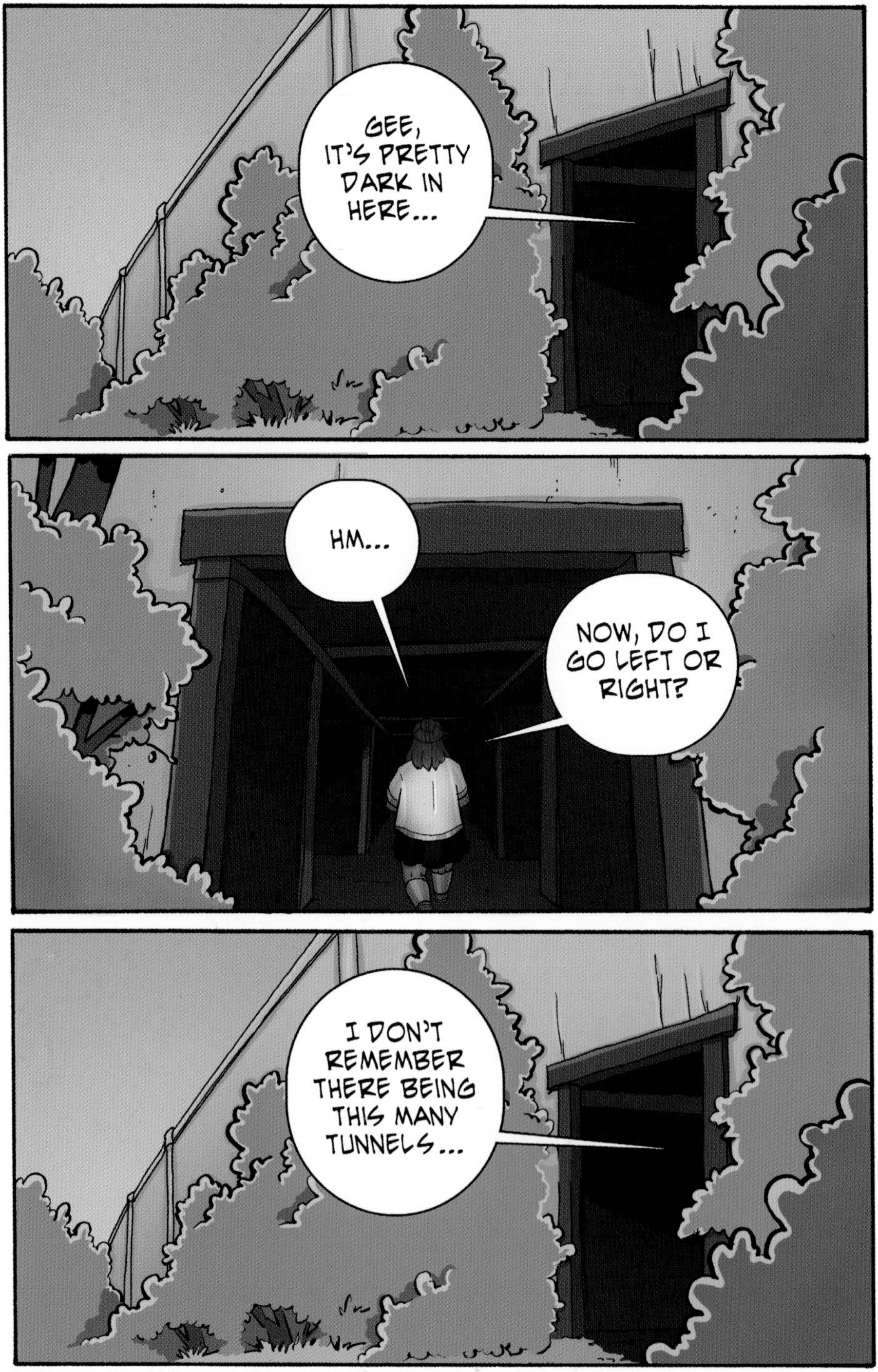
GEE, IT'S PRETTY DARK IN HERE...
HM...
NOW, DO I GO LEFT OR RIGHT?
I DON'T REMEMBER THERE BEING THIS MANY TUNNELS...

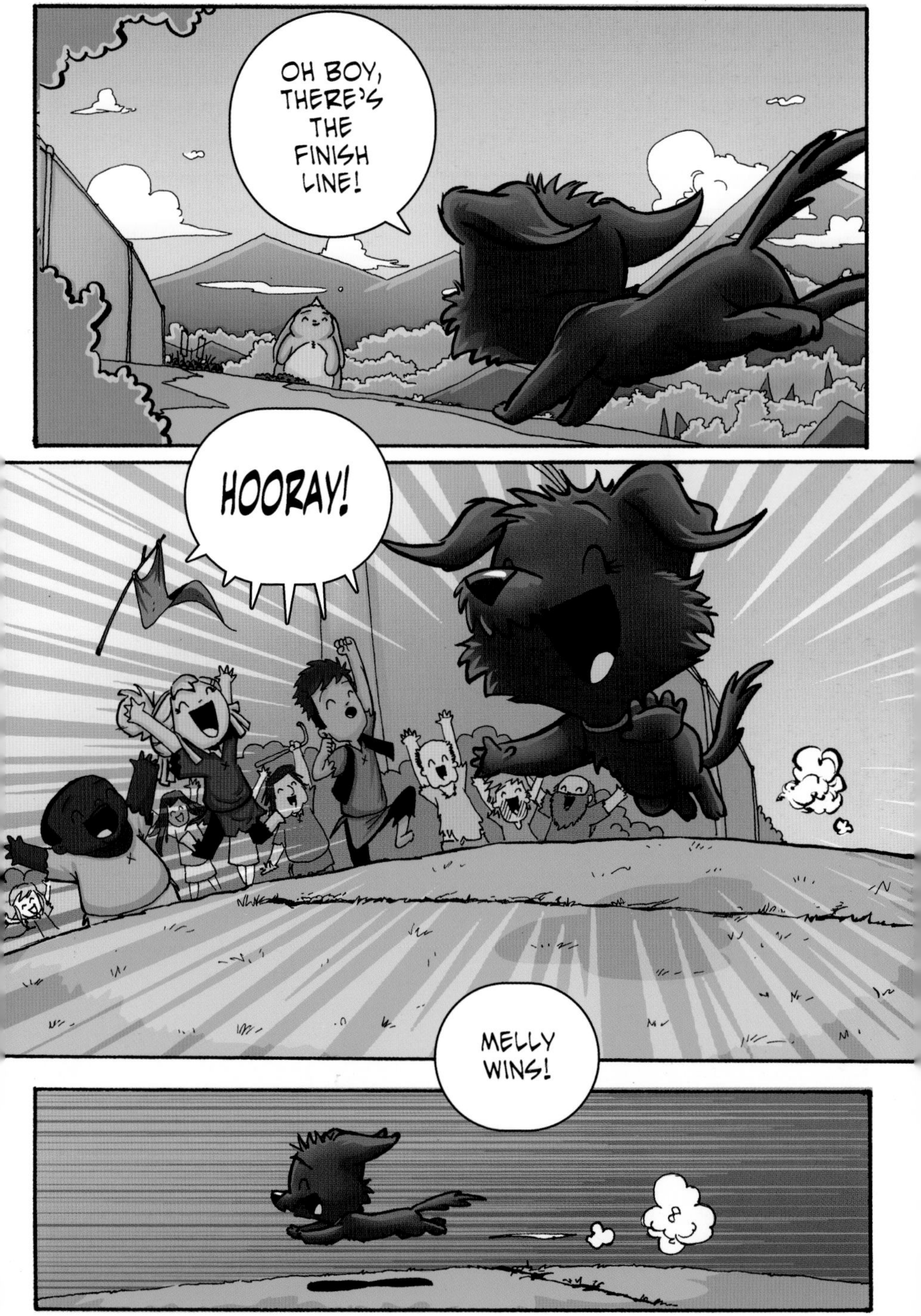
OH BOY, THERE'S THE FINISH LINE!
HOORAY!
MELLY WINS!

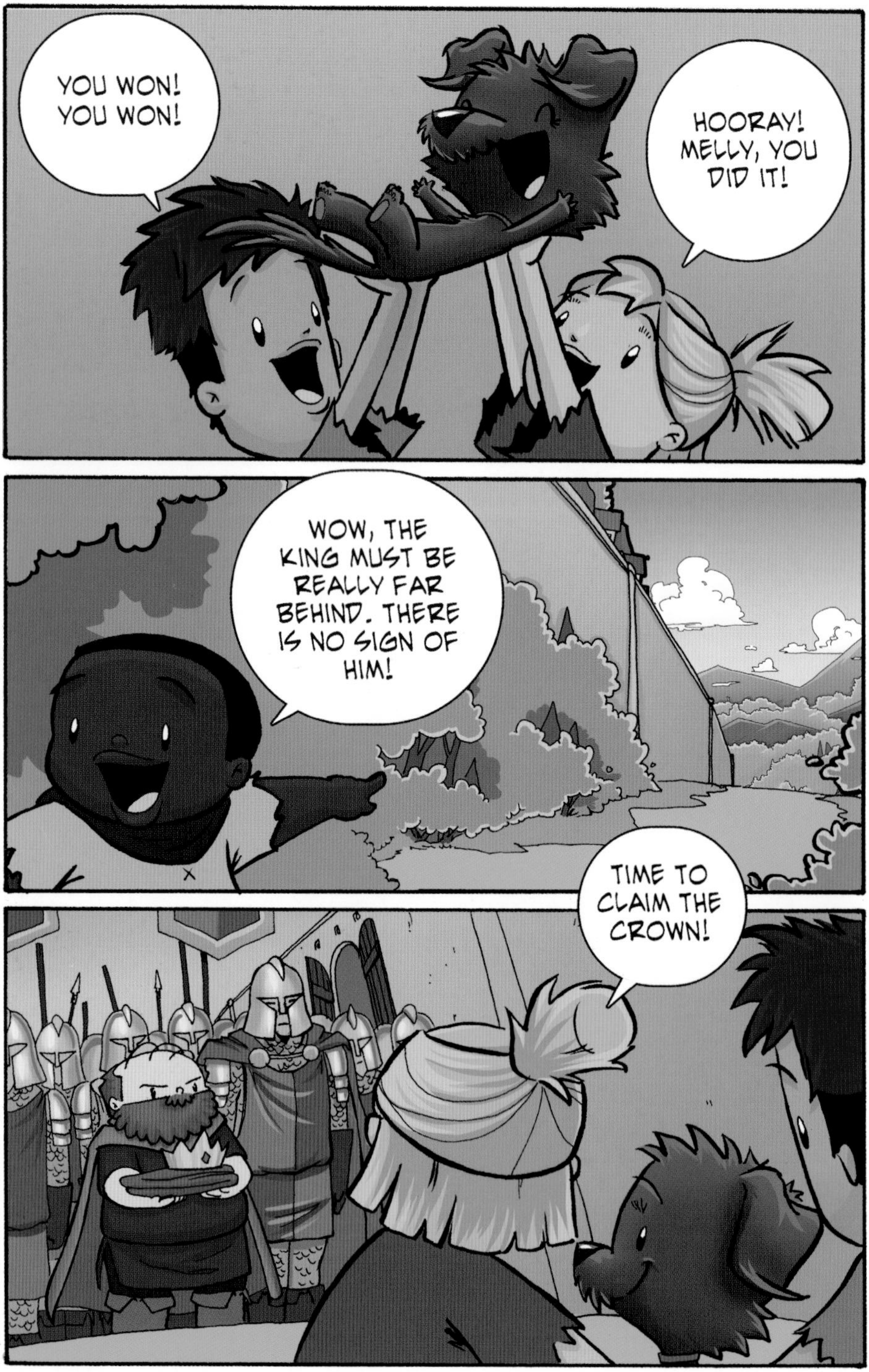
YOU WON! YOU WON!
HOORAY! MELLY, YOU DID IT!
WOW, THE KING MUST BE REALLY FAR BEHIND. THERE IS NO SIGN OF HIM!
TIME TO CLAIM THE CROWN!

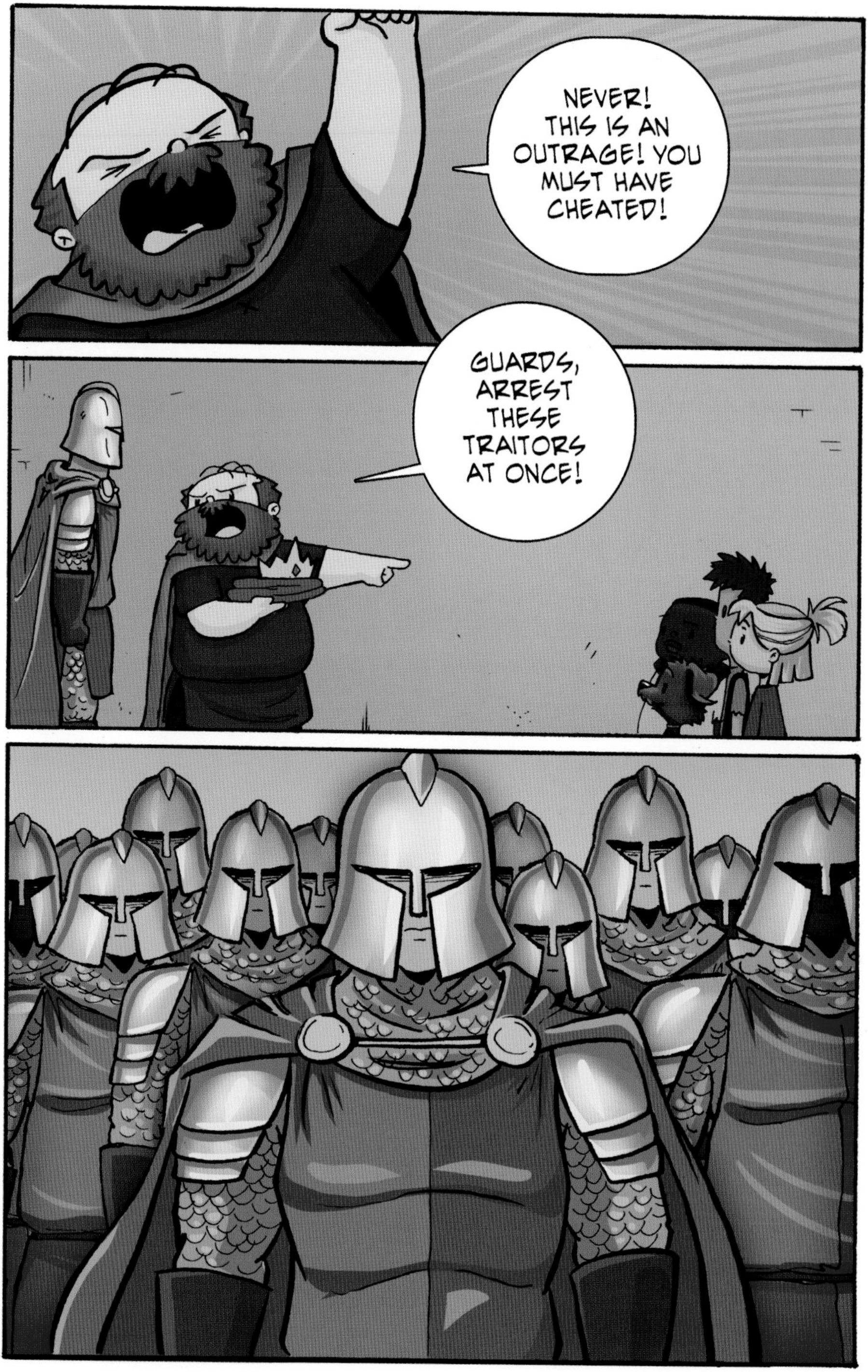
NEVER! THIS IS AN OUTRAGE! YOU MUST HAVE CHEATED!
GUARDS, ARREST THESE TRAITORS AT ONCE!

CHAPTER 8
GIFTS FROM ABOVE

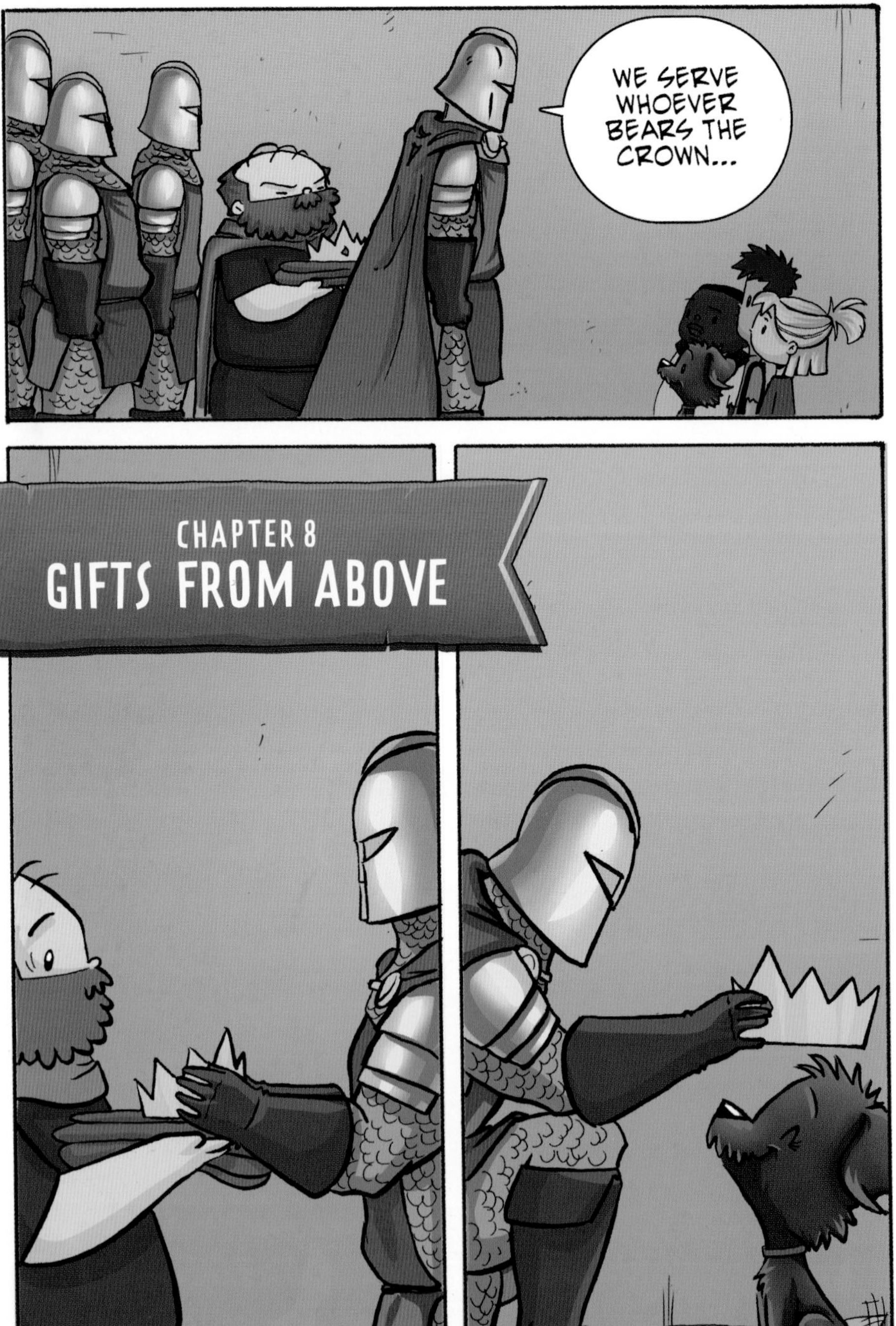
WE SERVE WHOEVER BEARS THE CROWN...

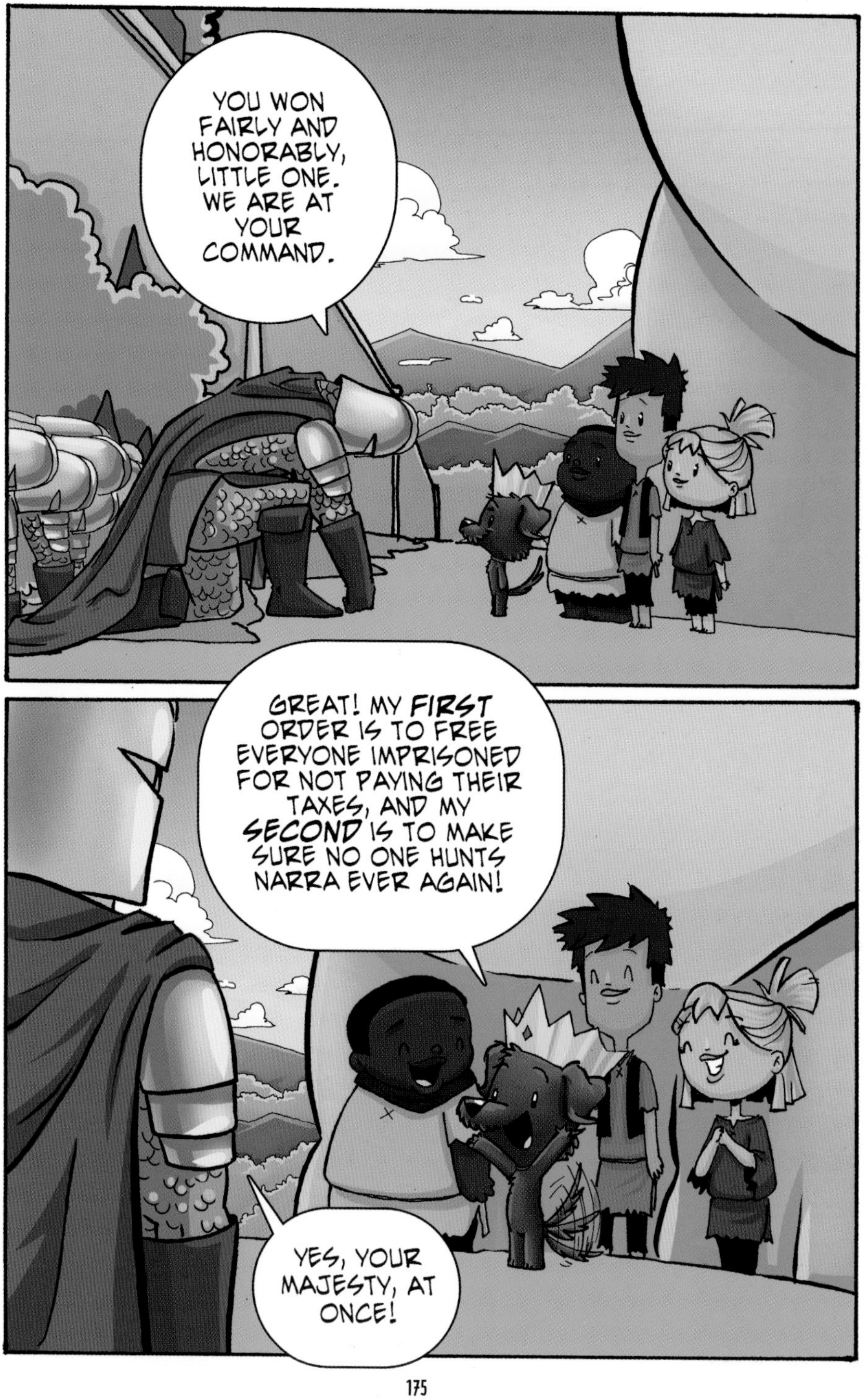
YOU WON FAIRLY AND HONORABLY, LITTLE ONE. WE ARE AT YOUR COMMAND.
GREAT! MY FIRST ORDER IS TO FREE EVERYONE IMPRISONED FOR NOT PAYING THEIR TAXES, AND MY SECOND IS TO MAKE SURE NO ONE HUNTS NARRA EVER AGAIN!
YES, YOUR MAJESTY, AT ONCE!

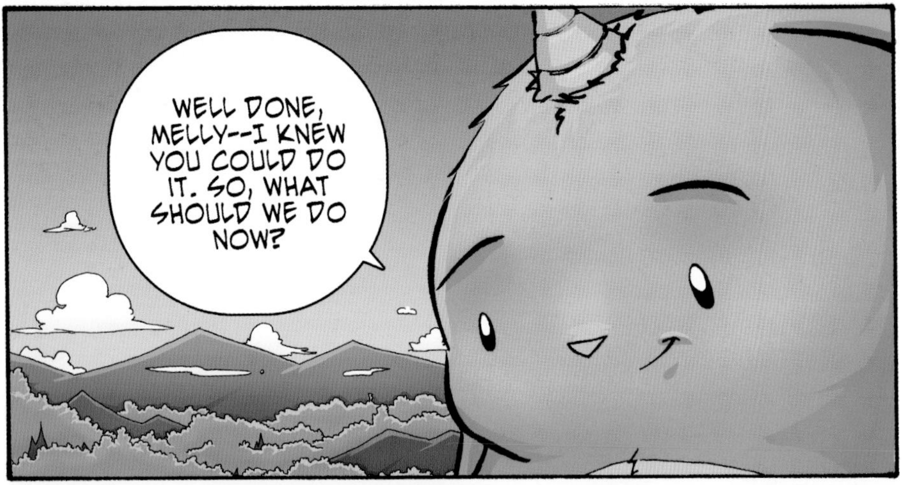
WELL DONE, MELLY--I KNEW YOU COULD DO IT. SO, WHAT SHOULD WE DO NOW?

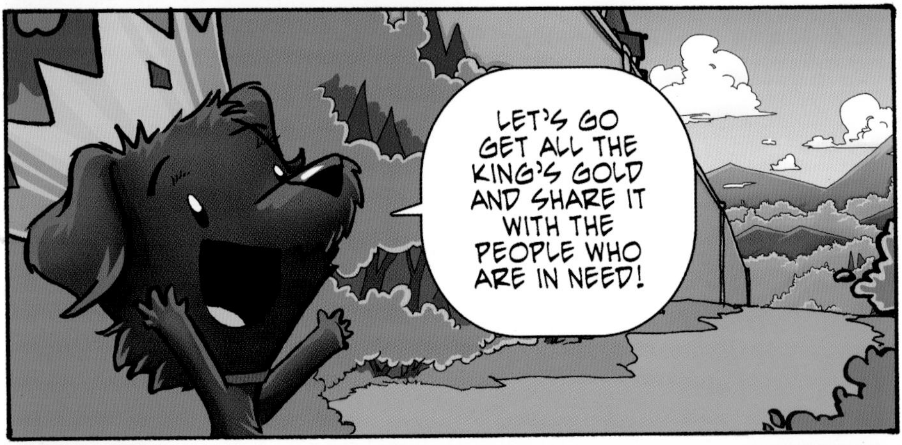
LET'S GO GET ALL THE KING'S GOLD AND SHARE IT WITH THE PEOPLE WHO ARE IN NEED!

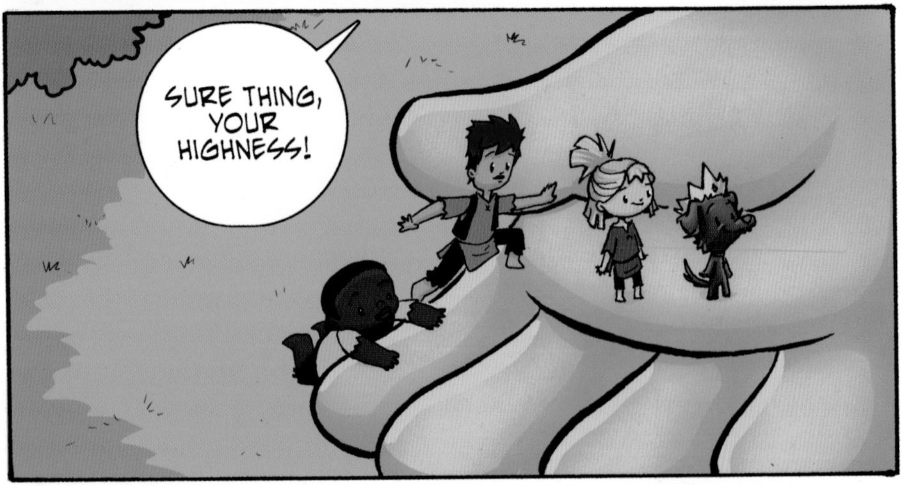
SURE THING, YOUR HIGHNESS!

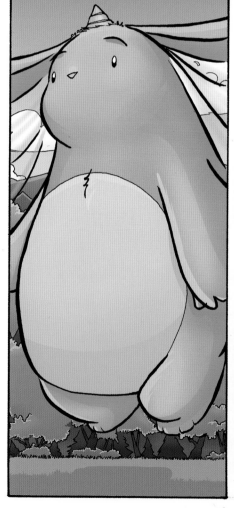

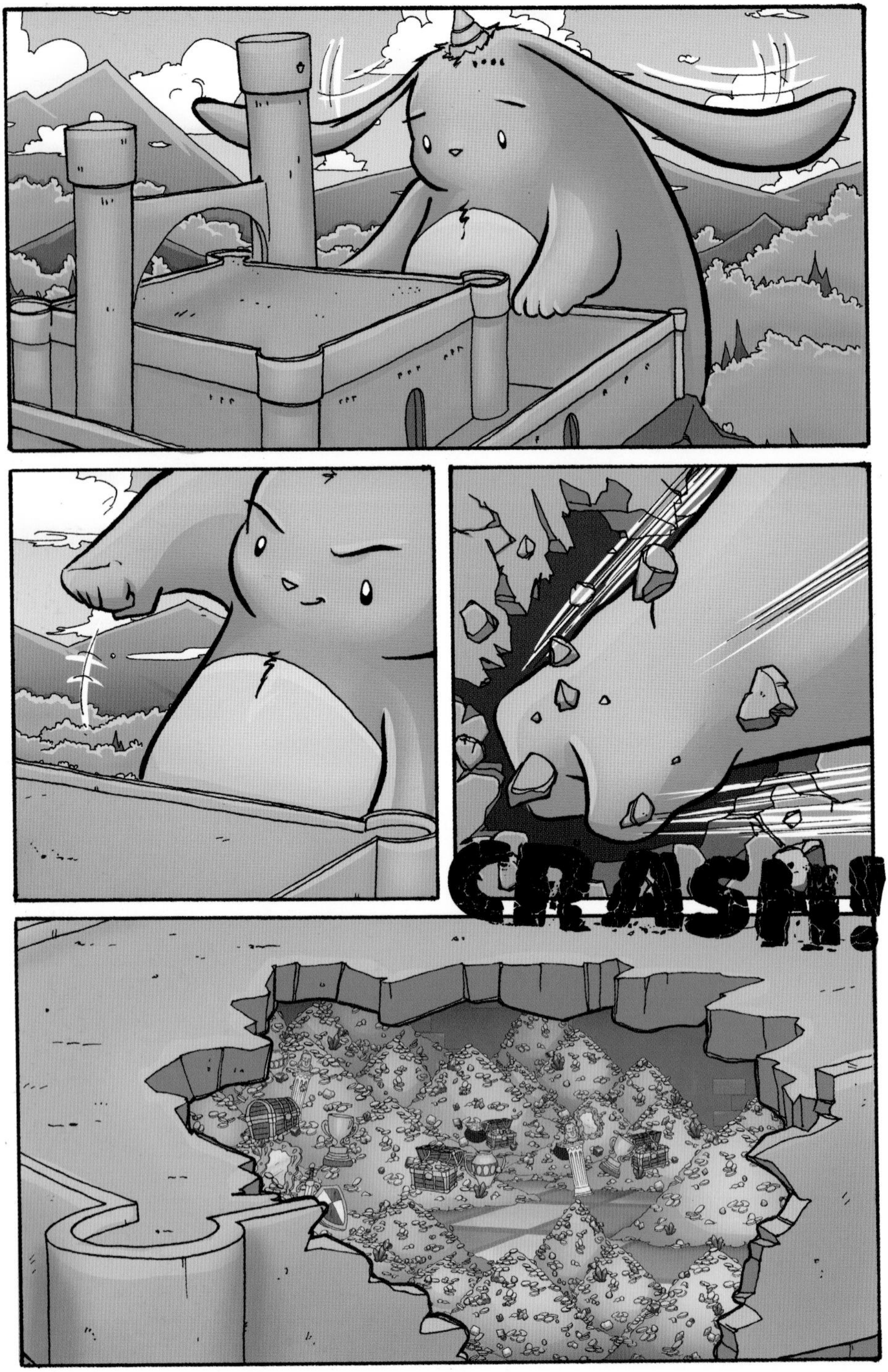
CRASH!

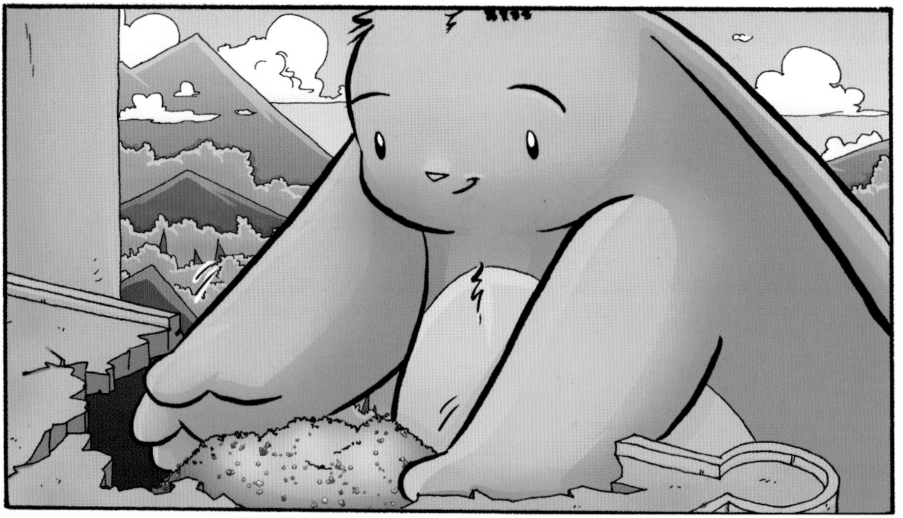
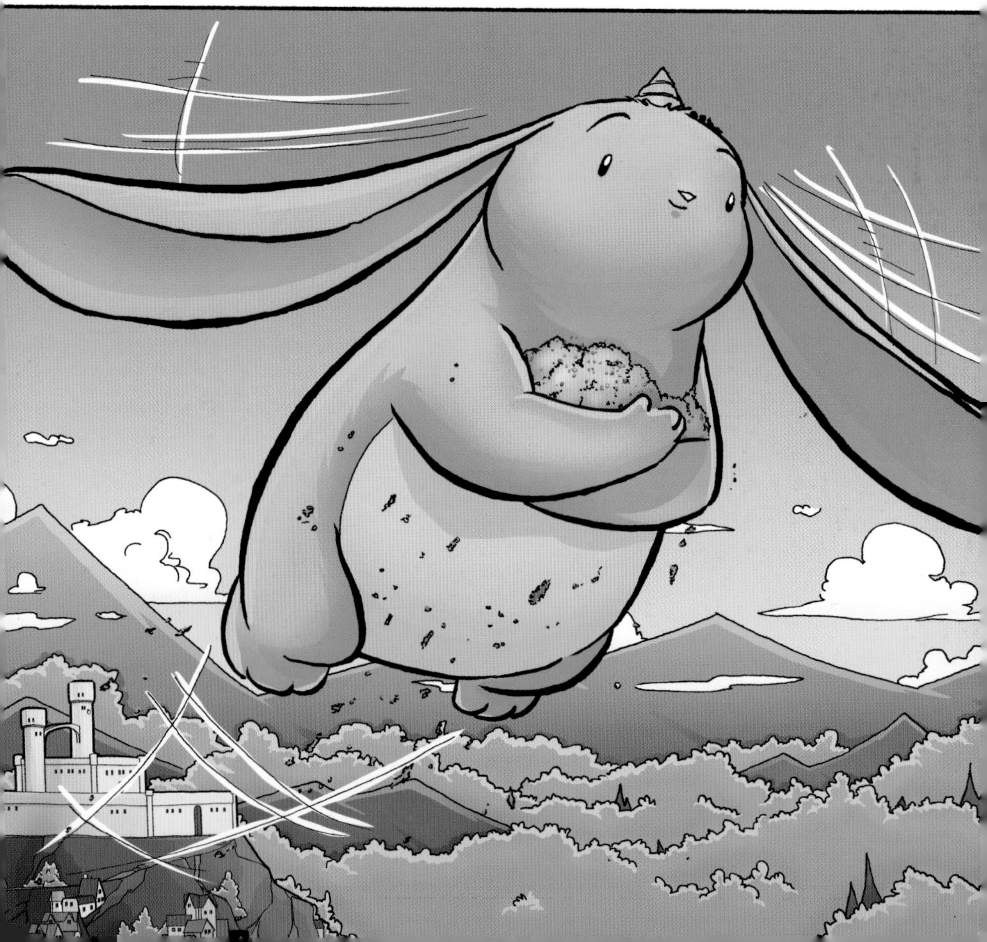

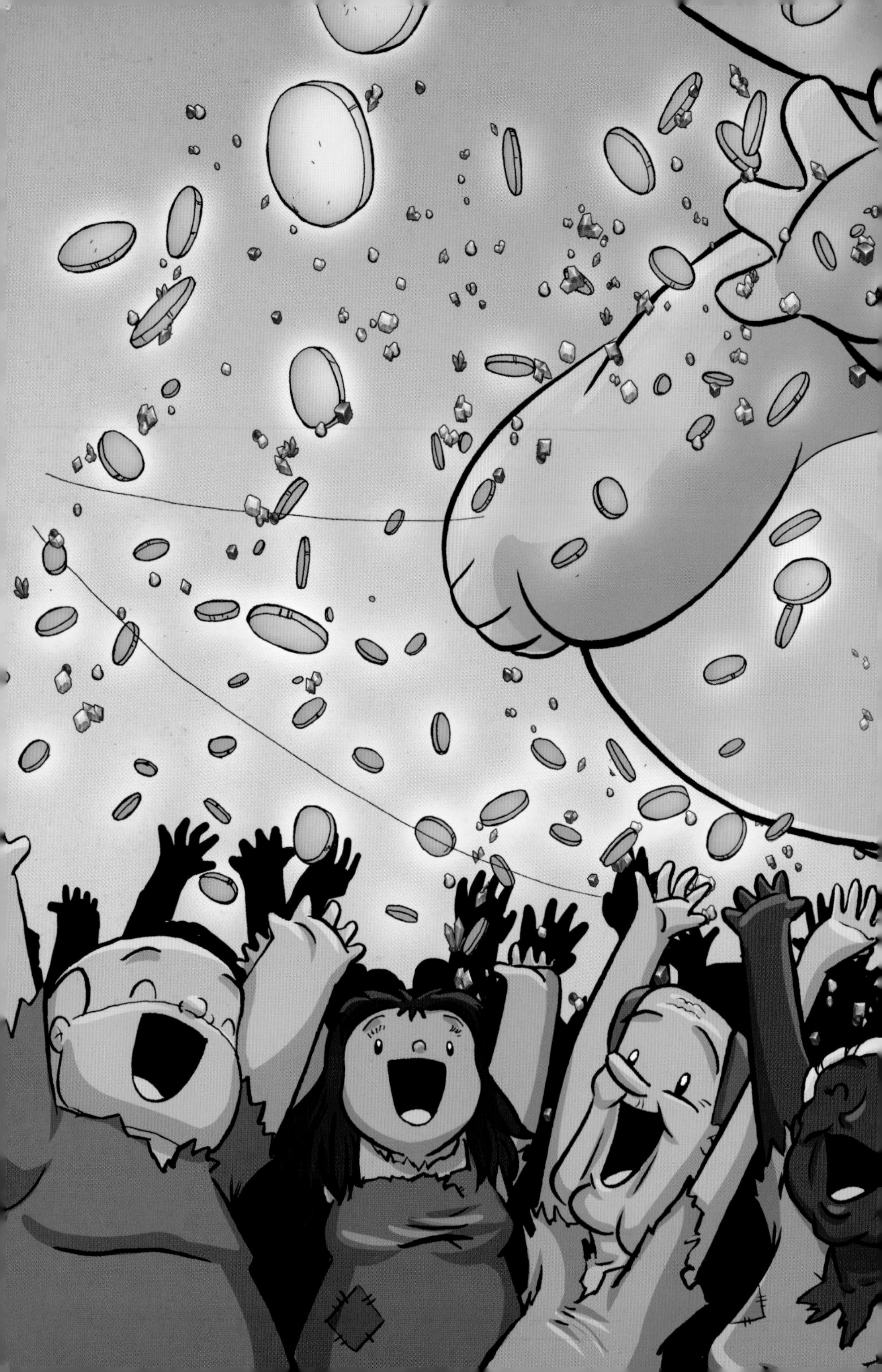

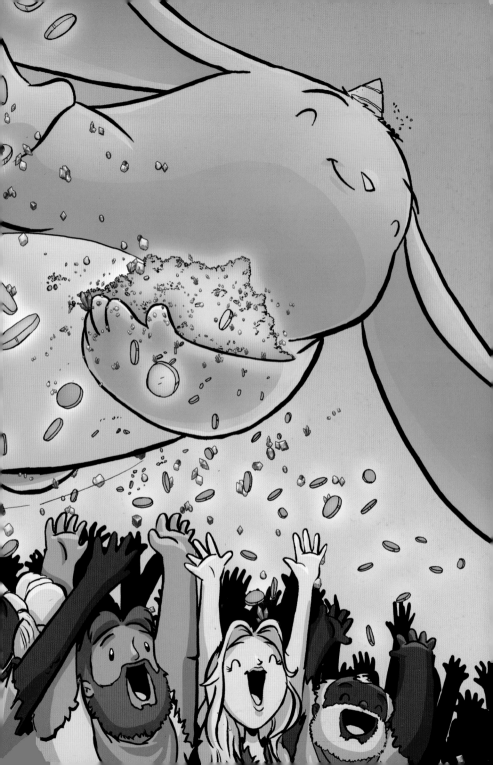

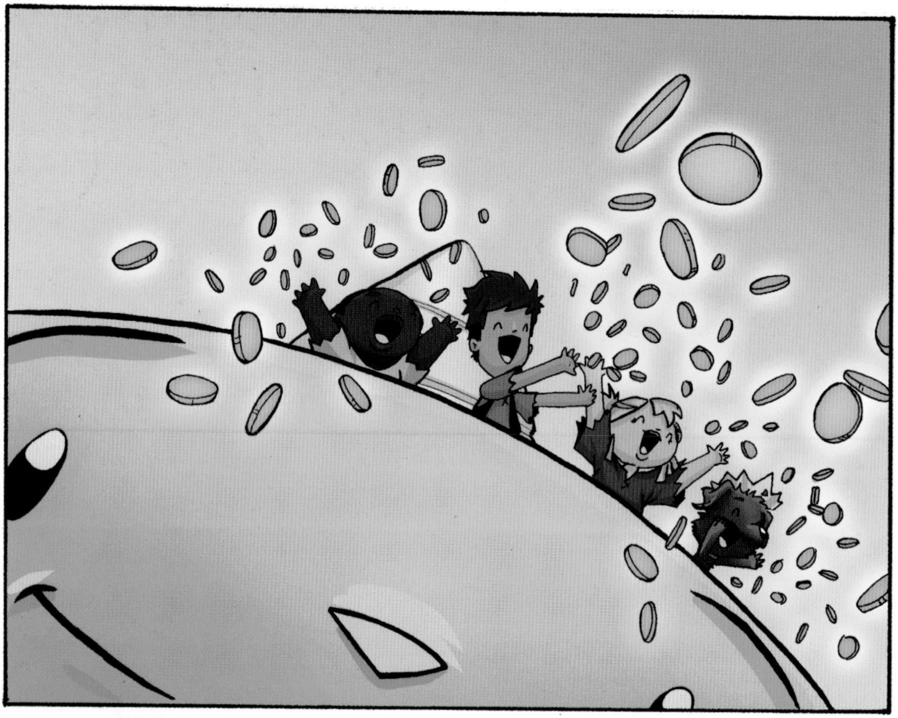

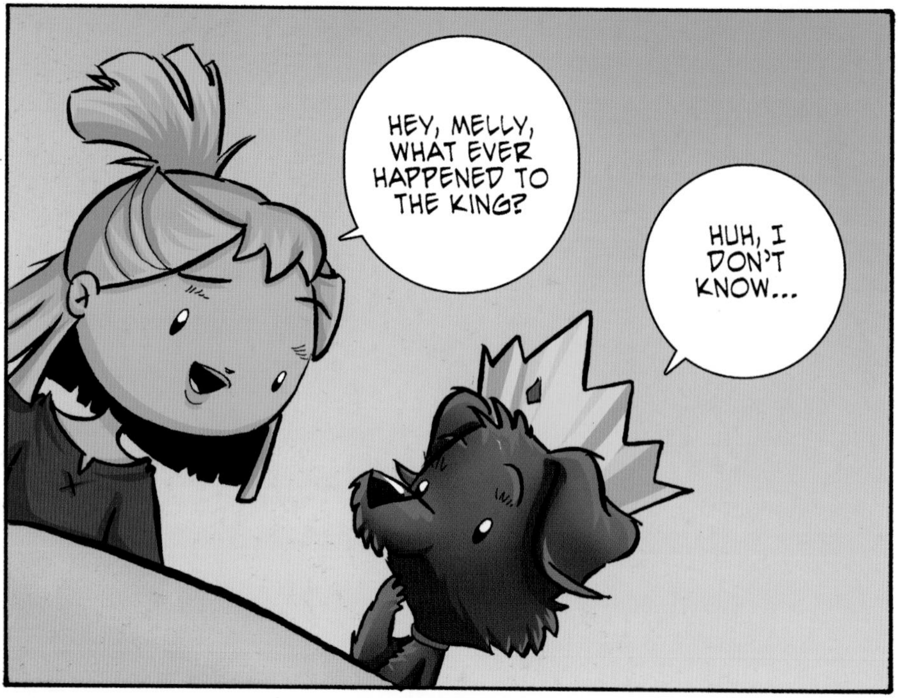
HEY, MELLY, WHAT EVER HAPPENED TO THE KING?
HUH, I DON'T KNOW...

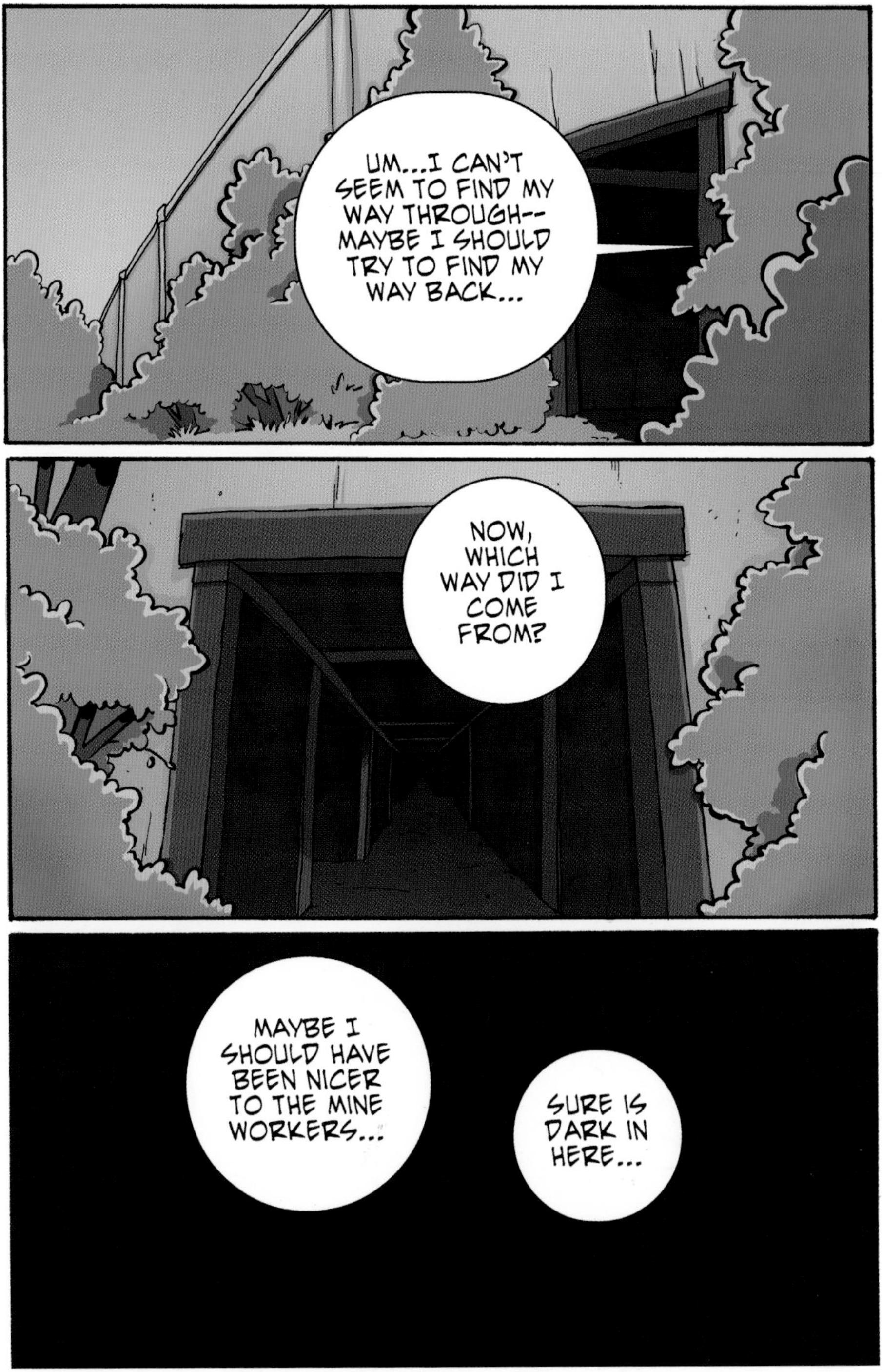
UM...I CAN'T SEEM TO FIND MY WAY THROUGH-- MAYBE I SHOULD TRY TO FIND MY WAY BACK...
NOW, WHICH WAY DID I COME FROM?
MAYBE I SHOULD HAVE BEEN NICER TO THE MINE WORKERS...
SURE IS DARK IN HERE...

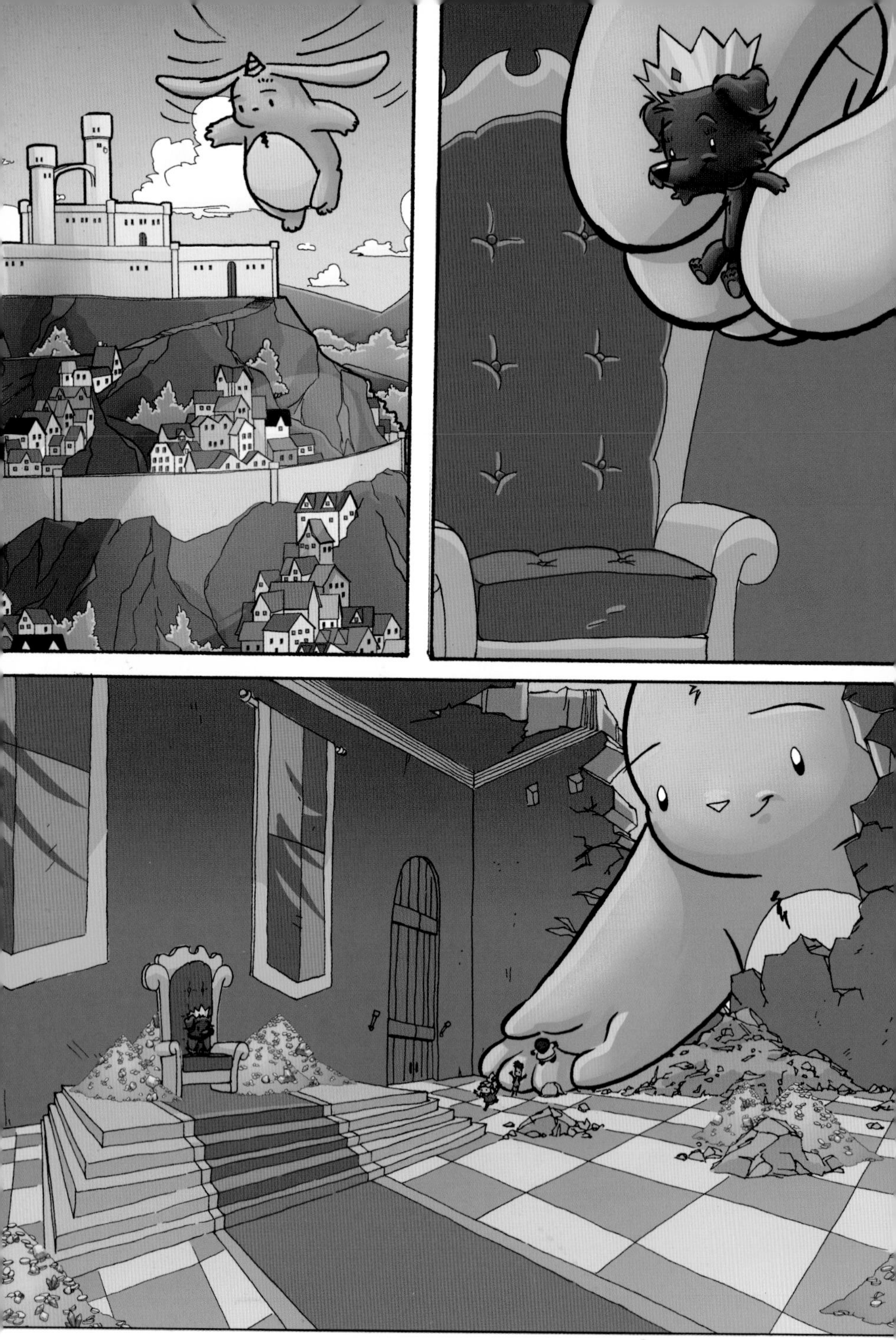

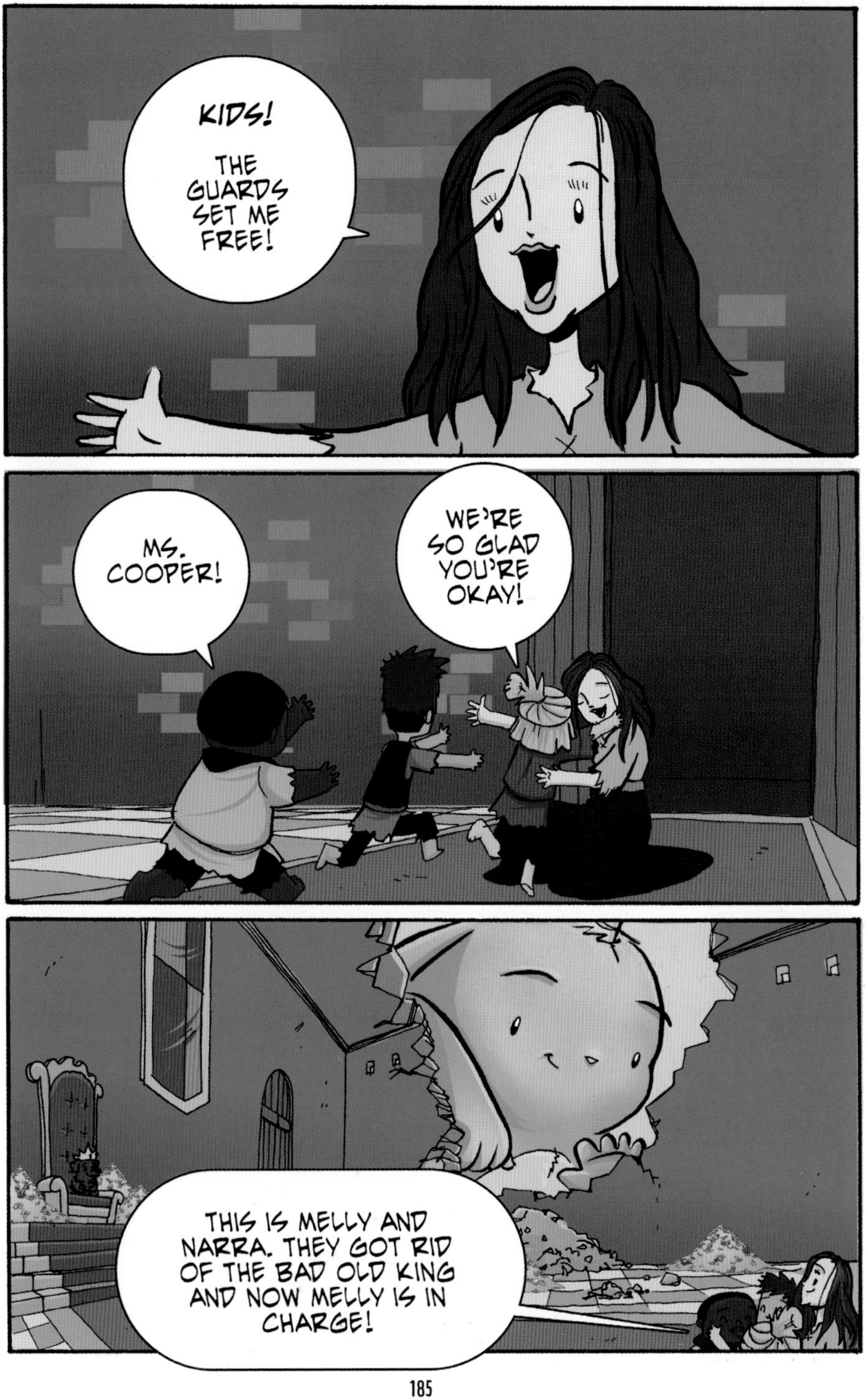
KIDS!
THE GUARDS SET ME FREE!
MS. COOPER!
WE'RE SO GLAD YOU'RE OKAY!
THIS IS MELLY AND NARRA. THEY GOT RID OF THE BAD OLD KING AND NOW MELLY IS IN CHARGE!

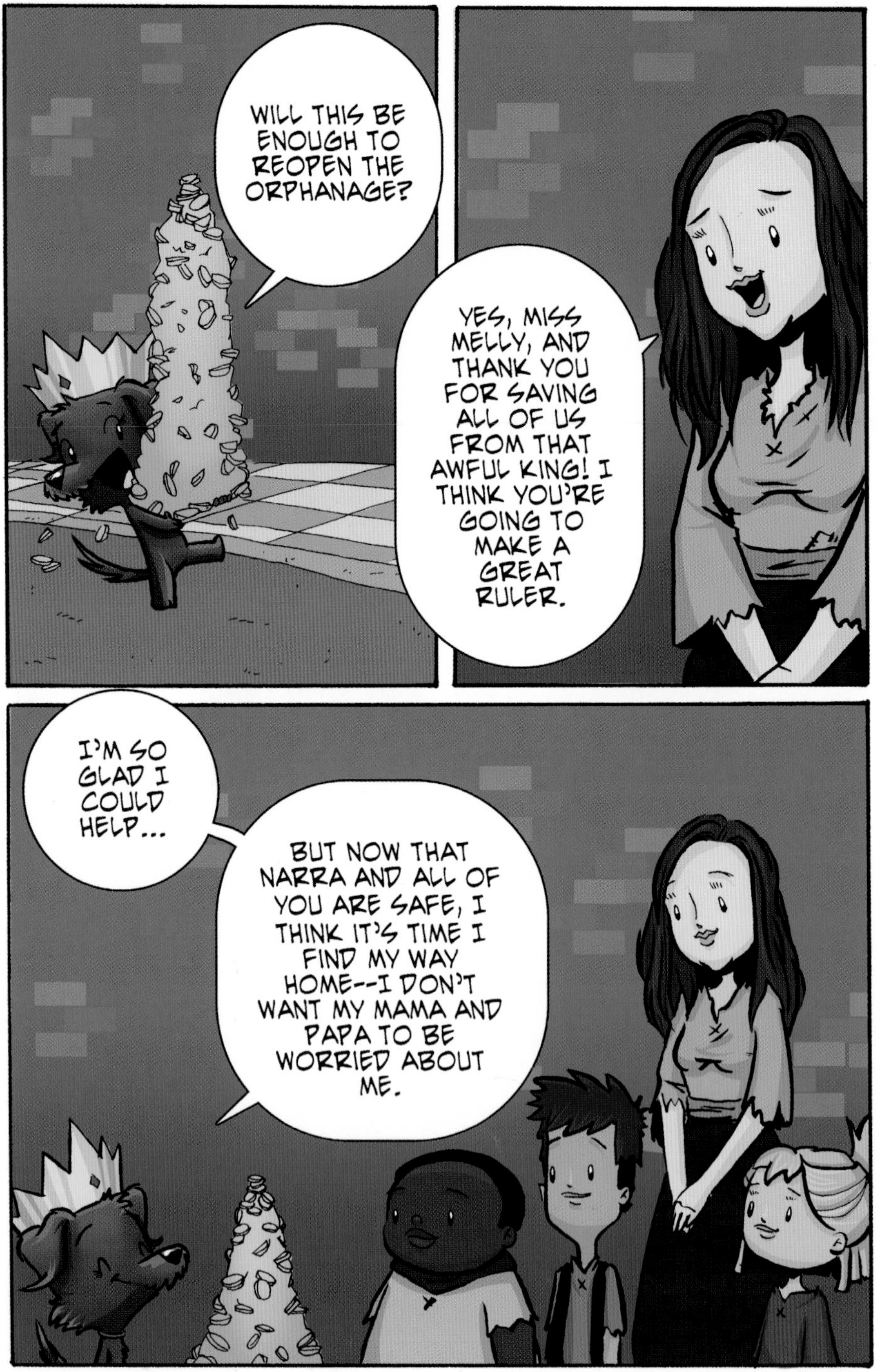
WILL THIS BE ENOUGH TO REOPEN THE ORPHANAGE?
YES, MISS MELLY, AND THANK YOU FOR SAVING ALL OF US FROM THAT AWFUL KING! I THINK YOU'RE GOING TO MAKE A GREAT RULER.
I'M SO GLAD I COULD HELP...
BUT NOW THAT NARRA AND ALL OF YOU ARE SAFE, I THINK IT'S TIME I FIND MY WAY HOME--I DON'T WANT MY MAMA AND PAPA TO BE WORRIED ABOUT ME.

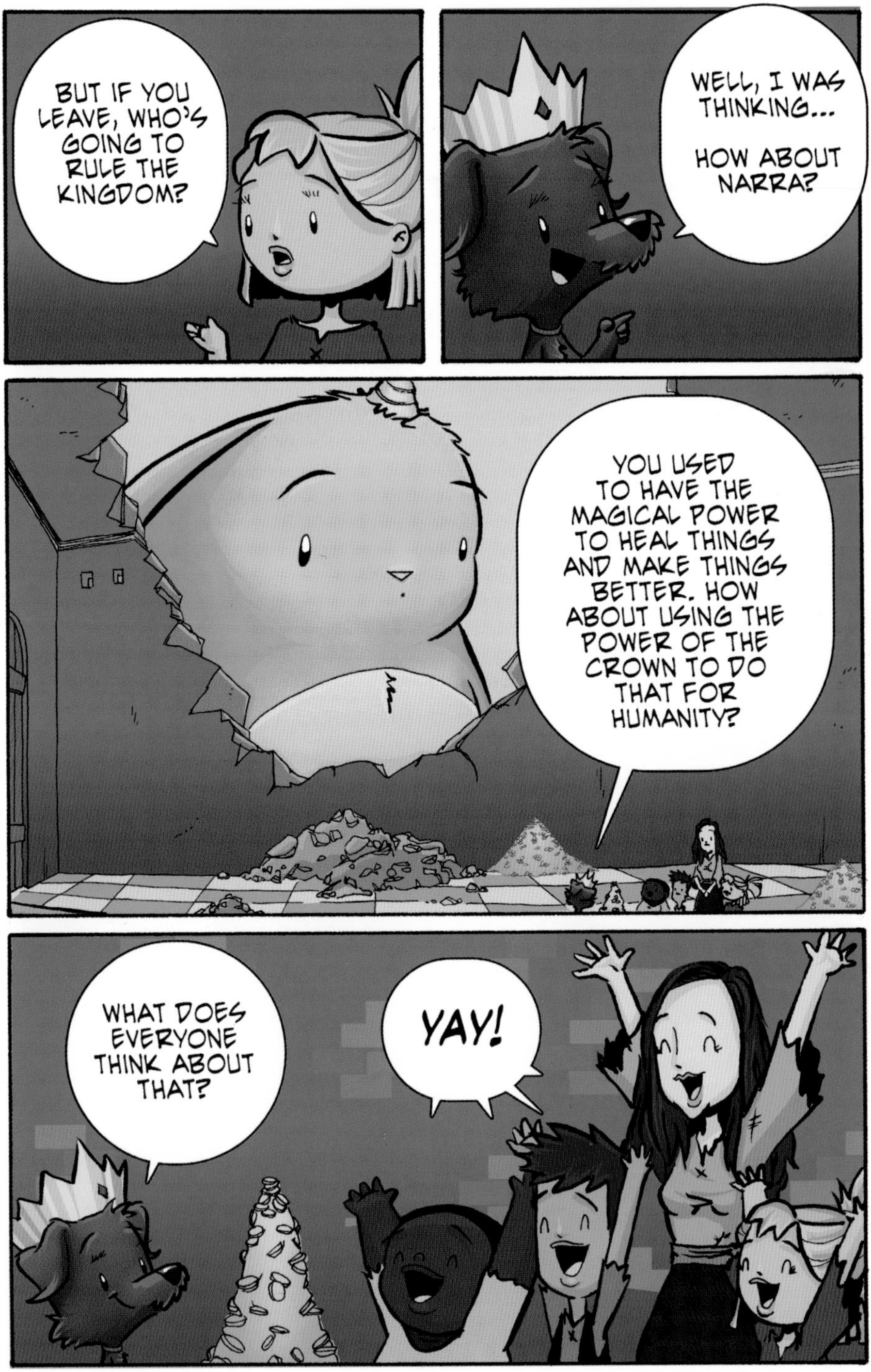
BUT IF YOU LEAVE, WHO'S GOING TO RULE THE KINGDOM?
WELL, I WAS THINKING...
HOW ABOUT NARRA?
YOU USED TO HAVE THE MAGICAL POWER TO HEAL THINGS AND MAKE THINGS BETTER. HOW ABOUT USING THE POWER OF THE CROWN TO DO THAT FOR HUMANITY?
WHAT DOES EVERYONE THINK ABOUT THAT?
YAY!

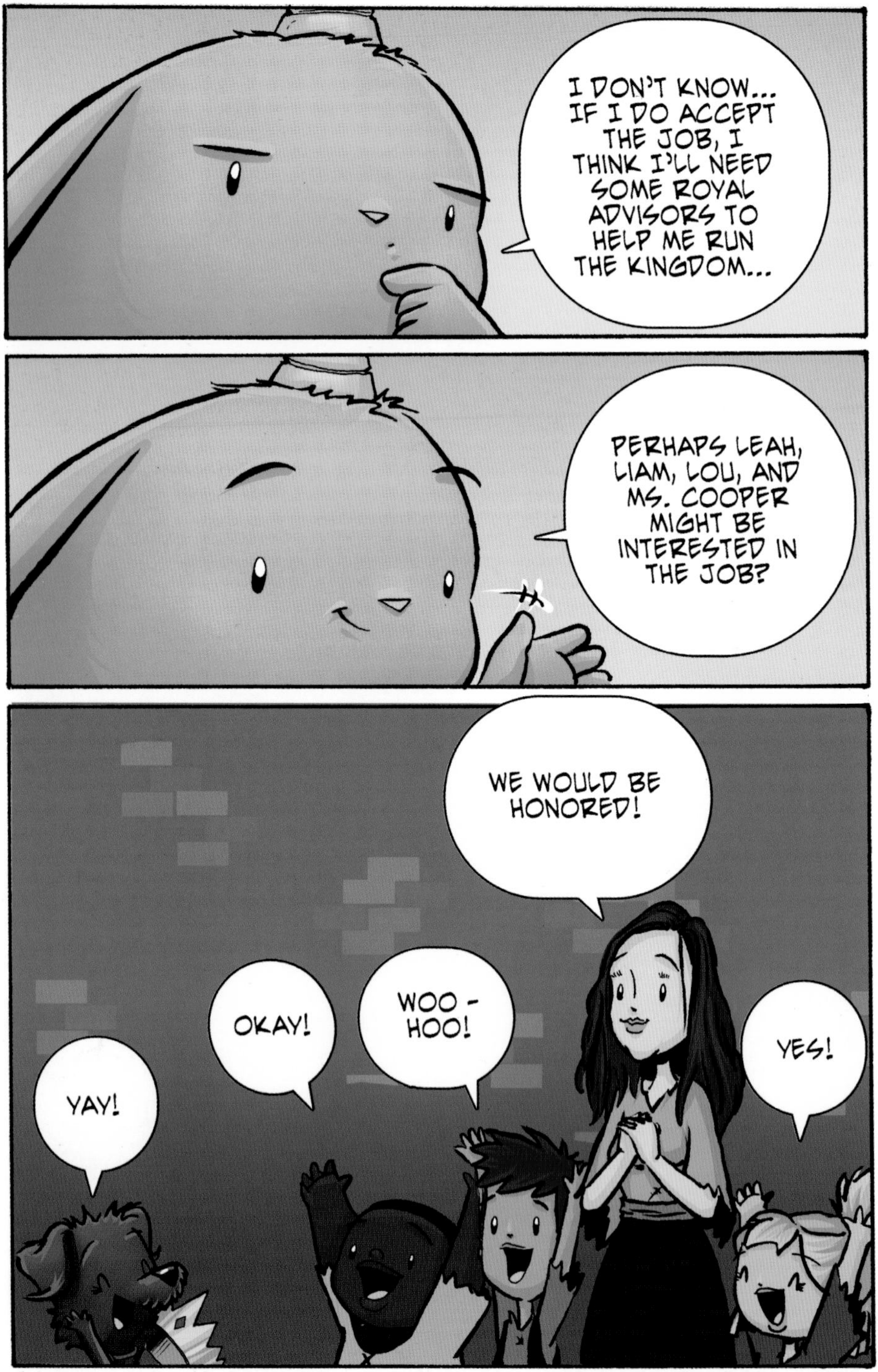
I DON'T KNOW... IF I DO ACCEPT THE JOB, I THINK I'LL NEED SOME ROYAL ADVISORS TO HELP ME RUN THE KINGDOM...
PERHAPS LEAH, LIAM, LOU, AND MS. COOPER MIGHT BE INTERESTED IN THE JOB?
WE WOULD BE HONORED!
YAY!
OKAY!
WOO-HOO!
YES!

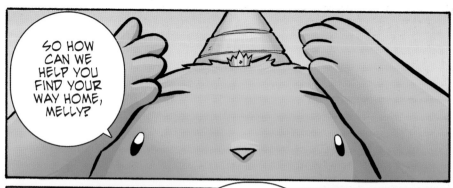

SO HOW CAN WE HELP YOU FIND YOUR WAY HOME, MELLY?

MINE'S THE HOUSE THAT SMELLS LIKE BATHROOM SPRAY AND SOMETIMES CHICKEN NUGGETS...

DOES ANYONE KNOW THAT ONE?

UM... I'M NOT SURE I...

GAK-HURK!

SHOOP!

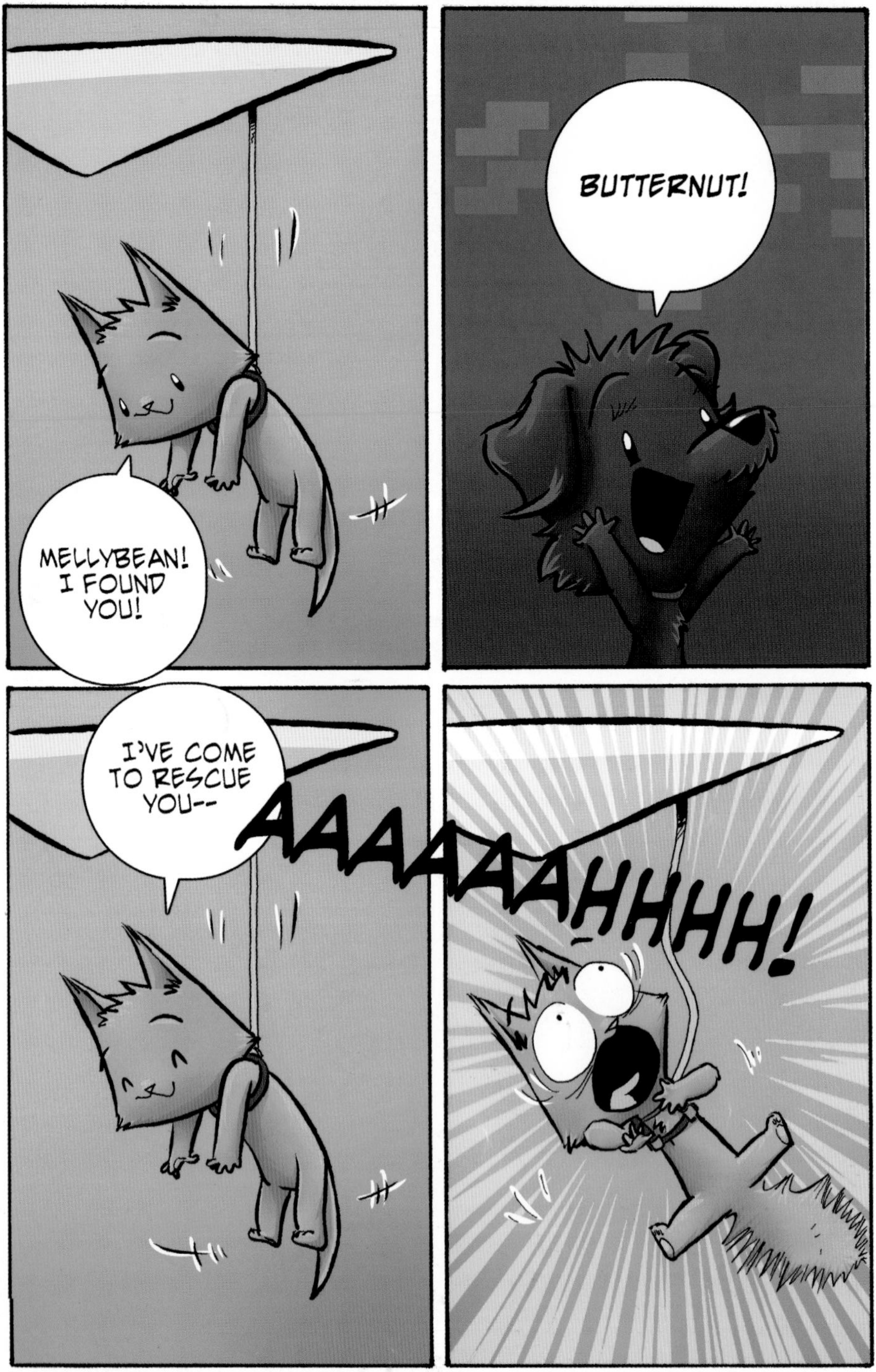
MELLYBEAN! I FOUND YOU!
BUTTERNUT!
I'VE COME TO RESCUE YOU--
AAAAAAAHHHHH!

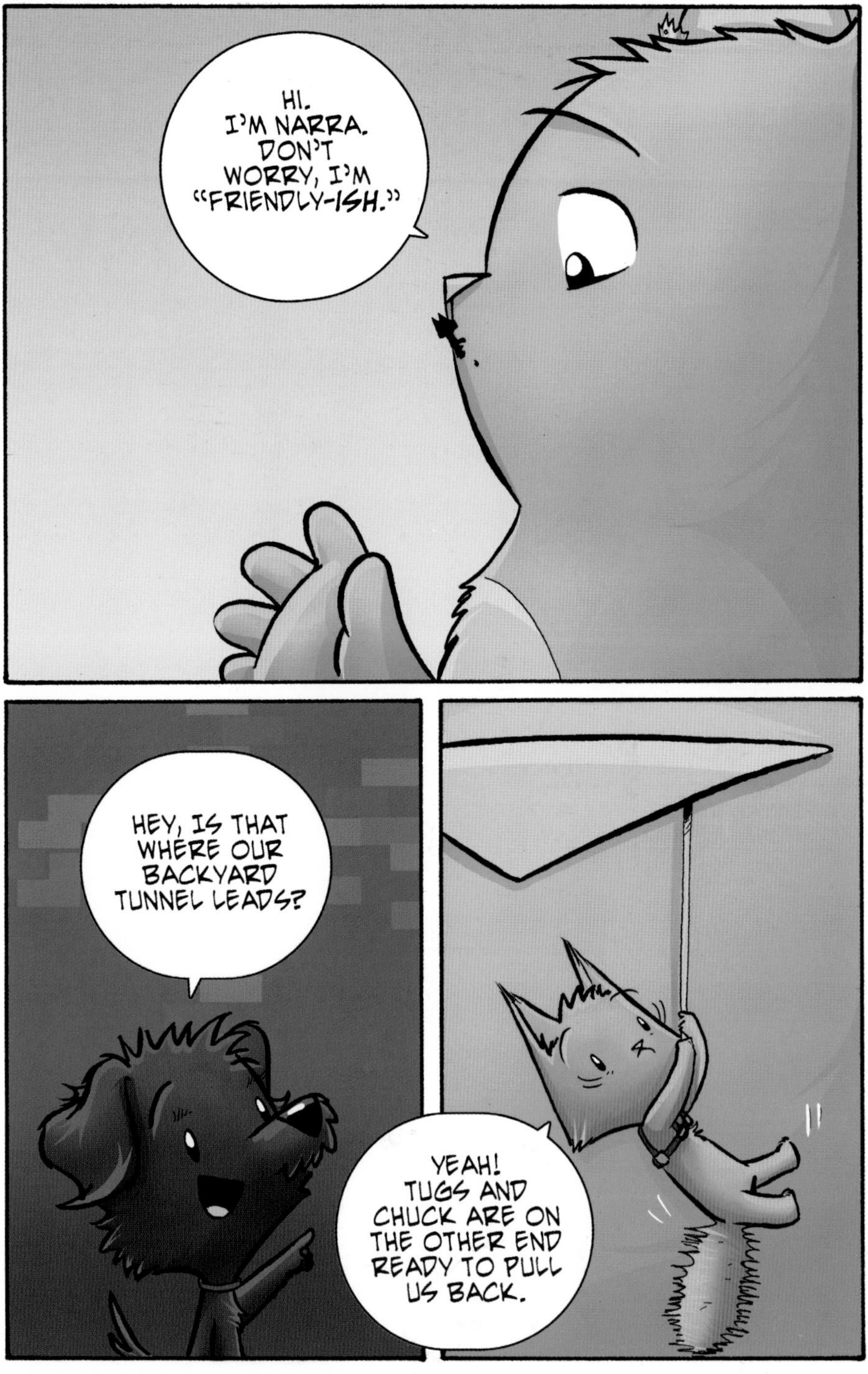
HI. I'M NARRA. DON'T WORRY, I'M "FRIENDLY-ISH."
HEY, IS THAT WHERE OUR BACKYARD TUNNEL LEADS?
YEAH! TUGS AND CHUCK ARE ON THE OTHER END READY TO PULL US BACK.

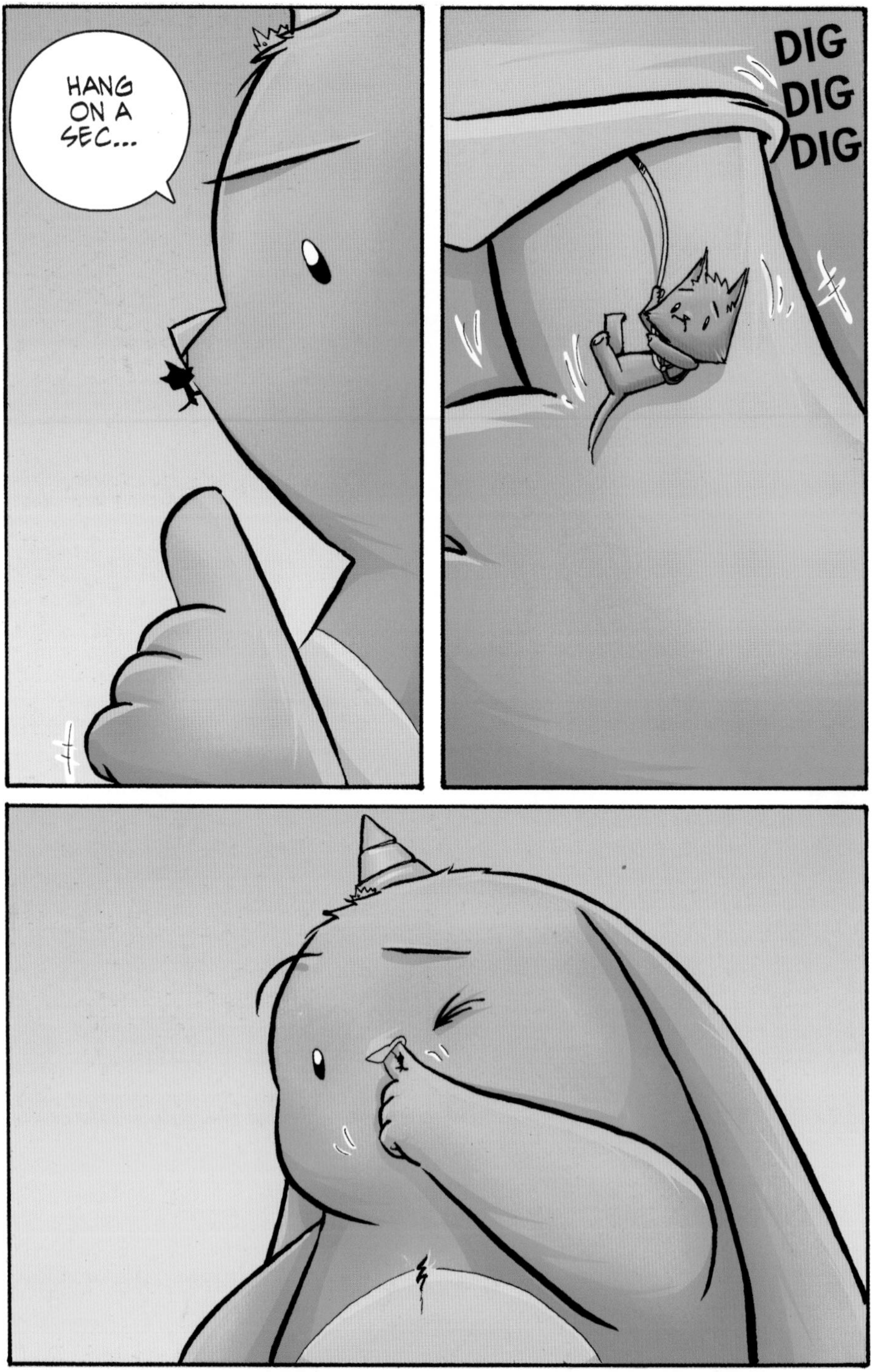
HANG ON A SEC...
DIG
DIG
DIG

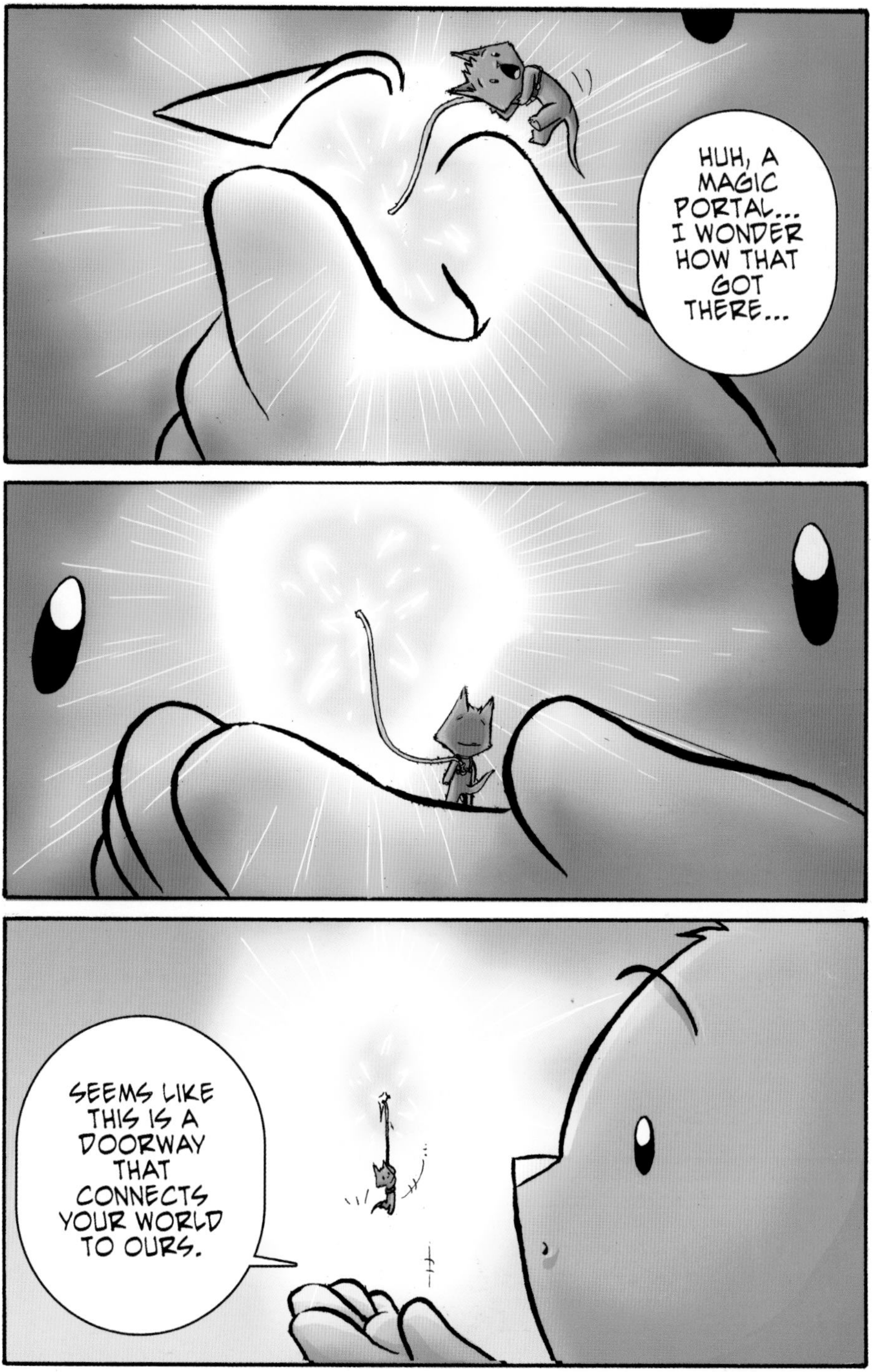
HUH, A MAGIC PORTAL... I WONDER HOW THAT GOT THERE...
SEEMS LIKE THIS IS A DOORWAY THAT CONNECTS YOUR WORLD TO OURS.

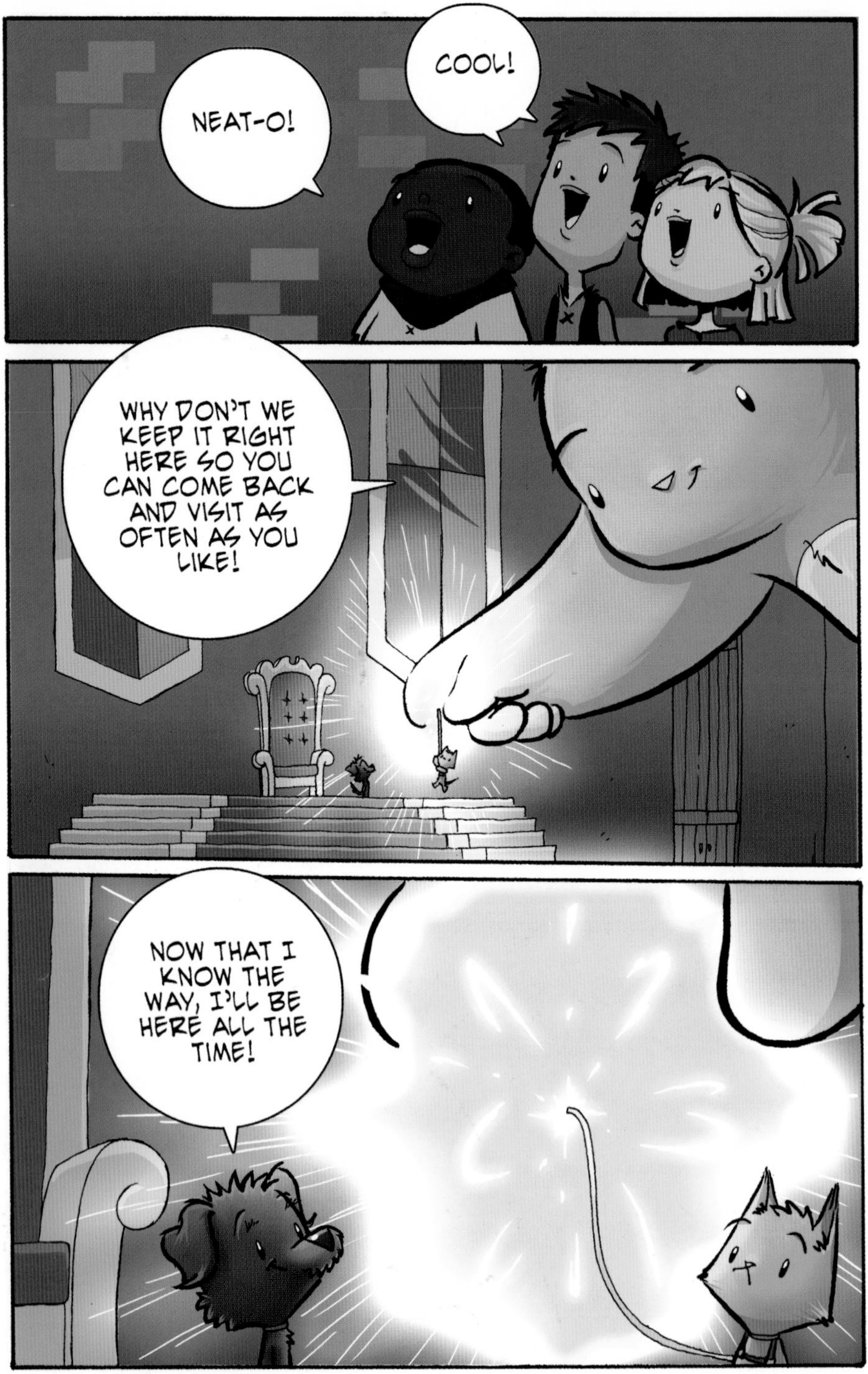
NEAT-O!
COOL!
WHY DON'T WE KEEP IT RIGHT HERE SO YOU CAN COME BACK AND VISIT AS OFTEN AS YOU LIKE!
NOW THAT I KNOW THE WAY, I'LL BE HERE ALL THE TIME!

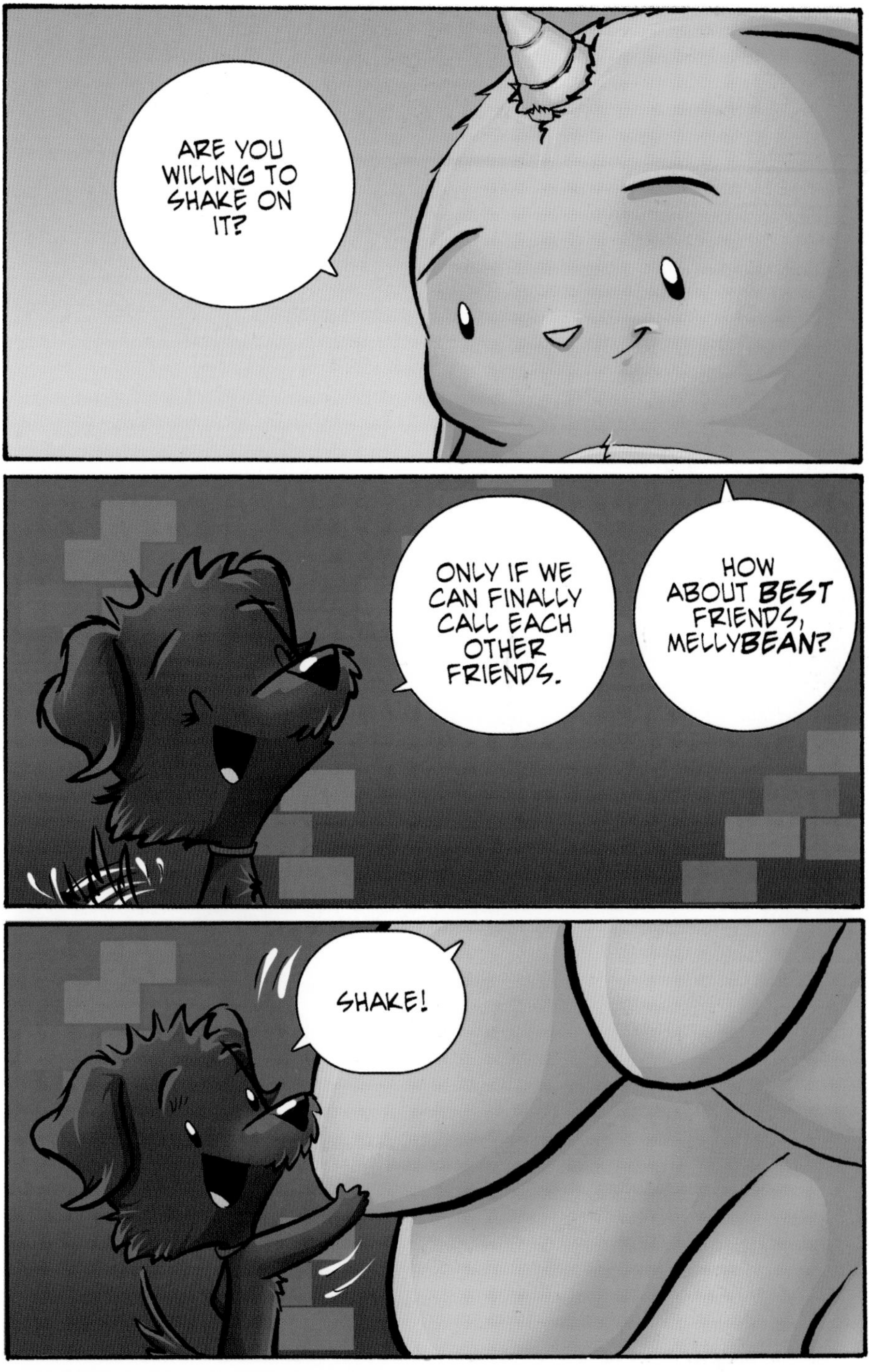
ARE YOU WILLING TO SHAKE ON IT?
ONLY IF WE CAN FINALLY CALL EACH OTHER FRIENDS.
HOW ABOUT BEST FRIENDS, MELLYBEAN?
SHAKE!

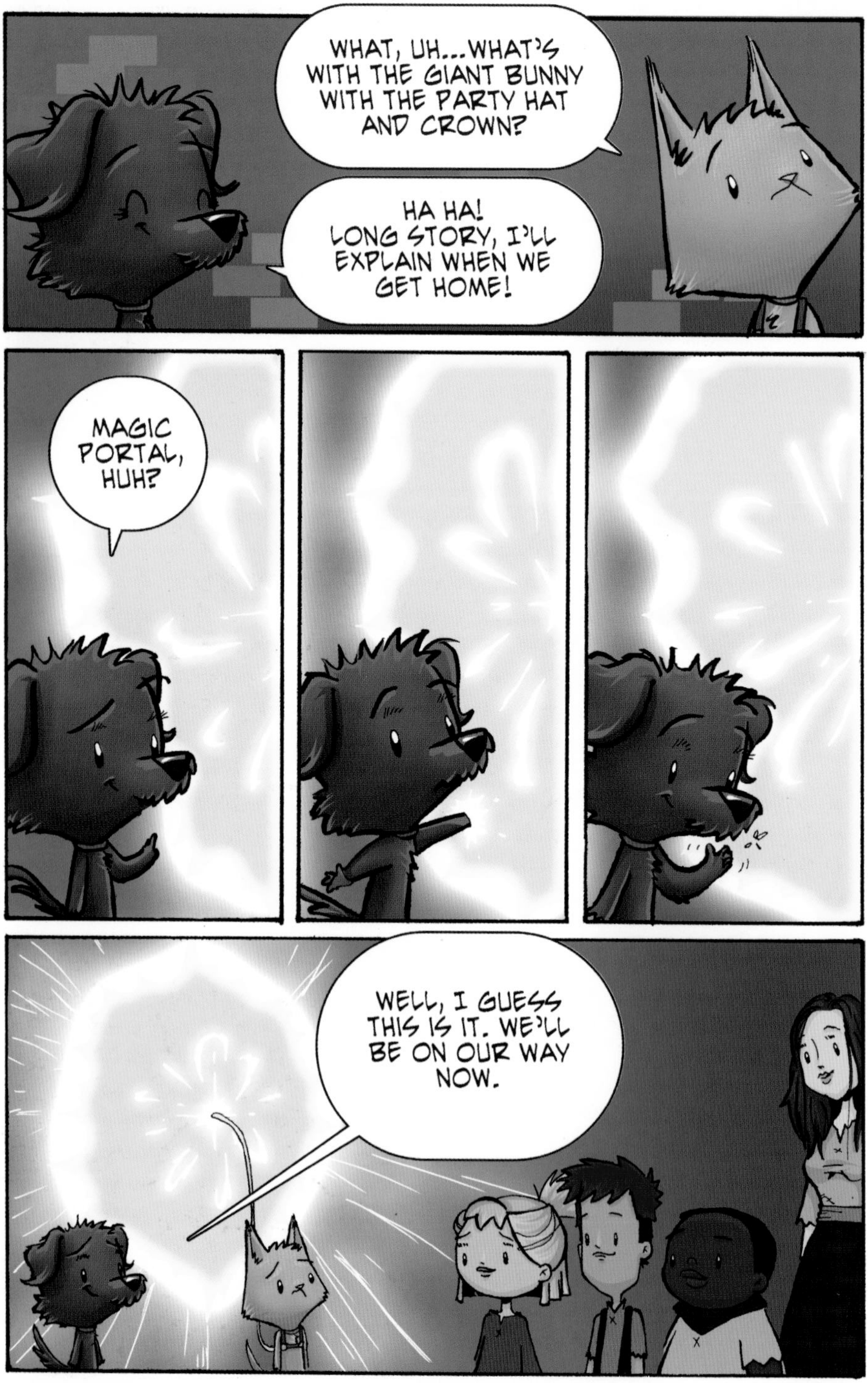
WHAT, UH...WHAT'S WITH THE GIANT BUNNY WITH THE PARTY HAT AND CROWN?
HA HA! LONG STORY, I'LL EXPLAIN WHEN WE GET HOME!
MAGIC PORTAL, HUH?
WELL, I GUESS THIS IS IT. WE'LL BE ON OUR WAY NOW.

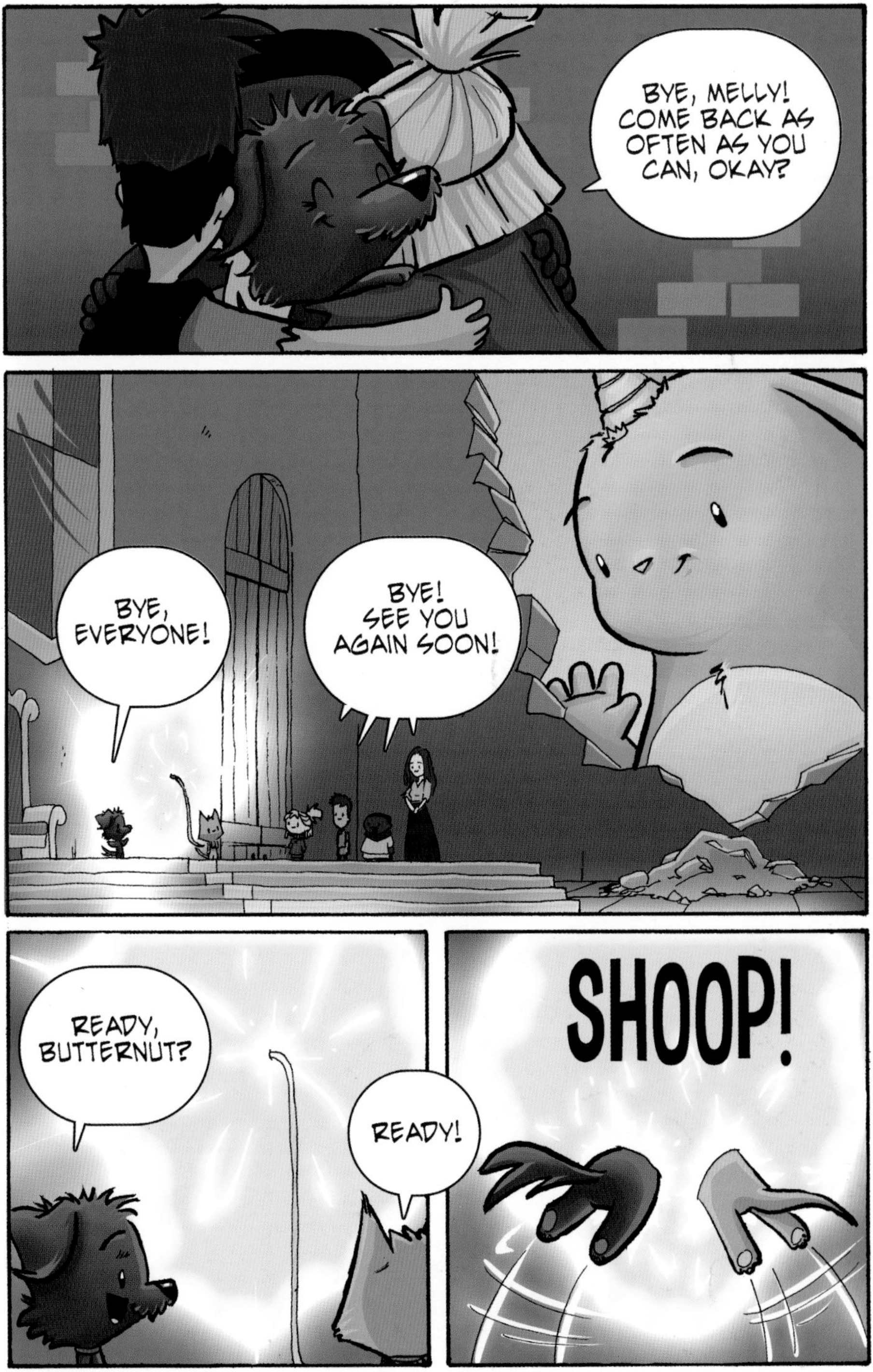
BYE, MELLY! COME BACK AS OFTEN AS YOU CAN, OKAY?
BYE, EVERYONE!
BYE! SEE YOU AGAIN SOON!
READY, BUTTERNUT?
READY!
SHOOP!

CHAPTER 9
NONE THE WISER

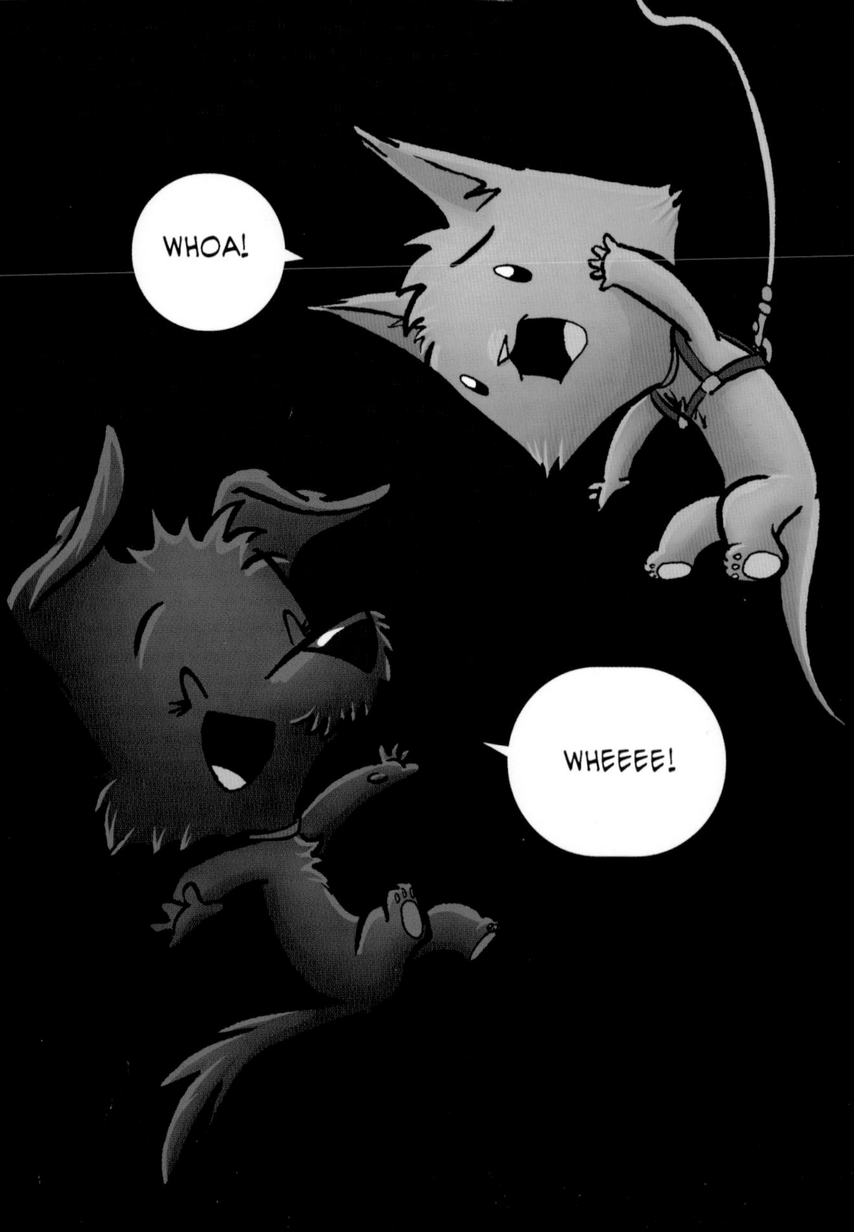

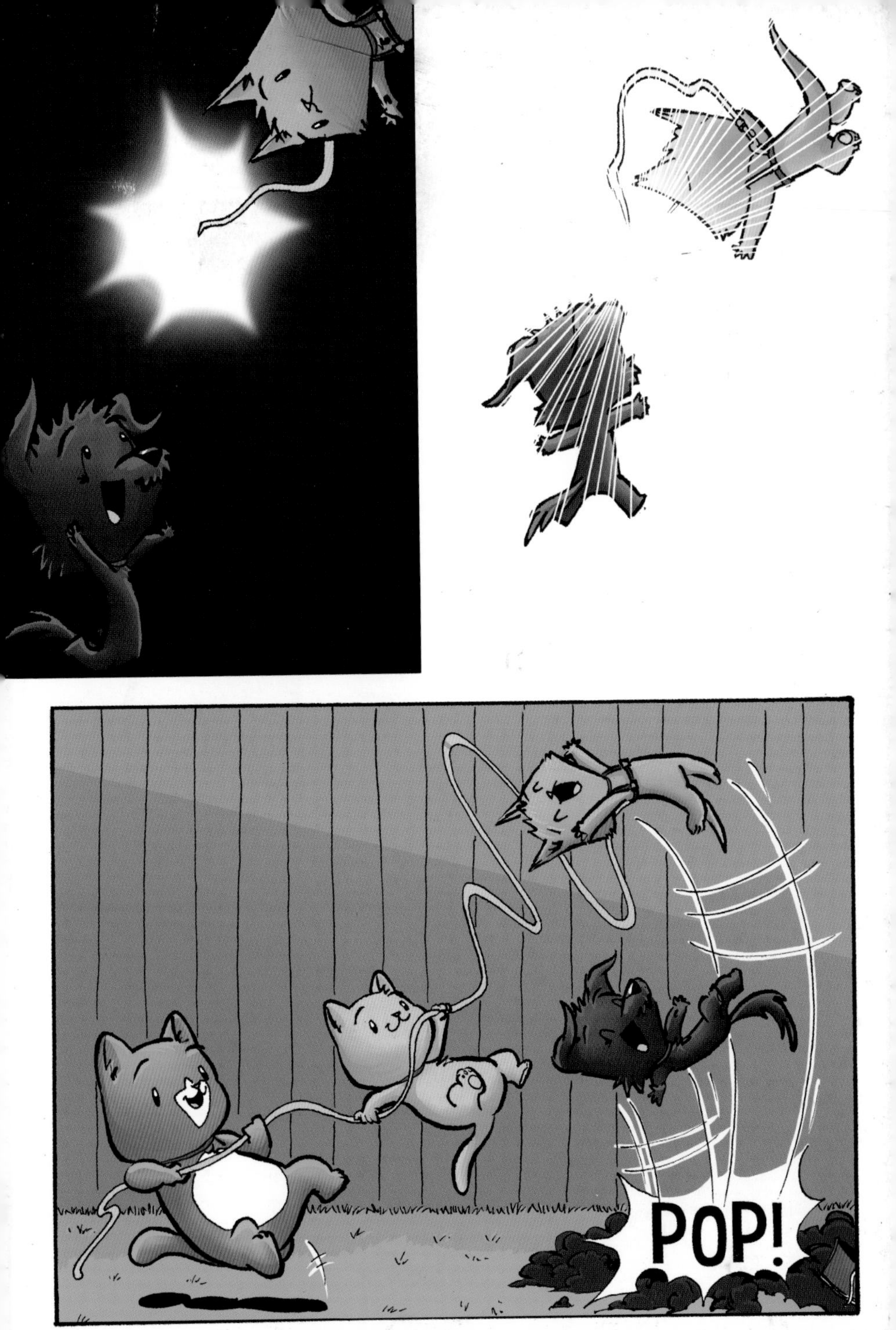
POP!

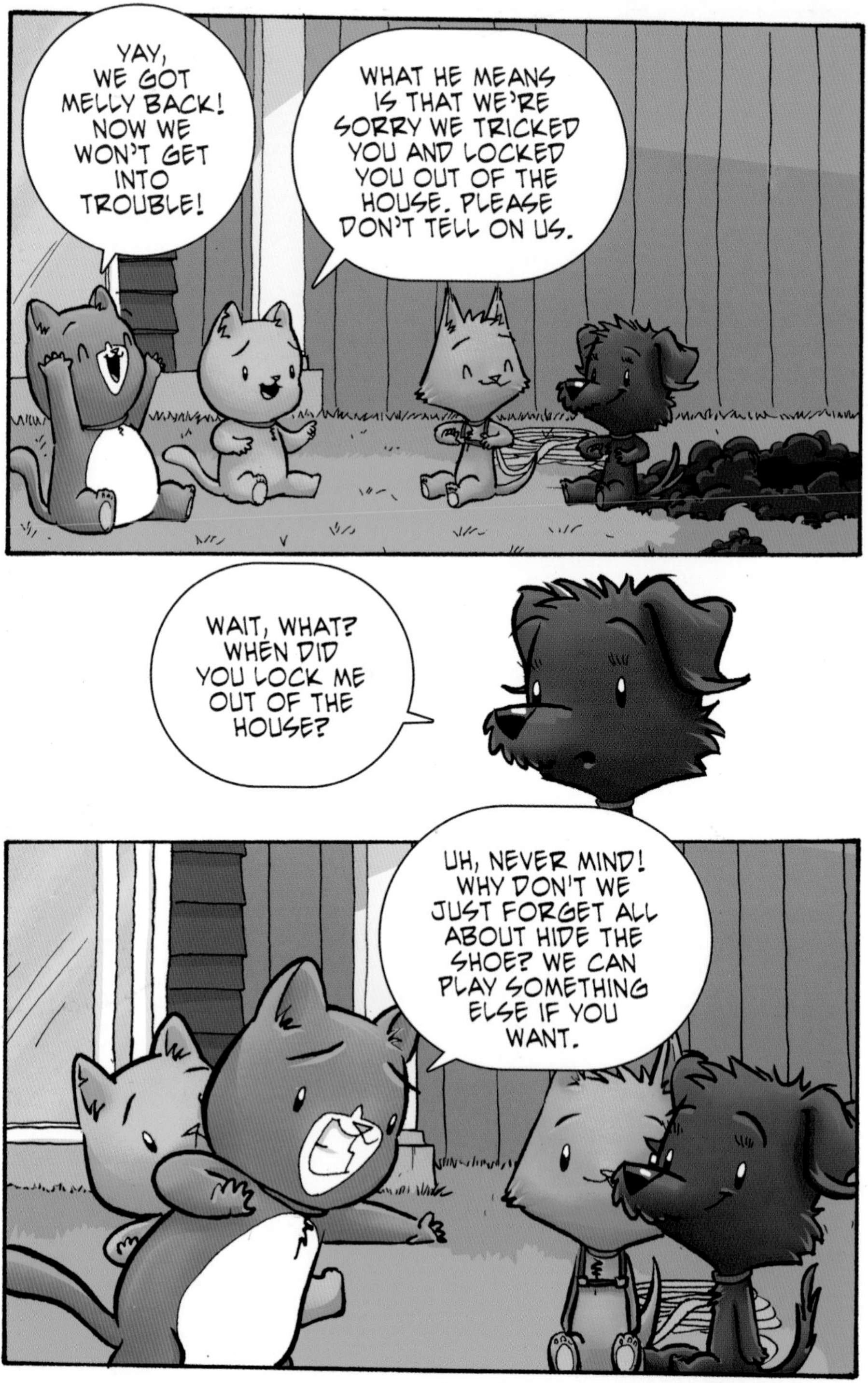
YAY, WE GOT MELLY BACK! NOW WE WON'T GET INTO TROUBLE!
WHAT HE MEANS IS THAT WE'RE SORRY WE TRICKED YOU AND LOCKED YOU OUT OF THE HOUSE. PLEASE DON'T TELL ON US.
WAIT, WHAT? WHEN DID YOU LOCK ME OUT OF THE HOUSE?
UH, NEVER MIND! WHY DON'T WE JUST FORGET ALL ABOUT HIDE THE SHOE? WE CAN PLAY SOMETHING ELSE IF YOU WANT.

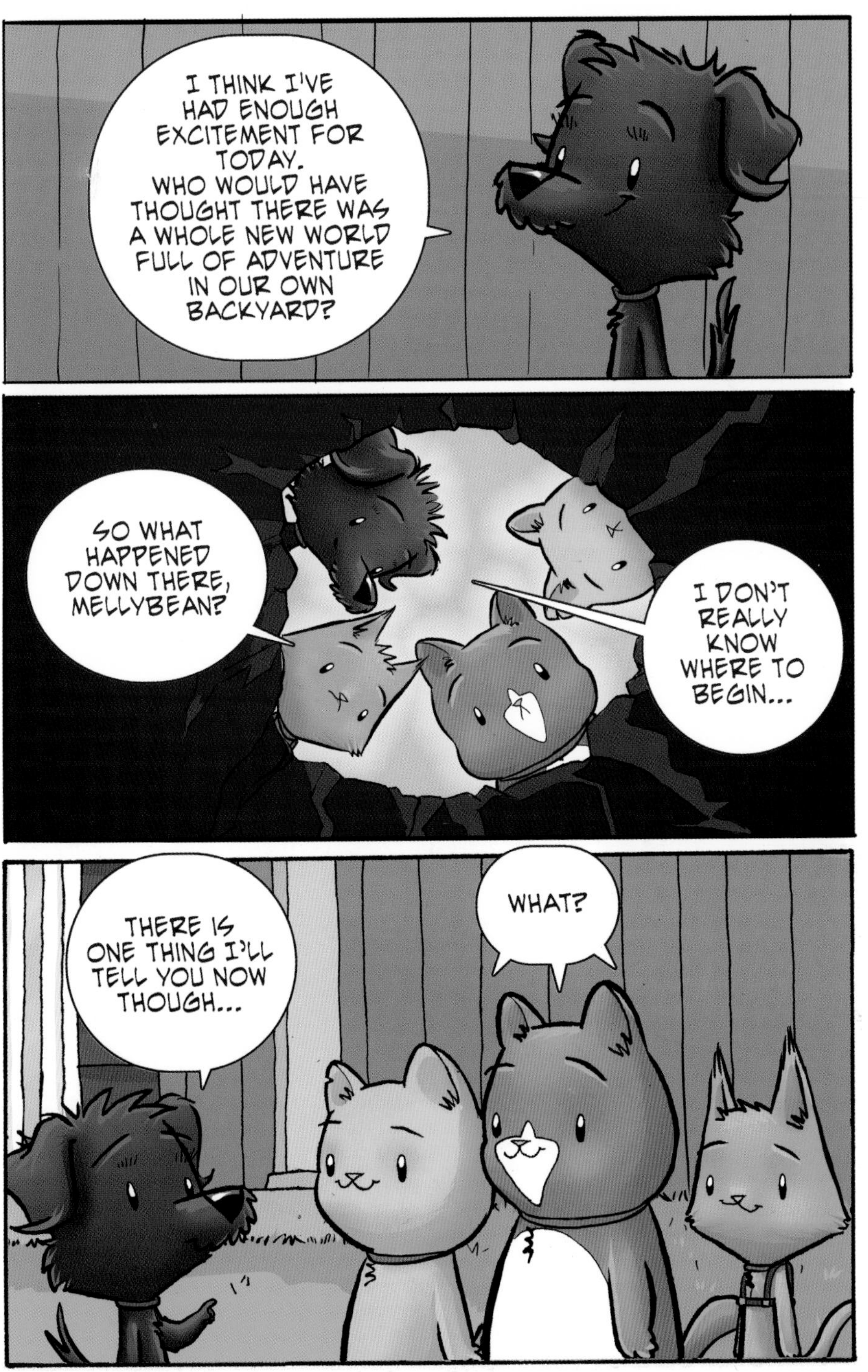
I THINK I'VE HAD ENOUGH EXCITEMENT FOR TODAY. WHO WOULD HAVE THOUGHT THERE WAS A WHOLE NEW WORLD FULL OF ADVENTURE IN OUR OWN BACKYARD?
SO WHAT HAPPENED DOWN THERE, MELLYBEAN?
I DON'T REALLY KNOW WHERE TO BEGIN...
THERE IS ONE THING I'LL TELL YOU NOW THOUGH...
WHAT?

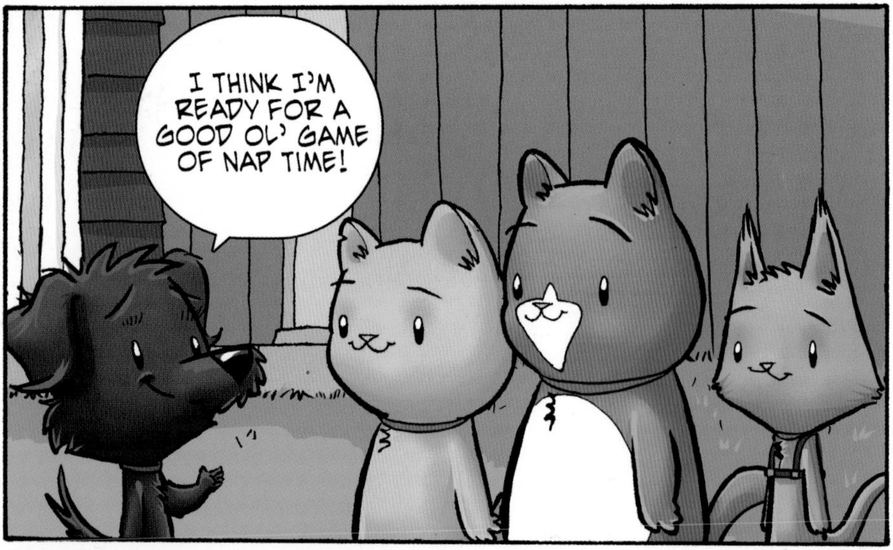
I THINK I'M READY FOR A GOOD OL' GAME OF NAP TIME!

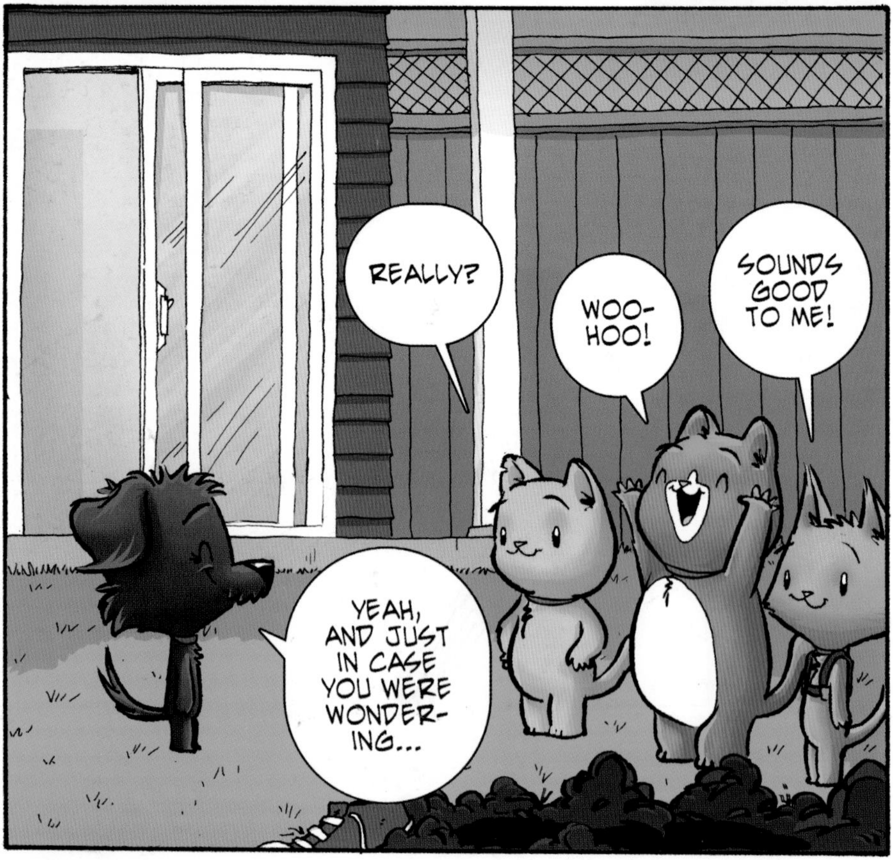
REALLY?
WOO-HOO!
SOUNDS GOOD TO ME!
YEAH, AND JUST IN CASE YOU WERE WONDER-ING...

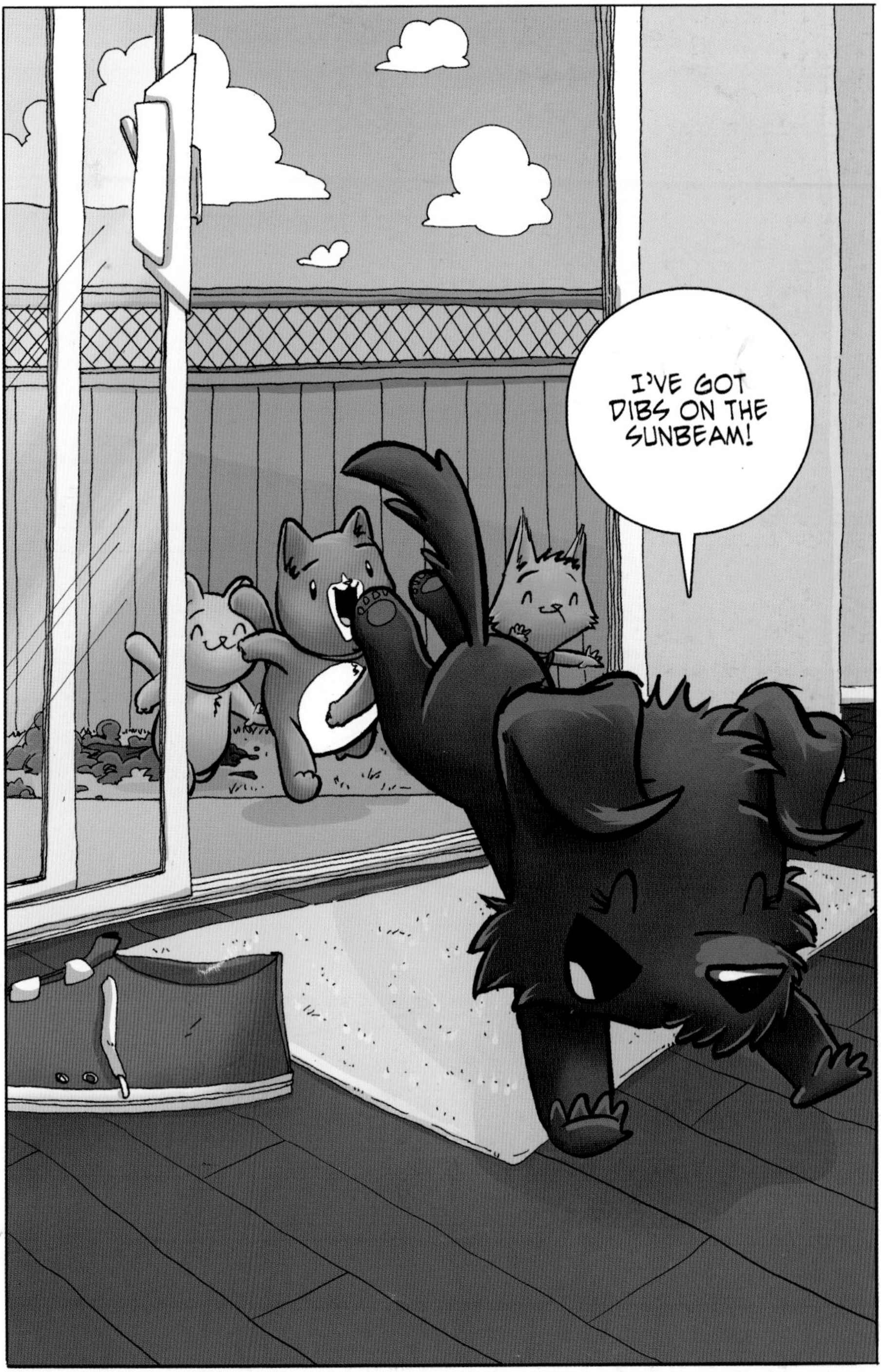
I'VE GOT DIBS ON THE SUNBEAM!

AUTHOR'S NOTE

Ever since I was four years old (learning to draw by tracing *Garfield* comic strips) I wanted to be an author. Now, at age forty, that dream has finally come true, and I couldn't be more grateful to everyone who helped make this possible. So from the bottom of my heart, thank you!

This series is about how one ordinary person (a pup in this case) can make a big difference just by being themselves. You don't have to be the "Chosen One" or "gifted" to make an impact on the world or in someone else's life. Just being you is enough, which is one of the many things my dog Melly has taught me.

That's right! It might be hard to believe, but Melly—and all of her feline friends, actually—are based on my real-life pets. In the summer of 2018, my girl-friend (who's now my fiancée!) and I adopted a two-month-old puppy we named Melody (and affectionately nicknamed Melly or Mellybean). The real Melly will always try to get Butternut, Tugs, and Charlie (Chuck) to play with her—and though she often tries to steal the cat's stinky food, they get along great and all share the love of a good sunbeam. Melly is hands down the most courageous and adventurous one of us, making new friends wherever we go and braving the great outdoors. We're an odd little family of misfits, and having this book to live out magical adventures that we'd never really get to go on is such a treat, and it means a lot to me to get to spend time living with and writing stories about ones I love so much.

Mellybean, both the real dog and the book, has changed my life, and I hope her adventures will bring as much joy to you, reading them, as they have for me writing and drawing them. I can't wait to see where her story will take us to next!

PHOTOS COURTESY OF THE AUTHOR

741.5 M
White, Mike
Mellybean and the giant monster /

JUN

JUNGMAN
06/22